THE CONTRACT MAN

A P BATEMAN

COPYRIGHT

Text © A P Bateman

All rights reserved

Author contact: authorapbateman@gmail.com

Author website: www.apbateman.com

ALSO BY A P BATEMAN

The Alex King Series

.

For my family. Crazy, loud and lovely.

CHAPTER ONE

He studied the face of the teenager next to him, noting the scars on his otherwise youthful face. How old was he? Sixteen perhaps even seventeen but surely no older. It was the eyes which deceived. They belonged to someone who had seen and lived a great deal of life at its harshest. More than they should have. They were the eyes of a middle-aged man, perhaps older still.

The boy's hands shook momentarily then tightened, forming a firm grip around the battered wooden stock of the old Russian-made Dragunov sniper rifle. He sighted his right eye an inch or so away from the telescopic sight then gradually closed his left eye allowing his target to come into full view.

"Keep it steady. The target's six hundred metres. Wind's three to four, right to left," the man paused as he glanced at the youth beside him. "Put the crosshairs a foot above and two to the right." He swallowed, his teeth grit together in frustration as the youth carried out his orders with slow methodical movements, just as he had been taught. Only now, weeks after he had first met him, taught him the finer skills of long-range marksmanship he wished that it was *he* who was taking the shot. "Keep the mark on him, then re-sight when he stops walking."

The youth grinned, then blinked profusely as a trickle of perspiration contaminated his eye. He moved his head and readjusted his aim. "This is for my people..." he smiled, forcing two decaying teeth over his dried and cracked bottom lip. "This is for Allah..."

The man tapped the youth on the back of the head. "Quiet," he said. "Don't even think it. Think only of the target, the wind and the bullet. When that bullet gets there almost two seconds after you squeeze the trigger, you'll have time for another shot. You should be ready for a follow up."

"But we don't take more than one shot from a firing point," the youth said, his eye still on the image in the scope. "Never. That's the rule."

"We do today," the man kept his eye on the spotting scope. "That man to the target's left – your right – is Jamil Betesh. I've been after him for two years. I'm not leaving here without a shot."

"Very well," the boy said nervously. His hand visibly shook on the weapon's stock. "Would you not prefer to take the shot?"

"No, it belongs to you." The man thought of the boy's family. Thought of how the man in the sights beheaded them, their hands bound, begging on their knees...

The boy breathed out a long slow and steady breath and the man knew he was ready. The boy squeezed the hair-trigger then visibly flinched as the heavy rifle recoiled violently against his bony shoulder and discharged a loud, near-deafening 'crack'.

The man kept his well-trained eye against the rubber eyepiece of the spotting scope, waiting for the bullet to find its mark. It did so a full two seconds later and the man in the lens crumpled to the dusty ground, flailing his arms wildly.

The older man quickly turned to the boy who was readjusting his aim on the heavy rifle. "Akhim! The target's down, but not out!" He forced his eye back against the spotting scope and then took a deep, steadying breath. "The bastard's moving about all over the deck. It looks like a shoulder wound. He's not going anywhere, leave him for now and put one in Betesh."

The new target was crouched over the wounded man, his assault rifle held loosely in both hands. There was a moment of indecision as he surveyed the mountains and the clump of rocks they were sheltered behind. The boy fired again, and the wounded man fell completely still.

"I said Betesh!"

The man grabbed the rifle and pushed the boy roughly aside. He checked the breech was closed and that the next round had chambered cleanly and sighted quickly in on the crouching man. Only he wasn't. He was running, and he was making good ground towards the Toyota pickup truck. And the fifty-calibre machine gun fixed on top. There would be a moment when he stopped running and mounted the bed of the pickup truck and at two seconds of travel, more likely a second and a half now the barrel was warmed, there was a chance of hitting the man as he slowed. The sides of the vehicle were high, but the rear wheel would provide a step. The man kept the rifle moving in time with the target. He overtook slightly, aimed at a point approximately three feet above the rear of the vehicle and squeezed.

Jamil Betesh stepped onto the tyre and heaved his weight upwards. The 7.62mm Swedish-made match grade soft-nosed bullet had left the barrel at eight hundred and ninety metres per second but hit Betesh square between the shoulder blades at a little under six hundred. The terrorist fell into the bed of the pickup and wouldn't be getting up.

The man squinted through the scope at the first target, which was lying somewhat twisted but perfectly still. He scanned the scope across the ground and already an ISIS fighter was on the big Browning in the back of the truck. He worked the cocking lever and brought the weapon round towards them. The big weapon's range was twice that of the sniper rifle, with approximately twice the power and was fed by a two hundred round belt coiled in the ammo box that was clipped to the side of the weapon. It didn't have the accuracy of the sniper rifle, but with tracer rounds staggered every tenth bullet, it would be a case of simply guiding the bullets in with all the skill of a child playing with a hosepipe. The man took a steadying breath, breathed out slowly until he had expelled all the air and squeezed the trigger. The fighter dropped out of view. He took another breath, methodically breathed out once more and fired into the action of the massive machine gun. He saw sparks through the clear image in the scope and hoped it would be enough to buckle the metal and put it out of commission.

The first rule of sniping had been broken. More than two shots fired from the same location could prove fatal. Ideally, one shot, one location. The Islamic State fighters now knew their exact position. The pair had previously wet the ground with water from a flask to eliminate dust clouds blown by the muzzle when the weapon was fired, and the taping of the barrel vents with duct tape had eliminated muzzle flash, but the weapon was loud and resonated through the mountainous terrain on either side of the valley. They were now as good as pinpointed.

The man turned to the boy as he dropped the rifle onto the ground and picked up his dusty pack. The boy was staring tearfully at the ground. He'd avenged his family, but the man knew the numbness, the emptiness of revenge and he could already see that the boy was not feeling the elation he had expected, had spent time dreaming of. He had merely started to grieve properly at last. The man slid off the rock and into the dried-up gully as gunfire erupted from the valley below. Almost three seconds later, in unison with the echo from the mountainous sides of the valley, bullets pinged and sang around them. Six hundred metres away and firing at an elevated position was pushing it for AK47s but the bullets seemed to be arguing to the contrary and both men ducked their heads as they threw themselves flat onto the hard earth.

The boy fumbled with the safety on his AK47, but the man shook his head.

"Too far. Let's get out of here instead."

The boy reached for the sniper rifle. Again, the man shook his head.

"But it will help my people, a rifle like that is like the hand of Allah!"

"Not part of the plan." The man turned towards the ridge, then suddenly sensed the closeness of the ensuing volley of gunfire. "Right now, we need the feet of your bloody Allah!" He caught hold of the youth's collar and pulled him as he ran along the dusty gully.

The two men bolted from the temporary cover of the gully and out into the open vulnerability of the plateau. Again, a volley of gunfire erupted some way behind them, ever closer, but this time the drone of engines at full stress was clearly audible.

The ground was rocky, almost a moonscape, making progress difficult as they set out across the plateau which would take them to the brow of the hill and the relative safety of the tarmacked road several hundred feet below.

The engine noises seemed ever closer, gaining on them rapidly. The man could tell that they were quad bikes. He hadn't seen them in the recce and there had been no mention of them in the intelligence report. But he knew they were a game changer.

Another volley erupted violently behind them, but this time a mass of dust and fragments of rock exploded just a few metres to their right.

"Down!" The man grabbed at the youth's shoulder and pulled him towards the rugged outcrop of jagged rocks. It acted as precious cover, but in a firefight if you're taking cover, you're taking fire. So, the man pulled the boy to his feet and he half guided, half hauled him towards the next pile of rocks. "Akhim!" he shouted. "We have to fight. We're not going to make the extraction point. As soon as we take cover aim and take steady single shots. Reload and keep heading for the extraction point."

Both men got down behind the rocks and took up firing positions. The man raised the Heckler and Koch G3 rifle and sighted on one of two ISIS fighters. Both were at two hundred metres and he dropped one with one shot and the other straight after. The rifle was old and battered but well maintained and he always used Swedish match quality ammunition when he could. By contrast Akhim was firing long bursts of fully automatic fire and doing nothing more than eroding the rock formations ten thousand years prematurely. The man knew the Kurd would use the weapon like that. You just couldn't train some people. The man got to one knee, aimed over the boy's back and fired three successive shots at a fighter who was taking aim from a crouched position one hundred and fifty metres distant. The fighter went down. He grabbed at the boy again and the two were running hard once more.

The next burst of gunfire sounded closer, raining bullets around their pounding feet and throwing pieces of debris into their faces. Above the dense sound of the impacting fragments and ricocheting bullets, a soft 'thud' was clearly audible.

The boy went limp, dropped his assault rifle with a clatter. He was a dead weight in the man's hand. He pulled hard and thrust the youth behind the welcome cover of rocks just in time for the next salvo of bullets.

The sound of more quad bikes filled the air. They were closer now, so close he could smell the poor petrol mix and burning oil. He shook the boy's limp arm. The boy was unconscious and there was a lot of blood on the ground. The man turned around and checked the ground behind. There were many fighters now. It was reaching a critical point where saturation was about to happen. He needed to thin them out. He aimed the big rifle and fired well-aimed single shots. He had both a power and accuracy advantage over the ISIS fighters with their AK47s, but they had numbers. They were also close, at the ideal operating distance for their weapons. He thought momentarily of the 9mm Makarov pistol in his shoulder holster and made a mental note of the single 9mm bullet he had earlier put in his shirt pocket. MI6 didn't go in for cyanide capsules anymore, but there was no way he was going to be the star of another ISIS beheading film on the internet. It was a strange notion, because as he fought on yet another battlefield in a fifteen-year career, for the first time he could remember, he genuinely wasn't scared. His resolute decision was liberating in the extreme. Now, he was fighting extremists on their terms. He stood again, took careful aim and dropped another two ISIS fighters. He turned back to the boy and checked him over. The 7.62x39 mm bullet from the AK 47 assault rifle had penetrated the youth's shoulder, tumbled after losing velocity and had exited through his elbow, taking most of the flesh clean off the bone. The boy was coming around and stared up at the man, his eyes wide, his lips quivering as the sudden bout of shock started to set in. The man knew he was going to lose consciousness again before long.

"Akhim!" he shouted. There was no response, so he slapped the youth across his cheek, snapping him back.

Teardrops trickled down the youth's face and he struggled to speak through the excruciating pain. "Am I to see paradise, Mister English?" he rasped, his throat suddenly dry.

The man slipped the pack off his shoulders and hastily unfastened the straps. He shook his head, as he attempted to comfort the boy. "No Akhim, just the doctor, when I can get you there." He tugged at the medical pack and quickly pulled out a pair of surgical scissors and a large dressing. He worked quickly and expertly, first cutting one of the webbing straps off the pack to use as a tourniquet, then binding the atrocious wound with a gauze and bandage. He jabbed a morphine ampoule into the youth's other shoulder hoping it would reach his heart faster.

A sudden clatter of gunfire erupted to his right, sending a thick cloud of dust and rock fragments high into the air. The man rolled for cover, picked up the G3 and aimed it quickly towards the edge of the rocky outcrop.

An ISIS fighter had moved forward, reaching the rocks as the man had tended to his wounded colleague and without taking careful aim had snatched a random burst of gunfire. He was now backed up against the rocks awaiting another opportunity.

The Englishman only needed *one* opportunity. He was close, was used to his weapon and the peep sight was working well up to two hundred metres so far. He slipped onto his stomach and quietly edged his way to where the soldier had played his hand. He held his breath, waiting for a sound, something that would give him the advantage. When it came it was slight enough, but nonetheless, a definite sign to the well-trained ear. A light metallic sound, the sound of an

AK47's sling clip rattling as the soldier moved. The true professional has no need for a canvas strap attached to his weapon, he always carries it. The fighter had unwittingly thrown in his hand. The Englishman eased himself forwards, then sensing the other man's presence and guessing at the distance, he swung out of the shadows and into the bright desert light. The ISIS fighter held his weapon firmly, close to his chest, the barrel pointing upwards. He was sweating profusely, and his lips were mouthing silent prayers towards the clear blue sky. He was young and clearly frightened. The Englishman needed nothing more. He brought the rifle up to aim, catching the man's surprise clearly in the weapon's sights. A single shot and prayer time was brought to an abrupt close.

He flung himself back into the welcoming shadows just as a volley of gunfire erupted from the outcrop of rocks near two abandoned quad bikes. He felt the displaced air from the bullet near his face and ducked his head involuntarily in reflex. Too close by far... When the volley was over he swung back, dropped to one knee and fired seven or eight shots at each quad bike and rider. Bullets tore through the wheels and into the engines. The riders scattered, firing wildly. One fell and lay still. As the next volley of gunfire sounded, he was back behind cover and changing the weapon's magazine. It was his last one. Twenty rounds left.

He turned his attention back to his companion. Akhim seemed to be high, as if he were tripping on acid. His eyes were large and glazed over and his lips were pursed into a pathetic grin as the effects of the opiate started to kick in.

"You got them?"

"Just one," the man replied quietly. He bent down and caught the youth by the lapels of his tattered jacket then hoisted him cleanly to his feet and positioned him over his right shoulder.

The clatter of assault rifles sounded off some way behind

him and then the sudden engulfing explosion of a grenade detonating just a few metres from their rocky sanctuary made the man take flight. He struggled momentarily then shifted the weight further up his back. With the casualty firmly in place he began his frantic retreat down the steep rocky gradient towards the road, as the four remaining pursuers suddenly enjoyed a surge of bravado and maintained their vicious onslaught.

Ahead of him the battered Land Rover pickup pulled off the road and two men leapt out and down to the dry and dusty ground. Both carried AK47 assault rifles with collapsible shoulder stocks. They opened fire, releasing a salvo of copper-coated lead above their heads.

"Akmed! Four, I think, directly behind us!" The Englishman stumbled over a small boulder, dropping the rifle in a bid to break his fall. He landed heavily, but instantly forced himself back to his tired feet. Ignoring the weapon, he regained composure and headed towards the two men. "Shameel! Get back into the bloody vehicle and get us moving!"

The overweight Kurd hesitated, staring disbelievingly at his wounded brother, then did as he was ordered. He got back into the Land Rover and quickly reversed it closer to where the Englishman was staggering over the scattering of rocks.

The second Kurd, who was tall and thin, especially in comparison to his companion, stood to the right firing continuously from the hip. The bullets sent clouds of dust and rock fragments into the air but had negligible effect on the advancing ISIS fighters who were now firing from prone positions high up in the rocky outcrop and getting their rounds dangerously close.

The Englishman eased the casualty into the rear of the open jeep, then picked up the AKS74 assault rifle from the rear seat, unfolded the metal shoulder-stock and held it firmly against his shoulder. He liked this weapon. It wasn't as powerful as an AK47 but that meant that the recoil was less, and the ease of aim was better for rapid shots. He flicked the selector switch down two clicks and fired single rounds in rapid succession towards the pattern of muzzle flashes which glittered away on top of the distant ridge.

Two fighters jumped up in unison and disappeared back over the ridge, very much aware that the bullets were becoming closer with every shot. The other two were set on staying and the man felt bullets tear through the air near him. He wasn't going to stand and have a duel with them. He crouched low and ran to the Land Rover. The thin Kurd was still spraying the hillside with wild abandon. He fired the weapon dry then ran for the cover of the vehicle. He leapt up into the bed and changed the magazine then started firing again. The spent brass cases fell into the young Kurd's face. The Englishman covered the wounded boy's face, placed a comforting hand on his forehead. The overweight Kurd floored the accelerator and the vehicle slid sideways then gained traction as the tyres suddenly met with the potholed tarmac road surface.

Alex King shook his head in dismay as he took his hand off the dead Kurd's forehead. He had suspected that shock would finally take the boy but dying in the back of a Land Rover with friends was better than dying at the hands of the vicious and sadistic ISIS terrorists. He said nothing to the youth's jubilant brothers, they had earned the right of a little celebration. Instead, he placed the assault rifle on the bench seat beside him, took out the silk print map from his jacket pocket and quietly started to plot his escape.

CHAPTER TWO

The hallway was dark. A security light would occasionally light up the car park outside, in turn illuminating inside the building a little. Enough to make his work easier. The man carefully applied the adhesive tape to the highly polished brass plate of the door handle. It was a vaguely sticky yellow tape used by decorators when painting. Easy to apply and easier to remove without any adhesive residue. The tape covered the plate completely skirting the keyhole. With the protective barrier between the bright metal and his picklock he carefully inserted the tool into the lock confident of leaving no tell-tale scratch marks.

His companion held the torch for him keeping the red-filtered beam trained steadily on the opening of the lock. For now, it was only feel which mattered. He eased the pick into position, gently holding the gate in place before inserting the larger, titanium-tipped key. He worked the lock delicately, sensing the contour of the mechanism. He was an experienced locksmith, yet still he practiced on several types of locks each week. It was a skill that required constant honing. Finally, he eased the gate a complete turn to the right. With a smile which beamed satisfaction bordering upon relief, he glanced up at his colleague and nodded.

"We're in!"

"Right, keep to the plan. You check for a safe and I'll do the filing cabinets." The second man nodded and flashed the red beam efficiently over the oak panelled walls of the tidy office. He was searching for the most probable place for a safe to be concealed.

A solicitor's office is a working office. Files, documents or even evidence must be kept secure, but also it should be easily attainable. However, the documents they sought were dormant files. Placed with the law firm for security. They would be secure and out of the way of the day to day affairs. This aided their search. Such was the material matter that the two men felt confident that secretaries would not by chance happen upon it. They had already searched the solicitor's house over a period of three separate days, timed during school time and within the busy gym, lunch and coffee sessions of the solicitor's wife.

What they had determined in the briefing sessions was the documents would be held in a private safe. They had no reason to believe, nor evidence of offsite security storage being used. Such was the thinking and motive behind the storage of the documents that a third party would be required as intermediary.

Ahead of him on the wall and between two ornate brass wall sconces, a large landscape oil painting was the central feature. It was the most obvious, possibly cliché location, but it also seemed to be the most probable. He walked around the imposing, mahogany desk, eased the leather chair aside, then gently felt around the rim of the frame for any traces of an alarm system.

"Have you got something?" his companion asked, walking over and standing just a few feet from his shoulder.

"I'm not sure," he paused, easing his fingers all the way around the gilt frame. "No alarm system, not that I can make out anyway." He cautiously stepped around to the side of the painting and attempted to peer behind, using the pencil torch with its eerie red glow. "It's fitted flush to the oak panelling, which is unusual."

"If you say so." His companion did not attempt to hide his impatience. "So, have you found something or not?"

He gently spread his arms out across the painting and caught hold of the two top corners then gradually eased the painting away from the wall. He turned and grinned at his colleague as the painting moved smoothly out, swinging gracefully on its custom-made hinges, revealing the metal safe door behind. "I would say so," he replied somewhat smugly.

His colleague stepped forward and placed the small canvas bag on the mahogany desk. "Right, you go downstairs and start preparing the alarm system for reactivation while I get this unlocked."

"No. Have you forgotten?" he paused, shaking his head defiantly at the man who was technically his superior. "Two to confirm."

The man grit his teeth, relenting under duress. "Very well," he paused, trying to reassert some authority. "Get the tools out for me. And this time, hold the torch steady."

CHAPTER THREE

"I suppose all in all, it wasn't a complete shambles." Donald McCullum looked at the three men in turn, then turned his eyes back to the front page of *The Times*. "There isn't a direct finger pointed at us, it could well have been anybody." He dropped the paper on to the pile of broadsheets and tabloids, all with similar headlines and looked up expectantly for a reply. It was not long in coming.

"That's as maybe, but the fact remains, a specialised piece of NATO equipment was left at the scene." Martin Andrews smirked. "The whole idea was to make the job look Russian funded. Right down to the discarded rifle and the second-rate ammunition. Thanks to your man, the whole illusion has been shattered. I understand he used match grade bullets?" He shook his head. "No, he disregarded the briefing. The Russians want a pipeline out of the Caspian through Iran, Iraq and into Turkey – the gateway to the west. These ISIS idiots are ruining their plans and it was as good a time as any to throw some mud on their faces. I mean, look at the Ukraine. We were caught napping there, as was the rest of the world. We had a chance to systematically remove known terrorists by assassination and point a finger at the Russians, leaving them with the reprisals to follow."

"Our transatlantic friends are simply livid," Marcus Arnott paused, noting an apparent flaw in his manicure. "To be honest, we can't blame them. Nor can we expect them to sit back and await terrorist attacks on their own soil. They don't want tit-for-tat. They will pick their targets, but they will be big, like Osama Bin Laden or Saddam. Or they'll do it just before an election..."

McCullum shook his head. "They were all too quick to suggest that Colonel Al-Muqtadir be eliminated. All too pleased that we agreed to take care of it. And we did, Al-Muqtadir is out of the picture, well and truly." The Deputy Director for Foreign Operations sat back in his leather chair and picked up his cup of tea. He sipped thoughtfully. "With the elimination of Colonel Al-Muqtadir went the very real threat of ISIS building a permanent foothold in Northern Iraq, like they did with Syria. We proved the Iraqi colonel was imbedded with the terrorist organisation. The Iraqi government has moved troops further into insurgent territory and we've sent a clear message that the west will not tolerate fraternisation with terrorists."

Martin Andrews shifted uncomfortably in his seat, becoming somewhat irritated with his colleague and technical equal. "Nobody is denying that, with Colonel Al-Muqtadir's death, the building of an ISIS stronghold has come to an end. Or is at least stalled. What we all have a problem with, is the fact that your agent messed things up! For reasons best known to himself he let an untrained Kurdish rebel take the bloody shot!" He paused, just long enough for his words to sink in. "Here we have a man, a highly trained, highly motivated individual with fifteen years operational experience, letting a boy do the job for him. What in God's name was he thinking?"

"In all honesty, I think Alex King should be recommended for psychological assessment." Arnott looked at everyone in turn then frowned when they failed to react as he had expected. "Come on, the man must be completely deranged!"

"You'd be amazed how different life can be in the field, Marcus." Peter Stewart, who had been silent until now, leaned forward and picked the copy of *The Times* up off the desk. "Alex King is a damned good agent, I should know, I helped train him."

The three men remained silent. Peter Stewart was a listener, a tough, no nonsense Scotsman who spoke little, but when he did, everybody tended to take notice. Recruited by MI6 two decades ago from the SAS, and as head of the Operational Training Wing, he was certainly more qualified to talk about life in the field than anyone else.

"If Alex King wanted to let the Kurd take the shot, then I believe that he had a good reason, but until I have questioned him about the incident, nobody makes damned fool remarks about psychological assessment..." He turned his solid frame towards Arnott and held a cold, hard stare. "Understand?"

Marcus Arnott looked away, apparently having discovered another blemish on his fingernail. He turned his attention back to Donald McCullum, blanking Stewart, who sat to his left. "If you don't mind me asking, what was the damning evidence that King left behind?"

"A navigational aid called an NGS1. Based on a Magellan, only NATO designed and developed." McCullum shook his head despondently. "It was in his kit bag."

"Magellan?" Arnott inquired, somewhat baffled.

Stewart coughed quietly, then looked at Marcus Arnott with glee. "A Magellan GPS. Global Positioning System. It's a hand-held piece of equipment which relays your position to three separate satellites, then sends your exact fix back to you. This NATO developed version has extra features and can relay off jet liners and other aircraft without them knowing. Takes reference points from their digital markers, their radio beacon signals. It can use mobile phone masts as well. Theoretically you can never be lost with one."

Arnott ignored him, keeping his eyes on McCullum. "Then how did he manage to lose it?"

"After the assassination, the Kurd helping King was fatally wounded. Before he died, King tended to the man's wounds, but Al-Muqtadir's bodyguards and ISIS fighters got too close, King was forced to flee, leaving his kit bag behind," McCullum paused. "The Kurd was part of the liaison team that the CIA set up six months ago, for just such missions. Enthusiastic rebels on the payroll, but lending deniability."

"And as a result of tending to this boy's wounds, Iraq now know that it was a British operation," Arnott stated flatly. "As do the Russians *and* Islamic State terrorists. As do the entire world's press, evidently."

"No. As I said earlier, I beg to differ. They know that it was most probably an operation funded by the West." McCullum looked at his understudy defiantly. "They do not know for sure that it was Britain. The Yanks do but won't tell tales on us. Not yet, at least."

Andrews chuckled sardonically. "No Donald, but ISIS have guessed correctly and have threatened out and out terrorism to Britain as a result. The Russians are putting pressure on America to volunteer any information they may have."

"Very well!" McCullum held his hands up in a gesture of mock submission. "If the department needs a head for the chopping block, then let it be mine that rolls!"

Andrews shook his head. "Nobody wants your head Donald. You're in line for the top job, we all know that. But I think that we might all be better placed if we can come up with a suitable solution, and fast," he paused, looking at the other two men. "The directive was put to us, and we reacted. Donald and I both agreed that Colonel Al-Muqtadir was a valid target. As is it was, Donald was the one who signed off on the executive order. Had it been myself, then you two would be seated in *my* office, albeit served with a superior brand of Cognac and not dishwater tea," he smiled, trying his best to ease the tense atmosphere. "Marcus, you were invited here because of ISIS's recent threat of *a blanket of fire* as they so theatrically put it. As head of domestic terrorism, we wondered what your views on that threat may be."

Arnott sat back in his seat and shrugged his shoulders. "As regards to deterring terrorism on our own soil, that's still Five's main directive. All my department can offer is intelligence from overseas, possible links with other organisations et cetera. If the threat is deemed to be real, then we can liaise with MI5 and Special Branch and offer them intelligence from our various contacts. The newly formed Joint Intelligence Group is where we're putting most of our data these days. Information is better than it was, but nobody likes sharing at the very beginning of their operations. Other than that, my department cannot really make a move at this end without stepping on other people's toes."

Andrews nodded, understanding the need for protocol. He also recognised someone playing a long game. Marcus Arnott was distancing himself from MI5 as much as he could. The new protocols were not that effective. However, with the situation as it was, SIS, or MI6 as it is more commonly known, could not afford any more embarrassments. He turned his attention to Peter Stewart who, characteristically, had remained patiently silent. "Peter, you were actively involved in training Alex King. In your opinion, was he one of the best men for the job?"

The big Scotsman eased his solid frame forward in his

chair and methodically replaced the newspaper on the desk before picking up the thin china mug containing the cool remnants of his tea. "Aye, well." He sipped some of the liquid then replaced the cup to the leather coaster. "To tell you the truth, at that level of operative there is barely a trait which separates them. At present, SIS have ten agents who are trained to mono-tactical level. That is to say, suitable for high-risk solo operations. When we require larger logistics, we make effective use of the SAS or SBS."

"Yes, yes. I know the situation," Andrews replied impatiently. "But was Alex King the best man for the task?"

Stewart frowned. "As I said, there is barely a discernible difference between the current agents. It would be extremely difficult, probably foolhardy, to choose between them. They are all trained to the same exacting standards, any one of them would have been deemed suitable."

Donald McCullum coughed quietly and smiled at the big Scotsman. "Peter, we all know the *official* line concerning the evaluation of Special-OPS agents, but off the level, was King the *best* agent that we could have sent?"

Stewart leaned back into the leather chair and looked at each of the men in turn. "Of the ten agents that form the current Special-OPS Unit, King is rated equally within the top three. That is to say, each man has his good and bad days. However, over the past five years, King has performed the highest percentage of successful operations. Of course, he doesn't know that. It wouldn't pay if an agent suddenly started to have delusions of grandeur. What King has though is experience. Typically, field agents are aged from twenty-seven to thirty-five. That's the best balance of fitness, stamina and durability as well as valuable life experience and tactical decision-making skills. King is our oldest tactical agent at forty-two. He's among the fittest though and passes all the regular mental agility tests."

McCullum did his best to hide a triumphant smile. He turned to his equal number and shrugged. "What more could we do? We sent the best man that we had, we can't be held responsible for the way an agent performs in the field."

Andrews nodded thoughtfully but looked dubiously at his colleague. "True, but the fact remains, we are left in the middle of a most awkward situation, one which could easily escalate into an international crisis," he paused, resting the cigar against the rim of the nearby ashtray. Like all government buildings there was a strict no smoking policy that was ignored at the higher levels. "What we need is a quick solution, one which ultimately takes the British SIS out of the equation. Tell me, what transpired from King's debrief?"

Donald McCullum shook his head. "I have not had the opportunity to interview him, yet," he paused, holding up his hands in front of his face in a defensive gesture. "I had pressing business at the weekend, I didn't get the report until yesterday."

Andrews looked dumfounded at his colleague, wondering what could have been so important as to take priority over the official debrief of a high-priority field agent. He knew that McCullum was extending his social circle, both within the intelligence community and among politicians, it was McCullum's chosen track for securing the Director General's position when the current DG left his post early next year.

"Who filed the report?" Arnott asked, looking at the document folder on McCullum's broad desk.

McCullum frowned. "King filed it himself, before taking his official leave."

Marcus Arnott nodded. "And does King mention that he let the Kurd take the shot?"

"No. That little gem of information came from Langley, via an extremely irate CIA field agent who was working as a liaison officer with Kurdish rebels in northern Iraq. He was forced to leave after the area became too hot with Iraqi soldiers and ISIS hit and run fighters."

"Presumably this band of merry men knew that King was British?" Andrews pursed his lips together as he ruminated out loud. "Then the answer is simple, we have no alternative," he paused, glancing at the Scotsman beside him. "King will have to go back to Iraq and tidy the loose ends."

CHAPTER FOUR

The girl swept a hand through her mane of anthracite black hair and giggled childishly, baring brilliant white, oversized teeth. She set her champagne glass on the smoked glass table, smoothed down the blue satin skirt, which had started to ride high up her slender thighs and then gently reached over to stroke the man's clean-shaven chin.

Junus looked across at his companion and grinned wolfishly. "I think she likes you my friend. If you like, business can wait until later..."

Charles Bryant laughed, brushing the girl's hand away and picking up his gin and tonic. "Are you joking?" He glanced at the girl, then chuckled to himself as he sipped some more of his aperitif. "The last time I saw a mouth like that, it was wearing a bit between its teeth!" He roared with laughter, then stared at his Indonesian friend who had missed the joke. "You know, a *bit*, as in a horse's mouth."

The tiny Indonesian concentrated hard then laughed, somewhat overdoing it, as he suddenly gained enlightenment. "Oh yes, I see what you mean." He glared at the girl and suddenly clapped his hands together. "Tidak terimah kasih!"

The girl's expression fell as she was unceremoniously dismissed. She picked up her drink, then walked back towards the bar, swaying her hips excessively as she worked the room.

Bryant glanced around the quiet bar and nodded towards the booth at the far end of the room. "Now *her,* well that would be a different story altogether."

Junus turned around and stared at the three girls who sat together, quietly sipping from over-decorated cocktails. One of them stood out, altogether more beautiful. She had sharper features than the other Javanese girls and she was elegantly tall. She smiled sweetly across at them, then flicked a loose lock of hair away from her eyes before seductively licking sugar crystals from the rim of her cocktail glass.

Junus turned back to his friend and grinned lecherously. "My friend, you have a lot to learn about Asia." He picked up his bottle of *Bintang* and took a long pull on the neck before placing it back down on the table. The beer was icy cold, and the bottle was wet with condensation making the label start to peel.

"What do you mean?" Bryant watched the girl as she sensuously rolled a cocktail cherry between her slender fingers, then popped it between her pouting lips. "She's a beauty."

Junus chuckled. "In Asia, when something looks too good to be true, that is because it usually is. *His* name is Numan, and he's Balinese. He works three of the local bars and for practical reasons, only goes so far," he paused shaking his head. "Ironically, he is one of the best-looking *girls* in Jakarta."

Bryant stared at the 'girl' in amazement, then turned back and faced his colleague. "I'll be blowed..."

"You could well have been!" Junus creased with laughter and picked up his bottle of Indonesian beer. "It's the only service he offers!"

Bryant smirked, shaking his head in dismay. He picked up his gin and tonic, swilled back the remnants then clicked his fingers at a nearby waiter. "Another round, my good man," he paused, staring at the vacant expression upon the waiter's face. "One Bintang and one gin and tonic. This time kindly see to it that the tonic is brought separately, in its bottle."

The waiter nodded, then ambled his way leisurely back to the bar, where a hugely overweight barman started to prepare the order.

Bryant looked back at Junus. There was something amiss, something that he could not quite put his finger on. He had been doing business with the tiny Indonesian for the best part of five years, ever since Bryant's company, CB Mineral Tec, had contracted to supply machine parts for a contract which Junus' partnership had won to build a hydro-electric plant and dam in Sumatra.

CB Mineral Tec had severely undercut the opposition, but Bryant's ploy had worked. He had lost a considerable sum of money funding the under-priced project but in doing so he had soon found a powerful ally in Junus Kutu, an ally who had since found CB Mineral Tec a good many profitable contracts. Since then, the two men had worked closely together, under the age-old adage governing everyday life in Asia: *You scratch my back, I scratch yours.*

Bryant maintained offices in Singapore, Jakarta, Darwin, Houston, Johannesburg and Aberdeen, covering all aspects of mineral and oil exploration and mining, as well as arranging joint ventures with fellow companies on a plant and work-force hire system. Usually cheap Filipino and Indonesian labour.

Junus, by contrast, was involved across a much wider spectrum than minerals and specialised construction programs. Junus Kutu was a major player in the Indonesian archipelago. If it was precious and buried deep in the ground Kutu was involved in getting it out. If a business had interests in Indonesia, Kutu could see that its shares and worldwide interest soared. Whether it was hotels, restaurants, tourist theme parks or national airlines - Junus Kutu could get the relevant planning permission and operating permits and in return for his fee and a substantial block of shares he would see to it that the businesses thrived. Altogether Junus Kutu was an extremely powerful and influential man. Charles Bryant liked him a great deal.

The waiter placed Junus' beer on the table then went to great pains to show Bryant that he had brought him both a chilled glass of gin, *and* a separate bottle of tonic.

"Yes, yes, thank you." Bryant waved the young man away, then picked up the mixer bottle and carefully poured half of the tonic water onto the thick pile of ice. "Will they ever get it right?" he asked, shaking his head in dismay. "You finally get them to serve the gin and tonic separately and then the bloody idiot forgets the lemon!" He glanced up suddenly, realising that he might well have caused his friend offence.

Junus smiled benignly. "Bloody natives, eh?"

Bryant sipped a cold mouthful and turned solemnly to the small man in front of him. "Come on then, Junus. I have a strange feeling that tonight isn't just for chatting about girls or catching up with each other because I happen to be in town for a couple of weeks," he paused, setting the glass down onto the table. "And I don't think you want to talk about regular business, or you'd have taken me to a decent restaurant and not this place."

Junus Kutu glanced around the room, which was starting to fill up with the sort of people who seemed to frequent the place, and many others like it. "What, you don't like this place?"

"If the best-looking woman in here is a bloody bloke, then no!"

Junus laughed out loud, then leant forward conspiratorially. "Tell me my friend, what do you know about the current
state of Indonesian politics?"

Bryant frowned. He was painfully aware of the sudden
upheaval of recent years, of Golkar, the once governing party
devolved, then reformed and put in as a major part of a coalition. Many felt they were gaining power by stealth. And the
growing unrest among the smaller, previously more independent islands threatened to domino into separation of power.
It had made the exploration and mining projects increasingly
difficult. However, his views might well be entirely different
from those of his friend, and if there was one lesson that he
had learned well in Southeast Asia, it was not to offend one's
business associates. He picked up his glass and slowly sipped
the refreshing contents before turning warily to his companion. "Why do you ask?"

Junus smiled wryly. "I see your predicament, but I need
your valid opinion. Come, my friend, you are a well-travelled
fellow and what's more, you have spent a great deal of time in
my beautiful country."

Bryant kept hold of his glass, smoothing his finger around
the condensation which trickled down the side of the vessel.
He gnawed subconsciously at his lip, then nodded. "All right,
if you wish. I know that your country is officially a democracy, and that *Golkar* was an invention of necessity, but when
all is said and done, the fact remains, the alliance is dominated heavily by the military. The core of the alliance, the
farmers, the fishermen, even the professions, are mere after-
thoughts."

Junus nodded thoughtfully and sipped at his bottle. "True.
But things are better now we are a coalition democracy, do
you not think so?"

Bryant nodded cautiously, suddenly suspicious of where

this might be leading. "I suppose so, but things certainly got a bit hectic when the rupiah crumbled."

"I am not disputing that," he paused, eyeing his companion closely. "But between you and me, business is good now, no?"

Bryant nodded. "It's up and down, but yes, the ups outweigh the downs."

Junus smiled. "Exactly. Tell me, what is your single most dependable resource within your company?" He held up his hands defensively. "Please my friend, bear with me on this."

Bryant frowned, then shrugged. "Oil. That is probably where I get the most contracts."

"And where do you receive the most contracts for oil exploration and production?" He sipped his beer, then added, "On a global level."

Bryant stared at the little man cautiously. "Indonesia. Why do you ask?"

"Last year, my country produced five hundred million barrels of oil. With proven reserves of eight point five billion barrels. With these figures, Indonesia is the world's leading oil producer," he paused. "But you already knew that."

Bryant nodded, keeping his wary eyes on his companion.

"Not only do we produce the most oil, we produce in excess of four point eight billion cubic metres of natural gas. We produce the most tin, at approximately twenty-eight thousand tons, the most copper, at around three hundred thousand tons, *and* four million tons of coal. Add this to the two hundred thousand tons of iron ore, the two million tons of nickel and the five hundred thousand tons of bauxite, and I think we know why your principal office is now in Jakarta."

Bryant remained silent as he looked suspiciously at Junus Kutu.

"Relax, my friend. I do not mean to offend. I only wish to put things into perspective."

"I'd say that you've achieved that, Junus. But frankly, I don't see where this is heading. Of course, my biggest interests are within your country, but that is where a great many companies' interests lie."

Junus held up his hands. "I am aware of that. It is other people's interests that have put me where I am today, and a great many others like myself. But let me just outline one more point. Mining makes up for thirteen percent of gross domestic output and more than seventy percent of the country's export earnings. Impressive, isn't it? But what if I were to say that it only employs one percent of the country's total work force?"

Bryant shrugged. "Machines do most of the work and companies need skilled labour to operate them."

"This is true of a great many things and personally, I can understand it. I am a businessman. A westerner at heart." He shook his head sombrely then sipped another refreshing mouthful of beer. "But the trouble with your average, ignorant Indonesian is that he is just a simple peasant, a native. It's in the blood."

Bryant stared at him impassively, not wanting to risk agreeing with what he thought to be perfectly true.

"Now, if someone influential, someone with a great deal of power and support, were to try and change things, try to get an ignorant population's support by promising to deliver their dreams to them on a plate, then in the long term, things could soon become extremely difficult for people like us. People who, when all is said and done, exploit both this wonderful nation and its people," he paused, studying Bryant's apparent blankness. "Now, if this influential person had the support of the underpaid yet loyal military and the people of the smaller islands, who as recently as the sixties or seventies, were independent – hell, were headhunting and performing acts of cannibalism - then business as we know it could be changed dramatically."

Bryant nodded. "Situations change, governments change. That's just an aspect of business risk."

"Very well, I accept that. But what if this influential person could swing the people one hundred and eighty degrees? What if he could take a nation which is hampered by extreme right-wing corruption, and turn it into a communist state?"

Bryant laughed out loud and picked up his glass. He gulped the last remnants, then turned around and waved to a waiter who was hovering near the bar. Junus Kutu remained silent as the waiter ambled to their table, then stood in front of them silently, awaiting their order.

Bryant placed his order for a large gin and tonic, this time emphasising the addition of a slice of lemon. He turned to Junus, who simply held up his empty bottle for the waiter to see what he was drinking. Bryant turned back to his companion as the waiter strolled casually back to the bar. "My dear Junus, I think that you have had perhaps a little too much sun. Either that, or you have drunk one too many beers!" He smiled as he shook his head. "A country cannot just change to communism. For a start, it's a dead, discredited policy. The Soviet Union collapsed, all the satellite countries separated. It doesn't work, nobody believes in the concept anymore."

"When people have nothing, then they will clutch at any straw. The grass is always greener. Isn't that what you say?" he paused, checking that he had used the correct colloquialism, then continued. "Indonesia is the largest country in South East Asia, its islands total over thirteen and a half thousand, over six-thousand of them are inhabited, yet these six thousand islands make up the fifth most populated country in the world. Its people are among the poorest. No other country produces so much for its economy yet returns so little to its people. Civil unrest is abound, and poverty is rife."

Bryant looked up at the pretty girl who was hovering in front of them, smoothing her hands over a shapely pair of hips. She smiled seductively, pursed her lips to form a kiss. "You want good time?" she asked in a sing-song voice. "I give you good time, mister."

Bryant held up his hand dismissively. The girl ignored his motion and made to sit down.

Junus leant forward and shook his head. "Tedak!" he snapped.

The girl glared at him, her features changing dramatically. "What wrong, you gay? You no like women? You have small cock!" She stormed away then turned around after a few paces and loosed a rapid outburst of *Bahasa Indonesian,* before finally walking back to the booth where Numan, the best looking 'girl' in Jakarta, was seated with three others.

Junus stared at Bryant and shrugged. "You see, those girls are the lucky ones. They are the ones who are pretty enough to be of some use. What about the ugly ones, what does this country hold for them?"

Bryant frowned. "But I still don't understand what you're saying. You said if *someone* could turn the country around. Who do you mean, and what do you know?"

Junus smiled. "My friend, I know more than the government, and believe me, they're extremely worried indeed. What I am about to say must be purely confidential."

Bryant nodded. "Of course. But why are you telling me this?"

The Indonesian waited for the waiter to place the two drinks on the table, then leaned forward to whisper conspiratorially. "There is something going on right now. If we, as businessmen do not act, then our interests in this nation are finished."

"Finished?" Bryant smiled. "My dear Junus, governments change all the time, but business always goes on." He reached forward and tipped a little tonic into his iced gin, then picked up the glass and took a shallow sip. He placed the glass back to the table and smiled. "You just have a few more pockets to line, that's all."

"Governments change, I will grant you that, but I have very interesting information indeed," Junus paused. "During the course of my life, I have made a great many useful contacts. However, unlike many businessmen, I go to great pains to keep in touch, in good favour."

Bryant felt a lump in his throat, wondering whether their relationship outside business matters was merely one of convenience for Junus Kutu. He picked up his glass, grateful for the distraction, and took a few small sips.

Junus did not detect Bryant's sudden change of mood, merely picked up his bottle and took a large gulp, before staring intensely at his companion. "What I am about to tell you now is in the strictest confidence. To mention it carelessly in this country could result in your untimely death," Junus paused to see whether he had his friend's consent to continue. Bryant simply nodded, intrigue getting the better of him, as it always did. "I have friends within the present government, useful friends," Junus paused, raising an eyebrow, as if to emphasise the purpose of these so-called *friends*. "At this moment in time, the Indonesian people are ready for a change and being mostly a poorly educated race, they do not realise that change at this moment in time could be terribly destabilising for the entire nation."

Bryant nodded, all too aware of the government's struggle to keep the economy afloat. Like most, he had suffered financially from the instability and unrest, but as with most troubled times, when the dust finally settled, there was even more money to be made than before.

"The government are panicking. Deep down they know that they are failing the people. Sure, we have the concept of Pancasila, the Five Principles, but do they deliver them? Of course not!

"As the Republic of Indonesia is spread over such a huge area, with over six thousand inhabited islands, the nation is divided into twenty-seven governed provinces. These provinces are ruled by separate local governments, who are required by the constitution to operate the philosophic concept of *Pancasila,* or the five principles. These principles are - the belief in one supreme god; just and civilized humanity; the unity of Indonesia; democracy; and equality. With a population of almost two hundred million, three hundred and thirty ethnic groups, two hundred and fifty distinct languages and practicing believers in every religion on Earth, it is easy to see how ineffective the concept of *Pancasila* really is." Junus eyed the room carefully, then stared at Bryant. "I also have a great many friends in the military. There is unrest within the ranks. It would appear that it is not just the civilians who yearn for change. Sure, the president ousted many of Soharto's old chiefs, but their replacements are merely puppets for the old regime." He looked nervously at his friend, then sipped another mouthful of *Bintang.* "There is a man who can threaten the current state of Indonesia, perhaps even the entire Malay Archipelago. The government know about him, but they are too scared to make a move. They cannot even use their own security service, for the fear that the man's agents have infiltrated it, along with a great many departments within the government."

Bryant looked at him nervously and frowned. "I don't understand Junus, I don't know what to say."

"Say nothing, just listen. This country is on borrowed time. The PKI, the Communist Party was banned in the sixties, but like most such organisations, it did not die but merely slept. Now, it is ready to awaken and with a paymaster who can make a difference," Junus paused, then anticipating Bryant's question he leaned forward in his seat until there was barely a hand's distance between them and whispered quietly into his ear. "China..."

CHAPTER FIVE

Junus Kutu dropped a ten thousand rupiah note into the copper bowl on the small round table beside the exit. The old woman smiled a toothless grin of appreciation, then nodded to the tough-looking man at the door. The muscle-bound Indonesian nodded his own silent thank you, then opened the door and let the two men out into the busy street.

Bryant felt the humid wave of overheated air suddenly engulf him, as he stepped from the comfort of the air-conditioned bar and into the density of the crowd. He smelt the pungent mixture of aromas which is almost any town in Southeast Asia. Fried rice, chilies, ginger, garlic, tamarind and a host of exotic spices mingled with sweat, urine, excrement and vehicle fumes, all combined into a single nauseating miasma which can half paralyze the primary senses. The smell of Asian towns and cities.

"I hope you don't mind talking out here?" Junus Kutu smiled at his friend as they negotiated a narrow side street and stepped into a dimly lit walkway. "I feel it would be safer if we kept on the move."

Bryant frowned, sensing that his companion was enjoying

the situation of secrecy and conspiracy perhaps a little more than he should. However, even Bryant had to admit to himself to an unsettling sense of danger and intrigue.

Kutu stopped at the entrance to the next street, which fed onto the main road. He looked at Bryant, then nodded towards the cluster of tiny stalls to the side of the pavement. "Hungry?" he asked.

Bryant studied the selection of stalls against which he habitually warned all his young executives, explaining in lurid detail the dangers of hepatitis through to botulism and salmonella. He watched as the men and women cooked over fierce propane flames, using woks and thin bottomed pans, turning the food over with large wooden tongs, as the oil spilled out and ignited in the heat. Every so often a lorry or bus would rattle past, spilling fumes into the midst of the ramshackle kitchens and season the mix of frying spices, ginger and garlic with a note of imperfectly burnt diesel.

Bryant looked further down the street towards the air-conditioned mall, and its selection of western fast food restaurants, including a *Wendy's*, *MacDonald's* and *Pizza Hut* then turned back to his friend, not wishing to hurt his feelings or to insult his judgment. "Sure, I could do with a bite."

Junus Kutu smiled. He led the way towards the group of canvas coverings and browsed over the produce on offer. Bryant followed the man's gaze, forcing himself to ignore the food, which was a little too heavily garnished with flies for his own taste.

Kutu smiled at Bryant and shook his head. "You come to my country five or six times a year but insist on eating from only the most expensive restaurants in Jakarta. Or the fat and sugar rich junk food of the West! You are seriously missing out, my good friend!"

"If you say so." Bryant mused, as he stared at a large bowl

of finely sliced lamb or goat, trying to work out what could possibly have been added to tint the meat green at the edges.

"If you like, I will order for the both of us," Kutu announced amiably, sensing his companion's indecision.

Bryant nodded, then turned back towards the hustle and bustle of the heavy traffic. He watched the scooters, some with three adults balancing on, weave between the cars and buses, then stared in horror as a blind woman stepped out into the traffic and proceeded to wave her stick at the fast-moving vehicles. The drivers responded by sounding their horns and launching into a crescendo of abuse. Still the woman continued on her path, unperturbed by the hazards, until she scuttled across both lanes and to the relative safety of the pavement. Bryant turned back to Kutu, then watched as a wizened old man arranged a selection of meat-filled skewers over a charcoal grill and dropped some blanched noodles into a wok of smoking hot peanut oil and added a handful of diced chilies. He worked quickly, tossing the noodles to keep them from sticking to the hot metal, then spooned a selection of fresh smelling spices into the pan, before adding a ladle of coconut milk. He reduced the mixture, allowing it to bubble furiously then stirred in a spoonful of fish paste, before taking the wok off the blazing inferno and setting it down onto the pavement.

Kutu smiled. "Ah! Dinner is served!" He stepped forward and accepted the plate which the old man handed to him. "Here, my friend, take this."

Bryant walked hesitantly to the stall, where he gingerly took the plate from Kutu, then looked for somewhere to sit. As if she had read his mind a haggard old woman who appeared to be in her late-seventies, walked out from the canvas covering and set a stool down in front of the stall. Bryant nodded a thank you and perched on the rickety stool, amid the busy pavement.

"You like satay?" Junus Kutu held up the tiny skewer, then dipped the meat into a thick chili and peanut sauce.

Bryant nodded. He *loved* satay but was used to eating it in expensive restaurants with pretty waitresses and credit card readers. He nodded, then took a bite of marinated lamb.

"Try the noodles, you'll not taste any better, not in the whole of Jawa Baret."

Bryant nodded and took a mouthful of the thick noodle mixture. Kutu was certainly right, Bryant had not tasted better in Jakarta. He placed the spoon on the rim of the plate then picked up another skewer and bit off a mouthful of the spicy lamb.

Kutu chuckled to himself, beaming brightly at his friend. "You have been missing out, admit it! You see, all these expensive restaurants employ Sri Lankan chefs. They have good training in Sri Lanka and the chefs learn all the cuisines. They are some of the best hospitality chefs in the world, but they do not know the basic, people's food of Indonesia. Their satay is good, but not like the satay I grew up with. Not like my grandmother cooked."

Bryant smiled, he *had* indeed been missing out. He had also missed out on stomach upsets and more serious illnesses, for which no doubt, he would soon be making up. He finished his mouthful, trying his best not to think about the green meat as he chewed, then stared intently at the little Indonesian. "You mentioned China," he prompted.

Junus Kutu set his own plate on the pavement and edged his stool forwards, until he rested barely a metre away from his companion. He then took a suspicious, but all too obvious, glance around and leaned forwards conspiratorially. "I did," he stated flatly. "China has always wanted Indonesia. She has influence with Vietnam, Burma, North Korea, even the Philippines. All that separates Indonesia from China is fifteen hundred miles of ocean, with friends conveniently placed all along the way."

Bryant nodded. "You're quite right, but if China made a move towards Indonesia, the rest of the Western world would react immediately," he paused, thinking of the consequences. "Where would that get them?"

Kutu shook his head. "Believe me, my friend, if China sneezes, the rest of the world will catch a cold." He stared at Bryant, picked up his plate and took another large mouthful of noodles. "An invasion is not China's plan. What they want to achieve is the governing of a country through dictatorship, by a leader and party completely loyal to Beijing. A sort of Chinese *franchise*, if you will. With the natural resources Indonesia has in abundance under Chinese control there will be no stopping them in business. They will bring their production costs down even further and be in control of at least a quarter of the world's oil, gas and coal." He spoke through his mouthful, but with the practice of a lifetime, spilt not the smallest morsel. "Tell me, have you ever heard of General Madi Soto?"

Bryant frowned and shook his head.

"No, I didn't think that you would have. Few have, even the government keeps his exploits quiet, but of late they have been having great trouble keeping a gag on him. Especially through mediums like *Facebook* and *YouTube*."

"Why, what is he saying?"

Junus shook his head dejectedly. "It's what they *can't* hear him saying that is causing the greatest problems. Nobody can get near enough, or if they can, they are found out and are 'disappeared'. The government is petrified that Soto's actions will cause a revolt among the people. He openly speaks of high minimum wages and guaranteed work for skilled positions, using retraining programs. He promises to keep unemployment down by using only Indonesian labour."

"Why don't the government just arrest him, lose him in the judicial system for a while?" Bryant asked, knowing full well that such things happened every day in Indonesia. Its record on human rights was among the worst in the world, but when a country produces useful minerals in such quantities, the rest of the world can afford to turn a conveniently blind eye.

"It's not as simple as that. The government can't get anywhere near him, he has growing support among the military, the police and key civil servants. Believe me, General Soto is becoming untouchable. If the government makes a move too soon, Soto is likely to become a political martyr, the people may start to revolt again. Lord knows, they cost us enough last time. However, if they do not act, then the coalition government's days are numbered. And believe me, a coalition is always what's best for Indonesia."

"Why are you telling me all this?" Bryant frowned. "What do you think I can do?"

"You?" Kutu smirked. "My friend, *you* can do nothing. *I* can do nothing; people *like* me can do nothing. But, if we get together, then we may just have a chance to rescue this situation."

CHAPTER SIX

Peter Stewart pulled the Vauxhall Insignia across the road and eased to a halt on the well-worn grass verge. He switched off the ignition but waited for a moment before getting out of the car allowing himself to take note of his surroundings.

The weather was mild for the time of year, although the past few days had witnessed the sudden chill in the air which means that autumn was just about here. The leaves had long since begun to darken, and it would not be long before they started to fall.

He looked at his watch, pleased that he had made good time. Having left London at midday, it had only taken him just under five hours to reach his destination. He had arrived in Cornwall at a little after four and had taken another hour to thread his way down the A30 and then the A39 towards Falmouth. He had now lost count of the myriad roads he had now taken, each one looking the same as the last and all too narrow. The satnav had told him he was two hundred metres from his destination. He opened the door and stepped onto the muddy verge, careful not to step into the tiny network of puddles in the potholes which skirted the fringe of the quiet back road.

To his right, the autumnal-tinged foliage spread into a small copse, then petered out in a series of overgrown fields, which had clearly been neglected for some time. Across the narrow country road, matters were quite different, with neatly trimmed hedges and a huge expanse of cultivated fields, spreading out to the brow of a hill a mile or so distant, beyond which he could see a huge expanse of water with many sails gleaming white in the autumn sun.

Stewart locked the vehicle, then dodged across the puddles and into the belt of overgrown foliage. He carefully pushed his way through and stood at the hedge studying the property ahead of him.

The cottage was set in a thicket of trees and perennial shrubs, hiding all but the roof and chimney, which emitted billows of dark grey smoke.

Stewart scrambled up the hedge, snagging himself in the clutching thorns of the thick brambles. He gently disentangled himself from the sharp claws, taking great care not to let the natural barrier rip his clothing, then jumped down into the field below.

The sudden sound caught him completely off guard, making him flinch involuntarily. His heart leapt as he moved out of the way, his reflexes taking over. Having almost flown into Stewart's face, the cock pheasant darted to its left, continuing its panic-stricken call, as it flew out over the road and into the neatly kept fields beyond.

Stewart sighed deeply, as his heartbeat quietened. He glanced up at the distant cottage, then started to pick his way through the waist-high thistles which marked the perimeter of the overgrown field. After he had covered about sixty-metres he stopped walking and studied the building a little more attentively. It seemed larger than he had first thought and upon closer inspection he could see that the rear of the cottage had been extended into some form of conservatory, though constructed in such a way as to remain in keeping with the rest of the property. As he eased forwards, he could see that the conservatory took in a view of a nearby creek. The tide was out, exposing thick muddy banks with ducks, geese and swans feeding in the mud.

Stewart caught sight of the man and quickly crouched down amongst the tall thistles. He peered through his makeshift barrier and watched intently as the man walked from round the side of the cottage and stopped at the entrance of a small tool shed. The man disappeared inside, to emerge seconds later carrying a large axe in his left hand. He walked back towards the cottage, swinging the axe playfully, then turned the corner and disappeared from Stewart's view.

Stewart moved fast, leaping over the clump of thistles and running to the far hedge, skirting the border of the garden which unsurprisingly, was no less overgrown than the field. Stewart knew the man's schedule, knew that he did not spend much time here. The cottage looked in good condition, but regular gardening was not on the agenda. He paused for a moment and listened, straining to hear above his own, rapid heartbeat. Stewart smiled. To his distinct pleasure, he could hear the heavy axe thudding into a log. He peered over the hedge to make sure all was clear, then nimbly slipped over the obstacle and rested quietly in the overgrown grass. The axe's reports were still clearly audible as the man continued to work on a difficult log, raining blows with what sounded like considerable force. Stewart edged his way out of cover, moving quickly towards the far side of the garden. He stopped at a row of untended rosebushes and smiled to himself as he watched the man deliver another heavy blow to the stubborn log. From his position, Stewart could clearly see the man's shoulders, as he worked energetically with his back towards him. All that separated the two men was Stewart's barrier of rosebushes and just over twenty metres of flat ground. Stewart breathed steadily, deliberately calming his nerves, smoothing the flow of adrenaline. He stood up slowly, extracted the length of cheese wire from his pocket and gripped the specially adapted rubber handles firmly with both hands. Slowly, cautiously, he stepped out from the row of bushes and made his way across the stretch of flat ground towards his target.

The man lost his patience with the stubborn log and dropped the axe like a pendulum allowing the blade to slice into his well-worn chopping log. Leaving the axe embedded where it fell, he stepped around the small pile of logs and made his way towards the front of the cottage.

Stewart moved quickly, expertly, making lightning progress across the flat ground, but making next to no sound as he closed on the unsuspecting man. He tightened the length of cheese wire, holding his left hand higher than his right, ready to wrap the thin line around his victim's neck, then pull down with all his might. His right knee would hammer into the base of the man's spine, giving him extra leverage and if it worked well to that point, he would also put his foot into the back of the man's knee to drop him and gain even more leverage and pin the man's leg to the ground preventing a counter attack. Attack cleanly and swiftly, and the target would die within seconds with the garrotte; get it wrong, and it could take up to five minutes.

He closed in, now only five or six paces from the man, who was strolling casually towards the front door of the cottage. He tightened the wire, grit his teeth in an act of controlled aggression then moved in for the kill.

The man moved gracefully, dropping low to the ground and spinning in a tight arc, his extended right leg catching Stewart's left leg, as he raised his right knee for the attack. It

was a fluid motion, supple. The back of his calf catching
Stewart at the back on his knee, forcing the joint to give
instantly. Stewart was taken cleanly off his feet. He dropped
heavily on his rear, releasing the handles of the cheese wire in
a desperate bid to break his fall.

The man wasted no time, dropping down onto Stewart's
chest and straddling him, each knee resting on one of Stewart's outstretched arms. He caught hold of the cheese wire,
ran his right hand around the helpless man's neck, then pulled
tight, keeping his hands pressed firmly against Stewart's
chest. Stewart made a bid to inhale as the wire pulled tight,
restricting his airway but not yet slicing into the flesh.
Stewart looked up into the man's eyes and could not help but
shiver as the man stared down at him, the icy glacier blue
eyes piercing into his own.

Gradually, the wire loosened, allowing precious air to
enter his lungs. Then, in an instant the man rolled back onto
his heels and stepped aside, offering a hand and eventually a
cold, detached smile. Stewart caught hold of the hand warily
and accepted the lift to his feet. He stood facing the man,
then broke into a humble grin. "Nearly got you that time,
Alex."

"No, you didn't," Alex King smirked and handed him the
cheese wire. "Not even close."

CHAPTER SEVEN

Charles Bryant let the cool air play over his damp shoulders, then looked up into the vents of the air conditioning unit. He glanced at Junus Kutu and smiled. "I don't think I will ever get used to the heat."

Kutu smirked. "Of course, you won't, not if you keep coming to places like this! You have to shrug off modern technology if you want to accustom yourself to my country's climate."

Bryant shook his head. "No, this will do me just fine." He glanced around the foyer of *The Emperor* and smiled at his new surroundings. He much preferred the comforts of an expensive hotel such as this; as far as he was concerned, Kutu could keep his country's culture and customs, along with its fondness of open-air eating and the attendant dysentery.

The cool air was starting to take effect. He felt the clammy perspiration cool on his skin, and his breathing became easier, less strained than it had been in the stifling closeness of the polluted streets, a world away behind the glass doors of this new-found sanctuary. Bryant turned back to his companion and nodded towards the mirrored entrance to the lounge. "My round, what are you drinking?"

CHAPTER EIGHT

Stewart studied the ledges of the cliff face, noting the complex patterns of shading, the contours and the way the grasses of the cliff top seemed almost animated. The sea raged against the base of the cliff, pounding great spumes of white water high up the slope, just short of where the gulls took refuge deep in its precipitous ledges.

He turned his concentration away from the oil painting and glanced briefly at his agent. "Is this one of yours?"

King nodded, taking a slow, deliberate sip of coffee from the oversized mug, as he weighed up his visitor.

Stewart looked back at the painting, transfixed by its realism. "Where is it?"

"Part of St. Agnes Head. A stretch of rugged headland near Chapel Porth," King paused, knowing that Stewart was not familiar with the Cornish coastline. "Just over eight miles away, west of here. What they call the north coast. Or surfers' coast." He waved a hand at the creek in front of them which had started to fill with a rising high tide. "This feeds into the Carrick Roads a large waterway which flows out to the south coast. Or sailors' coast."

Stewart nodded, though he was none the wiser. He turned his attention to another oil painting, a more sedate study of a picturesque cottage beside a gentle stream, feeding a water wheel. "And this?"

King nodded, somewhat embarrassed at having a critic for the first time. "Yeah, that one's mine as well. Quite a recent one. I did it early this spring," he paused, reminiscently. "It's the last one I painted. It's a cottage near Fowey. I was driving past it once with Jane and she fell in love with it. I went back before the summer and painted it..." King trailed off quietly.

There was an awkward silence which Stewart didn't break, but he did raise an eyebrow, genuinely impressed at his agent's talent. He turned around and walked back to his chair, where his coffee mug rested nearby on the small, half-moon table. He sat down heavily and continued glancing round the room, scrutinizing every fixture and feature. The cottage was decorated and furnished in keeping with the structure's design. The walls were plainly whitewashed, and the prominent oak beams were stained dark. The furniture looked antiquated rather than antique and had seen much service. Stewart looked across the room and stared at King. He nibbled at his lip tentatively, raised an expectant eyebrow. "You know why I'm here, Alex. Don't you..." he stated matter-of-factly. "You have obviously read the papers. The Iraq situation looks as if it's going to take another turn. ISIS has threatened to activate terrorists in Britain in retaliation for both Colonel Al-Muqtadir's and Betesh's deaths."

"I know," King paused. "I read the papers."

Stewart nodded. "In that case, you will know how Iraq discovered that it was a Western-funded and organised operation."

"A piece of equipment left at the scene," King replied sardonically. "My NATO GPS, to be precise. I know, I messed up. I shouldn't have attended to my wounded team-mate, I shouldn't have left my pack behind."

"You shouldn't have let a boy take *your* bloody shot!" Stewart said, tight lipped. He was irked by Alex King's blasé attitude. "What the bloody hell were you thinking? Those Kurds were there to assist you, not do your work…"

King rose to his feet and stared down at Stewart, towering over him. "I was thinking of a boy and his family!" he snapped, shaking his head sorrowfully. "It isn't always so simple in the field, it's a hell of a lot easier to make judgment from behind a desk in the safety of a comfortable office. For Christ's sake, Peter, you know that – you wrote the bloody book!"

Stewart nodded, somewhat intimidated by King's aggressive posture. He knew the man well, he had trained him and above all he knew what the man was capable of. He remained calm, casually motioning King back to his chair. "Sit down, Alex. Tell me from the beginning, we have to sort this out." He relaxed a little, as the man returned to his seat. "If you decided that your team-mate should take the shot, then I believe that you were justified in making the decision. But I need to know why you did it. The shit has truly hit the fan on this, everybody's story has got to tally."

CHAPTER NINE

The waitress poured half of the tonic into the frosted glass on top of the ice and gin - so cold the ice popped and cracked - then placed the bottle carefully on the table beside Bryant's glass. She smiled sweetly at them both, then placed the chit in the centre of the table, unsure who would be paying.

Bryant watched the attractive young girl walk back to the bar, admiring the sway of her hips. He turned back to Kutu and grinned wolfishly. "Now, if *she* is available later, that would be a different story! I might see how far a big tip will take it." Junus Kutu shook his head pitifully, making no effort to hide his disgust. "What's the matter?" Bryant asked, somewhat irked at his companion's sudden change in attitude.

"You still haven't worked it out, have you?" he stated flatly. "You come to my country and make a fortune from its assets and its poverty-stricken people and you have not had the decency to learn anything about it. You do not know the customs, and you certainly know nothing of our protocols."

Bryant glared at the tiny Indonesian. "What the hell do you mean?"

Kutu leaned forward, resting his chest against the rim of the glass table. "You see one prostitute working the bars or the street corners and you presume that *all* the women are for sale! That girl has a job the majority would kill for. She is working in a quality establishment, free from trouble and she is earning a very good wage compared to her friends or family. She has no need to sell herself, body *or* soul Do you think that the women out there want to sell their bodies? Do you think they want to be dribbled over, sweated on, to be degradingly *used* by people who have money? Of course not! But they have no other option. They risk disease every time they commit to a transaction. Why? Because nobody has ever explained to them about condoms or safe sex. In short, because nobody cares."

Bryant stared down at the table, knowing full well that his companion was right. He had used the prostitutes in Jakarta many times, although at first merely in pursuit of a novelty. It was only later, after his wife had returned to England to look after her aged mother that he had begun to rely upon them. He remembered how the first young girl had laughed as he had pulled the condom out of the packet, how she had watched him intently, as he had fumbled with its application in the dimly lit room. He had not considered the possibility that the girl might not be accustomed to using them.

He looked apologetically at Kutu. "I'm sorry, I never really thought about it."

Kutu shrugged. "Westerners seldom do." He picked up his bottle of *Bintang* and drank a large mouthful, before setting the bottle back down on the glass table. "Perhaps this will be your chance to make it up?"

Bryant frowned, realising that Kutu was most probably referring to their earlier conversation regarding the Indonesian General. "What do you mean, Junus?"

The little Indonesian smiled wryly, as he stared harshly into Bryant's eyes. "Assassination my friend! The only way we can get our country back on track..." he paused, glancing briefly around the quiet bar then turned his attention back to his companion. "Assassination..."

CHAPTER TEN

"It was the most macabre scene that I have ever witnessed," King glanced at Stewart and shook his head. "And after my years of service with the firm, that is certainly saying something."

The Scotsman said nothing, he sat back in his chair and waited for his agent to continue in his own time.

King sipped the remains of his coffee from the oversized mug, then gently returned the vessel to the miniature pine coffee table in front of him. He turned away and looked blankly out of the nearby window, though Stewart knew that he was not admiring the view. "I slipped over the Turkish border with relative ease, then met my contact near the town of Zakho, just north of Amadiyah. He warned me of the worsening situation between ISIS and the Kurdish rebels and advised me to return home. He went on to tell me of the recent atrocities committed by the ISIS fighters and of the many families which had been murdered in the past few weeks. To be honest, I thought he was exaggerating much of what he told me, just to show his appreciation of me being there."

"And he wasn't?" Stewart interjected. He looked at King and shook his head despondently. "Come on, Alex, you've played the game and you've seen the sights; South American drug wars, African dictatorships, Iraq, Afghanistan and Syria. Do you want me to give you the complete list, just in case you've forgotten one?"

King held up his hand in objection. "No, I haven't forgotten, I see them vividly, every single night," he paused, staring intently at his controller. "ISIS are on a whole other level. We will not beat them. Not without fighting them like they fight everyone else. And we will never do that. So, we're fucked Boss. Simple as that," King sighed, shaking his head. "When we arrived in the village of Kalsagir we were met with the smell of burning flesh and the sight of children hanging by their feet from the street lamps and shop fronts. They had no heads. The bastards had forced the parents to watch their children die. Every woman under forty had been raped. Repeatedly. And every male, regardless of age, had been beheaded. Most of them tortured terribly first. We're not talking swiftly either. Heads were piled up, in some instances half a foot or so of spine still attached. Hacked off with farm tools, or pulled off slowly with ropes…"

Stewart shook his head in dismay, although almost thirty years at the operational end of MI6 had desensitised him to almost all emotion.

"Don't get me wrong, I have seen the sights, as you say," King paused, picked up his coffee cup, then returned it to the table after realising that he had already drunk it dry. "Soon after I arrived, the team of rebels that I was to work with drove into the village in a battered truck."

Stewart nodded, he was familiar with the set-up and knew of the Kurdish rebel network of CIA funded freedom fighters, code-named; 'New Dawn'.

"The three men seconded to assist in my mission were

brothers. Akhim, the boy who was later fatally wounded in our retreat, was in his mid-teens. His siblings, Shameel and Akmed were older, in their thirties.

"They entered the village and were met with the news that their younger brother had been executed. Their eleven-year-old sister had been raped by six soldiers, and their father had been castrated and then beheaded," King paused, a look of sorrow in his hard, grey-blue eyes. "The boy, Akhim, barely shed a tear. He did not grieve, nor did he show anger. He merely greeted me, took me to where they had stockpiled the Russian equipment and offered me food and a bed for the night. His only wish was to exact revenge on the person responsible for ordering the atrocities against his family. Everyone knew who had given the order – Colonel Al Muqtadir in collusion with ISIS. He ran the northern sector without mercy and had deep sympathies with ISIS. He used ISIS to finish what Saddam started with the Kurds." King looked at Stewart, he seemed distant but slowly drew back in. "Akhim worked with me for the entire month. He showed me the best place to zero the rifle without detection and he surveyed the killing ground with me. Not once did he let the death of his family members interrupt *my* mission. I have never met such a dedicated, committed person in all my life. I decided to let him take the shot. Take revenge for his family."

Stewart nodded, understanding King's motives. Anyone would understand *why* King had acted in such a way. The problem that Stewart now faced, was *how* he was going to tell King that he would have to return to Iraq and eliminate the rest of his team.

CHAPTER ELEVEN

Donald McCullum replaced the detailed photograph to his desk, then turned ponderously to the next enlarged print. "I'll be damned," he mused quietly to himself.

"Sorry?" Marcus Arnott looked up expectantly, taking his eyes from his copy of the file.

McCullum shook his head dismissively. "Oh, nothing, I was just thinking out loud," he paused, shuffled the photographs and then held one up for Arnott's attention. "Look at this, Folio Seven."

Arnott rearranged his pile of photographs and looked at his copy, gingerly balancing the remainder of the file on his knee. He stared at the photograph and whistled, astonished. He glanced up at McCullum and frowned. "And King did all that, on his own?"

"Yes. All five of them," he paused, studying the macabre scene. "Notice that all of the men were armed."

"What about the woman?" Arnott asked, his eyes set on the ragged-looking bullet-hole just above the woman's left eye. "Was she armed?"

McCullum smiled wryly. "Well, I don't know. But by the time the police reached the scene, yes she was..."

Arnott nodded, turned his attention back to the photograph, studied the scene once more then looked back at McCullum. "He took out an entire Al Qaeda cell on his own?" He shook his head in bewilderment. "What was *our* line?"

"The government released a statement, detailing the operation and its objectives. MI5 and the SAS were working together alongside the Special Branch Anti-Terrorist Squad, gathering intelligence for the arrest of the cell by the Special Branch. Specialist armed officers were at the scene and reacted when the terrorist cell compromised them and started shooting."

"And they bought it?"

McCullum smiled wryly. "Hook, line and sinker. King was sent in at a moment's notice. The rest of the security forces never knew anything of his mission, nor even that he had been there."

"But the kill was chalked up to them all the same," Arnott stated flatly.

McCullum nodded. "Of course, things would be different now. This all happened some time ago. As head of Domestic Terrorism, you would be privy to such information now, as was your predecessor," he paused, studying Arnott intently, ever aware that the man was far safer as an ally. "That is why I have taken steps to remove Alex King's security blanket. With my position as Director General all but formally confirmed, I cannot afford any embarrassing incidents, now or later. As my future Deputy Director General, you can appreciate my predicament, can you not?"

Arnott nodded, managing not to appear over enthused at his future, unexpected promotion. "Of course, I can, Donald. You can count upon my unwavering support, as always," he paused, replacing the macabre photograph on the pile. "Does King have any more of these files?"

"Yes. I suspect that there is at least one more. So far, my agents have managed to locate two, both held in separate locations. They are still in place for now, merely confirmed of existence. These are copies photographed by smartphone and emailed over. If and when, all of the files will be lifted simultaneously. All have been stored in solicitors' offices, with instructions for the solicitor to publicise the material should King ever die in suspicious circumstances." McCullum shook his head in bewilderment. "Of course, I understand King's desire to cover himself, empathise with him in fact. It has not been unknown in his field for an employer to become tired of an employee and want to dispense with his services. But that generally isn't our style. King has obviously grown paranoid over the years. He must live with a lot going on inside his head, I'm sure it's the same for many field agents," he paused. "But there's an obvious problem. We might be happy with King's success rate. We *might* want King for as long as he can work for us. But what happens if he dies undertaking an assignment? It's risky work and could certainly have nothing to do with us betraying him, but my arse would be well and truly shafted all the same. The details of all of King's contracts, along with graphic photographs, would be all over the papers and on the television news. God knows what would be made of it on the internet. Investigative television shows all over the world would be wanting the full story. Why are the Secret Intelligence Service still ordering assassinations after the cold war? Who signed the orders? Who decides that financing assassinations is an acceptable or moral use of taxpayers' money?" McCullum smiled sardonically. "Well, as rotten luck would have it Marcus, the buck stops here."

CHAPTER TWELVE

"So apart from the obligatory bollocking, what are you here to tell me?" King stared icily at his former instructor, then broke into a smile. "Am I finished in the service, has the firm taken exception to my first major mistake?"

Stewart nibbled nervously at the inside of his cheek, then shrugged. "You made a mistake, Alex. At some stage or other, it was inevitable. You couldn't buck the odds forever," he paused, glancing away momentarily, though the motion was all too obvious. "The chiefs are in a stew. They are trying to wriggle out of the situation and if they can't come up with a solution then they will have to come up with a scapegoat."

King frowned. "The odds have always been well stacked against me, but I've always managed to pull off my missions. Surely one mistake shouldn't threaten my employment?"

Stewart shook his head dejectedly. "That isn't always the penalty. There are other solutions, as you know..."

King glared at the Scotsman. "Are you threatening me?"

Stewart shook his head dismissively. "No, not I, not personally."

"Then who?" King rose to his feet, stepped forward to

pick up Stewart's empty coffee cup. "Another?" he asked casually.

Stewart nodded. "Yes, thank you." He watched King walk to the kitchen, then turned his eyes back to the detailed coastal landscape as he spoke. "The top brass. They want you to go back to Iraq and clean things up. It's not so much the missing equipment and finger pointing, it's that you became too involved with an asset. Having a boy take such an important shot instead of an agent with a decade and a half operational experience isn't sitting comfortably with them. As far as they're thinking, what could you do next?" He smiled, relaxing a little. It had been much easier to pass the buck, let him know that the order came from the top, to tell him his orders while the man was in another room. "It's as much about testing your commitment as anything else..."

"Who gave the order?" King called, echoing from the tiny kitchen.

Stewart grinned. This was becoming much easier than he had first anticipated. "Martin Andrews," he replied casually, raising his voice a little. "He seems to be tidying the situation on behalf of McCullum, who is busy preening himself for the top job."

"Some things never change..." King had entered the room, standing at Stewart's shoulder, holding a single mug in his left hand. "Here you go, white with one sugar, right?"

Stewart nodded eagerly and reached up with both hands to accept the oversized mug.

King moved fast, dropping the empty mug into Stewart's lap then side stepping as the man made a desperate bid to dodge what he thought would be a shower of scalding coffee. By the time Stewart had realised that the mug had been empty, King had the small cook's knife in place against the man's throat, its razor-sharp edge resting gently against his carotid artery. "Is that what you came here to do, then?" King asked, staring coldly into his old friend's terrified eyes. "Cleaning up the situation, were you?"

"No! For Christ's sake, Alex!" He shook a little, realising how quickly death could come if King chose not to hear him out. One slice and the carotid artery would be severed. Continue to drag the blade down and across, and so would the jugular vein. Unconsciousness would follow in less than a minute, death in another two after that. "Earlier... outside, I was just playing our little game. Testing your reflexes, that's all!"

King pressed the knife firmly against Stewart's visible pulse, knowing that he was safe to press, so long as the blade did not actually slide across the skin. "Well they're better than yours, that's for sure. You should have given up as soon as you flushed that pheasant from cover. Too long behind a desk, you're out of touch. I saw you coming from behind, watched you in the reflection of my car's passenger window."

Stewart swallowed hard, moving the edge of the knife a little. He froze, waiting to feel the warm trickle of blood, then seemed relieved when none was forthcoming. "Take it easy, Alex. I'm unarmed and I'm just the messenger. You know that I don't make the decisions. Christ! I even told McCullum that you were the best, that if you allowed someone else to take the shot, then you surely had good reason!"

King smiled. "*I* know that I had good reason ..." His expression dropped, as he stared coldly into Stewart's eyes. "But will the likes of McCullum and Andrews understand? Frankly, they won't give a damn. As far as they're concerned, they need the situation resolved immediately and without having anything smelly left on them."

Stewart did his best to nod in agreement then felt the cold steel as the blade moved ever so slightly and thought better of it. "They have a job to do, Alex. They're not romantics, nor are they truly realists. They're mechanical. They make decisions that affect many innocent people and they never give it a second thought," he paused, as a bead of perspiration trickled down his brow and into his unblinking eye. "Alex, you work for the firm. You know the rules and the methods. Does it truly surprise you that they would resort to sacrificing you as a scapegoat? Of course, it doesn't. You knew as well as I that you would be called to go back and clean up the situation. You were waiting for the call."

King watched the tiny trickle of blood run down the side of Stewart's neck and disappear inside his collar. Deep down, he knew that Stewart was right, he had expected that someone would come. There was no way that the situation would correct itself, they never did. Stewart relaxed with a great sigh, as King took the blade from his neck. He dabbed his fingers against the tiny incision, then frowned as he looked at the blood smeared on his fingertips. He pulled a handkerchief out of his trouser pocket, then stared angrily at King.

"There was no bloody need to cut me!"

"Teach you to talk with a knife at your throat." He stared at the minuscule cut and laughed. "Don't worry, you'll live."

CHAPTER THIRTEEN

Charles Bryant sipped from his chilled glass of gin and tonic, purely to steady his sudden, unexpected bout of nerves. He replaced the glass on the mirrored table, catching a brief glimpse of his own reflection as he turned towards his companion. The sight had troubled him. If *he* could see the worry in his face, then surely Junus Kutu would see it also.

Kutu stared impassively at his companion and casually sipped from his cold bottle of *Bintang*. He had consumed quite a few beers throughout the evening and was now resorting to taking slow and shallow sips. "What is the problem, my friend?"

Bryant leaned forwards, resisting the sudden temptation to glance at his own reflection a second time. "What the hell do you think? You are talking about assassinating a prominent General, a potential political leader!"

"Exactly! Believe me, my friend if General Madi Soto becomes leader of this nation, then your business interests here are finished." The little Indonesian looked icily at the Englishman and shook his head despondently. "That is *your* fate. Now, do you want to hear mine? For myself, and a great many people like me, our business interests will be dead in the water. You can trade elsewhere; you have other interests. Mine have remained exclusively to the country that I love. I have some interests in Malaysia, but not even ten percent of my business in real terms. If Soto challenges this coalition government and wins, which I think will be the case, then he will grant China a monopoly on Indonesia's external business. All of her mineral contracts, certainly all of her defence contracts and most probably all of her other growth industries."

Bryant shook his head. "Come on Junus, you must be exaggerating! China is opening herself up, spreading her legs for the rest of the world to take a fuck. Look at the transition of Hong Kong. The take-over went smoothly. And now look at China's footing on the industrial world stage. They couldn't overstep the mark, if the rest of the world sanctioned China, who would they sell to?"

"They still have the worst human rights record. And countries would be too scared to sanction her. Which is exactly what they know to be true. The world cannot function without China. And if you turned on her, you couldn't possibly win. Did you know they have more personnel in their military, both serving and on call-up notice than there are American and British people put together?" Kutu looked at Bryant expectantly, but the man said nothing. "You mention Hong Kong. There are practically no westerners left in corporate positions anymore. China appears to be breaking down her barriers, but she is far removed from her Russian cousins. The Soviet Union broke down the barriers and has been in trouble ever since. Nothing but poverty or billionaires. Now they want their countries back. Look at the Ukraine. China is slowly opening the barriers, to become stronger. Beijing knew that she could not grow in strength behind closed doors. They took a different route, but they're the same bastards as they always were."

Bryant shrugged benignly. "Fair enough. But what you are saying about assassinating Soto is ludicrous! Why should such a task be left to people like you and me? Why are you even suggesting it?"

"Because, my friend, you seem to think that somebody else will do it. Do you know that in every major catastrophe that mankind has ever known, somebody has always thought that somebody else would deal with it? Think about it," he paused, the seriousness in his face almost disturbing in its intensity. "The Indonesian government is weak. The leader is merely another Suharto glove puppet threaded neatly in by Golkar yet lacks the man's distinctive qualities of leadership. The government is terrified that if they put together a plan to remove Soto, then Soto will hear of it and counter their move with the full support of the military. They know that the people are ready for change, maybe even an extreme change. A full one hundred and eighty degrees. If somebody does not take extreme action, then Indonesia will soon be merely a name, directly answerable to Beijing."

"Then what can *I* do?" Bryant looked at the Indonesian and frowned. "What do you want from me?"

"Just your support, for now. Just the knowledge that you would be behind me and represent Indonesia's best interests," he paused, slowly picking up his beer. "You are well connected my friend. You know people outside this country, as I do not. At a later date, that may prove invaluable."

"What do you mean?" Bryant stared at him warily.

Kutu smiled. "My friend, I think that I have indulged quite enough for one night." He looked at the diamond-encrusted Cartier on his wrist, then glanced casually back at his companion. "It is getting late. I think it would probably be for the better if we talked tomorrow. Shall we say, midday at my house? We could have lunch by the pool."

Bryant picked up his glass and drank the last remnants of his gin and tonic surprised at the abrupt end to their meeting. It was as if the cunning little Indonesian wanted to leave him hanging. He replaced the empty glass on the table and smiled at Junus Kutu, deciding to play along. "Sure. I have some business to attend to first thing, but I shouldn't be much after twelve, say... twelve thirty?"

Junus Kutu left through the automatic glass doors of The Emperor and the thick wave of heat engulfed him as his foot touched the first of the marble steps. He smiled for a second, thinking of Bryant's imminent discomfort when he would walk out into the night after he had finished his newly ordered drink.

He walked tentatively down the slippery-looking steps, then stepped onto the uneven pavement, dodging the hordes of pedestrians and street traders who hustled about, attempting to sell cheap Chinese made wares and tourist souvenirs.

Kutu looked around for a taxi then grinned with relief when he noticed a blue Toyota crawling by the roadside with a brightly illuminated taxi light on its roof. He made a dash for it waving frantically, knowing full well the difficulty in finding a vehicle at nearly two in the morning. To his relief, the taxi slowed to a halt and waited beside the pavement with its engine idling. He knew the firm. It was a good one he could trust. Kutu stepped forwards, opened the rear door and flopped exhausted and weary into the back seat.

He did not notice the slightly built Indonesian man watching him from across the street. The man was wraith thin and wore cut-off jeans as shorts and a torn vest. He ran a hand through a thick mane of long, greasy hair then dropped his cigarette stub to the pavement and ground it under the sole of his thin bottomed sandal. He smoothed his thumb and forefinger nervously over his wispy moustache and then swung a leg back over the saddle of his motor scooter and kick started the engine.

He waited for a moment, allowing the taxi to enter the steady stream of traffic, then slowly drove the scooter off the pavement and followed the taxi from a discreet distance.

CHAPTER FOURTEEN

The hood blinded not only his vision but the rest of his senses. He remembered reading somewhere that the remaining four primary senses are accentuated by the loss of another, but this case seemed altogether different.

He felt the weight of the man's heavy boot resting against his left kidney. He had taken a severe beating less than an hour ago and the pain had not yet subsided. His only fear lay in the uncomfortable knowledge that there was almost certainly more to come.

The exhaust fumes seeped through the truck's wooden floorboards, making him nauseous close to the point of vomiting. He tried to turn onto his stomach to relieve himself of the toxins but instantly felt a sharp pain against the side of his knee as the guard delivered yet another blow, forcing him to cry out in protest.

"Abdul!" the woman cried out in response to her husband's shout.

The second guard kicked out, from where he sat on the truck's bench seat, catching the woman in the face. She screamed, then lay still, sobbing, her face pressed against the solid wooden floor.

Abdul Tembarak grit his teeth in frustration. Calling out her name would only give the guards another excuse to administer further punishment. He thought of her, spread against the floor of the truck, with no protection from the bumpy road, her limbs tightly bound together, the hood pulled over her face, fastened around her neck with plastic duct tape. He could hear her struggling to breathe through the thick fabric, the heat was intolerable and the air in the fume-filled vehicle felt so thick, he could almost feel it pressing against his flesh. He felt the urge to call to her, to calm her, to let her know that everything would be all right. Only he couldn't. He couldn't lie to her anymore. Her innocence would be her undoing. She knew nothing, how could she tell them what they wanted to hear?

The truck slowed dramatically, its engine straining as the inexperienced driver dropped through the gears too quickly. Abdul felt himself slide slowly along the wooden floor, until he encountered his wife's legs, then blinked a tear, knowing that this would be the last time he would ever touch her.

The truck swung in a tight arc, stopped suddenly, then shuddered backwards, as the driver attempted to reverse in a straight line. After several attempts, the driver switched off the engine and started to shout instructions to the other soldiers.

Abdul heard the heavy wooden tailgate drop, then felt somebody catch hold of his ankles. He knew where he had arrived, knew the fearsome reputation of the Yogyakarta Military Installation and Intelligence Centre.

With a sudden, overwhelming disregard for his own safety, he took his last chance to speak to his young wife, the mother of their baby son. "I love you, my darling! I always will!"

"Abdul! Abdul! Where are they taking us?" She sobbed uncontrollably, then cried out as the guard kicked her again.

He heard the guards laughing as he was pulled out of the truck and dropped heavily onto the gravel. He knew what was in store for his wife, what they would do to her before the morning came. His mind started to fill with the graphic visions, the crystal-clear images, as recounted to him and many others, by those who had been fortunate enough to leave.

Abdul Tembarak started to sob for his wife, knowing that the gentle, sheltered life which she had lived up to this point, would be no preparation for the night which lay ahead.

CHAPTER FIFTEEN

Stewart paced over to the lounge window and stared out at the fields beyond the front garden. There were no other houses for as far as he could see, only patches of woodland and row after row of hedges crisscrossing the fields like the stitching on a patchwork quilt, until they met the sea beyond. He walked into the kitchen and peered through the tiny window. The view was much the same, apart from two similar cottages that were visible approximately half a mile away.

"See anything of interest?"

Stewart flinched visibly; he had been convinced King was still upstairs packing a travel bag. He turned around, somewhat irked by the way the man had entered the room so silently. "No, just nosing about. Not many neighbours to disturb you," he commented.

King nodded. "It's nice and quiet, that's what I like about it," he paused, glancing out of the window towards the nearest cottage. "But there are more houses nearby than you'd think. Much of Cornwall is like that, there's no wilderness down here. There's probably ten houses within a two-and-a-half-mile radius."

"But no nosy neighbours," Stewart said, almost enviously.

"No."

"What about girlfriends?"

King looked at him sharply. "What the hell do you mean by that?"

Stewart held up his hands defensively. "Nothing, I was just asking. You haven't had a relationship since... I was just wondering Alex; it's been three years..."

King walked over to the back door and quickly turned the key. "Well, it's none of your business." He reached up and slipped the key on top of the door frame, then turned to stare at Stewart. "Do you think it's easy to meet people or hold down a relationship in this profession? You've been there you should know. I'm not ready for all that, haven't felt I can move on yet..." King paused. Stewart could see the man's eyes were suddenly glossy, moist. Not cold and hard as they had been earlier. "Jane was MI5. She knew the score, knew the job. Alright, she was a liaison officer and not in my game, but she knew the hours, the commitment and the need for secrecy. That's why we worked as a couple. How do I start up something with somebody else? How do I explain my absence, my need to take off at a moment's notice? Besides, it doesn't seem right..."

Stewart nodded. He knew. He had lost his first wife also. But he'd moved on too quickly and had two successive divorces as a result. Not until he had started working in training and administrative roles had he found a solid relationship for himself. And by then he had been too old to start a family. His wife Margaret was a divorcee with three grown children of her own, but he had missed out on a family of his own and regretted it every single day.

"Well, maybe it's for the best," Stewart paused somewhat awkwardly. "I've always said all the best agents are single and childless. Nothing clouding their judgement..." He looked at

King and nodded towards his packed travel bag. "Ready to save the world again?" he asked with a wry smile, trying to break the sudden tension.

"Ready to do the dirty work for somebody else," King replied. "But it beats the hell out of me sitting here and wondering if it's all worth it..."

"Well, worth it or not, I hope you've left a note for the milkman, you may be gone for some time..."

CHAPTER SIXTEEN

They pushed him backwards and he fell heavily onto the concrete floor and rolled into the centre of the room, unable to make any attempt to break his fall with his hands bound tightly behind his back. The two guards laughed callously, then bent down and dragged him across the room to the single wooden chair, where they sat him down and roughly dispensed with the stifling hood.

Abdul Tembarak breathed deeply, almost feeling light-headed as the sudden rush of air entered his grateful lungs. He glanced up at one of the soldiers and immediately wished that he hadn't. The guard lashed out, catching him across the face with a painful, open-handed slap then turned to his companion and grinned. The two soldiers both laughed. Abdul smarted at the blow and kept his eyes towards the floor, not wishing for more of the same. He knew that this was merely the warm-up before the main event. He had listened to former prisoners, the lucky ones, the few who had left the camp alive. They had told of the many men and woman brought here for interrogation, the ones who had been lost in the system, or more often, the ones who had simply not made it to the next morning. He stared at the floor and tried to remember his training. His mind was fogging over, too preoccupied with thoughts of his wife and child.

The two soldiers had stopped laughing and had walked around him towards the heavy steel door of the cell. They hovered near the door for a moment, talking in low voices, then switched off the light and closed it.

Abdul raised his head and looked round the room but could see nothing in the complete darkness. He shifted on the wooden chair, easing himself into a more comfortable position, shifting his weight away from the vast areas of bruising.

The soldiers had come for them at a little after midnight. There had been no warning, no tell-tale sign, not even to Abdul Tembarak's well-trained ear. The doors and main windows had been assaulted simultaneously and within seconds the house had been full of soldiers and the beatings had begun. The hoods had been expertly applied, and their limbs bound tightly with the plastic duct tape. The soldiers had then begun to search the house and during the ensuing commotion, Abdul had clearly heard an authoritative sounding woman asking a soldier where the couple's baby was.

He knew when he had been spotted, knew the exact damning moment. The bank was full of people on General Madi Soto's payroll. The MB & C Bank of Indonesia handled all of Soto's official accounts, so it was only obvious that the man would have eyes and ears in place.

This was to be Abdul Tembarak's brief: to infiltrate the MB & C Bank of Indonesia's head office in Yogyakarta and look into General Soto's accounts. He was to identify inside contacts and follow them to possible outside contacts, or go-betweens. Cover identities and histories, known as legends, had been created for Abdul and his wife and the couple had been housed in the bank's adequate accommodation.

As far as Tembarak's wife was concerned the posting had been just another short-term accountancy contract that her husband had taken on a freelance basis. As a forensic accountant he had various contracts all over Indonesia. The couple lived well and travelled every few months. She was unaware of his intelligence work. To the manager and the staff of the bank, Abdul Tembarak was working on behalf of the accountancy department of the bank's headquarters, MB & C International, in Jakarta. He was undertaking a new initiative within the bank's infrastructure, random auditing and evaluation of accounts.

He had worked for the past seven weeks and had positively identified two of General Soto's informants; a woman who worked in Accounts and a man who had recently been promoted into Foreign Investments. He had followed them to their independent liaisons and suspected that neither informant was aware of the other's presence at the bank. That had not surprised Tembarak; it was typical of General Soto to run a single cell system, which would reduce the chance of the pair getting to know each other. Tembarak had followed the young man to his liaison for the third time in as many days but had become over-confident. He had got too close. When the man had taken a quick, cursory glance around, Tembarak had been in full view. He had reacted casually, smiling and acknowledging the chance meeting, but deep down he had known that he had aroused the informant's suspicions. From then on, it seemed as if the young man was onto him. Every time he looked up from his paperwork, the man from Foreign Investments was staring at him. Every time he went for a coffee break, or to lunch, the man from Foreign Investments was near. Even the unavoidable toilet break was fast becoming embarrassing.

Tembarak had contacted his controller within the Internal Security Service, but the man had been reluctant to withdraw him. The information he had already gathered had been invaluable. It was purely down to Tembarak's efforts that the government now knew the full extent of General Soto's plans for a leadership bid, and details of his subsequent funding from what, upon further investigation, had turned out to be a bogus company in China. There was also money coming in from accounts held in Switzerland and the Cayman Islands, the money transferred there from various IP addresses, but two had been traced to a Chinese investment group in Hong Kong. The Internal Security Service controller advised his agent to keep his head and continue to uncover more vital information. Easily advised from the safety and comfort of an air-conditioned office. That last conversation had been two days ago, now Abdul Tembarak sat alone in the blackness of a concrete cell.

He bowed his head, thinking of his young wife and child. Ignorant of the fact that her husband was a government agent, ignorant that her presence had unwittingly provided his cover, time and time again. Soon the tears started to flow, before long, Abdul Tembarak was sobbing out loud, grieving for the death of their union and the fate which certainly awaited his wife at the hands of their captors. He knew that he would die here. What he had a small chance of controlling was when. If he could keep his wits, he might be able to barter a deal for his wife. And if he could hold on long enough, his absence may just be noticed.

CHAPTER SEVENTEEN

Alex King stood at the front door of his cottage, waiting for
Stewart to return with his vehicle. He had watched the man
trudge across the field, back towards the road, smiling at the
sight of him picking his way through waist-high thistles in a
smart, double-breasted, navy suit. It had not occurred to
Stewart to take the lane adjacent to the house, which led
straight to the road, and it had only briefly occurred to King
to tell him. Instead, he had decided to remain silent, much
preferring to watch.

King looked out across the patch of garden, and the overgrown fields beyond. He had intended to turn the property
around from near dereliction, into a dream home, a chocolate
box cottage. It had been his dream since his early childhood
in Lambeth. Growing up on a council estate, with only his
mother supporting five children, times had been hard. With
his two sisters sharing their small bedroom and his mother
and string of lovers taking up the flat's largest bedroom, the
young Alex King had only ever known cramped surroundings,
sharing the flat's smallest bedroom with his two older brothers. Only back then, his name had been Mark Jeffries.

The young Mark Jeffries grew up quickly, through necessity rather than choice. Circumstance made for a short childhood. He never remembered his father and although there had been plenty of men in his mother's life, they were not the sort to be interested in kicking a football around the playing fields or forming any type of quasi-paternal kinship with the young children of the Jeffries family.

Mark Jeffries had heard the word prostitute, even whore, but did not understand their meaning. 'Tom', 'tart', 'brass', 'alley mattress' and 'shag-piece' were other expressions shouted on the estate, but the young Mark Jeffries had no idea of their meaning, nor that they all referred to his mother. It was his eldest brother who had finally, and vividly spelt it out, describing in detail what it was that his mother did, what put the food on the table, the clothes on their backs. Mark Jeffries did not believe him, he had never believed anything that his brother had said and never spoke to him after that. Again, it had been through circumstance, not choice.

The woman had a kindly face and had given each of the children sweets before they had taken their little car journey. Life at the children's home had been good at first. There had been plenty of room, plenty of food and even the daily showers were not all that bad. The Jeffries children had all made friends quickly, but it was not long before they were all being found separate homes and a new category in which to be placed, one that could almost have passed for a brand-new surname - Foster.

The young Mark Jeffries had many new parents, all by the name of Foster. They were nice houses and families at first. He spent time in a large house in Hertfordshire, a cul-de-sac in Reading and a mews in Belgravia. After that the settings were less austere. He couldn't seem to help getting into trouble. Next had come the three children's homes in inner London, the remand centre in Bromley and the young

offenders institute in Slough. At nineteen he had seen the
inside of two prisons and by twenty-one he managed to see
his third. He was a fine boxer, weighing in at middleweight or
light-heavy, depending on how well he got in shape, but
lacked the discipline to be world class. He had made money
from taking dives in the ring and fighting gypsies in construction skips on building sites at night. When he wasn't taking
dives for the money, he was half killing his opponents with
savage body blows.

A misunderstanding with a local criminal gang made life
difficult and after winning money double crossing a betting
syndicate Jeffries needed a change of location. He found a
position working at a dock in Portsmouth. His accommodation was cramped, but the money was regular, and he could
re-establish himself. He had long since lost all contact with
his brothers and sisters and he had heard at fourteen that his
mother had died from a heroin overdose. There was nothing
for him in London anymore, and a new life on the south coast
seemed a good move.

And then came the turning point, the one incident to
turn his life around. It came from out of the blue, as is so
often the case. A night out with fellow dock workers, a few
beers too many and one too many admirers of a woman. The
fight broke out in a notoriously rough Portsmouth pub, one
frequented by a good many sailors on shore leave, as well as
the hard-drinking soldiers of the Royal Marines.

Jeffries took on the group without fear, dealing with them
as they came. When the police finally arrived and contained
the incident, two young Royal Marines lay dead on the floor
of the bar, the other three were hospitalised for the duration
of their leave. Jeffries eluded the police at first but was later
arrested outside his lodgings. The court case had been
straightforward, swift even. Independent eye witnesses had
provided much of the evidence and the pathologist's report

had recorded the two men's death as a direct result of the injuries inflicted by Jeffries. His attack on the soldiers, all of them highly commended with service in the Gulf and Northern Ireland behind them had been described as 'wild and barbaric'. He was sentenced to twenty years' imprisonment, commencing at HM Prison, Dartmoor.

Peter Stewart had taken a great deal of interest in the Jeffries case. The incident had not gone unnoticed by the SIS, at the time regularly on the lookout for criminal informers, messengers and go-betweens. Impressed at Jeffries's natural ability and obvious potential, especially as he had received no recognised training, he felt compelled to pay the man a visit. The proposition was put to him, accepted immediately and a cover story put into operation. Subsequent orders were signed, the Official Secrets Act was brought into play, certain prison staff given the day off and Jeffries escaped. After a lengthy search, a body (that of a homeless drug addict killed in a hit and run in Bristol) was found in a quagmire near Rough Tor, in the heart of Dartmoor. It was later identified as one Mark Thomas Jeffries, twenty-five years of age originally from Lambeth, South London. That had been seventeen years ago, a world away, and distanced by what seemed like a lifetime's training. He was a different man now. He had talked to the service counsellors about the two Royal Marines he had killed, found it hard to deal with at times. He consoled himself that he worked now solely to protect his country and carry on what they had stood for. He knew their birthdays and the date of their deaths and he remembered them. He knew he could never truly make amends, and that was his penance because it ate away at him, consumed him. He donated a sizable amount each month to *Help for Heroes*, the armed forces charity by way of recompense.

Alex King watched the dark green Vauxhall Insignia drive slowly down the bumpy lane, weaving between the large potholes. He walked into the driveway, then took a quick glance back at the cottage, noticing the smoke which still billowed out from the chimney. The log fire would not last long untended, and he had long since got out of the habit of keeping perishable food in the house, finding it far more practical to purchase the essentials daily from the grocer's and butcher in the nearby village and keep a well-stocked freezer.

The cottage had been based on a lifetime's dream, but like most dreams, it had not been properly thought through. Due to the nature of his business, King spent up to eight months away from home each year, returning to the cottage for a few days, then taking off at a moment's notice, only to return weeks, often months later. The property needed almost constant attention and had soon fallen into disrepair. He had worked hard on the building but gave up on landscaping. Nevertheless, King took a final look at the house and experienced an overwhelming feeling of comfort, knowing that however dilapidated it looked now, he would soon be yearning for its creature comforts as he sheltered from the night-time cold in a gully somewhere in Northern Iraq.

CHAPTER EIGHTEEN

The noise came suddenly, snapping Tembarak out of his grief in an instant. He stared into the pitch darkness, searching in vain for its origin. He had no idea how much time had passed since his arrival, he was sure that he had been in the cell for at least half an hour, but the sound told him one thing only; he was not alone. Again, he heard it, very faint, perhaps a sharp intake of breath, but nonetheless, it was clear to him that he had company in the dark.

"Why do you grieve so?"

Tembarak jumped at the sudden sound of a man's voice, only inches from his left ear. He strained to see a face, but still could see nothing. The next sound was that of thick-bottomed boots scraping on the concrete floor, as the owner of the voice turned around, then walked back across the cell towards the door. Suddenly, the light in the centre of the ceiling flickered for a second and then threw the room into a brilliant whiteness. Tembarak squinted, protecting his eyes until they slowly adjusted to the sudden light. He looked at the walls in front and to each side of him and found himself confused by the cell's design. He had been told by former inmates of the plain concrete floor, the un-plastered concrete block walls and of the damp and smell of decay. This cell, however, was whitewashed from floor to ceiling, anything but damp, and looked newly built. He turned around, intending to study the view behind, then immediately wished that he hadn't. The blow was hard and fast, expertly aimed at a point behind and below his right ear. He felt the sudden rush of blood flow to his brain, and a flash of stars darted in front of his eyes. He started to sway, then felt his head wrenched backwards, pulled back with such force that he feared his neck would snap.

"Name?" the faceless voice shouted, echoing eerily in the sound-proofed room. Abdul Tembarak suddenly realised that it was hopeless, the initial assault had been carried out with such force that he knew he would be unable to resist telling him what or who he was. The beatings would be swift and hard, and he would break. He just needed to hold on long enough.

CHAPTER NINETEEN

"Right, they're off," the man paused, watching the Vauxhall Insignia through powerful binoculars, as it pulled out of the narrow entrance to the drive. "We'll give them about ten minutes or so, then go in."

"Do we know of any security systems?" Pryce asked his superior, as he watched the Insignia drive away. "Someone like King will surely have *something* in place."

Holmwood shook his head. "The intelligence reports show nothing. Stewart hasn't texted, so he didn't notice anything. King is away for most of the year, so unless he has a security system which uses the telephone lines, direct to the local police station, we shall be quite safe. Besides, someone in King's line of work tends to keep a low profile, doesn't want to create any unnecessary interest with ringing alarm bells and such like. When he's down here, he lives the life of a virtual recluse."

"Do you know him?" Pryce asked, keeping his eyes on the stretch of road ahead.

Holmwood shook his head. "No. I'd heard of him though, before we started searching for his security blanket, but only the usual canteen gossip. He's been a bit of a legend, almost a myth within the firm," he paused, turning towards Pryce as he spoke. "There aren't many of them left. I don't know how many, just a handful. It's all tech now, satellites, airstrikes and Predator Drones. We used to call these guys reapers but ended up being told not to. Fucking priceless, being told not to call someone something, then being told that people like that didn't exist in the modern MI6." He laughed, shaking his head. "Those guys built the bloody service. Nothing like James Bond and all that suave and sophisticated bollocks. These guys were a different deal. They never lasted long, the risks were too great. MI6 has always had agents who work alone, especially during the Cold War. Sometimes they've had to kill. We've never called them assassins, but everybody knew what they were. But King is a separate entity. He's used when there's going to be a killing. Then he's put back in the box. The thing is, since Al Qaeda and ISIS raised their heads the few men like him have been used a lot," he paused. "Perhaps too much. They're prone to burn out, to paranoia, to make mistakes. For now, he's an effective tool. He doesn't spy, he doesn't inform, he doesn't process intelligence or run assets. He kills, plain and simple."

"What happens if he burns out and starts making mistakes?" Pryce asked.

Holmwood stared out of the window across the valley and towards the sea. He remained silent for a moment, then said quietly, "You don't want to know..."

CHAPTER TWENTY

General Soto stood a few feet in front of Tembarak, smiling with a terrifyingly sadistic menace in his eyes. Tembarak knew at that moment that there was madness in there somewhere.

Soto's immaculately pressed olive uniform was emblazoned with a vast array of military ribbons, as well as the general's gold insignia on each lapel. Slung low on his right hip he wore a western style cowboy holster which housed a non-military issue revolver, nickel-plated and finished with ivory grips, interwoven with thin threads of silver. On his left hip, he wore a large Bowie knife, with equally decorative hilt and handle.

Tembarak looked up at the man, realising that he was even more imposing in person than in the photograph which he had been given at intelligence headquarters in Jakarta. At over six feet tall, General Soto was unusually tall for an Indonesian, and weighing at least thirteen stone, he was also extremely powerfully built in comparison to the clear majority of his fellow countrymen.

Soto squatted on his haunches, so that his eyes were at

the same level as Tembarak's, then spoke in a low voice, slow and deliberate, as if addressing a naughty child. "What... is... your... name?"

Tembarak looked away, turning his eyes to the floor. "Tembarak. Abdul Tembarak."

Soto smiled, then stood up straight. He walked around his prisoner and bent down and picked a large manilla envelope off the floor. He opened it, then walked back around into the man's view. "Well, Abdul Tembarak..." He slid a large colour photograph out of the envelope and looked at it disapprovingly. He turned it around for his captive to see. "What I want to know, is why did you have this photograph of me in your possession? And who are you working for?"

Tembarak stared at the photograph in dismay, realising his grave error in keeping it. No amount of pleading innocence would remove him from this situation, but he would have to play the game for as long as he could. For as long as he held information, he would be kept alive. Long enough for his controller to realise that something had gone terribly wrong? He hoped so...

Soto lashed out suddenly, catching Tembarak across the cheek with the back of his hand. "I asked you a question!" He bent down and caught hold of Tembarak's ear, wrenching his head violently towards him. "Who are you working for?"

Tembarak's mind raced, working through the few options open to him, trying to think back to his training for this sort of scenario. But *that* was exactly what it had been; training. No amount of training could ever have prepared him for this, knowing that his life really was in danger. His overwhelming desire was to plead his wife's innocence, to tell General Soto that she knew nothing of his work. However, if he jumped straight in with this revelation, Soto would be all too aware of his weak spot. He would have played his hand too soon. What he needed was to buy some time. Enough time to get his head straight and work out his cover story, even if it meant taking a beating. General Soto released his grip on Tembarak's ear and slapped him hard across the face. "Who are you working for?" he asked quietly, yet with an underlying impatience in his tone. "Believe me, what you feel now is nothing compared with what you will encounter later. If you cooperate now, things can soon be comfortable once more."

Tembarak knew better than to be sucked in by the sort of promises that are the small change of every interrogator's stock in trade. The promise of the beatings to stop, the promise of food and water, the promise that things will return to normal – all simple variants on the game of stick and carrot. However, if he didn't give Soto something, it would not be long before the interrogation became much harsher.

General Soto stared down at him and shook his head in dismay. "I was hoping that it would not come to this, I do so hate unnecessary violence." He reached down to his belt and caught hold of the butt of his revolver. He drew it quickly, western style, with practiced grace. Tembarak stared at the revolver, unsure of Soto's intentions. Surely death would not come this quickly? His mind raced, as he watched him spin the gun around his index finger by its trigger guard.

"Just like Clint Eastwood, no?" He smiled ruthlessly, then in an instant, he spun the weapon around, caught it by the barrel and brought the butt down across the side of Tembarak's knee.

Tembarak screamed as never before. He had heard the bone crack upon impact and had to fight an overwhelming desire to vomit. He closed his eyes as he wailed, unable to bring a comforting hand to the wounded limb.

Soto tutted, then shook his head dejectedly. "I was hoping to refrain from this sort of treatment. You are obviously an educated man; you do work in a bank after all. Talk to me. Talk to me, and then you can go home."

Tembarak grit his teeth together, trying to quell the agonising pain, and the accursed frustration that he could not defend himself. There was only one option left open to him. He decided to stick closely to the accountancy story. With any luck, he would be able to create the impression that he was in fact investigating the MB & C Bank of Indonesia's Yogyakarta branch and had stumbled across General Soto's involvement with the bank by pure chance. If he could prove that he truly knew nothing of the general's business, then perhaps he could protest his wife's innocence later.

CHAPTER TWENTY-ONE

Holmwood looked around the kitchen then walked over and opened the fridge. It was empty, apart from an unopened carton of UHT milk and tub of spreadable long-life butter, a jar of strawberry jam and a few cans of beer. He closed the door and bent down and opened the small door to the built-in freezer. Neatly stacked packets of rump steaks, each one weighing about a pound, packs of minced beef, loaves of sliced bread, various packets of frozen vegetables, some pizzas stacked all down one side, a few whole chickens and some ready meals. He closed the door, then turned to Pryce as he entered the room.

"Not exactly a gourmet, our friend King. Must live from day to day. Plenty of tins in the cupboard though," he paused, then shook his head. "This is all wrong, not King's style. We know about the files in those solicitors, offices, this would be the last place for him to keep anything confidential."

Pryce nodded. "I agree, but McCullum wants this place searched, so what else can we do?" he paused and frowned at Holmwood. "What is all this for anyway? Are they going to dispense with King's services?"

Holmwood stared coldly at him. "Doesn't pay to ask too many questions in this job. Sometimes, the less you know, the better." He turned around and walked out into the lounge. "Right, let's make a start. You take the downstairs, and I'll take upstairs. Take pictures of everything first on your phone, so we can put things back in the right place. Don't make a mistake; a man like King will notice in an instant."

CHAPTER TWENTY-TWO

Abdul Tembarak struggled to get his head together, making positive use of his time alone in the cell. He knew from his training that solitude was all part of any successful interrogation but had not expected to be left alone for what now seemed to be such a considerable length of time. Although he could not be sure of how long it had been since General Soto had left, he suspected that it had been at least four hours, possibly more.

The bright light had been left on, reflecting harshly off the whitewashed walls, which seemed to make it harder for him to concentrate. The tight bindings around his wrists were making his arms ache painfully and cramp starting to nibble threateningly at his calves. He was terribly thirsty as well. But overriding all these discomforts was the agony shooting through his knee. It pulsated and throbbed like nothing he'd known before.

He was trying to work the story out in his mind but realised that he would have to be careful and remember everything that he had said. The room was certain to be bugged, recording every word spoken by the two men, to be used later, when he was exhausted, confused and unable to remember the lies. He would be asked to repeat all he had said, over and over, until he made a mistake. Then, all he had said would be analysed and compared to previous statements, as Soto tried to trip him up and trick him into telling the truth.

He had told General Soto his cover story; that he was investigating the bank and randomly auditing its expenditure. He omitted to mention that he had discovered details of both Soto's official military budgetary and personal accounts, or that he had identified two of his spies. The photograph was the major obstacle. Soto had asked how he had come by it and had administered a fierce beating when Tembarak had hesitated before answering. This however, had worked to the man's advantage, as he had faked unconsciousness, forcing the General to leave the cell, no doubt to check his explanation.

Tembarak had remained slumped in the chair with his eyes closed for a considerable time, agonising over an explanation for the photograph, but the harder he thought, the more distracted he became, his mind turning back to his wife, and what she might be enduring at the hands of the young, undisciplined soldiers. And his baby. Where was he? Who was looking after him?

Without warning, the heavy steel door of the cell burst open, slamming forcefully against the concrete wall. Tembarak flinched, startled by the violent intrusion. He shivered, knowing that whoever had entered the cell was now standing directly behind him.

"You are a liar!" Soto shouted accusingly at the back of Tembarak's head. "I have checked up on your story and MB & C International have never heard of you!"

Tembarak's mind raced. His 'legend' had been inserted into the company's records over three months ago and extended back for two years. Any routine check into the company's employment files would find Abdul Tembarak's details alongside the real personnel data. Besides, who could Soto have checked with at this hour? Although he had lost track of time, Tembarak knew that it could not yet be eight o'clock, the opening time of the head office in Jakarta. No, Soto was tricking him, trying to trap him into an admission. He would have to remain adamant, but ever careful not to antagonise him into further acts of torture. "I am not a liar," Tembarak protested. "I have worked with MB & C International for two years, as a freelance. I was posted to the MB & C Bank of Yogyakarta just over a month ago."

General Soto walked around to face Tembarak and stared coldly into the man's frightened eyes. "I know *when* you came to Yogyakarta and I know *what* you have been doing ever since you arrived," he paused, then nodded over Tembarak's head, at a second man who had just entered the cell, accompanied by the sound of something being wheeled, screeching wheels in need of oil.

He looked back at Tembarak, then shook his head dejectedly. "Unfortunately, you do not seem to be cooperating with me, so I will leave you in the capable hands of Sergeant Grogol. He is a master of his profession, having served most of his time in East Timor, extracting confessions from the radical *Fretilin* revolutionaries."

Tembarak made to turn his head but thought better of it. He looked up at Soto and shook his head pleadingly. "Please! I am telling the truth, I am an accountant, I work for MB & C International!"

General Soto smiled, and turned to the stocky man behind Tembarak. "Sergeant Grogol, I have some business to attend to elsewhere which shouldn't take me more than a few hours, kindly make sure that our new friend here is telling the truth upon my return."

CHAPTER TWENTY-THREE

Sergeant Grogol was short, with a prominent belly which strained over a pair of tight trousers, and an even tighter belt. From the straining belt hung a canvas holster, containing a worn Browning pistol, complete with officer's lanyard ring and cord, which he wore wrapped around his neck. It was clear that Sergeant Grogol did not intend to lose his trusty weapon.

Grogol smiled down at Tembarak, then turned to the trolley, which he had earlier wheeled into the room and taken great care in positioning to the right, and slightly in front of Tembarak's feet. He arranged the tools of his profession neatly on the wooden trolley, then turned to the two guards who had accompanied him into the cell, with an abruptly shouted order.

"Strip him!" He watched the two soldiers grab hold of his prisoner, then shook his head in frustration. "No! Don't untie him! Here..." He reached down onto the trolley and picked up a pair of surgical scissors, then held it out in front of him. "Take these and cut the clothes off him. And be careful not to cut the flesh." He stared at Tembarak and smiled sadistically. "That's my job..."

Tembarak tried to struggle, but it was useless. He was in great pain from his knee and he felt as if he had lost the use of his limbs; sitting bound tightly for so long had cut off the circulation, giving him acute cramps whenever he attempted to move.

Grogol chuckled as he watched the guards cut away lengths of fabric and discard the pieces to the floor. Before long, Tembarak was naked, breathing heavily and sweating profusely.

"Good, good," Grogol paused, looking at both soldiers. "Now, hold him still and don't let go."

Tembarak struggled frantically as the two guards caught hold of him and attempted to restrain him. He tried to stand, but his knee buckled under the weight and he cried out in pain. Grogol laughed raucously, then glared at the two soldiers as they struggled to hold him still. "Keep him still!" Without warning, he kicked out, catching Tembarak's kneecap with the side of his heavy boot. Abdul felt the knee give way, forcing him back into the wooden chair. His head swam, and he could not even bring himself to scream, only panted for breath as the fiery pain surrounded his knee, then slowly subsided, ebbing away leaving him nauseous. Both soldiers caught hold of him and held him tightly, as they fearfully watched their master.

Sergeant Grogol nodded his appreciation, then reached over to the trolley and picked up the first implement of torture and waved it slowly in front of Tembarak's face. It was a long, needle-like tool, with a rubber grip.

"This is the first of many tools that you will become aquatinted with as time goes by. Its uses are many, but today we will be using it for probing," he paused, and gently touched the tip of the needle with his finger. He then turned his finger towards Tembarak and smiled, as a trickle of blood ran down the side and across the back of his hand. "As you can see, it is sharp and requires very little pressure to insert."

Tembarak flinched, shaking his head despairingly. "You're sick! I have already told General Soto who I am and what I am doing in Yogyakarta!"

Grogol smiled. "Well, then I think we shall start with the basics and work our way upwards." He turned the implement over between his fingers, then tapped the edge of the needle impatiently against his knuckles. "How do you know that the man who first questioned you is General Soto?"

CHAPTER TWENTY-FOUR

Sergeant Grogol turned to the smaller of the two soldiers and nodded towards the cell door. "Get some water! Hurry!" He waited for the man to scurry off then bent down and lifted Tembarak's eyelid with his thumb. He stood back and shook his head in mock compassion while he waited impatiently for the soldier to return. He had not expected his prisoner to pass out so quickly, having experienced so little of his repertoire. He stepped back, tapping his foot impatiently on the concrete floor as he waited through the unexpected interval.

The soldier returned, barging hastily through the doorway, not wishing to keep his master waiting. He hurried over to Grogol and handed him the two-litre plastic bottle, apologetic to have held up the process, even so briefly. Grogol snatched the bottle, then caught Tembarak by the hair and pulled his head savagely forward. He poured some of the water onto the nape of the man's neck, then pushed his head back and splashed a little into his face.

Tembarak slowly regained consciousness and looked drowsily up at his interrogator, who was grinning once more. Sergeant Grogol looked down at the needle-like instrument, which was embedded deep into Tembarak's damaged knee. He raised an eyebrow expectantly at his prisoner, then cocked his head to one side, as if to emphasize his growing impatience.

Abdul Tembarak stared down at the handle of the instrument, and the patch of blood around his knee. He could feel the metal in the cartilage, and the burning sensation around the area, but suddenly became acutely aware of the loss of feeling in the lower part of his leg.

"I will ask you the question again," Grogol paused, as he bent down and gently caught hold of the instrument's handle. "What were you doing with the photograph of General Soto?"

Tembarak's mind raced. He knew that he would feel the excruciating pain again unless he gave the man an answer, but the more he tried to think, the more he could only imagine the pain which lay ahead. He looked pleadingly into Grogol's evil, piercing eyes and shook his head profusely. "Please! I have already told you, I can't remember!"

Grogol twisted the instrument, then swept it around in a full circle, probing at the damaged cartilage and scraping the needle's point around the bone. Tembarak screamed a desperate wail, then an urge to vomit too strong to overcome. He retched down into his naked lap, then fought hard not to choke as he struggled to get air back into his aching lungs.

Sergeant Grogol released his grip on the instrument and stepped backwards, his expression twisted in disgust, as he watched the vomit drip from Tembarak's lap and then to the pristine whitewashed floor. He stared coldly at his prisoner, then smiled menacingly.

"Abdul Tembarak, you are not helping yourself. There will come a time when you will not be able to withstand any more pain. It comes to *everyone*, sooner or later." He stepped forwards and grabbed the instrument once more, forcing

Tembarak to suck in deeply and tense in anticipation of the inevitable pain. Grogol smiled, and merely pulled the instrument effortlessly from the man's leg. He studied the tip of the needle, which appeared to have bent slightly against the bone. He returned it to the trolley, before staring back at his captive.

"You *will* talk before long, even the toughest men weep in my company. You may call it a gift, but I have the ability to realise when I have taken things too far. I rein back, only to continue later. Nobody ever dies before they have told me everything." He watched the man's stubborn pout, his tough jaw-line and hard eyes, then nodded in realisation. "You are an agent. A spy for this weak and decadent government." Tembarak shook his head, but Grogol held up his hand to silence him. "Other men cry. They beg. And then tell me all that they know. You are different, you have clearly received training." He stepped back and rubbed his chin thoughtfully with his thumb and forefinger. "But the question is, how much your pretty young wife knows?"

Tembarak tensed, all too visibly, at the mention of his wife. He looked up defiantly at his captor and shook his head. "She knows nothing!" he protested vehemently. "She can't tell you anything!"

"Maybe not," Grogol grinned sadistically. "But we shall see just how much pain I can inflict upon her, before *you* start to talk." He turned to the shorter of the two soldiers and grinned triumphantly. "Private! Bring the woman to me!" He watched the young soldier hurry out of the cell, then rested his back against the wall and smiled benignly down at Tembarak. "He will not be long; the guards should have finished amusing themselves with her by now."

CHAPTER TWENTY-FIVE

Holmwood sifted through the pile of paperwork, methodically placing each document face down on the bed, noting the exact order in which he had checked them. He looked up as Pryce entered the room but could instantly tell by the man's expression that he had found nothing of great worth.

"Any luck?" Pryce asked, as he perched on the foot of the bed.

Holmwood chuckled sardonically, then placed another household bill on the pile and picked up the next document. "You must be joking! King is far too cagey," he paused, then nodded towards the chest of drawers near the door. "You can have a look through there if you've nothing better to do."

Pryce sighed dejectedly, then walked over to the pine unit and eased the top drawer open. He studied the array of clutter, then patiently picked his way through, making certain to leave nothing out of place. The two men used the cameras on their smartphones to record everything they touched. Every detail could be recreated before they left.

"Anything?" Holmwood asked, as he carefully replaced the pile of documents in the empty drawer.

"Nothing. Just a few photographs and some letters." He studied the piece of paper in front of him, then smiled.

"What is it? Have you got something?" Holmwood stood up excitedly and made towards him.

"Check this out..." Pryce grinned, then put on a face of exaggerated sadness. *"My darling Alex, by the time you read this, I will be gone. I am so sorry that I had to leave you this way, but..."*

"Put it down!" Holmwood snapped irately. "For Christ's sake!"

Pryce stared at him, dumbfounded. "What's your problem? I was only having a laugh! It's just a Dear John letter..."

"Have some damned respect! We are looking for part of his security blanket, not the poor bastard's personal letters!" Holmwood stared at him coldly and pointed towards the drawer. "Just put it back and get on with the search."

Pryce folded the letter, then returned it to the drawer. "I don't know what your problem is, it's not like you know the guy."

Holmwood caught hold of him by his collar and pushed him back against the chest of drawers. "I think

it was a letter from his wife. Just before she died... She had ovarian cancer. They lost a child because of it. She wasn't alright, couldn't cope with losing the child and being terminally ill. Blamed herself for the child's death. She took a massive overdose..." He released his grip on his colleague and shook his head. "Sorry... You weren't to know, Stewart filled me in, gave me some background on the guy. Look, doesn't this piss you off just a little? For God's sake, all this guy has done for the past fifteen years or so is serve his fucking country! All he has done is kill people without questioning the motive, so that complete bastards like Donald McCullum and Martin Andrews can take the credit for resolving the situation and further their careers!" He paused, sitting down on a nearby leather chair, worn and doubling as a clothes horse. "Jesus! The thought of somebody going through *my* things just sickens me. I've done some dodgy things for the firm. What if they decide that they don't want me any longer?"

Pryce straightened his collar, then looked at him bitterly. "It's not as if you've killed anyone is it?" he stated flatly. "What reason would you have for keeping a security blanket?"

"Jesus, Richard!" Holmwood stared at him in disbelief. "I've set up arms deals with the IRA, I've robbed banks in Belfast and made it look like terrorist fund-raising, just to give the SAS the green light to go hunting. I've even spread disinformation to engineer stock market panics and bankrupt innocent companies just so terrorist funds get lost in investments," he paused, shaking his head despondently. "I've helped plant evidence, so the police can make a charge stick. I robbed a diamond exchange to flush out terrorist money-men... And all in my country's best interest. And do you know who orders me to do these things? The same people in the same meetings who order King to kill, that's who."

CHAPTER TWENTY-SIX

"They left the bar and walked through the streets. I followed them from a distance, just like you told me to," he paused, taking a packet of cigarettes from the hip pocket of his faded jean shorts. "They stopped at a food stall, then sat down and ate. They were there for about twenty minutes." He opened the packet, extracted one and slipped it between his thick lips, then reached into his back pocket and pulled out a cheap, plastic lighter.

"My dear friend, you are quite mistaken if you think that I shall permit your filthy habit in my office," the effeminate-looking Indonesian stared at him coldly, then adjusted his silk necktie, more out of habit than from necessity. "Just continue your report... Where did Junus Kutu take the man after they had finished eating?"

The scrawny Javanese stared at the lighter, then slipped it back into his pocket, but kept the unlit cigarette between his lips, in a vain gesture towards saving face. "They went to The Emperor."

"And?" the man prompted.

The Javanese swept a hand through his mane of unkempt

hair with a shrug. "I couldn't get in, there is a strict dress code... But I did manage to follow Kutu back to his house."

The man rubbed his chin thoughtfully then smiled at the scruffy-looking Javanese. "So, who was the mystery man with whom Junus Kutu met?"

The little Javanese shrugged and shook his head. "I... I don't know. I stayed with Kutu..."

The man sighed tiresomely and steepled his fingers, resting his elbows on the leather-bound desk. "A little pointless, one might say. You already know where Junus Kutu lives... don't you think that it would have been more beneficial to follow this new addition to the equation? Surely anyone Kutu is meeting must be considered a potential threat?" he paused and took a small brown envelope out from the inside pocket of his tailored jacket, then set it down on the desk in front of him. He tapped the envelope thoughtfully and smiled. "You know what this is, don't you?"

The scruffy little man stared longingly at the envelope and grinned. He knew what it contained, he also knew how long it would have taken him to earn selling tacky gifts to the tourists or giving them short lifts through the busy streets on the back of his motor scooter. He held out his hand expectantly, then hesitated as the man in the tailored suit kept his hand on top of the packet.

"This is a great deal of money to you, no?" He waited until the man in front of him nodded eagerly, before he continued. "When you have found out who Junus Kutu's mystery appointment was, you shall receive the payment, as agreed." He held up his hand and silenced the little Indonesian as he started to protest. "Be aware I do not tolerate insubordination. As I said, when I know who Kutu was meeting with, you shall receive this. Now, be sure to shut the door behind you on your way out..."

CHAPTER TWENTY-SEVEN

Abdul Tembarak heard the cell door open but forced himself to resist the temptation to turn his head. He knew by now that to do so would undoubtedly bring further punishment.

The two tough-looking soldiers wheeled the hospital style bed in front of him, then applied the brakes and stood back, as Sergeant Grogol walked eagerly over and inspected the bed's position. He looked up at the two men and grinned sadistically.

"Yes, that is good, thank you." He turned around and looked towards the door of the cell, then smiled excitedly, as another two soldiers roughly manhandled the woman through the doorway and dragged her towards the bed. "Ah! This is good, she still has some fight left in her!"

Tembarak turned his head and watched in horror as the two men dragged his naked wife through the cell then pushed her down onto the metal framed bed. All she wore was a thick canvas hood, similar to those they had both worn in the truck.

Sergeant Grogol hurried over to the bed and shouted instructions to the two men, ordering them where to position

the woman's limbs, as he untangled the thick webbing straps
from the rails of the bed. Tembarak bowed his head, as his
wife fought frantically with the two men, lashing her legs out
and flailing her arms wildly.

Grogol reached through the barrage of limbs and grabbed
the woman by the throat, digging his fingers under her windpipe. He pressed down steadily, with what appeared to be all
his weight, and the woman's frantic fight ceased instantly.
Grogol continued to press for another five or six seconds,
until the woman lost consciousness. He turned to the two
grinning soldiers and nodded towards the webbing straps.
"Restrain her and make sure that there's no slack in the
bindings."

The two soldiers did as they were ordered, and bound her
arms tightly, first at the loops, which fastened around her
elbows, and then at the wrists, which pulled her arms firmly
back against the bed. Next, they pulled her legs apart and
fastened her ankles and knees to the side-rail, which ran
along the entire length of the bed. Abdul could not bring
himself to watch as the two young soldiers leered at one
another like randy adolescents and gestured obscenely at his
wife's crotch and her open nakedness. He stared to the floor
and started to sob. He knew that it was over, these monsters
had broken his resolve so quickly, far sooner than he would
have ever thought possible. All he could do now was comply
with Grogol's questioning and tell the man everything. He
had watched the two of them manhandle his wife and had
been sickened. He knew that it would have been easier for
them to wheel the bed into the cell with his wife already
strapped in place, but that would not have had the same
effect on him. To observe the degrading scene, to feel for his
wife's violation and to be enraged that other men should see
her naked, as only he should, was all part of Grogol's sadistically sickening formula, one which he was sure the man had

taken a great deal of time and thought, as well as pleasure, to perfect.

"I take it that I have your undivided attention now?" Sergeant Grogol smiled, staring down at him impatiently. He nodded towards the woman, who was coming around and groaning. "Think carefully before you answer my questions."

"Abdul?" she called out meekly, embarrassed at the thought of her husband seeing her in this undignified state. "Are you there? Why are they doing this?" she sobbed.

Tembarak hung his head and looked up tearfully at the stocky Indonesian. "Please, I will tell you anything you wish to know, just let my wife go."

"Abdul, why are they doing this?" She wept, as she struggled feebly against the thick webbing straps. "Abdul?"

Grogol laughed heartily, then shook his head in mock compassion. He walked over to the woman, and savagely wrenched the hood from her head. She raised her head and stared desperately towards her husband. "Abdul!"

Tembarak's eyes watered, as he looked back at her and shook his head sorrowfully. "I am so sorry, my darling I never meant for you to get hurt..."

"That's enough!" Grogol snapped. He looked down at the woman and sneered. "My dear, your husband does not appear to have told you everything about himself," he paused and reached down, letting his hand rest gently on her right breast. He left it there. She struggled momentarily, then submitted as she looked into his cold, cruel eyes. Grogol squeezed the woman's soft breast and looked back at Tembarak. He smiled as he watched the burning, impotent hatred in the man's eyes. "Allow me to fill the gaps," he looked back at her. "Your husband is a spy. A government spy, who has been investigating business of no concern of his."

She looked away from Grogol, towards her husband,

shaking her head disbelievingly. "No! He is an accountant, he has been working for a bank!"

Grogol laughed raucously, then let his hand wonder over to her other breast. She tensed, then caught the man's terrifying expression once again, and conceded to him. He looked down at her, his head cocked to one side. He let his finger circle her nipple as he spoke. "What is wrong, my dear? Do you not like to be touched?"

"Only by my husband!" she spat at him contemptuously.

Grogol chuckled, then moved his hand slowly across her belly and down to her inner thigh. She tried to close her legs, but the straps held her firm. She shuddered as his fingers moved steadily upwards, then stopped just short of her tiny mound of pubic hair. He looked at her and smiled, turned towards Tembarak and cocked his head to one side. "Shall I call in the guards yet?"

CHAPTER TWENTY-EIGHT

The house seemed well protected. A three-metre boundary wall separated most of the property from the main highway, and to the east a wire mesh fence divided the beautifully kept gardens from the acres of rice paddy spreading to the horizon without impeding the view.

The house itself was of colonial Dutch construction, though much of it drew from other European influences, more in keeping with mainland Spain than Indonesia. The building's plan was a giant L, high up on a manmade hillock, laid out in a series of terraced gardens and patios, which led down over a drop of some thirty feet, to the large patio and pool area at the bottom. Beyond that lay a vast expanse of gardens laid out to lawn, incorporating a small putting green as its central feature.

The man moved further through the overgrown brush, carefully studying the ground, ever watchful for any of Indonesia's many varieties of venomous snakes. With similar care, he cautiously pushed the low-hanging branches aside, knowing that they were the favourite retreats of the country's even wider variety of poisonous spiders.

As he pushed himself through a curtain of overgrown foliage, he stopped and peered through the canopy, then crouched down on the dusty ground, satisfied that he had found the perfect vantage point. The area of thick brush lay midway between the grassed verge of the highway and the endless expanse of rice paddies, spreading as far as the eye could see, each tiny plot of rice at a different stage of growth and separated from the next by tiny earthen walls.

From there he kept watch on the house, which lay approximately one hundred and fifty metres from the high wire fence. He was not sure if the fence was electrified, although he was certain that it was more of a visual deterrent than anything else. However, he could see that the high wall to his right was generously topped with broken glass securely cemented in place. This simple, yet effective method ever popular in Indonesia could prove almost impossible to breach and he knew a great many would be thieves who had fallen foul of such a security system.

The man glanced at his cheap wristwatch, a poor imitation of an Omega diver's watch and cursed aloud. It was only just midday; the sun was at its highest and would remain at its hottest for another three hours. He had ignored the necessity of bringing water with him and had no idea just how long his vigil might take. He had no choice but to observe Junus Kutu and hope that it would not be long before he met with the mystery Westerner again. He knew that he had made a mistake in following Kutu from the Emperor and would not receive his fee until he could put a name to the westerner's face.

———

Junus Kutu stepped through the double sliding doors to the edge of the narrow terracotta patio. He stood for a second or two, his fists resting firmly against his hips as he surveyed the gardens in front of him. *"Not bad for a fisherman's son from Surabaya,"* he mused quietly to himself. In fact, it had become his daily ritual. Every day, when he stepped outside for the first time, he would contemplate his property and reflect on what he had achieved, then acknowledge that achievement. It had been his father's parting advice. The old man had been proud of his son's determination to break away from the family's time long tradition of shrimp fishing. Since his early childhood, Junus Kutu had admired the few businessmen of Surabaya and had always said that he would be just like them, only *more* successful. His father had laughed at the time, but had given him what guidance he could, and had explained the need for a formal education. With much favouritism towards his youngest son, the only one of his offspring to show any ambition outside of fishing and shrimping, his father had sold much of the family's possessions to finance Junus' college education in Jakarta. His only wish was that Junus appreciate all he achieved and help the family out financially once he became a successful businessman. To date, Junus Kutu had kept his word.

He walked out onto the terracotta path, then followed it downwards, as it meandered through the crop of baby palms to the first terrace, where the winding stone steps led down to the kidney shaped pool and patio below. The steps were cut into the tiny hillock, with beds of flowers and exotic plants to either side. Junus did not know what the majority of the plants were called, nor did he care. All he knew, was that Adu, his hard-working gardener had chosen them for their beauty, their compatibility with other plants and contribution to the soil, and he was happy with that. While Adu worked hard tending the gardens, cleaning the swimming pool, performing general maintenance and expelling snakes from the property, his wife Marie worked in the house as a cook

and house maid. The couple had been in Junus' employ for
nearly ten years and shared the small annex to the rear of the
building.

––––––

The man remained crouched, resting on his haunches as he
watched Junus Kutu walk across the patio and past his swimming pool towards the pool house, which lay just out of sight
behind the large stone wall. He cursed as he lost sight of Kutu
and rose to his feet. Still he could not see and decided to
move further to his left for a better view. He swept the
branches aside, ever watchful for spiders and looked back at
the property once he reached a small clearing. He wiped the
heavy perspiration from his brow then squinted against the
sun, as he caught sight of Kutu, who was walking directly
towards him. He was carrying something in his right hand.
The man strained his eyes as he tried to fathom out what the
object was. It glistened against the sun, as Kutu turned it over
in his hand. The man's heartbeat raced. Was it a gun? Surely
Kutu could not have caught sight of him at this distance? He
tensed, as Kutu continued to march purposefully towards
him. He was only eighty metres or so away from him when
the man suddenly realised what it was that he was carrying.
Although there was nobody to witness his mistake, he felt
foolish all the same. He eased back from the edge of the
foliage slightly and continued to watch, as Junus Kutu
dropped four golf balls onto the neatly mown green, then
lined the putter up with the golf ball and the cup.

––––––

Junus Kutu had only recently taken up golf, for in his mind,
any sport where you only walked and never broke into a run,

let alone a sweat, was inappropriately described. Nevertheless, he knew that golf was, and always had been, an effective way to meet new business contacts or discuss business matters with clients, who might be caught off guard in the more sociable, relaxed atmosphere. Having decided to partake of this wonderful business aid he had approached the task with his usual commitment. He had engaged Java's leading golf course contractors to set up a first-class putting green, complete with easy approaches to the pin, as well as the more difficult, left to right to left, with a large degree of break. Kutu now had a green with one of the easiest possible putts, through to probably one of the most difficult and demanding in the world, with a large variety in between. Nor did practice end there; Kutu paid a highly revered golf professional from a nearby course to visit him twice a week for a variety of practice, from chipping onto the green, through to distance driving, far into the rice paddies beyond. The paddy workers would return his 'lost' balls for five hundred rupiahs each. It was Kutu's strategy not to set foot on a golf course until he was well above average in all the game's disciplines.

He stepped up to the ball, lined the putter up with the hole, took a step back, then placed both feet reasonably close together, just as he had been taught. Keeping his back straight, he bent his knees then took the weight of the club in both hands and realigned the club with the ball. Taking great care not to catch the back of the club on the ground, he smoothly brought the club backwards, then let it swing gently forwards like a pendulum, albeit guided with a little force. The face of the putter clipped the ball gently, and it sped rapidly towards the hole. It arched around to the left and came to rest three inches short and to the right.

"Not enough juice!"

Kutu turned suddenly to see Charles Bryant jog down the last few steps. He raised his hand in a welcoming gesture and cursed under his breath, annoyed that the man had seen him in practice. He knew that Bryant was an avid golfer and spent a great deal of time at Gleneagles and St Andrews when he was overseeing work in his Scottish office.

"A little bit more, and you would have slipped over that left to right break and ended up right in the old girl's crotch!" Bryant stepped up onto the putting green and kicked one of the balls gently into the position from where Kutu's ball had started. "Do you mind?" he asked, holding out his hand for the putter. Kutu bit his lip, as he passed the club to Bryant, who scrutinized the instrument expertly. "Not a bad piece of kit, I use Mizuno myself. Graphite shaft, with titanium head, works like a dream." He stepped up to the ball, placed the head of the putter an inch away, and gently tapped it as he spoke. "See, with a little more power ..." He watched, as the ball rolled towards the hole and dropped straight into the metal lined cup. "...the ball should go in!"

Kutu nodded politely, hiding his chagrin, as he walked towards the patio, turning around to observe Bryant setting up for another putt. "Come, let us have a drink." He turned around, just as the man took his putt, knowing full well that the best way to foil a show off is to ignore him. Nevertheless, as he stepped up onto the patio, he heard the hollow sound of the ball meeting with the inside of the hole and groaned inwardly.

———

The man had rubbed his eyes, unable to believe what he had just seen. Prepared for a long wait and inured to the prospect of never seeing the Westerner again, which would lose all hope of regaining his fee, he could never remember such joy as he felt now, seeing the tall white man walk down the steps to the paved patio. He knew that to watch them now would be pointless, for there was no way that he could tell what they were talking about. Even if he had brought along his father's old binoculars with him, he knew that he would not be able to lip-read the two men. Such skills were only known to the highly trained, or every Hollywood hero.

Watching carefully for snakes or scurrying scorpions, he moved from his position and made his way back towards the highway, where he would wait on his motor scooter for the Westerner to leave.

———

"You're early." Junus Kutu checked his watch and looked back at Bryant. "I didn't hear you arrive."

Bryant smiled, as he looked around the patio for a suitable seat. "You wouldn't!" He pulled a bamboo sun lounger out from the wall, then perched himself comfortably. "It's my new car, silent as the grave."

Kutu looked at him, and knew that he was expected to ask, even though he knew nothing about cars. "What is it?"

"A BMW i8." Bryant smiled proudly. "It's a fantastic sports car with Porsche performance but electric motors and a really economical engine. Run the electric and engine together and it is lightning quick. Keep to just electric and it's virtually silent. Got to be seen to be embracing environmental innovation in this job these days, doesn't hurt for it to be seen outside the oil offices. Mind you, I must be mad to drive one here, the way half the population drive," he paused, smiled and added. "The other half aren't much better either!"

Kutu smiled politely, knowing that Bryant could not help being so insulting, it was just that the man was so self-consumed, he never thought before he spoke. He looked at his watch again, then nodded towards the house. "Shall we have that drink, then?"

Bryant laughed out loud. "All taken care of. That tasty wench you keep up there is already fixing us a couple of martinis. I told her how to make them, plenty of dry Vermouth, a little gin, and a good splash of Vodka. Shame you haven't got any proper Vodka, but anything tastes good in this heat," he paused, suddenly aware of his host's change of expression. "You don't mind me telling the help what to do, do you? After all, it's no good keeping a dog and barking yourself..."

CHAPTER TWENTY-NINE

"Stop! Please!" Abdul Tembarak struggled against his bindings in a hopeless bid to break free. He fell back against the chair, exhausted and in great pain from his injured knee. "Please, I'm begging you!"

Sergeant Grogol laughed, as he watched the young soldier feel the woman's breasts, then run his hands lower down her naked body. He turned towards Tembarak and shrugged. "They do not get the chance to be with women, not their own kind, anyway. You see, they are Muslim," he paused. "Myself, I am from a predominantly Christian background. My teachings are very different, possibly more lenient. These boys are from the strictest of Muslim sects, like so many of our recruits. They cannot have sex with the women of their own community until they are married, therefore they experiment with each other, not because they are all queer, but because they never get the chance to be intimate with a woman. That is why they are showing so very little respect for your wife."

"But *I* am a Muslim..." Tembarak pleaded. He was cut

short by a vicious back fist from Grogol. He looked up at the man with contempt and spoke through the metallic taste of blood on his swollen lips. "*She* is a Christian. Devout. What does your Christian teachings tell you about the treatment of another man's wife?" He braced himself for more beating, but none came.

"Abdul! Abdul! Make them stop!" she screamed, as the young soldier started to unbuckle his belt. "Please! Tell him what you know!"

Grogol chuckled and smiled at Tembarak. "These are devout Muslim boys from the country. She is Christian and of no consequence. You are Muslim, but your marriage with this woman makes you *Kaffir*. A Muslim who has let his beliefs slide. You are worse than Christian to them. After they have finished amusing themselves with her, I can purify her if you like. She will be as clean as the day she was born. You wouldn't even know they had been there." He bent down to the trolley and picked up a tiny bottle, then casually read the label, as the soldier climbed up onto the table and positioned himself on top of the helpless woman. "You would be amazed what Hydrogen Peroxide can do to a woman's parts..."

"Stop!" Abdul Tembarak screamed desperately. "I will tell you everything, just stop him from..." The words failed him, and he started to sob. He looked up at Grogol pleadingly and shook his head tearfully. "I will tell you *everything*..."

"Grogol smiled as he walked over to the bed and watched the young soldier finally fumble himself into position. Without warning, he lashed out and pushed the startled youth harshly to the floor. Grogol, of all people, knew the importance in not playing his hand too early. If he had allowed the man to penetrate the woman, then Tembarak might well have given up all hope. With that very real threat hanging over her, Abdul Tembarak would *always* be willing to talk. Sergeant Grogol turned to the disgruntled youth, who was busy covering his flagging manhood as he hastily refastened his combat trousers. "Private! Go and call for General Soto!" he paused, staring gleefully at Tembarak. "Tell him that our prisoner is finally ready to talk."

CHAPTER THIRTY

Kutu looked up expectantly as he watched Marie walk down the last few steps, careful not to spill the contents of the two glasses, which rattled on the metal tray, balanced precariously above her right shoulder on the palm of her hand. She walked towards the two men, smiling amiably at Kutu, who reached out and pulled the small round table a little closer to where they were seated.

Charles Bryant smiled, as she placed his glass down next to him. "Thank you my dear!" He picked up the glass and drank thirstily then shrugged at the woman, who had just placed Kutu's glass down onto the small table. "Not half bad," he announced critically. "It's terribly hot, I think that I could do with another, if you don't mind... A little less gin, and a touch more dry vermouth and ice next time, thank you. Oh, and maybe an extra olive?"

The woman nodded impassively and turned towards Kutu, who shook his head. "No thank you, Marie. Just one for Mister Bryant, please." He waited for the woman to begin her return journey up the winding steps, then turned towards Bryant, somewhat irked at the way he had given his employee orders. "Have you given any thought to our conversation last night?"

Bryant sipped, then set his glass back on the table and leant back into his chair. "Well, what can I say? At first, I thought that you had some sort of business proposition for me, then you start to talk some rubbish about assassinating a prominent Indonesian Army General! It took me by surprise, to say the least..."

Junus Kutu smiled and sipped slowly. He rested his glass against the arm of his sun lounger, then looked intently at his companion. "It intrigued you though?"

"Intrigued? Of course, it bloody did!" Bryant frowned, as he looked icily back at his host. "You were serious, weren't you?"

"Deadly."

Bryant looked around nervously, suddenly apprehensive. "Why are you talking to me about it?" he replied cautiously. "I'm warning you, Kutu. If you are trying to set me up ..."

"Oh, don't be so bloody melodramatic! I *have* a business proposition for you, it's just not as straightforward as the usual contracts, that's all."

"Bullshit! You are talking about killing a man! How can that be regarded as a business proposition?"

"Because it will save the fate of a great many businessmen for a start. Including, may I hasten to add, you!" The little Indonesian glared at him, then settled his features into a friendlier smile. "As I mentioned last night, General Madi Soto is on China's payroll. He is planning a nationwide revolution. By promising the impossible and therefore planting unrealistic dreams into the population's minds, he will gain an overwhelming majority of the people's support. However, it will not go to a democratic vote, he will use the military and his other supporters to take control of the country."

Bryant shook his head. "But how do you know this?"

Junus Kutu smiled wryly. "I have a great many contacts all over Indonesia. Some of them are highly placed within the coalition government," he paused, taking a small sip from his chilled martini. "As I said, the government are in a quandary, they have their heads in the sand. General Soto has spies and informants everywhere, including deep within the administration. They are scared that if they make a move too soon, Soto will find out and launch his revolt."

Bryant nodded, realising their predicament. The coalition government was finished. But he knew it was the only type of government to work in such a multicultural country.

"However," Kutu smiled jubilantly. "Some rather influential, and highly successful, businessmen and politicians have come up with a solution. These men, and I may hasten to add, not all are Indonesian, have proved that it is not only the socialists who rule this great nation, and have its best interests at heart. A price has been put on General Madi Soto's head and I have been tasked with arranging the hit."

Charles Bryant remained silent, choosing only to pick up his glass and empty it. If nothing else for the distraction. He replaced it on the table and looked up, as Kutu's housekeeper once again, walked down the last few steps. The silence continued while she set the glass down before him, then, sensing that the two men were engrossed in an extremely private matter, walked back towards the steps. Bryant picked up the fresh martini and took a generous mouthful, which included the pitted olive. He held the glass in his right hand, thankful for the prop, then stared coldly at the little Indonesian. "Are you bloody insane? What the hell do you know about setting up a hit?"

Junus Kutu smiled wryly. "A damned sight more than I did three months ago, I can tell you that. The Internet is the most anonymous place, but it takes a great deal of time to sift through and make sense of the underlying meanings. To date,

I have contacted three men, but we have still not got so far as discussing the hit. They are wary of being set up by investigative reporters, or worse, and quite frankly, so am I."

Bryant nodded, understanding the man's predicament. In an age when investigative reporting ruled television ratings, it was only to be expected that contacting these ambiguously advertised services could present more than a few problems.

"But after I had been working on contacting a potential client, I suddenly remembered something that you once told me, several years ago." Kutu smiled amiably. "As you know, I tend to remember everything that I am told. You made it quite clear, when we were discussing the Sekampung Dam project in Sumatra, that you could get an aerial survey done and it would not cost us a penny," he paused, waiting for the man to recall the conversation. When he caught a flicker of enlightenment in Bryant's eyes, he continued. "I said that aerial surveys are not so expensive for the cost to be a factor, but you pressed that this would be no ordinary survey. That certain contacts you had made over the years could get their hands on high-resolution satellite footage, photographed to order. You told me that someone influential owed you a favour..."

Charles Bryant remembered the incident well. He had boasted unduly, hoping to impress his new-found business associate. It was true, he *had* been owed a favour, but as circumstances had played out, the two men had lost the Sekampung Dam contract to a very dubiously priced tender submitted by a Dutch construction company. The need for the satellite footage never arose and the conversation had receded from his mind. He turned towards the little Indonesian and smiled. "My word Junus, you really *do* remember every little snippet, don't you?" he stated flatly, as he picked up his glass and sipped a deliberate mouthful. "What use do you think I can be now? To be frank, I haven't spoken to my contact for quite some time, he may no longer have any influence."

"Believe me, he will. You see, remembering our conversation got me thinking... Many companies have satellites, they are merely necessary tools for information. Mobile telephone companies could not operate without them, nor in fact could the media. But answer me this, who numbers a camera-operated satellite among his facilities? Unless your contact works for a weather station, then I suspect that he is working within the government," Kutu paused, watching Bryant's expression intently. "The thing is, if your contact were a politician, then his influence is all but extinct. I mean, since we last spoke of this matter, a new government is at the helm, steering your country towards similar mistakes," Kutu smiled wryly. "So, if your contact has any influence whatsoever, then maybe he holds a more tangible position, a Civil Servant perhaps?"

Bryant folded his arms defensively and stared icily at his host. "Go on," he said, with a sardonic smile. "You've obviously given this plenty of thought, don't let me interrupt your flow."

Kutu ignored the remark and looked at him heavily. "You see; I have carried out some extensive research. Any intelligence retrieved from your government's satellites is directed straight to GCHQ in Cheltenham. Depending on its sensitivity, it goes via certain departments and is duly processed and sent to the body who needs it most. Analysts from every British intelligence organisation are on the staff of GCHQ, to see that all intelligence remains strictly confidential."

Bryant shifted awkwardly in his chair, then held up his hands dismissively. "What the hell do you want me to say?" he asked, somewhat perplexed at the situation. "You've done your homework; I'll give you that. But what has any of this got to do with my contact? I'm not going to divulge the position of my contact to you, besides, *I* was talking about satellites, *you* are talking about an assassination!"

Junus Kutu smiled wryly and continued to pontificate, unaffected by Bryant's outburst. "That is how the government and all its departments receive their information. However, I have it on sound information that the Secret Intelligence Service, or MI6 as it is better known, can operate its own satellites and process all intelligence exclusively," he paused, picked up his martini glass and sipped a small, delicate mouthful of the now tepid liquid. "There is only one way in which your contact could off-load satellite data and that is certainly not through the red tape and protocol of GCHQ."

Bryant gave his friend a contemptuous look, furious that he had pressed a delicate matter so far and so indiscreetly. He knew for a fact that Junus Kutu would never have allowed such probing into his own contacts. "Okay," he paused, glaring angrily at his host. "You've got me. Why don't you finish your speech? I can see that you're simply dying to draw a conclusion."

"My dear friend, I am sorry if I got carried away, I did not mean to offend." Kutu shook his head dejectedly, as if he were the wronged party. "Perhaps it would be seemlier for you to tell me about your contact, if you don't mind?"

Bryant looked away. "Well I bloody do!" He glared back at the little Indonesian, unable to hide his rage. "Who was your Golkar contact who allowed you to build three hotels on a holy burial site in Bali? Who was the Japanese businessman who paid you to pull out of the electronics deal in Sumatra?" Bryant stood up suddenly and stared down at him. "See? How do you like it?"

"The Japanese businessman was called Suzuki Tomatzo and my Golkar contact was none other than President Suharto himself. He hated the Balinese and their separate principality." Kutu rose to his feet and smiled, gesturing for Bryant to return to his seat. "Please, Charles, bear with me on this. I need to know two things."

Bryant grudgingly returned to his sun lounger and shrugged. "All right, I'm listening." He glanced at his wristwatch, then looked impassively at the Indonesian. "Not for long though, I have a meeting later this afternoon."

Junus Kutu knew that this was merely an effort to save face, but he acknowledged Bryant's change of heart with a nod of appreciation. "I will not take long, and I *do* apologise for my lack of discretion," he hesitated, pleased to see that Bryant was relaxing a little. "Firstly, is your contact working within one of the intelligence services, say, MI5 or MI6?"

Bryant nodded. "What's the second thing?"

"Is he still influential?"

Again, Bryant nodded. "Now, I think you had better tell me what you have in mind."

Kutu leaned forward in his seat and smiled. "Gladly," he smiled. "But first let us have some more drinks, and Marie is standing by with some chilled lobster salads. If you're hungry?"

Bryant nodded. Kutu rang a nearby bell and within a minute his maid was walking down the steps with a tray of prepared dishes. Kutu asked for more drinks and she dutifully nodded. The lobster was thick and juicy, only just cooked, and was served with a variety of dips, crisp salad leaves and a tasty salsa of cucumber, tomatoes, coriander and chillies.

Bryant put down his fork and dabbed his lips with a napkin. "I went to school with him. We weren't all that close, but we wound up at the same university. We attended the same lectures. Well, some of them anyway. We both took a business degree. We became close during Freshers' Week; familiarity I suppose..."

"And you kept in touch afterwards?" Kutu asked through a mouthful of lobster.

Bryant nodded. "We played rugby for our school and then for our college. People who play a sport together tend to socialise together. We got drunk a lot at university... A lot of us kept in touch."

"So, what is his position within the intelligence service?"

Bryant shook his head. "No way! I'm not telling you his position, or his name!" He reached for his drink. The ice had already melted away in the heat.

"I could find out, I already know that you studied together, and it would not be difficult to search your former university for records of the rugby team."

Charles Bryant tensed. Kutu was sharp, he would have to be more careful in future. He looked at the Indonesian and faked a smile. "I know Junus, but let's be fair, you sought my help. So far, I have given it. If I walk, you will be no better off, it's not you who has the contact."

"Very well, perhaps I have been a little overzealous. But tell me, how do you come to have something over this man?"

"I haven't, I just did him a big favour some time ago, the sort of favour which can be called in, if the need arises," Bryant paused. "Let's just say, thanks to my advice, he made an awful lot of money. We both did."

Junus Kutu smiled. He had also partaken in many such arrangements. "Well, Charles, I may just have a suitable proposition for both you and your intelligence service friend."

Bryant laughed raucously. "I don't see how! My contact is far from James bloody Bond, in fact since our rugby days, I don't think he's done anything more strenuous than shuffle papers, along with most of our Cambridge counterparts! Really Junus, you have been watching far too many films!"

"I am not ignorant though," the little Indonesian

commented flatly. "I know for a fact that the intelligence services employ such people. People who can kill the likes of General Soto. I know that there are not many, but they still exist in that rather murky world of intelligence."

"I have a friend who can re-task the odd satellite, perform an in-depth company search, or investigate someone's banking records, not assassinate third-world Generals!" Bryant paused, very much aware that he had probably caused the man great offence at classifying his growing country as third world. "Look Junus, I am a businessman, I have never thought about killing another man in my life. What's more, my contact is a pen-pusher, a paper-shuffler of the first order."

Kutu smiled. "It is because *you* are a businessman that you are here. It is because *I* am a businessman that I speak with you at this very moment. And if your contact is open-minded, then we can all be in business together," he paused staring at the Englishman intensely, perhaps with the most intense stare that Charles Bryant had ever experienced. "Just answer me one question; can your contact act on his own, make his own decisions?"

Bryant nodded. "Pretty much, he *is* high up the ladder."

Kutu smiled triumphantly. "Then, my friend, we may well be in business!"

"That is assuming one hell of a lot!"

"Allow me to explain," Junus Kutu leant back against his chair and smiled at his potential partner. "As I mentioned earlier, certain influential people have taken it upon themselves to rid Indonesia of the tyrant, General Madi Soto. Because of my renowned and I must say, deserved reputation, I have been tasked with hiring an assassin for the job. The payment is to be no higher than the equivalent of five million pounds. To the consortium, it is an affordable amount, a necessary expense. However, I am a businessman, and five million sounds an awfully large amount of money just to pull a trigger, don't you think?"

Bryant nodded courteously but remained silent.

"If your contact could arrange for a British agent to eliminate Soto, then perhaps the five million could be put to better use?"

Bryant smiled, suddenly very much on Kutu's wavelength. "How would you suggest the money be spent?"

Kutu sucked air through his yellow teeth and grinned. "Say, two million apiece for both you and myself, a tax free one million for your contact and a hearty thank you and a well-deserved pat on the back for the assassin?"

Bryant laughed heartily. "Sounds acceptable to me!" He picked up his glass and shook it gently, letting the slice of lemon bounce off the sides. "What say we have another drink, before we put the wheels in motion?"

CHAPTER THIRTY-ONE

General Soto stood before Abdul Tembarak and shook his head regretfully. He held himself as if posing for a dictator's political portrait, with his legs shoulder-width apart and his fists resting against his hips in a posture of stylised defiance.

"I am told that you are ready to speak." He glanced at Sergeant Grogol, then returned his eyes expectantly to his prisoner. "Let there be no mistake, if you do not speak the truth, I will have *every* man in this battalion use your wife like a cheap, desperate whore. Afterwards, I will have Sergeant Grogol take out his plastic surgery implements and skin her slowly, from her toes to her pretty little head."

Abdul Tembarak felt himself start to shake uncontrollably. He tried desperately to quell the emotion but understood that he now had no control over himself. He had been told of General Soto's fearsome reputation and had been told that the man had no mercy. Although he had doubted much of what he'd heard as scaremongering and exaggeration. The man could not operate like this. Indonesia was a democracy. There had always been talk of human rights violations in the judicial system and inside the prisons, but not within the military. The military could only act by instruction from the government. The police were in command until superseded. Only now did he grasp that every word had been true. Soto was operating within his own remit. He was nothing more than a criminal with the military behind him.

"Well?" General Soto asked quietly. "I am waiting. Start with your name, age, rank and the objective of your mission. Understand me Tembarak, I have many contacts within the government, I will know when you are lying."

"Let my wife go first," Tembarak pleaded. "When she and our child our safe, I will tell you everything."

General Soto laughed out loud and shook his head. "No, I have another idea. You think you can bargain with me?" He turned to Grogol with a sadistic smile. "Sergeant Grogol, kindly remove one of the woman's toes." He turned back to Tembarak with an impassive shrug. "You had your chance. Now, you can listen to your wife's pain…"

It was all over quickly. As Grogol had selected the set of snips Tembarak had struggled to get the words out of his mouth. He begged and pleaded, but General Soto had held up a hand, indicating that it was too late for talking and that nothing Tembarak said now would matter. She had struggled desperately, but as the snips went over her toe, she had ceased for long enough for all in the room to hear an audible snap as the blades sliced cleanly through the joint of a toe. Her screaming was frantic and Tembarak sobbed as Grogol held up the toe and smiled at him. By way of final humiliation, General Soto had ordered the two young soldiers to hold Tambarak still, whilst Grogol had forced the severed toe into his mouth, then wrapped a length of duct-tape across his mouth and face to keep his lips together. Tembarak forced himself to resist the urge to vomit as he felt the toe with the side of his tongue. He felt the wetness and could taste the saltiness of his wife's blood at the back of his throat. He

breathed deeply through his nostrils, knowing the importance of refraining from vomiting. If he did so with his lips
fastened, he might well drown.

His wife continued to sob, as she writhed awkwardly on
the bed. He glanced at her for a second, then turned his eyes
back to the floor. He felt the tiny toe roll forward slightly,
then completely helpless, he lost all self-control. He felt the
bile rise from the pit of his stomach and fought for air as it
surged against his breath and retched into his mouth. There
was no way that he could fight the inevitability of the situation and within seconds he found himself completely starved
of air. He struggled in his seat and wrenched his hands up in a
frantic bid to free the tape from his mouth. The bindings
held firm, and his hands remained involuntarily in place.

General Soto smiled and bent down in front of his prisoner as he convulsed frantically on the straight-backed
wooden chair. "Would you like me to remove the tape
Abdul?"

Tembarak could not hear the man's voice, only his own
heartbeat as he fought in vain for the slightest amount of
precious air. General Soto wrinkled his nose in disgust, as he
caught the edge of tape, ripped it from Tembarak's face and
stepped back just in time to avoid the eruption of vomit
which spilt out onto the concrete floor. Tembarak spat onto
the ground and took in deep mouthfuls of stale air. He panted
frantically, then relaxed a little, relieved to be alive.

"Are you willing to talk now?" General Soto paused and
glanced briefly at the naked woman. "Or do we have to
remove another piece of your wife first?"

Tembarak shook his head frantically. It was no good,
nothing in his training had prepared him for this, all he
wanted to do was co-operate. If it gave him the slightest
chance of survival, the slightest chance to save his wife from
further torture, he would tell them everything. Any man

would do the same. He looked up at General Soto. "My name is Abdul Tembarak. I am thirty-two years old," he paused, blinking away a tear from the corner of his eye. "And I am a field agent with The Republic of Indonesia, Internal Security Service..."

CHAPTER THIRTY-TWO

Alex King was used to the Secret Intelligence Service's approach to its more diverse work. There were no regular offices for agents like him. No secretaries to chat-up between missions. Not even a chance to talk shop with other agents. All he ever saw were functional, plain rooms with MDF tables and plastic chairs. A place where a projection screen could be pulled down or sometimes an interactive whiteboard used, and a laptop powered up and the details of an operation discussed. After the briefing with his operation liaison officer he was on his own again.

He followed Stewart into the tiny room and shivered involuntarily as he closed the door behind him.

"It *is* a bit chilly in here, isn't it," Stewart agreed. He walked over to the old-fashioned radiator and placed his hand on top. "Typical, the budget doesn't seem to run to heating for our department anymore." He bent to adjust the thermo-stat then turned and smiled. "That should do it. By the time we've finished our briefing, the place should be just about tolerable."

King nodded and sat down on the nearest chair. The cold

did not bother him, he hadn't even noticed the room's temperature. The involuntary reaction had stemmed entirely from what he knew lay ahead.

Stewart dropped the file onto the nearby desk then perched himself casually and somewhat selfishly on the warming radiator. King stared at the red file and felt a sudden, rising anger. He knew the SIS colour coding system and realised that the entire operation was now a giant hot potato. The files had always been designated into three categories: buff or manila indicated a present, highly sensitive matter. Red was for ongoing situations, so far unresolved or needing further attention. Completed assignments were blue. The fact that Colonel Al-Muqtadir was dead was insignificant; the operation was now seen as a failure.

"I know what you're thinking," Stewart stated flatly. "Well, between you, me and a hell of a lot of people, the operation has been hailed as a success. If your GPS had never been found, then it would have been tea and medals all round."

King nodded. "Yes, but I don't see the significance. So, the Kurds had a GPS. You can buy similar in camping and outdoor leisure shops."

"Aye, but what the analysts say goes. You know that. They say that the NGS1 GPS system was not your average, everyday piece of kit that the Kurds might get hold of. As soon as the Iraqis found it, they pointed a finger at the west. Considering the ISIS attack on British soil last year, they pointed the finger at Britain."

"Well whatever happened to good old-fashioned lying?" King asked. "They would have pointed the finger anyway. The fact that I used an archaic piece of Russian hardware would not have made any difference! Shit, I could have used a .50 calibre Barratt or a Macmillan and taken him out from five times the distance! The irony is that they would never have got close to us and we would have been able to make a clean getaway. The bloody GPS would never have been lost in the first place," he paused, shaking his head in exasperation. "Why couldn't the analysts have foreseen that in the first place?"

Stewart shrugged impassively, almost distancing himself from his agent. "Lord knows. All I know is, that you have to go back and finish the job." He opened the file and took out the cover page. "Akmed and Shameel Faisal are the priority, they worked directly with you and helped you to escape back into Turkey," Stewart shrugged. "I'm sorry, it just has to be done..."

King stood up and paced across to the window. He pulled the blind down, kinking it slightly as he peered down to the murky river below. "For God's sake, the whole village knew why I was there, do you want me to take care of them as well? Two men knew me, but they didn't even know my bloody name! This is bogus. The area is hot, and ISIS are being cleaned up by a new front of Iraqi soldiers, desperate to prove they're not behind extremism. They're a capable bunch these days, they won't have made it easy for the likes of me to operate."

"Akmed and Shameel are the targets. Let's keep it at that," Stewart paused. "You will have a different liaison officer this time, someone to help you back over the border. Or organise assistance in other ways."

King released the blind and glared at the big Scotsman. "A babysitter, you mean," he stated flatly. "Someone to make sure that the job gets done. Why don't you just get him to do the job, wouldn't it save a whole lot of trouble?"

"He's a *she* actually. The name's Juliet Kalver. Pronounced Carver, for some obscure reason," he paused and pointed to the file on top of the desk. "Her picture is in there, towards the back."

"Doesn't sound very local to the region," King mused as he sifted through the thin pile of documents and maps.

"She isn't. She's a Yank, works for the CIA. She's from a Hispanic background but speaks perfect Arabic. Kalver is her husband's name," he paused. "She's been operating in the region for just over five months."

"So, it's a joint operation now?" King smirked. "Big brother wants to make sure little brother does his chores..."

"It's become messy, Alex. The US has requested we clean house."

"Doesn't hubby mind her doing this sort of work?"

"Shouldn't do, he's dead."

King found the enlarged photograph and pulled it from behind the rest of the paperwork. He stared at the woman's features and into her dark eyes. There was beauty there, but an eerie sadness prevailed. He suspected that the woman had seen a great deal of life's suffering. He replaced the photograph and turned back to Stewart. "What about my insertion?"

"Ah, yes. Thought you might like this one. No late-night border dodges for you this time."

"No?"

"No. The Turks are patrolling non-stop on the Syrian and Iraqi borders. Pressure from Europe and the sudden influx of ISIS supporters. Stupid Muslim girls and boys from Birmingham and Leeds or whatnot..." Stewart smiled. "The border has really heated up this week. The press is all over it. So, you're doing it like I used to... parachute drop, almost directly over Kalsagir."

King frowned and tapped his fingers on the desktop. "Sounds a bit risky to me. Why don't I just slip over the border just north of Amadiyah? Anyway, how the hell are you going to explain an aircraft over Northern Iraq?"

"To answer the first of your questions, the border is

simply too hot. As I said, they're all over it. Not only are the Turks finally getting security right, but the Iraqi army are patrolling night and day, your chances of getting into Iraq would be slim. Secondly, we've come up with a solution for the aircraft. We've arranged for a private pilot to veer off course from Southern Turkey. In which time, you will exit the aircraft and open your chute at approximately two hundred feet."

"You're joking..."

"No, my friend, quite serious. It will be at dawn, so you'll just about be able to see the ground when you jump. The coordinates are vital, so you will have to double-check with the pilot."

"What the hell will I be flying in?" King asked, somewhat bemused at the scenario.

Stewart coughed apprehensively. "An old Cessna one-seven-two. The starboard side has been fitted with a sliding door and a footrest," he paused and smiled wryly. "But your contact will be at the drop zone to meet you."

"What about the pilot, what happens to him?"

"Ahh," Stewart paused nervously. "Our office in Istanbul have identified him as a double-agent. Not for any particular organization, just a bit of a freelance profiteer. He sells information to whoever he thinks will be most grateful. One day it's the Iraqis, the next it's Al Qaeda. But rest assured, he has cost us lives and we want rid of him."

"Easier said than done at just a few hundred feet."

"I'm sure you'll find a way. You usually do."

King nodded, then returned his eyes to the file. "What about this Kalver woman, what happens to her?"

"Nothing. She is the CIA's new girl wonder. She will stay behind and continue to conduct New Dawn. She will help you to get out of the country. How you do it is all down to you."

"If the border is too hot for insertion, then surely it is too hot for exfiltration?" he paused, then nodded knowingly. "That's it, isn't it? If I get in and get the job done, everybody is happy. It doesn't matter that I might not be able to get back out..."

"Frankly Alex, yes. You know the score, get it done. How you get home is up to you. As usual, you will be issued with a considerable amount of unaccounted expenses. How you use them is also up to you. Personally, I would recommend using them to your advantage. Use your noggin. Beg, borrow and steal. Put a bit by for retirement..."

King sifted through the remaining paperwork, then turned to the Scotsman. "Where do I meet the pilot?"

"You will be met at Istanbul International Airport by a liaison officer, then transported immediately to an airstrip in Southern Turkey. There, you will meet the pilot. As you can see from the brief, there's only a small window of opportunity. You will be back in the air almost as soon as you arrive. From there, the pilot will *stray* into Iraq."

"Sounds tight."

"It will be. Believe me, CIA reports are all confirming the worst. The Iraqi intelligence service is close to discovering who was behind the hit. It is only a matter of time before they get to the Faisal brothers."

"Well there you go. Job done."

"It's not going to play out like that. The cards have been dealt."

CHAPTER THIRTY-THREE

"Charles Bryant?" He shook his head in bewilderment, then stared at the man in front of him. "Are you sure?"

The scruffy-looking Indonesian nodded and retrieved a tattered sheet of notepaper from his back pocket. "Charles Bryant, company director of CB Mineraltec." He slid the paper across the desk, then leaned back in his seat and beamed a grin of immense satisfaction. "I followed him all the way to his company's offices in east Jakarta."

"And you are sure that this man was Bryant?" The man placed his hand inside his jacket but hesitated. "Because if you are wrong..."

"No! The man was Charles Bryant. His vehicle's registration number is right there on the piece of paper!" He took out his rather basic cell phone and thumbed the screen. "Here, I got a picture of him..."

The effeminate looking man looked at the slightly blurry image and nodded. He gave back the phone and took the thick envelope out of his inside pocket and placed it on the desk, but he kept his hand on top of the packet. "This is a great deal of money to you," he stated flatly. "Would you like to double it?"

The scruffy Indonesian looked suspiciously at the smart, effeminate looking man behind the desk, but nodded a little too eagerly.

"Good." The man picked up the package and slipped it back into his inside pocket. "I'll keep this safe for you, until you return."

The scruffy man visibly sank in his seat as he watched the man's cruel smile. "What do you want me to do?" he asked, dejected at losing sight of his payment.

"I want you to follow Bryant, find out what both he and Junus Kutu are up to. I want to know who else Bryant meets and if possible, I want you to find out what he talks about." He subconsciously adjusted his silk necktie, then glanced down at his slim gold wristwatch. "Go back to Bryant's offices and follow him home." He looked thoughtful for a second or two then took a gold fountain pen out from his inside pocket and scribbled on a piece of notepaper. "Here, take this," he said, then waited for the scruffy man to take the paper and start to read. "It's Bryant's address, just on the outskirts of the city, near Bekasi. We have done a great deal of business with Mister Bryant over the years." He smiled sardonically, with a brief chuckle. "Now it certainly looks as if we may well be doing some more."

CHAPTER THIRTY-FOUR

"Do you take me for a fool?" General Soto shook his head as if he were answering the question for him. "Of course, you don't! So then, why treat me as one?"

Tembarak spat out a mouthful of blood and looked up at him pleadingly. "I am not! I cannot tell you any more than I already know!" He watched the man as he raised the revolver above his head. "No! Please don't hit me again! I don't know anything else!"

General Soto brought the revolver's barrel down onto the side of Tembarak's damaged knee, then swiped upwards catching him in the face, just as he had done not two minutes before.

Tembarak cried out in agony, then looked down at the floor as he continued to bleed from the mouth. He felt the saltiness in the back of his throat but was more distressed at the discomfort of not being able to hold his hand to the pain, to comfort the injury. He felt the shards of broken teeth with the tip of his tongue, spat them out onto the bloody floor in front of him.

General Soto spun the weapon around his finger by the

trigger guard western style then slipped it expertly back into his hip holster. He caught hold of Tembarak by a handful of his hair and pulled his head upwards until their eyes met. "Do you want the soldiers to amuse themselves with your wife?" He waited for the man to shake his head, then smiled, as he saw the desperation in his eyes. He released his grip, and Tembarak's head dropped down, resting his chin against his bloodstained chest. Soto smiled once more. He waited for Tembarak to look back at him, then in an instant, he whipped the revolver out from his holster and spun it around his finger again, before the barrel came to rest directly in front of Tembarak's eyes. "Do you know anything about handguns?"

Tembarak knew a little. He had passed the compulsory small arms course in training, but he did not answer. Instead, he watched the General's childish display, which seemed to have the two young guards quite transfixed.

"The revolver is seldom used by the armies or police forces of the world. Your average soldier rarely needs to use a handgun at all." Soto started spinning the revolver around his finger again, then brought it to a halt instantly, with the hammer cocked and his finger resting on the trigger. He turned the weapon back towards Tembarak and aimed the barrel at the centre of the man's forehead. "You see, ever since the end of the First World War there has been a push for weapons to fire at greater rates of fire and have more and more capacity for ammunition. All this has really done is increase the supply of bullets. Back in the First World War soldiers averaged one point five bullets per kill. In the Second World War that increased to forty bullets per kill. By the time Vietnam ended for the Americans it stood at a quarter of a million bullets per kill..." Soto studied the large revolver in his hand then turned his eyes back to his prisoner. "I think some of the old ways are best. Teach a man to shoot well. Make every bullet count." He thumbed the cylinder catch and dropped the six .357 magnum bullets into the palm of his left hand. He grinned at Tembarak as he slipped just one of them back into the cylinder and snapped it shut. He placed the remaining bullets into his trouser pocket, then pulled back the hammer to 'half-cock' position and spun the cylinder with his left hand. The cylinder spun like a bicycle wheel, then ran out of momentum and stopped. Soto continued to smile, as he cocked the hammer and walked over to Tembarak's wife, who lay still on the bed.

"No!" Tembarak shouted at the top of his voice. "Please!"

General Soto rested the muzzle of the barrel against the woman's temple and squeezed the trigger. There was a loud, distinctive click as the hammer dropped down onto an empty chamber and the woman, who had been completely unaware, visibly jumped. She looked at the revolver, then started to scream. Soto smiled and pulled the hammer back halfway and spun the cylinder once more. "The correct way to do this is to keep pulling the trigger until someone dies, taking it in turns of course. That was how the drunken Russian soldiers perfected the game on cold Siberian nights. However, I have found it more entertaining to keep spinning the cylinder, that way the game can go on and on..." He looked across at Sergeant Grogol and smiled. "Grogol once kept a man sweating for an hour. That's impressive for one in six odds. What are the chances of me doing the same with your wife?"

Tembarak shook his head. "Please! I have already told you everything. I was sent to the bank to investigate your accounts. I was to come up with names and details of all your financial transactions. To date, I have come up with nothing..."

Click.

"No!"

"Quiet!" Soto cocked the hammer and pointed the revolver back at Tembarak and squeezed the trigger.

Click.

He pulled back the hammer again, then aimed the weapon at the woman's head. Again, he pulled the trigger.

Click.

General Soto looked at him and pulled back the hammer once more. "Three shots without spinning the cylinder. At best, you have two more..."

"I don't know anything else! *They* know about your aspirations for leadership and they know of your deal with China. They wanted me to find out more. But as I have told you, I don't know anything else!"

Soto looked at him and shook his head belligerently. "*They* know nothing of my plans with China! The coalition are just fumbling in the dark! Sending idiots like you to get themselves killed!" He looked at Tembarak and shook his head contemptuously. "To think that you would risk your own life, and that of your wife's, for such an impotent, weak-minded government. Can you not think of a higher, greater good which you could serve, for which you would be prepared to die?" He looked thoughtful for a moment, then turned to Sergeant Grogol. "Get the woman cleaned up and her wound seen to, then have her locked in a holding cell," he paused and looked at Tembarak briefly. "While you are at it, have this man cleaned up and find him something to eat and drink. After that, put him in a cell on his own and report back to me."

CHAPTER THIRTY-FIVE

She flicked through the pages of the passport, taking in the vast array of visas adorning its back pages with a combination of admiration for the traveller and a hint of jealousy, having never had the opportunity to travel herself. She turned back to the photograph and studied the man before her. A shade under six-foot, broad shoulders, muscular chest and trim waist. His hair was dark, but the odd grey was showing through which was not indicated in the photograph. His features were a little more prominent now, the wrinkles more pronounced; but she could see that the man had not gained weight in the six years since the document had been issued.

Alex King watched her closely, aware that his visa stamps made for impressive reading, although he omitted to tell the Turkish customs officer of the other two passports, each under a different name, and the two *clean* passports in his own name which were stitched into the lining of his travel bag. The clean passports held visas which would not offend certain countries. You wouldn't get into Israel with a recent Syrian or Iranian visa for example.

She closed the passport and handed it back to him, then turned blankly towards the next man, who stood approximately five feet away behind the thick yellow line separating the queue of travellers from her desk. King thanked the woman, slipped the passport back into his jacket pocket, picked up his one, medium-sized travel bag and headed towards the exit. He was used to travelling light and never carried more than one bag. That way he could be sure of exiting airports quickly and never had to wait for his luggage, which he knew could easily be misplaced or delayed. He bypassed the hordes of anxious holidaymakers preparing for the scramble ahead and made his way through the green passage and into the crowds of eager taxi drivers, luggage carriers and travel reps.

He studied the crowd casually, then cringed at the sight of a slightly built young man holding a small handwritten placard, baring the blatant legend - *MR. KING*. He walked on past the young man, to check if he was alone. He studied the man's build then looked to see whether he was carrying anything which might spoil the lines of his well-tailored linen suit. Satisfied that his new companion was both alone and unarmed, King walked over and smiled politely. "I'm King. You are expecting me?"

"Alex King of the London office? Yes, I am," the young man drawled, in what King guessed to be a naturally upper-class accent. "I've been looking forward to meeting you actually. Glad to be working with you."

King nodded, uninterested in his new companion's aspirations. He looked warily around the large foyer, then turned back to the young man. "Do you have transport?"

The man nodded, and King held his bag out for him to carry. He liked to establish the pecking order early on. "Come on then. We'd better be going."

The young man took King's bag and led the way through the foyer towards the vast taxi rank skirting the perimeter of the building. He continued past the row of cars, then turned his head back to King as he walked.

"My name is Richard Houndsworth," he announced amiably, then slowed his pace to allow King to walk alongside him. "I will be accompanying you to our destination. The time window will be extremely narrow, but not to worry, you can catch up with some sleep on the flight."

"Where are we going now, then?" King asked, as they reached the end of the taxi rank. "Are we not just catching an internal flight to somewhere nearer the border?"

"We are, but not from here," Houndsworth paused, then nodded towards the nearby car park, motioning King to follow him across the road. "We have a helicopter, fuelled and ready to go. It's just a few minutes' car ride from here. We have to stop off halfway for a refuel, but that should only take half an hour or so." He fell silent as they approached the first row of cars, then briefly glanced at his key-fob. He looked across at a nearby Toyota Corolla, double-checked the vehicle's number plate with the key fob and then walked decisively towards it.

King watched him intently, realising that this was the first time that the man had set eyes on the vehicle. He had obviously been dropped off at the airport and was merely following the instructions and directions he had been given. King noted that the security surrounding this operation was tight. He had already been ordered to kill the pilot of the light plane and started to doubt whether the pilot was really a double agent, or whether he would just be another loose-end, like King's two Kurdish companions. And how the hell was he going to kill the pilot? Unless they had another pilot arranged for the mission a plane crashing down with a dead pilot was going to do a bit more than ruin the element of surprise... He looked across at Richard Houndsworth as he slipped the key into the lock and started to wonder what was in store for his new-found companion.

CHAPTER THIRTY-SIX

"He can't be bloody serious!" Arnott exclaimed loudly. A little too loudly for Donald McCullum's liking.

"The important thing is to remain calm," McCullum said quietly. He looked across at Stewart and raised an eyebrow expectantly. "Where is Alex King as we speak?"

Stewart frowned. "In Turkey," he paused, deciding that he would probably need to be more specific. "He should have just landed in Istanbul. Richard Houndsworth, of the Istanbul office, should have met him by now."

McCullum kept his eyes on Stewart and nodded. "All right, there is little we can do but allow the operation to continue as planned." He looked thoughtful for a moment. "I think that everyone will agree that this is not only necessary, but probably most prudent." He waited for the two men to nod in unison, then continued to question Peter Stewart. "Did you suspect that King was doing something like this?"

Stewart glared back at him. "Of course not!"

"Well he *is* one of your field agents, you are meant to keep close tabs on them at all times," McCullum shook his head, almost dumbfounded. "Why was this not spotted earlier?"

Stewart glared contemptuously at the Deputy Director General. "Because until now, nobody has ever ordered that his private life be violated!"

"He is a specialist for the SIS. He *has* no private life!" Marcus Arnott interrupted.

Stewart ignored him, deciding to keep his attention focused on McCullum. "What I am saying is, it is not regular procedure to go through an agent's possessions. This was only stumbled upon *after* the order was given. What King does in his private life..." he glanced across at Arnott. "...should ordinarily be no concern of ours."

"Writing a book of his bloody memoirs is very much our concern!" Arnott responded. He held up a sheet of the printout which had been given to them both not ten minutes earlier. "If it's half as compelling as this, it'll be a bestseller within weeks!"

"I'm not disputing that it will be a problem for us, I am just saying that there would have been no way of knowing." Stewart looked across at McCullum and shook his head dejectedly. "For God's sake, Donald, I had no idea! How could I have?"

McCullum shrugged. "He's your agent, you helped to train him. You're the one who should have been keeping tabs on him. Instead, because he's a one-off, the best at what he does, you cut him some slack. Perhaps a little too much," he paused, then glanced down at the sheets of paper in front of him. "It was all very well allowing the man to go off into the countryside painting his bloody pictures, but now we know he was diverting his artistic flair into other channels."

Stewart remained silent. He was familiar with the technique, having seen it time and time before. He knew that he was already being set-up as the scapegoat, he would not be surprised if his signature had found its way onto several sensitive documents already. "I'll talk to him. Remind him of the

Official Secrets act, let him know that the nature of his work may have the faint whiff of murder about it. He'll change his mind when he thinks what a few life sentences will do for him..." He looked at McCullum, who was shaking his head emphatically. He sighed in resignation. He'd tried at least. "All right, what do you want me to do?"

McCullum smiled. "You can take a handful of men and step up the search for his Security Blanket. Two components have been located, Holmwood is certain that there should only be one more, given both King's patterns and locations worked or time on leave," he paused, glancing at Arnott. "In your opinion, what can be done to destroy King's chances of getting his memoirs into print?"

Marcus Arnott shrugged. "Well he's signed the Official Secrets Act. Legally he can't divulge any pertinent information. He could always write under the guise of fiction though. Like those former SAS types do. He could write some extremely embarrassing and sensitive situations regarding SIS into his story. Publishers and literary agents tend to keep a firm lid on any future projects. Finding out whether King has a contract will prove nigh on impossible."

"What makes you an expert suddenly?" Stewart asked, a trace of cynicism clearly detectable in his voice.

Arnott looked at him. "My sister, old boy. She was a school teacher, plodded away writing romantic fiction for a decade. When she retired, she wrote a sort of romantic thriller. The book sold quite well, didn't get anywhere near the bestsellers, but netted her a fairly considerable sum all the same."

"The trouble is, the sort of thing that King is writing about is bound to sell well. Espionage, assassinations, intrigue; God only knows how well it could do with the appropriate marketing. And *that* factor is a given. An actual government assassin writing espionage thrillers... That's gold to a good publicist," McCullum sat back in his seat and frowned. "And then there's the internet, self-publishing, blogs... But we're digressing. King is writing his bloody memoirs and we categorically can't allow it to go any further. He also has sensitive documented evidence of missions he's participated in locked up in various legal offices. It simply ends now. King is a loose cannon. Who the hell does he think he is? Trying to hold the firm to ransom? No, he needs to be taken out of the picture altogether."

"Assassinated?" Stewart asked dubiously. The Scotsman looked perplexed, he'd never come across this sort of action in his entire career, let alone been a part of it.

"Maybe not," McCullum said. "He's about to drop into a living hell on Earth. If we can locate and lift the rest of his security blanket before he starts running about in a war zone, then maybe we'll get lucky and ISIS or the Iraqis will do the work for us..."

CHAPTER THIRTY-SEVEN

The helicopter was a Gazelle. It needed a few body repairs and a coat of paint. The paint didn't bother King as much as the repairs. The aircraft had hit something or had a minor crash. Which made King think about the pilot. Maybe a vehicle had backed into it in the hanger. King hung on to that thought as they walked from the car across the dirt yard to the helicopter.

"She's a bit of a dog, but she'll get us there all the same." Houndsworth stood next to him, still carrying the bag like a loyal butler. He turned towards the old metal hangar and pointed to a man sitting in the back of an open Jeep reading from a newspaper and keeping his bare shoulders out of the sun. "That's the pilot. He does a bit of work for us from time to time and has agreed to take us to the border."

King watched the man, then turned back to Houndsworth. "What are we waiting for then?" he paused, studying the Turk in the back of the Jeep. "If the time frame is so tight, why the hell don't we get going?"

Houndsworth shrugged. "He is a bit temperamental, perhaps he's waiting for us to go to him?"

"But the bloody chopper is over here!" King kicked a small pebble across the dusty ground, then looked at his liaison officer. "Don't you think that it might be a good idea to find out what's going on?"

The young man nodded, put down King's travel bag and walked hastily across towards the rickety looking hangar.

King turned around and looked out across the dry plain, which spread out far into the distance. It reminded him vaguely of Northern Iraq and the task which lay ahead. Getting into the country would be easy enough, as long as the American woman, Juliet Kalver, was at the rendezvous to meet him. If not, then he knew the coordinates of the village and could tab there within a few hours. No doubt his two good friends would be pleased to see him again and would offer him a bed for the duration of his stay. King turned around cringing suddenly at the irony. Richard Houndsworth was walking back towards him, stumbling briefly on the rough ground, but quickly regaining his footing as he walked despondently towards the helicopter.

He looked apologetically at King, then shrugged. "He says that he cannot leave the hangar until his brother-in-law arrives to look after the place."

"What?" King looked at him and shook his head. "Are you joking? For Christ's sake Houndsworth we have an operation here!" He looked across at the pilot, who was nonchalantly turning the pages of his newspaper. "I'm not putting my arse in a sling because your pilot hasn't got his act together. Go over and tell him he flies now, or I will go over, slot the bastard there and then and fly the fucking chopper myself!"

Houndsworth trembled as he saw the expression on King's face. He looked briefly into his hard, glacier-blue eyes, then glanced to the ground, never wanting to make eye-contact with this man again. He turned back across the dusty ground, a shiver running down his spine as he thought of what he had just experienced. No wonder Alex King was an assassin, there was nothing behind his eyes but death.

King watched from the helicopter as Houndsworth talked to the arrogant looking Turk. He studied the Turk's mannerisms and Houndsworth's own body language and could tell in an instant that the young liaison officer was getting nowhere. King could see that he not only lacked vital experience, but also the authority or presence to win over the Turkish pilot. He turned around and opened the left-hand door to the bulbous fuselage, then dropped his travel bag onto a rear seat. He looked back at the two men and could see that the pilot took exception to his aircraft being touched by anyone. King left the door open and walked calmly across the waste ground towards the hangar. Richard Houndsworth looked away from King, turned frantically to the Turk and started to converse with him quite animatedly in his own semi-fluent grasp of the language. The Turk stuck his chin arrogantly in the air as if to ignore the Englishman's warning. He dropped his paper in the Jeep and jumped to the dry earth. "Get into the chopper, Houndsworth," King ordered him quietly.

The young man looked at King, feeling useless in the middle of the situation. He turned to the pilot in desperation and started to plead with him not to ignore his warning. Then looked back at King, before turning to walk dejectedly back towards the helicopter. King looked at the Turk, who was now holding himself defensively in an amateurish fighting stance. King noted the width of his stance, estimated the percentage of weight over each foot. The man's hips were pushed forwards, so any punch aimed his way would be powered only from his arms and not the crucial power driven from both hips and torso. He also looked stiff and slow. But that was never a certainty.

"You threaten me bastard? You come and see what you

get!" The Turk bunched his fists. "We no fly. Not until Ismail comes to look after building."

King walked openly towards his man, his hands by his sides. "No. We have a schedule to keep. You are being paid well for your services. You will fly now." He stared at him, his eyes cold, hard and steady. "Understand?"

The Turk suddenly stepped forward and swung his right fist, at the same time mouthing obscenities in Turkish. King twisted to his left and pushed the man's arm a few inches aside with his left hand, brought up his right arm around the arm. King's right hand connected with the side of the man's neck with his bunched thumb catching the carotid artery. At the same time, King caught hold of his right hand with his left and turned the strike into a vice-like hold. He kicked out the man's lead foot for good measure and the two-hundred odd pounds sagged increasing the effectiveness of the hold. The man was struggling to breathe, and King knew that the blood supply to his brain was being pinched. The man would have blurred vision by now, along with a pounding pulse in both ears. He released his grip a little then said in fluent Turkish; "Get into the chopper and fly us like you agreed. It's your choice. I can fly it if necessary. But then we won't need you. Do you understand what I mean by that?" The Turk nodded, and King cautiously released his grip and the man sagged to the dusty ground.

CHAPTER THIRTY-EIGHT

Charles Bryant sipped the gin and tonic and closed his eyes. The drink was generic. Made from mass produced ingredients and all the better for it. The gin was *Gordons*. Looked down on by aficionados these days, but consistently good. The tonic was *Schweppes* and the ice was made from water that was safe to drink. The lemon was Sicilian but tasted no different to him. It was the best G & T he'd had since leaving Britain for Indonesia.

He was flying business class. He always did. Economy was too tiresome, and first class was a waste of money. Besides, business class was tax deductible. He would enjoy a few of these gin and tonics, but only until he reached Dubai. From there he would drink espresso and later tea. He would then arrive in London level headed and within the drink driving limit. His Mercedes C63 AMG Black was securely parked at a luxury car specialist near Heathrow and he would enjoy the drive through Hampshire to his home on the outskirts of Winchester.

Bryant had decided that this business with Junus Kutu was too important and too sensitive to risk anything other than a face to face meeting with his contact in the intelligence services. If nothing came from it then he could be back in Java in a few days. He would have wasted money on the flight, but from speculation came accumulation and two-million tax free was incentive enough. His biggest worry was broaching the subject of taking another man's life.

CHAPTER THIRTY-NINE

Donald McCullum set the page down on the desk and picked up the next instalment of the printout, his eyes never leaving the words in front of him. Not for a long time could he remember feeling quite so compelled to continue reading.

The quality of writing and punctuation were surprisingly good, given that Alex King had not excelled at academic study, either in his formal education, or in training within SIS. The subject matter was compelling, and the style flowed easily, enabling the reader to cover a great many pages in a short amount of time.

He looked up, suddenly aware of a soft buzzing from the internal telephone line. He cursed inwardly, and replaced the page on the desk, before picking up the rather dated looking red telephone. "Yes?" he asked impatiently.

"Sir, there is a telephone call for you from a Mister Holmwood. That was all he would say, but he *did* give this month's security clearance code." The voice belonged to a young woman who was monitoring the service's switchboard. "Do you want me to put him through?"

"Please," he put down the receiver, then picked up the

white telephone, which was a secure link, external line only. "Holmwood?"

"Yes Sir. I'm just reporting to give an update."

"Well get on with it man..." McCullum glanced down at the unfinished page and found himself scanning the words as he waited.

"Yes Sir," Holmwood paused. "We have found a possible location for the missing merchandise..."

McCullum sat up expectantly in his chair, clutching the receiver tightly. "Go on," he prompted calmly.

"It's an invoice for services rendered, from what looks to be a small legal firm called Callington and Co. based in a nearby town called Falmouth."

McCullum smiled. It certainly fitted in with King's *modus operandi*. So far, he had used two small legal firms, one based in Hereford, the other in Blakeney, Norfolk. It would make sense to spread the files and to use a firm in the county where he lived would only be practical. Doubtless it would also appear to be just another small-time legal office, one of many. But there was a pattern. King spent a great deal of time in Hereford at the SAS base, where he trained and refreshed and sometimes instructed other MI6 and MI5 agents. Blakeney was a small town in Norfolk where SIS held a safe house for debriefing and a farm where training and evaluation took place.

"Sir?" Holmwood asked, made somewhat uncomfortable by the long pause.

"Yes." McCullum came to his senses, suddenly excited that he might well be nearing a conclusion to his most recent bout of problems.

"Do you want us to take a closer look?" Holmwood prompted.

"No, stay put." He glanced anxiously at his watch. "I am sending someone down to you to assume command. Clear?"

Holmwood hesitated. Then, realising that there was nothing that he could say or do, he conceded. "Yes, sir."

McCullum replaced the receiver, ending the conversation abruptly. He picked up the internal line and dialled the four-digit number from memory.

CHAPTER FORTY

The helicopter swooped low over the hilltop, then plummeted rapidly into the deep ravine. The engine struggled as the pilot pitched his considerable skill against overwhelming odds to control the speed of their descent. The sound of the rotor blades groaning through the steep turn seemed to drown the noise of the damaged engine and the look on the pilot's face said it all. They were about to crash.

He looked at the wounded man next to him. Blood pumped from his chest, oozing out in small floods in time with his heartbeat. The man's eyes were starting to glaze. He had seen the look before and knew that the young intelligence officer had little time left on this earth. He returned his attention to the view in front of him, and the ever-nearing landscape. The pilot struggled frantically with the yoke, heaving it backwards, and pressing his left foot as forcefully as he could against the stiff rudder.

He knew that there was little time left. If he did not help the pilot, if he did not put their previous differences behind him, they would both be dead within moments. He dropped the AK47 assault rifle between the two front seats, frantically seeking a position next to the pilot. The pilot glanced at him, then looked ahead as he spoke. "Left rudder, full yoke. I've got the cyclic on full!"

He reached down to his right to catch hold of the cyclic, then with his left hand, he aided the pilot on the yoke, at the same time as pressing his left foot flat to the floor on the rudder pedal. The helicopter seemed to react, but their descent was still far too rapid. There were pine trees looming ahead out of the mountainside, getting larger with every passing second.

"There's very little hydraulic fluid left, we need to slow now, or we're done!" The pilot clenched his teeth with the strain of the vibrating controls. "I'm going to try to auto-rotate!"

He looked at the pilot and kept his weight fully behind the yoke. There was nothing that he could do now. He felt like closing his eyes as the pilot shut down the engine and relied on physics to slow the falling aircraft. The helicopter slowed slightly, but far too late to avoid the treetops. He kept his grip on the yoke, then braced for the impending crash. Many things seemed to be passing through his mind, uninvited through his panic. Strange, inconsequential things, from his everyday life, only now, they seemed important. Had he wasted his time? No, he was sure he hadn't, after all, someone had to keep the world in check, perform the tasks that others were unwilling to do. He wished he'd asked Jane to marry him sooner... He suddenly snapped back to reality, back to the very real fate ahead of them. He glanced over his shoulder at the young man.

"Brace yourself, we are going to crash any moment!" There was no response, no flicker of life from the glazed eyes. He turned, realising that the man was already dead. He kept his limbs on the three separate controls ready to pull his body into a ball upon impact, to avoid entanglement with the rudder pedals and the yoke, which would flail around violently until the craft lay still. Then, as their last second in the air passed and the ground became ever closer, he suddenly realised to his horror that he wasn't strapped into his harness...

King woke with a start, his breathing irregular and the pulse pounding in his ears, as his mind relived the moment. He looked ahead, at the sun scorched earth and the rocky sided slopes of the valley, then breathed steadily, as his racing pulse began to slow.

"Are you all right?" Richard Houndsworth looked at him, his expression one of genuine concern. The man nodded, as if in understanding of King's mental turmoil. "Nightmare was it?"

King ignored him, choosing to look out of the tiny craft's side window instead. Once King had persuaded the pilot that to fly would be in his best interest, they had taken off in under five minutes. The pilot had rushed through the pre-flight checks and they had made suitable progress to their refuelling point near the small town of Sivigi, near Diyarbakir. It was a small airfield used mainly by a skydiving school and a training centre where English private pilots came to build up cheap hours on their logbooks. Stopping for no longer than it took to refuel the thirsty tanks and drink a couple of ice-cold Cokes, they were soon flying on towards their destination; a small airstrip outside the town of Hakkari.

Richard Houndsworth had insisted on talking for much of the way, mainly about chess and his other passion for collecting classic model vehicles. Everything from steam trains and vintage cars, to airplanes and steamships. King suspected that Houndsworth had been single for most of his adult life.

King looked up suddenly as the helicopter lost speed. For a second, he found himself gripping the edge of his seat and his heartbeat started to race. The pilot turned around, avoiding eye contact with King, and nodded to Houndsworth.

King relaxed, aware that they were in fact nearing their destination and the pilot was slowing down accordingly. He looked ahead, through the front of the cockpit and watched as the helicopter seemed to aim itself at a large aircraft hangar, then slowed considerably before starting its descent, at a more moderate pace, steadily towards the dusty ground.

"That's the pilot over there." Houndsworth pointed out of his own side window towards the hangar, which seemed semi derelict. "He's a Turk but works for us all the same."

King looked at the young liaison officer and realised that the man knew nothing of his own orders to kill the Turk. He glanced towards the hangar and took in his first target. He was of average height but carried a little weight. Broad shouldered and barrel chested. And he looked more like a Mexican bandit than a Turkish pilot, with his black hair slicked back and long moustache, which hung down to either side of a cruel-looking mouth. The 'bandito' as King now mentally referred to him, stood next to a young woman, with a mane of sun-bleached hair, which had tinged to a reddish blonde. The Turk muttered something to the woman, and she disappeared back inside the building. King looked back at the young Englishman and wondered just how much he knew of the mission. On the face of it, he seriously doubted that the young operative knew anything more than that he had to escort a man from Istanbul to Hakkari.

The pilot turned in his seat and nonchalantly signalled for them to disembark from the aircraft. The engine shut down, slowly losing its revs, but the din of the whirling rotor blades still flooded the cabin as King opened his door. The dust flew up from the ground in miniature whirlwinds and the chill of the night air blasted into the cabin, suddenly reminding King that he was only a few miles from the border with Iraq.

The two men adopted the 'helicopter run', crouched over and jogging away from the whirling rotor blades. King stood erect when he was just a few feet clear of the danger, but Houndsworth kept running in a crouch for another ten to twelve metres or so, which seemed comical to King. As they neared the derelict looking hangar the Turk nodded a greeting and stepped back inside the smaller of the two doors, out of the dust storm.

"It is good to see you again so soon!" he greeted Houndsworth with a smile, as the two men entered the cool, dark building.

"And you, Ozzy," Houndsworth paused, then motioned breezily in King's general direction. "This is Alex King, from our London office," he smiled, turning back towards the British agent. "And this is our man in these parts, Osman Emre... Or Ozzy for short."

King held out his right hand and stared into the man's eyes, as he returned King's gesture and shook his hand firmly. The grip was firm, if a little exaggerated for a handshake, indicating that the man not only possessed ample strength, but wanted others to know it. As Ozzy turned around and led the way through the hangar, King caught sight of the man's muscular neck, which was temporarily displayed by his ill-fitting crew-neck sweater. Maybe Osman worked out in a gym, or with his own weights. Maybe he was strong from formative years doing manual labour. Those muscles were stronger and lasted over anything gained from the gym. At just under six-foot-tall and approximately two hundred pounds King had both a height and weight advantage over the man but was pleased to have noted Osman's potential strength. He had gained some valuable insight into the target. It was simply a matter of increasing the odds in his favour, of discovering the target's strengths and weaknesses before he made his move.

Osman lived in a small house at the back of the hangar. It was a simple affair of concrete blocks, unpainted or plastered, with a tiled roof. There was a small patio area with a vented grill for outside cooking and what looked like a small herb garden and vegetable patch. A few chickens pecked around in the dry earth for insects, grubs and seeds.

Osman's wife was called Lorraine and was half French on her mother's side. She was at least ten years younger than her husband and her sun-bleached red hair was a curious feature, catching various lights it could be brown, red, blonde or almost orange. King found himself staring at it, then looking away fearing he was being too obvious. Fortunately, it worked for her, as she was very attractive. She had cooked them a simple but delicious meal accompanied by a sizable basket of assorted breads. King noted this must have been her French influence as accompanying the pita was classic pan and brioche, the best he'd tasted outside France. The meal had been assorted cuts of lamb marinated in fresh chilies, garlic and coriander before being pan fried in a little clarified butter and the rice had its flavour enhanced by the additions of a touch of saffron and cloves. There were lentils too, spiced with cinnamon and nutmeg as well as a large bowl of chopped nuts, apples and figs and a jug of spiced red wine. Osman also produced a bottle of arrack, the powerful illegal Middle Eastern spirit which is supposed to be distilled from pure date juice, but whose origins often include, rice, coco palm sap and other more dubious materials.

King looked at the woman and watched as she hospitably refilled Houndsworth's glass with a generous measure of wine, then looked towards him expectantly.

"No thank you," he picked up his glass of water and smiled. "I have a busy day tomorrow."

She smiled politely and refilled her husband's glass. Watching her tend him, King experienced a sudden pang of guilt that she would soon become a widow at his hands. He returned his attention to his meal and speared a small piece of the spicy lamb on his fork.

"Isn't it gorgeous?" Richard Houndsworth looked at him, amid chewing a rather ambitious mouthful of the tender meat. He turned to the woman and grinned. "This is absolutely divine. Lorraine, you must give me the recipe before I leave tomorrow morning."

King agreed that the meal was good, the lamb in particular, but Houndsworth's compliment was a little camp for his liking. He looked at the man, trying to fathom what he was doing in this line of work.

After Lorraine had cleared away the dishes, the three men remained at the dinner table in the couple's open plan kitchen and the talk had quickly turned to the next day's mission. Ozzy, as it had turned out, was an extremely likeable fellow and King suffered several more pangs of guilt at the thought of what lay ahead of him in the morning. He kept reminding himself that the man was a double agent, a thought which made the gruesome task a little easier for him to live with, although he was starting to have serious doubts about that story. He knew that the firm was going to extraordinary lengths to keep this mission under wraps.

"As you know Alex, this trip has been planned at the last minute. The plan was put into operation a mere two days ago," Houndsworth paused, taking a slim cigar tube out of his inside pocket. He unscrewed it, tipped out a panatela and ceremoniously clipped both ends with a small silver cigar clipper, before slipping the cigar between his rather thick lips.

Ozzy, on seeing the cigar, took out a stainless-steel Zippo lighter, snapped open the lid and went to flick the wheel.

"No thank you old boy," Houndsworth said curtly. "I have my own means." He took out a book of paper matches and carefully tore one off the line, then struck it against the matchbook's abrasive edge, as he smiled. "Besides, petrol lighters ruin the overall flavour and aroma." Houndsworth turned back to King and smiled. "As I was saying, it has been planned at the last minute..."

"You mean, rushed." King interrupted. "I only received my briefing this morning."

Houndsworth shrugged. "I guess they knew that the job would have to be done and planned accordingly. Getting someone to do it was left to the very last minute." He reached into his jacket pocket and retrieved a folded slip of paper, which he opened and read silently. He glanced back at King, then turned towards Osman. "These are tomorrow's co-ordinates; I trust you can get our man to the exact spot?"

The Turk grinned, taking the piece of paper from Houndsworth's outstretched hand. "To within one metre!" he paused. "Do you want to see the plane now?"

Houndsworth shook his head, as he blew out a thick, pungent plume. "No thank you Ozzy, that will not be necessary."

Alex King coughed, then turned to the Turk. "If you don't mind, I would very much like to see the aircraft." He side-glanced Houndsworth. "If you have no objections that is?" He was damned if he was going to have this little upstart answer for him; after all, it was not Houndsworth who would be jumping out of the plane at dawn.

Richard Houndsworth sensed the sarcasm in the other man's tone but decided to ignore it. He blew out another plume of smoke and smiled benignly. "No, of course not, old boy."

The aircraft in question was rather the worse for wear. King ducked under the port wing and looked at the cockpit door. The hinges were loose and looked as if they might part company with the rest of the plane at any moment. He reached out and pulled at the door handle, but there was no joy. He tugged a little harder, then looked blankly at Osman when the handle came off in his hand.

The Turk smiled, shrugging his shoulders sheepishly. "Don't worry, that's my seat," he said. "Wait until you see your side..."

King walked around the single propeller and glanced at

his own door. At least, the place where there should have been a door. He looked at the gap in the plane's cockpit, then stepped forward for a closer inspection. The door had been removed and the opening had been crudely enlarged, obviously to allow enough room for him to exit the cabin safely with the addition of a bulky parachute. Beneath the doorway's ledge, a small kick plate had been roughly fitted, to serve as his launching platform. Exiting the aircraft at such a low altitude would not allow much time for a mishap. The safer and easier the exit, the more time he would have to allow for any problems with his chute, which he would be opening at approximately two hundred feet.

"I thought a sliding door was going to be fitted..." King mused. He tapped at the edges of crudely cut fuselage.

"Couldn't get it to work," Ozzy replied. "This is safer to exit anyway. Only finished it this afternoon, so don't touch it, the resin might not be dry yet." Ozzy looked at his cobbled modification and shrugged. "What can I say? I didn't have a lot of time," he paused and pointed towards a stack of crates near the opening of the hangar. "By the way, that bag arrived for you this morning, along with the parachute. You'd better check it."

King nodded thankfully and walked over to the crates and picked up the medium sized khaki rucksack and the bulkier parachute, which came in a black nylon pack. He looked around for somewhere to check the contents and Ozzy, who sensed that he might need some privacy, pointed towards a narrow doorway. "Through there. The light switch is just inside the doorway, on the left." The Turk started towards the door, then turned around. "Do you want some genuine Turkish coffee, my friend?" he asked. "Lorraine may be more French than Turkish, but she makes a mean coffee all the same. How do you like it?"

King nodded. "Yeah, that would be nice. Strong and

sweet, thanks." He turned around and walked towards the doorway, cursing the man for having to be so pleasant. He stepped into the doorway and reached to the left for the light switch, found it instantly, then looked around the tiny room as the fluorescent light flickered into life. He was in an office. A tiny, functional office, but one which he knew was set up for more than mere charter flights, skydiving or contract surveying. There was an array of maps and charts on the walls, a large filing cabinet and a desktop computer jacked into a nearby router and telephone socket. Osman Emre either sent and received e-mail or was active on the internet. Standard operating procedure was to bypass wireless routers in favour of direct dial-up. It decreased the chances of email interception tenfold. However, it should never be left plugged in as hacking was easily performed with a constant internet connection. But maybe that was intentional. If there was another way people could glean information, it lessened the chances of proportionate blame. The man could always argue that he'd been hacked due to negligence rather than having intentionally passed on information.

King dropped the small rucksack onto the neatly organised desk and checked the fastenings. A combination padlock had been fitted. This was standard operating procedure and King had three designated passcodes. He tried one, and when that didn't work, he tried another and the lock unclipped. He looked warily inside, a habit formed over years of covert work, lifted the layer of clothing out and placed it on the nearby chair. The clothes were desert pattern camouflage fatigues. They were in his size and looked to have seen service. King wasn't entirely sure which nation's uniform they were, as the lapels had been removed. They looked like French Foreign Legion to him. Maybe the Frogs were getting the blame for this one. Who knew? He reached into the bag and retrieved a small handgun, a new 9mm Glock model 26, or baby Glock, complete with a small, bulbous silencer and two ten-round magazines, already loaded with hollow point ammunition. There was also a webbing shoulder holster and utility vest which was furnished with pockets and webbing loops to attach equipment to. The vest was ballistic rated to .45 and .357 magnum pistol loads as well as completely stab-proof. It wasn't going to stop a rifle round at close quarters, but it was a comforting feature knowing pistol, knives and shrapnel were less of a threat. He set the pistol and the magazines down on the desk, then reached inside and took out another weapon, a KA-Bar knife. Designed exclusively for US marines in World War Two, this was the latest version with an all-weather composite handle and plastic sheath. King slipped the knife easily out of the sheath and felt the edge of the blade with his thumb. The blade was razor sharp and the tip was honed to an extremely fine point, perfect for a silent kill. If the knife was positioned just behind the ear, it could be driven upwards, deep into the skull and brain cavity, and the target would be dead instantaneously. Far quicker than any other method.

There was a hard-plastic box about the size of a thick paperback which contained an assortment of detonators and wire along with snips, detonator cord, red head matches, plumbing tape, crocodile clips and four 5v batteries. King was trained in many methods to use these to detonate the four 250-gram blocks of Semtex plastic explosive in the bottom of the bag. For many operations he would have used PE4 or C4. However, not only was Semtex slightly more powerful, it was used widely by the Russians.

The bag also contained a compass, a standard issue medical pack, which was just about the most comprehensive first aid kit that anyone could carry, an empty two litre water bottle, which he would have to remember to fill, and something wrapped in a silk map of Iraq and the countries on its borders. He unwrapped the bundle and chuckled loudly when he saw the final piece of equipment. A NATO spec navigational aid, or NSG-1, identical to the one he had lost. Desirable as it was to have in his kit, it still seemed as though somebody within the logistics section had a sense of humour.

He gathered up the equipment and was about to put it back into the rucksack when he noticed a medium sized envelope tucked into one of the inside pockets. It was only protruding from the pocket by a few inches and could easily have been missed. He replaced the rest of the equipment in the bag, then perched on the desk and looked at the seal of the envelope. The seal had been double stamped with the official wax seal of the Secret Intelligence Service and had been countersigned by someone whom King had never heard of. His paranoia taking over, he felt the envelope for anything suspicious, such as a lithium battery in one corner, or wire around the edges, but all appeared to be normal. He carefully opened the seal and extracted the thick sheet of paper, then unfolded it and started to read.

It was extremely rare for an assassination to be sanctioned without written confirmation and now he had it from the most direct of sources - the head of the Istanbul office, no less. His orders were clear, the fact that he had started to take a liking to Osman Emre was now irrelevant. The double agent had been identified from the source and he had no other choice but to obey his written orders.

King looked around the office, then picked up the large metal waste-paper bin. He tore the sheet of paper and the envelope into quarters, dropped the pieces into the bin, then took out his survival field lighter and lit the small pile of paper. He watched as the paper caught and started to burn fiercely, until suddenly there was nothing but ash. When the flames had subsided, he reached into the waste bin and shook his hand around the flakes of burnt paper, breaking them into a pile of ashes. With all evidence of the letter destroyed, King fastened the neck of the bag, slung it casually over his shoulder, picked up the parachute and turned for the door. He would require a great deal more space to check over the parachute thoroughly. Alex King trusted nobody.

CHAPTER FORTY-ONE

Alex King stepped outside and breathed a deep lungful of icy air. The light was dim, and the air was still, which for some reason made him acutely aware of where he was and what tasks lay ahead. He walked over to the edge of the building and stared out towards the horizon, where a thin sliver of light was breaking over the distant hills, beyond which lay the vast plateau of Northern Iraq.

He glanced down at his watch, straining to see the luminous dials clearly in the half light. Allowing for the time difference in Iraq, which was one hour ahead of Turkish time and three hours ahead of London, they would not have to leave for another hour. His rendezvous with Juliet Kalver was not for another two hours.

Suddenly, he was aware of someone's footsteps behind him. He turned around and looked at Lorraine, who was standing just a few feet to his right.

"Gorgeous, isn't it?" She stated more than asked, staring at the streak of golden light on the horizon. She looked at him and smiled hesitantly. "I sometimes come out here before dawn and watch it until the sun is way above those hills," she paused, looking thoughtfully towards the horizon. "It has to be one of the loveliest sights in the world, especially in midwinter, when there's a scattering of snow on the ground."

King nodded. "Yes, it certainly looks beautiful from here." He looked at the sunlight, which was starting to edge over the highest of the distant hills. He also knew that it wasn't far in that direction to Northern Iraq and the ISIS terror which was growing daily.

"Would you like some breakfast? I have just made some for Ozzy and Richard." She smiled politely. "It's no trouble, eggs and toast all right for you?"

He nodded, then turned his eyes back to the splendour of the breaking dawn. "Yes please," he replied, but didn't look at her as she walked back towards the hangar, even though he had by now vanquished his feelings of guilt at the impending killing. A double agent was a double agent; there was nothing that he could do now but follow his orders.

At the table Lorraine had placed a large basket of toast, a plate of fried eggs with delicious looking dark yellow yolks and a pat of rich yellow butter. There was a steaming pot of coffee made from Arabica beans and a jug of milk. It was simple fayre, but King thought it one of the best breakfasts he'd had in months.

"How are you getting back to Istanbul?" Ozzy asked Houndsworth quietly, as he cut a piece of toast and dipped it into the soft egg yolk. "Is the helicopter pilot coming back for you?"

"Yes, but not until I have overseen matters here." Richard Houndsworth sipped a mouthful of the strong, sweet coffee and smiled. "Not that I can do anything once you have left the ground, but they want me to report back to them and let them know that the infiltration went according to plan. I will need to use your computer, if that's alright? I'll need to send an email."

The Turk nodded, as if he were half expecting the request. "Of course, I will key in the password when I get back and leave you to it." He turned towards King and grinned. "Not long now, my friend. After you have eaten, we had better get the plane out. Then I will do the pre-flight checks, while you gather your equipment."

King nodded, then moved to one side as Lorraine cleared his empty plate. He looked up at her and smiled. "Thank you," then he glanced back at Osman and nodded. "Okay. This won't take me long, if you want to do the pre-flight checks now, I'll be out in a few minutes to give you a hand with the plane."

Osman nodded and stood up from the table, then walked out through the adjoining doorway. Richard Houndsworth rose to his feet and picked up his coffee. "If you don't mind, I'll drink this outside," he paused awkwardly. "Lorraine tells me that the dawn is magnificent at this hour."

"Wait." King put down his empty coffee cup and stood up. "I have something to tell you... something important." He looked towards the door of the kitchen, unsure whether Lorraine would be able to hear. "It's about sending that message back to headquarters," he paused, then looked at the man decisively. "I can't tell you here. After we have manoeuvred the Cessna out of the hangar, meet me around the back of the building."

Houndsworth looked at him suspiciously and frowned. "Why?" he whispered.

"It's about sending that email," King spoke softly, preferring not to whisper, as that sound often travels more distinctly than a low voice. He glanced at the kitchen doorway again, then shook his head in frustration at the man's questioning. "I'll tell you when you meet me."

There was very little manoeuvring to be done. The plane was only slightly offset to the hangar's double doors and the concrete floor inside the hangar was smooth, which allowed the aircraft to travel easily as the three men pushed her towards the doors. Ozzy had shouted for someone to check that the starboard wing had enough clearance from the doorway, and Houndsworth had needed no further encouragement. He released his grip on the fuselage and trotted across to the hangar's entrance. Osman and King exchanged an ironical glance, as his sudden absence made no difference at all to the aircraft's momentum.

With the Cessna safely outside, Ozzy paid attention to the ailerons and sampled the fuel to check for water contamination. It was an important check. If condensation builds up, or rainwater leaks in the engine will misfire. Cars splutter and coast to the curb, planes crash.

King walked back inside the hangar and picked up the parachute and small rucksack, which was simply a smaller version of a British army-issue Bergen. He walked back to the Cessna, reached over the hastily constructed platform and placed both packs on the front passenger seat. He looked around for Richard Houndsworth, then decided that the man had already gone to the rear of the hangar.

"She's all set and raring to go, boss!" Ozzy announced excitedly.

"Great stuff! Now, go and kiss your wife goodbye and get yourself in the driver's seat!" King grinned. He was familiar with Ozzy's sudden excitement; it was merely adrenaline rising to the surface. He had seen it a hundred times before. He watched the Turk bound excitedly into the hangar and decided that he would be safely out of the way for a few minutes. There was still no sign of Houndsworth. The man had obviously done as King had asked.

The sunlight was now well above the distant hills and the dark sky above had turned from starlit night, to a beautiful, deep blue, although to the west, the sky was still dark. King walked around the side of the hangar and stopped when he saw Houndsworth leaning against a rusty old tractor. The young liaison officer looked up at him, then dropped his half-smoked cigarette and carefully stubbed it out with the toe of his leather brogue. "What's all this about Alex? What have you got to say that can't be said in front of Osman?"

King stepped around the edge of the building, his back blocking out Houndsworth's view of the rising sun, putting the man in the shade. "It's about sending your email. You won't be able to do it. I'm afraid you have run into an unforeseen problem."

"What the hell do you mean?" He glared defiantly. "What can *you* possibly know that *I* can't? You're just a cleaner that somebody sent to tidy up!"

King stared at the man and shook his head. "Well Richard, I am afraid that it is you who has been kept in the dark," he paused, glancing cautiously around before continuing. "You see, before I left, I was briefed about Osman. I was told that he was a double agent. He was selling information on to Al Qaeda and ISIS. I was ordered to kill him."

Houndsworth tensed. "Osman is a double agent?" He shook his head in disbelief. "I don't believe it!"

"Of course, you don't," King stated flatly. "That is because *you* know better. You know who is putting information into the hands of terrorists. The Istanbul office know, that's for sure."

"I don't know what you mean..."

King shook his head. "I was given a bogus story, one which would act as a cover and avoid tipping you off if anything went wrong. Call it what you want, but it was just the firm being cautious, as usual. They know you're the double agent, Houndsworth. It's over."

"It's bullshit! I'm not a double agent!" He dropped his hands down to his sides, then shook his head despondently. "I haven't a clue what you're talking about, honestly. I think I want to see a solicitor..."

"It's not going to work like that Richard. Your treachery has cost lives. Many lives. They've followed a money trail, no matter how cautious you think you've been, they've got you. They have been on to you for some time now, all they had to do was wait for an opportunity. The Director General of the Istanbul office signed the executive order personally. I opened it last night."

Houndsworth shook his head. "Wait... Just wait, okay? I'm not a bloody..." He moved rapidly, surprisingly so, dodging quickly towards the tractor. The tiny pistol was out of his pocket and in his hand in an instant. He had it aimed at King and his hand was steady. "Not so tough now, eh?" The young man smiled somewhat smugly. "Well, I've got the drop on you. Now, tell me... Do Osman and Lorraine know your orders? Do they know the firm suspect me?"

"I..." King started to speak, but side-stepped, unblocking Houndsworth's view of the rising sun, which was now above the distant cluster of hills. Houndsworth squinted, suddenly blinded by the unexpected glare of light. It was enough for King, who had the Glock out from his waistband and aimed steadily. He double-tapped the hair-trigger, sending two 9mm rounds into the man's forehead. Houndsworth dropped like a wet cloth, his body crumpling lifelessly to the dusty ground. King instinctively kept the pistol's sights on the corpse as he took a couple of steps to inspect the body more closely. The two neat little bullet holes were about an inch apart. There was no back to the head though, hollow points were horribly effective. There was a slight twitch from the right foot, but King knew this would stop in a moment.

He looked around cautiously, then caught the body by its shoulders and hastily dragged it around the back of the tractor, where a shallow drainage ditch cut past the hangar, feeding off the fields beyond. He dropped the body into the dry ditch, then bent to stretch the legs out, keeping the body from view as best he could. It was far from perfect, but it would have to do for now. He would task Osman to find a more suitable resting place upon his return.

King walked to the front of the tractor. He scanned the area for a few moments, then bent down and retrieved Houndsworth's tiny .25 calibre Beretta pistol. He tossed the weapon into the ditch, where it landed softly on top of the body. With the first part of his mission accomplished, King glanced at his watch and walked quickly to the waiting aircraft.

CHAPTER FORTY-TWO

Lorraine stood at the fringe of the narrow runway and waved her husband goodbye as he let the Cessna's engine build up revs. With the revs at an optimum he released the brakes and the tiny airplane lunged violently forwards.

"She's a bit jerky, but what can you expect on a budget? Should have been scrapped or rebuilt years ago." Ozzy steadied the yoke and eased on a little rudder with his left foot. "Besides, she's going to be trashed as soon as I get her back to the hangar."

King watched the scrubland accelerate by. He couldn't help feeling concerned about the condition of the plane, nor Ozzy's apparent disregard for his own personal safety. He turned towards him, as the plane's wheels left the ground, and the nose of the craft pointed upwards. "What do you mean?" he asked, staring at the huge gap in the fuselage next to him. The icy wind was blowing straight into King's face making it hard for him to talk.

The Turk smiled as he eased the aircraft into a shallow turn and decreased the pitch of climb. "We took on the aircraft hangar about eighteen months ago. Since then, we have used it as a sort of command post for surveillance operations in Iraq and Syria." He applied a little more left rudder to allow for the slight southerly wind, which was blowing them steadily northwards. The plane straightened, and he reached forward to push the throttle towards the control panel. The engine's tone relaxed a little, then Ozzy glanced back at his passenger. "With the no-fly zone still enforced, we could deviate slightly here and there and do a bit of camera work. We also dropped a few agents like yourself into places over the border. But things are getting a bit hectic. The Yanks have Predator drones buzzing all over the place. Because of increasing activity with ISIS, they're firing first and not even asking questions later. You can't see the drones, even though they're slow they fly too high to outrun. You scoot the deck at a few hundred feet and one-hundred and thirty knots, and they buzz around at sixty thousand feet in a holding pattern and can have eyes on you for a thousand miles..."

"So, what happens when you get back?"

The Turk smiled wryly. "Lorraine is preparing for that as we speak. After I land, there will be a fire and the hangar will be destroyed, along with this plane and our house," he paused, checking the compass reading and the attitude, or pitch level of the plane. "After that, we head off to Istanbul, report in and then get our next assignment." He looked at King and smiled. "We're a *real* husband and wife team. I met Lorraine eleven years ago, whilst working in Ankara, shortly after I was recruited into the service. In those days I was working as a lecturer in political studies at the university."

King stared at the pilot's muscular forearms and his bull neck. With his hair swept back and his bandit moustache, Osman Emre looked nothing like a political studies lecturer. In fact, he looked nothing like an SIS agent, which was probably why he made such a good one.

"I have a job for you when you return..." King turned and looked at the scrubland below, very much aware of the open doorway and Ozzy's rough attempt at creating a jump-off platform. "Richard Houndsworth was a double agent. Or a cash for information agent. A traitor nonetheless." He turned and looked at the Turk, who stared back at him open mouthed. "I received orders to kill him, and I did. His body is behind the hangar in a drainage ditch."

Osman shook his head in a manner which expressed disbelief, but not disagreement. "I would never have guessed."

"I know, that was why he was so successful," King paused watching the horizon as the plane lost altitude slightly. "You'd better get rid of him before you leave. The fire would be the best bet. He drew a weapon on me, that's still loaded and with his body. I think he may have been using your computer to email his contacts. Just a thought, seeing as he said he needed to email when you returned from dropping me off. I got the impression he'd used it before. If you can get the hard drive out and hand it to the communications department, they may get something off it."

Ozzy nodded, then eased the yoke forwards, bringing the aircraft into a steep climb. "All right leave it to me," he paused, then looked at him earnestly. "We're about to cross the border, it's best to do this at a low altitude, approximately two hundred feet. That takes us below Iraqi radar. We'll keep at that height for about eighteen miles. Hang on, it feels pretty hairy at that height..." He brought the aircraft out of the steep dive, then pointed at a huge double-spaced fence, snaking across the ground. "There, that's the border..."

King nodded and looked below. He had cut his way through the obstruction not long ago. The urgency had been frantic, both Colonel Al-Muqtadir's troops and ISIS terrorists had been extremely close to capturing him. As an 'unofficial' agent of MI6, he knew the British Government would have denied knowledge as a matter of course. His capture would have meant certain denial and Lord only knew what fate at the hands of his captors. Now he was back.

"Only another eight minutes before we reach the drop zone." Ozzy eased the throttle a little more towards the control panel and pushed down the right rudder. "We're approximately two minutes early, so I'm going to pull a medium turn and bring us back on the same approach. You'd better get ready!"

King watched the hostile terrain shoot past, a little too close for his liking. As Ozzy pulled the plane into a tight starboard turn, he was left straining against his harness with nothing to see but the ground below.

The Turk straightened the aircraft's attitude, then pointed towards the horizon. "Kalsagir is approximately six miles in that direction."

King nodded, checked a nearby rocky hillock for reference then scanned as far as he could in all directions. There was no sign of the vehicle and the female CIA agent, but she was not essential. He knew where the village was and would prefer to work without the hindrance of a babysitter anyway. He reached into his jacket pocket and took out the handheld GPS, switched it on and typed in the co-ordinates from memory. "No offence Ozzy, but I would rather double check our position." He smiled at the Turk, then sat back and waited for the three satellites to form a fix on his position. He was lucky, the task can often take as long as ten minutes, but on this occasion, he had timed it just right. "OK, that's close enough!" He slipped the GPS back into his jacket pocket and turned towards his pilot. "When you're ready! The light is good, and the wind is not too strong. Take us up to eight hundred feet and let me know when we're five seconds in front of the drop zone. When I exit, pull a sharp port turn and drop back down below radar. That way, you should only be a momentary blip on their screens." He unfastened his harness and checked that the parachute's straps were secure, then gathered up the rucksack, which was attached to a three-metre length of nylon cord, which in turn, was fastened to the base of his parachute. He eased himself out onto the platform and caught hold of the wing strut with his right hand. He glanced over at the pilot and grinned. "It's been a pleasure Ozzy..."

The Turk kept his eyes on the compass and the digital clock which had been mounted onto the control panel. "Good luck!" he shouted, his eyes not leaving the instruments. He held up his right hand and extended his fingers.

King looked out onto the ground below and started to count down in his head. With five seconds passed, he leapt out into the frigid air and released his grip on the rucksack. The engine's revs increased dramatically as Osman readied himself for the sharp turn. The jolt to his system was not only unexpected, but violent enough to knock the wind out of him. The icy air lashed savagely into his face and he felt himself bang hard against the side of the fuselage. Again, he felt the back of the parachute impact against the aircraft and as a direct result he started to spin like a top. With no control over the situation, he tucked his head onto his chest and prepared for another fearsomely hard impact.

Ozzy craned his neck to look for the source of the impact and leaned across the passenger seat, half expecting see King's corpse dropping to the barren ground. Instead, he watched in horror as he saw the man take another beating against the side of the plane. He dropped back into his seat and did the only thing he could to enhance the man's chances of survival, which was to close down the throttle and turn to starboard. The inertia should ease King away from the plane. The aircraft slowed dramatically, but suddenly came too close to its stalling speed. Ozzy yanked the throttle back out and cringed, as he heard the Englishman impact against the fuse-lage once more.

King flailed with his arms wildly, grabbing frantically for the nylon cord connected to his pack which was anchoring him to the aircraft. He caught sight of the rucksack, which had become entangled in the wing strut and knew that he had only one option. As the plane gathered more speed, he knew that he was due for another atrocious beating. He reached down to his belt and caught hold of the KA-Bar knife, gripping the polymer handle as tightly as he could, knowing full well that it was his only lifeline. He felt the plane slow dramatically and as he seemed to float with the sudden loss of speed, he reached out with his left hand and grabbed hold of the thin nylon cord. With an almighty swing, he slashed through the toughened cord and broke free, tumbling violently backwards as he parted company with the aircraft.

There was little time to spare. At less than eight hundred feet from the ground, he let go of the knife and reached around to his side, taking a firm hold on the release tag. He pulled instantly, then felt the parachute release and unfold. Moments later came the sudden, welcoming jolt as he slowed dramatically and drifted peacefully towards the ground.

Osman pulled the Cessna into a tight starboard turn and flew low over the area. He glanced at the compass, then scanned the area below. There was no sign of a body, but he had no idea of when King had finally broken free of the aircraft. All he knew was that the violent knocking against the plane's fuselage had suddenly stopped only moments after he had started his climb to pull out of the sharp turn. He quickly pulled into a rapid port turn and started to dive, until he was down to two hundred feet. There he steadied the plane's attitude and flew back over the area, well below the Iraqi radar.

King's breathing had started to return to normal, along

with his pulse, which had pounded frantically in his ears during the traumatic ride alongside the aircraft. He looked below and realised that he was approximately three hundred feet above the barren ground and that although he had lost most of his equipment and his knife, he was lucky to be alive. He watched the Cessna pull into the turn and then straighten up. What was the man doing? He was meant to be heading back towards the border. Then King grasped that Ozzy was scouring the area for him, searching for his body on the ground. He smiled at the thought and realised that in different circumstances, Osman Emre would be the sort of person that one could easily call a friend. Even after such a short acquaintance, the man was concerned for his welfare. Either that or, more realistically, he was confirming his death for his report back to Istanbul.

The airplane straightened and continued towards him. King watched, then to his dismay he saw that it was heading on a direct course. There was still a little height between the Cessna and himself, but King was dropping at a steady rate and would soon be on the same level as the oncoming plane. He tensed as he watched the approaching aircraft, feeling despair that there was no hope. He was dropping ever closer to the plane's flightpath.

Ozzy's heart sank. The Englishman had perished, he was certain. Already, the hostile terrain was proving impossible to search, as the daylight was not yet bright enough and the mass of gullies and dried-up wadis below could easily hide a camouflaged body. He looked up from the ground and glanced at the compass, then turned his eyes towards the horizon. He squinted through the dawning light, then gasped as he saw the object in front of him. There was barely time to react, as he pulled hard on the yoke and pressed the left rudder to the floor.

King knew that he was about to collide with the

oncoming plane and knew that the collision would be fatal. He reached up with both hands and caught hold of the cutaway tags. With only seconds to spare, he pulled hard and felt himself drop suddenly away from the oncoming plane. The wind rushed past him and he had to force his body rigid to avoid spinning out of control. He looked at the approaching ground, then pulled at the emergency cord, which would release his reserve parachute. The parachute fed out in front of him, wavered in the wind for a moment then suddenly opened into full canopy. King glanced at the ground, his eyes watering from the sudden rush of air, but there was no time to prepare for landing. He crashed heavily onto the hard, rocky earth and collapsed into a limp heap before rolling over onto his back and staring blankly up at the sky.

His last vision was of the Cessna banking into too steep a turn, its engines straining. His eyes flickered for a second, then closed. As he drifted in and out of consciousness, he heard the whine of the struggling engine, the shredding of the parachute on the propeller then the thunderous impact as the aircraft fell out of the sky and crashed to the rocky ground below.

CHAPTER FORTY-THREE

He was back inside the home for boys. The room was cramped, and not only was the single bed hard, but he was aware that it had recently been slept in by someone else. The ceiling was unfamiliar, and he felt the overwhelming sensation that he had been abandoned to fend for himself once more.

He concentrated hard, willing himself to return to his senses. He did not know where he was, and he did not know how he had arrived. The sight of the diving plane was his last recollection, and whilst he knew that he had sustained an injury from the fall, he could recall nothing else. He eased back the covers with his right hand and swung his legs over the edge of the bed, then suddenly realised that he was naked. His clothes were nowhere to be seen, and as he pushed himself unsteadily to his feet, he felt a shock of pain in his left wrist. It was a sharp pain, one which he had felt before. He looked down at the bandages wrapped tightly around his wrist and forearm and knew that he had sprained it in the bid to break his rapid fall. King rose unsteadily to his feet and felt a sudden wave of light-headedness wash over him. He reached up to touch his forehead gently with his right hand and felt bandages wrapping it. He probed carefully and was acutely aware of a painful lump on his brow. He looked at his fingers, which were now bloody.

He turned his attention back to the room, which was of timber construction and extremely basic design. There was no sink and no cupboards, yet the room lacked the air of a prison cell. He walked around the bed and searched for his clothes. When that search proved unsuccessful, he resorted to taking the thin blanket off the tiny bed. He hastily folded the blanket, then wrapped it round his waist like an Indonesian or Malaysian sarong, twisting and tucking the ends to hold it firm.

The dark curtains were drawn, but a thin shaft of light had crept through and was now shining into his face. He walked over and gently pulled the rough fabric back a few inches. The view was bleak, with only the barren plateau for scenery and a ridge of hills many miles away. To the left of the window, a battered Toyota 4x4 pickup truck was parked next to a well with a stone rim and a metal bucket hanging from a nearby wooden post.

He turned around and walked back across the room, then paused before cautiously opening the ill-fitting wooden door.

"You shouldn't be up yet." The woman stared at him nosily, then frowned in concern. "How are you feeling?"

"Okay, I suppose." King felt another wave of pain wash over his head and caught hold of the wooden door jamb to steady himself.

"Strange," she said. "Because you look like shit warmed up."

King looked down at the breakfast tray in the woman's hands and nodded towards the glass of orange juice. "Is that for me, by any chance?"

The woman balanced the tray on the palm of her left

hand, then picked up the glass and passed it to him. "It's tinned and tastes pretty awful, but it's all you can get out here."

King accepted the glass and drank thirstily. It tasted pretty good to him, but then again, his mouth tasted like a gorilla's armpit. He drained the remnants, then licked his dry lips. "Thank you." He placed the empty glass back onto the tray, then looked at the woman, studying her pretty but slightly haggard features. She was blessed with good bone structure and a shapely figure, but her eyes were hard, surrounded by a web of crow's feet and her lips were thin and cruel-looking. The woman had obviously seen the worst that life can offer. But, so had he. And he was no oil painting either.

He held out his right hand and smiled. "I'm Alex King, as you know. Thank you for helping me."

"You're welcome." She shook his hand, then looked towards the bed and smiled. "I'm Juliet Kalver, as *you* know. Now get back there and have some rest."

King shook his head. "No. Enough time has been wasted already," he paused, then went to look at his watch, which was also absent. "What time is it, by the way?"

"A little after midday. You've been out cold for around six hours."

He nodded. By the state of his headache, he could well believe it. "Where are my things?"

She smiled and pointed towards the bed. "Sit down over there and I will go and get them," she paused, then set the tray down on the floor. "If the Iraqi army came and found you with them, they would know who you were in an instant. I thought that, should you be found, it might be better if you were without any incriminating evidence." She turned to walk out of the room, then called out over her shoulder. "You gave them enough clues last time..."

King scoffed. "Thanks," he paused. "What about Islamic State?"

"They're skirting the border," she raised her voice for him to hear. King could hear her unlocking a drawer or box. "The Iraqis have them pinned down now that there's a new commander in the region. I suppose they have you to thank for that. They look like they're making some headway. The eyes of the world are watching to see if there are ISIS supporters within the military now. There are plenty of towns under ISIS control though," she paused. "It's unbelievable what they've done."

"I know. I've seen."

Juliet Kalver walked back into the room with the bundle of clothes and dropped them on the bed. "There wasn't any equipment. Are you travelling light or something?" she asked, smiling at him coldly. "I suppose that if you don't bring anything with you, you can't leave anything behind this time..."

King gathered up his combat trousers and hastily pulled them on, dropping the makeshift sarong at the last moment. He looked across at her, a little more comfortable with the situation, now that he had some clothing on. "I lost my equipment when I got tangled in the aircraft's wing. As for leaving equipment behind *this* time, well the whole bag is probably lying in the desert somewhere, along with my combat knife, which I had to use to cut myself free and the main parachute, which I had to jettison at about two-hundred feet."

"My, we did get off to a good start!"

"Shit happens, it's as simple as that. I left my GPS finder here last time and now I have returned to kill two good men as a consequence. It's a bogus mission to please *your* employers," he snapped. "There was nothing incriminating in my rucksack, it only contained a water bottle, a medi-pack, some detonators and Czech made Semtex and some civilian clothes for my exfiltration. My passports, money and GPS were all in my combats. As for the knife, well, it's just about the most popular combat knife there is. They sell them on the internet to anybody."

"And the parachute?" she asked, not in the least disturbed by his cold stare.

"Russian," King paused, and carefully pulled his sweatshirt over his bandaged head. He looked at her with a little more civility. "What about the pilot, is he dead?"

Juliet Kalver shrugged. "The plane went down at least a kilometre from where I found you. I could see a group of vehicles on the horizon and didn't want to chance taking a closer look," she paused, deciding whether to offer to help him with his boots, but thought better of it. He looked in pain as he tentatively pulled them on. "I saw your chute open - way off course - and followed cross country in the truck, then the plane doubled back and flew low across the ground. I lost sight of you, but saw your reserve open just feet above the ground. When I got to you, you were out cold. I got you into the truck, then got us the fuck out of there."

King listened intently, noticing that the woman's New York accent had gradually become heavier, indicating that she had not conversed in English for some time. He pulled on the thick khaki jacket. "Were the vehicles military or civilian?" he asked.

"Terror Wagons, I think. You know? Toyota or Nissan pickup trucks. So quite possibly ISIS." She reached into her pocket and pulled out the stainless-steel diver's watch, studied the face for a second or two, then passed it to him. "My husband had one just like it. A Rolex Submariner..."

"Popular watch," King acknowledged. He knew that a great many pilots, divers, special forces soldiers and intelligence agents end up wearing that watch, above all others, as if it were a piece of their specialist equipment. Not only were they extremely reliable and durable, they also held their value possibly better than any other watch, giving easy access to collateral in desperate times. He unclipped the bracelet's fastening and slipped it over his right wrist, suddenly remembering his bandaged left arm.

"It looks like a mild sprain, nothing serious," Juliet remarked, as she watched him struggle to fasten the clasp. "Your head took a bit of a knock. You cut it on a rock, but it was the swelling that was more worrying."

King reached up and touched the source of his pain. The lump was the size of an egg. "It'll go down in a while." He pulled off the dressing, then looked at her. "What about my pistol, it was in a shoulder holster?"

"The holster was empty. You must have lost it when the jump went wrong," she paused and smiled. "There's a spare mag, but we're not in Glock country. The 9mm rounds are worth hanging onto though. As for your GPS, well that took a bit of a beating, by the looks of it." She reached into her jacket pocket and took out a mangled mess of wires and plastic. "Not doing too well, are we?" she commented flatly.

"No," King smiled and rose to his feet, flinching at a sudden stab of pain in his head. "But I've still got my health..."

Juliet Kalver drove a battered Toyota pickup. King noticed that it had low mileage, good tyres and that the scoop in the bonnet indicated that it was the more powerful model. The bodywork was poor, but he knew that underneath it would be immaculately maintained and reliable. The CIA would always give their assets an edge. However, it bounced harshly over the potholed road, throwing up great plumes of dust in their wake as they drove at speed along the deserted highway.

King felt a little better now and knew that his injuries

were merely superficial, and would no doubt heal quickly. His head felt less painful and the lump had gone down considerably. His wrist was giving him less worry and with the improved movement and rapid drop in swelling, he realised that it had just been a moderate sprain to the ligaments.

Juliet Kalver drove the truck with wild abandon, swerving at the last moment to avoid the largest of the frequent potholes and at times drifting worryingly close to the drainage gullies on each side of the road.

"How much further?" King asked, shouting above both the engine's revs and the road's monotonous hum, as the stony surface wore heavily on the tyres.

"Approximately eight klicks, as you are probably aware," she paused, glancing at him briefly. "There is no need for small talk Mister King. You have an objective, and so do I. Yours is to kill the Faisal brothers, mine is to make sure that you do it."

King smiled at her. "Oh, I believe you will."

She looked back at the road, which was hardly distinguishable from the terrain to either side of it. "Your mistake cost the Kurds many lives. The CIA had built up a great many contacts and had supplied the freedom fighters with hundreds of thousands of dollars of equipment, to encourage them to take up arms against ISIS. The Iraqi army have gone in heavy handed in this past week taking the opportunity to settle a few debts and old scores with the Kurds under the guise of fighting Islamic State. Now the area is too hot, your mistake has cost us the entire operation," she paused, shaking her head despondently. "It's increasingly unlikely that we will be able to pick up the pieces."

"Crap!"

"What?" She looked at him in disbelief. "What the hell are you talking about?"

"Whether I lost the NATO GPS or whether I took it

back with me would not have made one bit of difference. The Iraqi government are angry somebody exposed their regional commander as an Islamic State sympathiser. They're even angrier that we pulled the trigger without consulting them. The Russians need that pipeline to go through the region without the problems they've been having, and we exploited that. We feel pissed off that they just took the Ukraine back and didn't give a shit what the west felt about it, so we tried to throw a little egg on their faces," King paused. "After knocking Saddam off his throne, the west has pumped billions into this country. We should have simply told them their Colonel was rotten and told them to do something about it or the money will dry up. But we went in for all this bullshit and it backfired."

"Because you fucked up!" Kalver scoffed.

"Because the CIA were pissed off that the Brits got there first. We identified the threat, took action but didn't keep them in the loop. This mission has nothing to do with cleaning house, and everything to do with the CIA letting MI6 know that they are the big boys and that if we are to work together in the future and have the US behind us, then we must perform a little test of faith. To see if we can be trusted. You're shutting operations down out here and you don't want the remnants of a failed operation armed, trained and disillusioned with a turnaround in foreign policy. Like in Afghanistan when it was the Soviets' problem. The CIA funded and trained the very same Taliban fighters we later spent ten years fighting."

"You're an asshole!" Kalver exclaimed. "You think you've got it all worked out..."

King shook his head and glared at her, as she swerved the truck round the body of a rotting goat. "Put your hand on your heart and tell me that the Faisal brothers' deaths will save the operation and put you back on track. Go on, do it!"

He laughed contemptuously. "Of course, you can't, because it's a bogus solution. It makes the CIA feel better and it gives them a hold on the SIS, who as we both know, will be reminded in due course of how Uncle Sam gave them the chance to redeem themselves. Your operation was heading towards the gutter long before I arrived, and long before Colonel Al-Muqtadir took a fucking bullet..."

Juliet Kalver remained silent and swerved the pickup truck around yet another dead goat. It would seem that Iraqi drivers didn't respect that the goats were somebody's livelihood. She looked at him briefly, then shook her head. "I am following orders, I was told of your mission and I was ordered to see it through. I don't plan the operations, I just complete them."

"How astute," he commented flatly. He watched the road ahead, then looked back at her suddenly. "Get off the road!" he snapped.

She looked at him in astonishment, her mouth gaping open.

"Do it now, woman!" King caught hold of the wheel and wrenched it across, sending them off the road and into the even harsher roadside terrain. "Can't you see the dust?"

The woman strained her eyes to see against the bright glare of the sun, as she stared blankly into the distance. There was dust drifting into the air, but it had to be over three or four miles away. She looked back at him and shrugged. "So, there's a lorry coming, what's the big deal?"

"Many lorries," King stated flatly as he watched the horizon. "The dust is spread out in a lengthy line. You know the territory, what need is there for a convoy of road trains this far north, and with the border all but shut down? They're military vehicles, I'd bet my life on it."

The CIA agent brought the vehicle to a halt and turned around in her seat and reached into the rear foot well of the truck where she retrieved a formidable pair of binoculars. She sighted on the dust clouds, then brought the binoculars up to her eyes, keeping perfectly still to avoid losing precious time. She adjusted the magnification slightly, bringing the vehicles into clear focus.

"Holy shit, you're right! There's about a dozen of them, all military!" She looked around her and turned back to him, panic-stricken. "There's nowhere for us to go. They'll stop and check us, that's the procedure in these parts!"

King turned around briefly, then looked back at the horizon. "Get us back on the road and turn us around. Quickly!" He waited for her to swing the vehicle back onto the road, then looked back towards the approaching dust cloud. "About two and a half miles back there was a dried-up river bed, get us to it," he said calmly.

She crunched the gears, located first and accelerated rapidly back up the road. The pickup bumped harshly as she drove flat out, no longer avoiding the potholes, dead goats or other obstacles which had been abandoned on the highway.

King studied the terrain, then pointed to his right. "Okay, slow down and pull off the road at that outcrop of boulders." He turned around in his seat and watched the dust cloud, which was still high up in the sky. "You see the river bed?" he asked. She nodded nervously. "Good, now slow down and get us into it..."

"I can't, it's too steep!" She stared at the drop as they approached, then looked back at him. "You do it!"

King shook his head. "No time! Just slow the revs, take us down into second gear and head for the drop. These things will go anywhere, just keep the engine bay away from large boulders." She did as he said, then at the last moment, she hit the brake. "No!" King reached his leg across the floor pan, then pressed hard against the accelerator. The Toyota lurched forwards and dropped heavily into the riverbed. The impact was heavy, but the pickup continued to advance over the huge boulders lining the course of the dead river.

"How the hell do we get out?" Juliet asked, as she looked at the steep walls enclosing them on both sides.

King pulled up the hand brake and knocked the gear stick into neutral, bringing the vehicle to a sudden halt. "We'll worry about that later." He turned back and noted to his relief that they were well out of view from the highway. "Right, now I want to get a look at those trucks."

"Why?" She looked at him as though he were insane.

"Why not?"

CHAPTER FORTY-FOUR

He eased himself forwards cautiously, taking great care not to raise the thick layer of dust above the sun-baked crust of sandy earth. With the sun on his back, he knew that he was in the best position to observe the approaching convoy.

Juliet Kalver had argued vehemently but King had been adamant. He needed to know more about the convoy. Fewer vehicles in the north meant that he might well be able to make good his escape over the Turkish border.

His desert pattern combat fatigues blended him effort-lessly into the barren landscape, and the scattering of large boulders and dried-up tributaries gave him what little cover he needed. He watched the convoy as it drew near, and even at this distance, he identified the two leading vehicles, which were driving abreast, as American Humvees. Behind these, also travelling two abreast, were old Soviet-made BTR-80 Armoured Personnel Carriers. Iraq took its equipment from its allegiances of the time.

He eased himself back a few feet and kept as low as he possibly could, with his chin resting against the warming ground. The convoy drove at a rapid pace, close to the limit for the two lead vehicles. King rose his head slightly to improve his view, but kept his movements deliberately slow, just in case any sudden movements caught a soldier's eye.

He counted the vehicles - fifteen in all. Four APCs, two Humvees, five old lorries with canvas sides, which could be carrying either soldiers or, more likely the supplies needed by the soldiers who were travelling in the APCs. Behind the old transport lorries travelled two vehicles, which King recognized as 130 Land Rovers. These towed artillery pieces. Behind these were two open backed Land Rovers. In the rear of the lead vehicle were two men dressed in civilian clothing. Sunglasses, jeans and leather jackets. Secret police for sure. The driver was the obligatory corporal and beside him sat a tough looking soldier, riding shotgun. Only it wasn't a shotgun, it was a .50 Browning machine gun mounted above the screen on a one hundred and eighty-degree mount.

King studied the remaining Land Rover then stared at the man who knelt in the rear. Head down, eyes blindfolded, hands bound behind his back. He could only catch a glimpse of him as the vehicles raced past, but he recognised the man's build and clothing all the same. Osman Emre was alive, if not well.

As the last two APCs shot past his position, King felt hopeless. A man's life would soon not be worth living. It didn't matter how tough a man was, the Iraqi secret police would get anyone to talk, sooner or later. When Ozzy talked, King would soon be hunted once more, and Iraq would know of a second British mission in their country. He hadn't even begun to clean house and things had become even worse.

King watched the convoy disappear into the distance.

"Happy now?" The tone was more than sarcastic, there was a hint of actual hatred towards him as he slid down the slope and into the gully.

King considered her hard eyes, then nodded. "Extremely.

Now I know that we're in trouble." He walked around to the driver's side and glanced at the key in the ignition. "I'll get us out of here if you like." He opened the door, not giving her the chance to object.

Juliet Kalver opened the passenger's door and climbed up onto the seat. "So, what did you see that puts us in so much trouble?"

He started the vehicle and selected first gear, then slipped the ratio lever into low. The vehicle crawled forwards slowly and King carefully eased through the myriad boulders and smaller rocks, taking great care not to ground the underside and risk damaging the drive shaft. "The pilot who flew me in is alive and looks reasonably uninjured. They have him prisoner and he will end up talking. Everyone does, sooner or later." He looked at her intensely. "The pilot is an MI6 unofficial, but no matter how much SIS deny it, the Iraqis and the rest of the world will know he's the real deal. He knows I was meeting a contact, and he knows the rendezvous point. It's not safe here at all. Once we get to Kalsagir, take the truck and get yourself out of there."

"Fuck you!" she snapped savagely, then stared at him with distaste. "Who the hell do you think you are? I'm in charge of this sector, *I* make the goddamn decisions, don't you forget it!"

King looked her in disbelief. "So, what do you suggest? I just thought that your operation would stand more chance of success if I distanced myself from you," he paused, sneering at her. "Of course, if you have a better idea, I'd love to hear it."

She stared ahead for a moment, then looked at him decisively. "Your pilot will talk, that's just a fact of life. Once we get out of this river bed..." she sneered. "If we ever do, then we head straight for Kalsagir, locate the Faisal brothers and you do your stuff. After that, we head straight for the border,

I know a good spot for you to get through. I have guards either side on the payroll. Leave *my* operation to me, I'll sort it out by myself."

King remained silent. Kalver was certainly tenacious, but far from open minded. If she chose to reject his suggestions, then he could be of no further help to her. He would simply have to do his job and leave her to the Iraqi army, who would no doubt catch up with her very soon. He looked at the left-hand side of the riverbed, where the bank seemed a little less steep. He positioned the Toyota at a slight angle, turned the front wheels into the bank and eased a little pressure onto the accelerator. The pickup shot violently upwards, then lost momentum. He applied more throttle, then slipped the stick into second gear, and eased off the power. The vehicle's engine groaned and strained, then the pickup crawled smoothly out of the gully, powered only by the engine's idling revs.

King grinned, thankful that it had been so easy. He slipped the gear stick into neutral, then pulled up the hand brake and looked at his passenger. "Right, better get yourself back in the driver's seat and get us to Kalsagir." He opened the door and stared coldly at her. "I'd hate to be late for a killing."

CHAPTER FORTY-FIVE

"Rather chilly location for an assignation, don't you think?" Bryant paused and smiled at his old friend. "I suppose that this is your regular rendezvous for discussing your dodgy dealings."

"I don't have dodgy dealings, only delicate matters for discreet and confidential discussion." The man returned his friend's smile, then sat down on the empty park bench and looked up at Bryant, who remained standing. "Please..." he swept a hand elaborately beside him. "Do take a seat, this is merely an extension to my office..."

Bryant sat down beside him, then shivered as a sudden gust of wind stabbed ruthlessly through him. "Well, back in Indonesia, my swimming pool and patio are the extension to *my* office," he paused, rubbing his shoulders to relieve himself of the cold. "For heaven's sake Sandy, why can't we discuss this somewhere in the warm? I only got off a bloody plane this morning, it was touching a hundred and ten degrees when I left!"

"Well, it will teach you to live in such a God-awful place then, won't it?" The man looked at Bryant seriously, then smiled. "Honestly Charles, this will suit us just fine. There's no prying eyes or twitching ears. Look around, there isn't anyone for a hundred yards!"

"Too bloody cold, that's why," Bryant muttered.

The man smiled, then studied his old friend's haggard and slightly bloated face. "Come on Charles, let's get down to it, I can only spare you half an hour, I have an important meeting after lunch."

"This meeting is important Sandy, *believe* me," Bryant paused then stared at him sceptically. "Tell me, what do you know about Indonesia?"

"Hah! What don't I know about Indonesia more like? That should be the bloody question!" he smiled, shaking his head. "The place has become a giant, political hot potato. Britain exports arms and the Indonesian government uses them to suppress the people. We export machinery, and the Indonesian government operates it with slave labour." He shrugged his shoulders and looked blankly at him. "What can I say? There is far too much money at stake to become politically correct. Britain makes a fortune, or at least helps to keep the deficit down, out of exports to Indonesia. And besides, it *is* an awfully long way away... It's not like taking a shit on our own doorstep."

Bryant nodded. "OK. Now, what do you know about its stability?"

"There is none."

"Care to elaborate?"

"You live there for half of the year, figure it out for yourself," he paused. "It's not like other countries where it's always kicking off, but there's always murmurs, always something simmering underneath. The tourists are oblivious of course, but let's just say, the country's future stability is uncertain."

"So is our own, that's not what I'm getting at," Bryant

shook his head. "What I want to know is; do you know what I know?"

"Just get to it Charles." He glanced at his watch, then shrugged impassively at him. "I *do* have a meeting to get to after all."

Bryant nodded, deciding to change tack. Sandy was a man of limited patience; besides, he was used to this sort of conversation. Every day, people would probe him on delicate matters, trying to slip him up. There was only one way for him to play it, and that was straight.

"There is a man high up in the Indonesian military by the name of General Madi Soto." Bryant watched his friend's face for any sign of familiarity with the name. His eyes flickered slightly and that was enough for Charles Bryant. "Heard the name then?" he asked.

"Few within the Foreign and Commonwealth Office haven't."

"Care to elaborate?"

"What's all this about Charles?" Sandy asked, looking at him coldly. "You are treading rather heavily on extremely thin ice, my friend."

"If you know what I know, then you will know that Indonesia, the lucrative gem within the shithole that is South East Asia is in big trouble."

"You seem remarkably well informed my friend."

Bryant smiled, enjoying the compliment, albeit on behalf of Junus Kutu. "As you know, if General Soto takes over, then the entire archipelago looks set to change dramatically. The West will lose all of its business interests and China will have a foothold in the country she always wanted."

"China? What the hell has China got to do with it?"

Bryant frowned at him. "You don't know?"

"Know what? For Christ's sake, Charles, tell me what you know!"

Bryant smiled wryly, then rubbed his shoulders, which were starting to feel numb in the chilly air. "Allow me to explain." He glanced at his wristwatch, then stood up abruptly. "But not until we are in a warmer location. How about a spot of lunch?" His companion glanced at his watch but said nothing. I'll take that as a yes." Bryant smiled, as the man rose uncertainly to his feet. "I fancy *The Ivy*. I took the liberty of booking a table. You can put it on Her Majesty's expenses. You can telephone the office and cancel your meeting. You're going to find what I have to say of great interest..."

CHAPTER FORTY-SIX

"I've certainly missed this!" Bryant grinned as he slipped the fork into his mouth and started to chew the piece of succulent meat.

"You don't get it cooked like that in Jakarta, then?"

"You've got to be kidding! Can't even tell what bloody animal it is half the time!" He sliced off another tender piece of Scotch fillet steak and wiped it through the rosette of *Sauce Béarnaise*. "This is what I miss the most; decent quality food, with an experienced waiter on hand."

"Can't have everything can you?" Sandy chewed his mouthful of grilled turbot and looked at Bryant nonchalantly. "You must make a fortune over there, sacrifices have to be made in certain areas."

"I suppose so," Bryant paused to cut through his portion of *rosti* potatoes, the best he'd tasted since his last visit to Geneva. "I trust you invested your little fortune wisely?"

The man looked at him warily, then smiled as he picked up his glass of chilled Chablis. "I thought that we were never going to mention that little deal," he stated flatly. "Or am I indebted to you forever?"

Bryant laughed out loud. "Of course not! My God, man, I could never have swung that deal were it not for you, it was the least I could do," he paused, taking a sip of full-bodied claret. "Now I am here again. I cannot go any further without you and am offering you a great deal of money for your trouble."

Sandy looked around cautiously, then frowned. "Tell me what you know about General Soto first, and after that, you can tell me what this has to do with China."

Bryant told his friend all he knew. He didn't mention Junus Kutu by name, but he told him that the man represented a group of worried businessmen and politicians. The two men ate their entrees and ordered dessert. Bryant went for a dark chocolate fondant with vanilla and white chocolate foam, his companion chose Scandinavian iced berries with elderflower cream.

"So, this..." he paused, trying to search for the appropriate word. "*Consortium* of businessmen have charged you with the task of coming up with an assassin. Tell me, what's in it for you?"

"I told you, my fee is secure," Bryant paused uneasily. "The five hundred thousand, is the assassin's fee. I just thought that if you could swing it for one of your secret agent SAS type Johnnies to do the job, then you might just as well have the fee for yourself," Bryant smiled nervously. He had tried his luck at the last moment and halved his contact's fee. Only now he was sure that the man in front of him, a man trained to spot liars and cheats at a glance, was all too aware that something was amiss.

"I'm fascinated how you concluded that General Soto is in league with China. Of course, our analysts have drawn similar conclusions, but it was just a theory. No one ever thought that it could be proven," he paused, looking thoughtfully at his berries, wondering briefly what it was that was Scandinavian about them. "Our agents cannot get near Indonesia and as for coming up with their own conclusions, the Indonesian government have their heads buried deep in the sand."

"Well it looks as if someone is about to take advantage and bugger them good and proper," Bryant commented flatly. "Anyway, you're not the only one with analysts. Serious businessmen spend millions on finding out things and predicting the future, it's only wise when so much money is at stake."

"So how did you come to be charged with doing the job?"

Bryant spooned a mouthful of chocolate pudding and dipped it into the white chocolate and vanilla foam. "My dear man, I was in the right place at the right time. Let's just leave it at that." He put down his spoon and stared at him coldly. "Sandy, I am giving you the chance to earn half a million pounds, tax free. Follow the investment guidelines which I gave you last time and your offshore bank balance will be blooming," he paused, then took the napkin off his lap and dropped it on the table in a heap, deciding that he had eaten enough. "Just answer me one question."

"Fair enough."

"Could it be done? Could we use one of your agents and make him think that he was simply following orders?"

The man gave up on the Scandinavian berries and put his spoon and fork down on the plate. He pondered for a moment, swilled some wine unhurriedly. "It would be difficult, but not impossible. Yes, we could get a man in place," he paused. "It's a highly specialist, highly difficult job. One would say, perhaps a suicide mission. Obviously, we don't send operatives on suicide missions, but should General Soto be killed, it would be hard to imagine an operative escaping cleanly. However, after the dirty work has been done, our man would become extremely soiled. Suffice to say; I wouldn't want him back... That aspect you would have to arrange yourself. I trust you could find suitable people to handle that?"

"I hadn't thought of that," Bryant paused. "I suppose the odds would be in favour of a vanload of armed villains? Not professionally trained, but exceptionally violent and above all, experienced." He knew of miners who would turn their hand to such things, he had heard that gold prospectors panning gold mining tailings on the edge of claims had been disappeared in such a way.

The man nodded. "The more the better, at least three or four, with surprise in their favour. Who knows? Maybe the Indonesian army will do the job for them..."

Bryant drained his glass. "In that case, I trust you could find such a man for the task?"

"Oh, that shouldn't be too difficult," Sandy paused thoughtfully, drained the rest of his Chablis and broke into a grin. "I have just the man in mind."

CHAPTER FORTY-SEVEN

Stewart pulled the Vauxhall Insignia into the driveway and eased off the accelerator as he bounced and weaved his way down the potholed lane. He swept around the corner, then slowed to a crawl as he searched for a place to park. The Ford Mondeo which had transported both Pryce and Holmwood was parked in front of the house, blocking most of Alex King's old Range Rover from view.

Stewart eased the vehicle up onto the nearby patch of grass verge and switched off the engine. He looked out over the overgrown field and stared thoughtfully into the distance. It all felt so deceitful. Alex King was his friend, one of his initial recruits. The two men had even operated in the field together, King as the sniper while Stewart had guided his shots into place over two thousand metres away through the spotting scope.

He looked back at the house, where Holmwood now stood on the doorstep, awaiting his imminent relief of charge. Within the next few hours, he would be putting a plan together to search for his old friend's lifeline; his security blanket. The sentiment was almost too much for him, the irony so thick he could almost choke on it.

He had found Alex King and he had saved him from a near lifetime in prison and he had given him the chance of freedom, and the new life which followed. He had shaped King into an effective tool of the Secret Intelligence Service but had also been a part of shaping him into a better person. Ironic, considering the man's line of work, but under the surface lay a well-rounded individual with a strong moral compass. King was not interested in money, just the best for his country and the safety of its citizens. And now? Now Stewart was going to pull the rug from under him, steal his security, and God only knew what would follow in the wake. God, and Deputy Director General Donald McCullum.

CHAPTER FORTY-EIGHT

As they entered the remote village, King stared at the burned-out vehicles by the roadside. The vehicles, mainly old four-wheel-drive SUVs and pickup trucks had been turned over onto their sides, or roofs and ignited with petrol by the look of it. Whatever had happened, the burning had not been the result of artillery fire or explosives.

"The Iraqi army," Juliet Kalver stated flatly. "Making hay while Islamic State militants are in the area. They are getting to strike at the Kurds under the guise of wheedling out ISIS." She looked at King. "They weren't doing this until you killed the regional commander. It's been a hell of a week..."

King remained silent as he surveyed the scene. The carnage of vehicles was scattered along both sides of the dusty road and seemed to convey an eerie warning as they approached the village, which to the few inhabitants remaining, had become their own, morose prison.

Juliet turned to him. "Where do you intend to do it?" she asked as she steered the pickup around a discarded wheel which had found its way into the middle of the road. "I think it will be better if it is done outside of the village."

King nodded. "Yeah, I guess they've had more than their fair share of killing recently..."

"I don't make the decisions," she glared at him. "God only knows what the hell you're doing in such a profession. Are you an assassin or not?"

King turned and looked out of the window, as they entered the deserted village. Her question had struck a chord. Each assassination *was* becoming more difficult afterwards, and it was not until he had sat down and started to write an account of his memoirs, that he had started to realise that he might soon be coming to the end of his career. He could still kill without question and he had never doubted his ability, but his enthusiasm before the kill ebbed further with every mission.

The killing of Richard Houndsworth had not been a problem. The man had retaliated, drawing a pistol from nowhere. In truth, King had enjoyed the sudden unexpected thrill of pure combat. Kill or be killed, it was always the easiest scenario to live with. However, King knew that pulling the trigger on an unarmed, helpless man would have been an entirely different matter. The sight of Houndsworth's tiny Beretta had evoked a feeling of elation, as the task had suddenly lost its emotional burden.

The assassinations were becoming harder to live with, that much was true, although it had not been until the order to kill the Faisal brothers that King had seriously thought of disobeying a direct order. The killings made no sense. The Faisal brothers were freedom fighters, Iraqi Intelligence was aware of that, as were the rest of the Kurds in the area. They had shifted from fighting with the Iraqis under Saddam to fighting insurgents with the British and Americans. They were now defending their land and people from Islamic State. The Faisal family were renowned and would one day be the stuff of legend. No, this operation had all the hallmarks of protocol. The mission had not gone entirely as planned, and the Americans wanted to crack the whip on the Brits' backsides. The British government's answer, as was becoming its tedious habit, was to stick its backside out and brace itself.

King turned his eyes back to the derelict looking houses in the centre of the village. He could see the changes of the few weeks since he had last been here. The town was even more dilapidated and had obviously undertaken a battering from the Iraqi soldiers, as well as ISIS insurgents, judging by the bullet holes in the walls and windows. It was a crazy situation and if the Iraqis put weapons, equipment and resources behind the Kurds they would no doubt fight Islamic State back over the border. Instead, while the rest of the world were not looking, they chose to settle old scores from a long-defeated leadership.

King turned to Juliet and frowned. "Is there anybody left in this town?"

"You could hardly blame them if there wasn't." She eased the truck to a halt outside a building which looked to have once been a cafe, then switched off the ignition. "Most of the men have been killed and the women and children have fled across the border into Turkey. All that remain are the old, who are stubborn to the bitter end, or the few men who are fighting a guerrilla war against Islamic State. They use the village as a stop-off or resupply point. As far as the village of Kalsagir is concerned, it died a long time ago."

King looked up as something caught his attention out of the corner of his eye. A man was watching them from the edge of the building across the square. His hair was long and most of it was tucked up under a floppy Australian bushman's hat, but for a few unruly strands which poked out like dreadlocks. He carried a battered AK47 assault rifle with a collapsible shoulder stock and tucked into the front of his belt, as if on display, was a large bowie knife.

King turned slowly to the American agent and spoke quietly. "We have company. Don't make it too obvious, try to check him out with a glance. He's across the square, to your left."

Juliet rolled her neck slowly, as if she were suffering from stiffness or an aching muscle. She glanced quickly towards the far building, then relaxed. "It's all right, that's Rocky. He's just checking us out, making sure that we're alone."

"What the hell sort of a name is Rocky?"

She smiled. "He's a bit of a movie buff. Took on the name after watching a load of bootlegged DVDs. You know, Rocky," she paused. "The boxer played by Sylvester Stallone in about a hundred movies..."

"I think it was more like five," he replied sarcastically. "Or maybe six. I lost interest after number four. So, what do we do now?"

"Now? Now we get out and get down to business," she paused, looking at him curiously. "Or are you going to disobey your orders?"

King glared at her, as she caught hold of the door handle. "Of course, I'm not... I just have a few reservations, that's all."

She pushed her door open, then shook her head as he reached for his own door handle. "No, you wait here. Rocky is a bit trigger happy, best let me explain who you are first."

"And who *am* I?" King asked cynically. "And who's Rocky? He was nowhere around here when I started setting up the hit over a month ago..."

She smiled at him, then slipped on a pair of small, round sunglasses. "You're my replacement, I'm just showing you the ropes before I hand the operation over to you, that's all."

"Really?" King paused, as he watched her slide off her seat and climb out of the pickup. "And you think he'll buy that?"

"No reason not to. The CIA are closing shop," she said. "As soon as the loose ends have been tidied. As for Rocky, he works with me. New Dawn has or had two cells. It's only now that they are being merged before we bug out."

King watched her walk casually towards the Kurd, then frowned as he mulled over her last words. So that's what he was here to do. He shook his head at the simplicity of it all. The whistle had been blown on Operation New Dawn and the Americans were using a British agent to do their dirty work, under the pretence that it was one of their agents who had led to the cover of the operation being blown in the first place. The fact that King had left his GPS behind had merely been a bonus for the CIA, who could now implicate Britain in the collapse of the operation.

King watched the woman as she conversed animatedly with Rocky, who seemed to be angered at her presence. The man shook his head vehemently and his eyes glowered angrily as he spoke.

King glanced around the inside of the pickup, suddenly very much aware that he was unarmed. Surely Kalver would carry a weapon with her? He eased his arms back behind his seat and searched with his fingertips for a hidden weapon. There was none. He turned back to the pair, who were now shouting at one another with rage and contempt. There was little else he could do. He gently opened the door and stepped casually onto the dusty earth.

The Kurd stopped his shouting and pointed the assault rifle at King, as he walked slowly, but deliberately towards them. King kept his eyes on the man, not daring to falter, or glance at the obtrusive weapon aimed threateningly at him from the Kurd's hip. He stopped just a few paces away and turned calmly towards Juliet Kalver, who was standing directly in front of the man with her hands on her hips, and a defiant pout upon her face.

"What's the problem?" King asked impassively, ignoring

the rifle's muzzle, which was now less than feet away from his stomach.

Juliet Kalver did not look at him. "The Faisal brothers are in hiding. Seems they accidentally blew up most of a border patrol with an IED meant for Islamic State insurgents. They are now the subjects of a dedicated manhunt. That's what happened here. Iraqi soldiers came back through here on a vengeance run. According to one of Rocky's contacts, the Iraqi border patrol are mounting a full-scale search tonight and will not halt until both Faisal brothers are dead. Every Kurdish rebel is getting out of the area, the Iraqi soldiers will show no mercy."

"So, what are you and our friend here getting so uptight about?" King asked pointedly.

"He knows where the Faisal brothers are hiding out. He knows, but he won't tell me."

King smiled wryly. "Can you blame him? He doesn't know who he can trust." He looked at her then shook his head. "Take your sunglasses off, he can't see your eyes, he has no idea how sincere you really are," he paused, as she followed his instructions. "Good. Now, apologise to him, and ask if we can get a message to the Faisal brothers. Tell him to say that; *Mister English* has returned and that he will be waiting for them in the village. Go on, tell him!" King turned around and looked at the dilapidated houses, which had clearly taken a hammering from small arms fire. He wasn't looking at the Kurd, but he could tell that the mood had already softened, and that Juliet Kalver was making some progress with the stubborn man. He turned around to smile at Rocky, who had lowered the rifle barrel and was now talking to her more calmly.

After many smiles and even more handshakes, the Kurd left, agreeing to give the message to the Faisal brothers but he made it clear that he could not promise that either of the two men would return to Kalsagir. It was agreed that both Juliet and King would remain in the village until dark, but if the Faisal brothers had not shown their faces by then, it could be assumed that they were not going to show at all.

Juliet Kalver returned to the pickup and drove it behind a row of buildings, while King set off to find a suitable waiting place.

King walked through the entrance of the small, deserted hotel and leant against the wooden veranda rail. He looked out across the square, and saw Juliet appear from around a large, stone building, carrying a bulky hold-all over her shoulder. King studied her as she approached. She was tall, and her figure was not only slim, but indicated that she was extremely fit, to judge by the way that her tight-fitting T-shirt showed off her abdominal muscles as she walked. He tried to guess her age but could only come up with mid to late thirties. Her eyes looked older though, hard and cruel. He could not help thinking that she was perhaps a little more attractive when she wore her dark sunglasses.

"Found somewhere?" she shouted as she drew near. The thick New York accent carried loudly, and King could not help cringing as he felt their presence being advertised.

He waited for her to reach the wooden veranda, then nodded. "Yes. If we take one of the rooms upstairs, there's a fire escape that we can use if we must. It drops down to a row of flat roofs."

"Perfect." She leapt up the four wooden steps, then dropped the hold-all onto the wooden decking. "You can look after that." She brushed past him, then turned. "There should be enough equipment in there for you to do the job, there's also a little food for us both."

King bent down and picked up the bag, then followed her into the foyer and up the first flight of stairs. "Keep going, third floor, second room on the left."

She jogged up the flight of stairs, her shapely legs and rear just inches from King, who followed closely. Perhaps closer than he had to. She kept walking, then paused at the second door on the left-hand side of the narrow corridor. "This one?"

"Yes," King nodded. "Ladies first."

"You can cut that shit out! I'm firm for feminism."

"Except when it comes to carrying a heavy bag up two flights of stairs," King smiled as she opened the door, then stood back for him to enter first. "Then all that women's rights bullshit goes out of the window."

"Of course," She smiled. "What do you expect? I'm a woman, I've got double standards to maintain..."

King dropped the bag to the wooden floorboards, then paced over to the window and peered into the bright sunlight. The view extended over the single storey buildings and out into the overgrown fields beyond. The farmland had long since reverted to desert and the harshness natural to these parts, and King could tell at a glance that farming had not been high among Kurdish priorities for quite some time.

"Sandwich?"

King turned around and looked at the woman, who was holding out a foil wrapped package for him. He nodded gratefully, very much aware that it was some time since he had eaten. "Thanks." He took the package from her and unwrapped it enthusiastically.

"Just canned corned beef and mustard in long-life pita bread, I'm afraid."

"That's fine, I'd eat anything. My stomach thinks my throat's been cut."

The pair ate in silence, King perched on the edge of the bed, Kalver in the single wooden chair in the corner of the room. King finished his sandwich, washed it down with some bottled water, then bent forwards and pulled the hold-all towards him. He unzipped the fastening and peered warily inside.

"It's all right, nothing's going to bite you!" Juliet laughed through her mouthful, then smiled. "Just a couple of weapons and ammunition, as well as a secure burst feed radio and interlocking aerials."

"What for?" King had used burst or squirt radios before. They recorded the message you made, then compressed it into a short message that anybody listening for could not decipher. It would literally sound like a blip. The recipient would then lengthen the message before listening to it.

"My control wants to know when the Faisal brothers are dead."

King turned back to the contents of the bag impassively. He picked up the first weapon, a 9mm Uzi machine pistol, unloaded but directly underneath were three thirty round magazines, each loaded with full metal jacketed ammunition. It wasn't ideal. The trouble with the Uzi was it spat out bullets and was not very accurate, nor did it have an effective range much beyond one hundred metres. It was not his first choice. He placed the Uzi and the three magazines on the bed, then picked up the Israeli made 5.56 mm Galil ARM rifle with folding shoulder stock. "Where the hell did this come from? A bit unusual to have two Israeli weapons in Iraq." He placed the assault rifle on the bed, then picked up the five loaded magazines.

"Apparently the Israelis tried a bit of a coup during the preliminary stages of the Gulf War, a team of Special Forces soldiers and Mossad agents performed a raid, but as they were not privy to the allies' plans, they ran into a bit of a fix. A team of US Navy Seals, who were performing sabotage missions in the area, gunned them down thinking they were Iraqi soldiers," she paused. "The Israeli government denied any knowledge but of course they would, the whole allied operation relied upon them keeping out of the conflict to ensure cooperation from Arab states."

King nodded and returned his attention to the bag. He reached in for the last of the weapons, a 9 mm Browning HP35 semi-automatic pistol. King checked over the weapon, pulling back the slide to inspect the empty breech, then inserted a loaded magazine and made the weapon ready. He applied the safety and tucked the pistol into his jacket breast pocket and picked up the Galil rifle. It was a good weapon, a copy of the Kalashnikov AK47 assault rifle, which had impressed the Israeli Army after witnessing its effectiveness in the hands of Arab armies during the 1967 Arab War. Israel had copied the tried and tested AK47 closely but had chambered the Galil for the smaller 5.56 mm NATO round and made small improvements on the AK47's sights, creating probably one of the world's most effective, sturdy and reliable assault rifles.

King glanced at the radio and the bundle of interlocking aerial segments, then pushed the bag back towards Juliet with his foot. "Why the insistence on sending a message?" he asked, looking at her closely. "Earlier, before you went to talk to Rocky, you said you were leaving." King watched her reaction, then smiled wryly. "You're not just leaving, are you? The CIA are shutting down the entire operation. Am I right? The decision to close the operation down was made a while ago, wasn't it?"

Juliet Kalver stared at him, her expression impassive. "You ask far too many questions for somebody in your profession..."

"I'm just sweeping up for you..." King sighed. "My people think that I'm sorting out a situation that has become tainted, when your people are really using me for damage limitation. If I am captured, or if Operation New Dawn becomes public knowledge, then there is a convenient British angle on the whole affair."

"I don't make policies."

"I know," King stated harshly. "You just follow orders, you made that perfectly clear earlier. The Faisal brothers are not being silenced because of a dumb mistake on my part, they've just outlived their usefulness to the United States, and know too much."

Kalver got up and paced to the window. She arched her back and stretched as she watched the deserted street below. "You should be used to it by now." She turned and looked at him, her features softening slightly. "It's all a game. So, what do you do now? Contact London tell them the Americans have out witted them?" She laughed. "Isn't the first time, sure as hell won't be the last..." King thought for a moment. Kalver filled the silence. "You'll create a shit storm. Muscles will be flexed, we'll win, and MI6 will have to do the job anyway. You're in place, the targets are near, and you've got equipment and a ride to a safe crossing I know on the border." She walked towards him. Her hips swayed a little. Her combats were tightly belted at the waist, her snug fitting vest top tucked in, showing off her slim waist. King noticed her figure, not for the first time, but with a little interest. It went against his feelings of dislike for her. "Just one more job and you'll be back in Turkey tomorrow night ..."

He watched her as she walked over to him. She bent over and picked up the Uzi. King noticed her breasts touch together fleetingly. He could see she wore nothing under her vest. She stood up straight and dropped the weapon onto the chair beside the bed.

"I've been out here a while," she said. "Death all around, horrible decisions to make. Nobody to talk to. Except the Kurds, but they're just assets. To be honest, they've barely evolved since the middle ages..."

"Why did you go in for a posting like this?"

She scoffed. "I thought I could heal myself," she paused. "My husband died on an operation. I mourned, took leave, went back to work on a desk and in the field. Everywhere I looked I had reminders of him." She sat down on the bed and looked at him. "It's weird. You miss them terribly when they go, but…"

King felt a flutter in his chest. He had loved and lost, knew the emotions. "But what?"

"The need doesn't go," she paused, stared at her feet then back into his eyes. "I miss him, but still need to be loved… I still need comfort and to be close to somebody…"

King knew, had lain awake at night conflicted by missing the person and desiring another body. The feeling of betrayal it left was sickening, though sometimes a frustrating barrier he wanted to lift. "I know," he said. He nodded. "I've lost someone too…"

She stared at him. Her eyes almost boring into his own. She pushed herself up and at him. For a moment he started to defend himself, bringing his hand behind her head and catching hold of her ponytail. His other hand caught her throat, but by now she was kissing him, and he kissed back, releasing his grip. Their tongues were frantic, exploring each other's mouths. She caught hold of his hand and moved it to cup her breast at the same time she reached down and felt him, rubbed him and gasped as he responded to her touch. They felt each other, tested the other's response as they tore at the other's clothes. Kalver pushed King backwards onto the bed, straddled him and pulled her vest over her head, dropping it to the floor. King ripped off his shirt, reached up and pulled her down onto his chest, kissing her once more, feeling her bare breasts against his skin. Both were lost in the moment, their pasts temporarily forgotten, neither having ever felt so alive.

CHAPTER FORTY-NINE

Juliet Kalver rolled onto her side, her back to him, her legs tucked up in the foetal position. She was breathing heavily, her hips rising and falling steadily. King rolled onto his back, his breathing equally as heavy. He wiped perspiration from his brow with the back of his hand, looked across at her. They had been completely uninhibited, had been in sync with the other's needs and climaxed in unison. They had gone from a mutual loathing to passionate tenderness in an instant, satisfying each other as if they had been lovers for years. He reached out and placed his left hand on her hip, allowed it to follow her curve and rest on the edge of her buttock. She flinched away, swung her legs over the bed and picked up her clothes.

"We've got a job to do," she said without looking at him. She walked off in the direction of the bathroom, clutching the bundle of clothing and covering her naked breasts. King noticed the tears on her cheeks. He suspected that they both may feel guilt afterwards, although he hadn't bargained on so soon. Surprisingly, he felt good. Relieved. It had been a long time and he enjoyed the closeness and tenderness, the satisfaction. Clearly Juliet Kalver hadn't found herself in the same place.

Hearing a vehicle outside, King got off the bed and peered out of the window down onto the street below. An old, battered Land Rover pickup thundered into the deserted village and swung in a wide arc, before coming to a sudden halt outside the row of derelict shops opposite the hotel. The dust cloud wafted in the wake of the vehicle, then gently dispersed in the light wind blowing between the empty houses. King recognised it as the Faisal brothers' where he had sat next to the young boy as he died and plotted his route out of Iraq just over a week ago.

The man Kalver had referred to as Rocky jumped from the rear of the vehicle and walked to the front passenger door where he nodded to the man in the front seat, who was scanning the buildings in front of him. He looked up at Rocky, then opened the door and stepped onto the dusty ground. He was tall, with deliberately slow, somewhat calculating movements, as he slung the AK47 assault rifle over his shoulder to let the weapon hang casually from its sling.

As the two men surveyed the empty streets, the Land Rover's wheels spun briefly on the loose earth before the driver turned and powered the vehicle rapidly across the deserted square, then disappeared behind the row of empty buildings to the left.

King watched the two men in the square below. He glanced at Kalver, who was now dressed and avoided eye contact. "Do you want to greet them?" he paused, turning his attention back to the two men in the street. "Akmed and your *friend* Rocky. It looks as if Shameel has gone to hide their vehicle."

"The Faisal brothers were told that you were waiting for them," she paused, almost uninterested in their arrival. "You'd best go down to meet them, I don't want them getting all jumpy now, do I?"

King sighed, turned from the window and crossed to the door. He paused briefly beside the bed, then picked up the Browning pistol and tucked it into his waistband. The Galil was fitted with a sling, and although he preferred not to use one a covert operation or in combat, as the sling clips often rattle and give your position away, he inserted a magazine, made the weapon ready and slung it over his shoulder. "What about Rocky?"

"He's operation sensitive," Kalver said sharply. "He needs eliminating."

"Really? Nobody mentioned that in my brief... What do you think this is... kill two, get one free?" King paused. "You've got everything worked out here..."

"That's the best way. MI6 may well make it up as they go along, but the CIA generally see the bigger picture."

"Right," King said, somewhat dubiously.

"Doing it now, are you?" Juliet Kalver took out a piece of gum and put it in her mouth. King thought her somewhat cruel looking mouth looked sensual as she chewed. It seemed to soften her features. "Might be better if we wait until dark."

King stared at her. "What the hell difference would that make?" He shook his head in bewilderment. "No. I'm not doing it now, I just feel a little safer with a weapon, that's all." He opened the door and stepped out into the hallway, closing the door behind him.

The woman was getting to him. She had displayed nothing but contempt for him since he had arrived, albeit crashing to the ground and needing her help. Now, moments after throwing herself at him, giving herself completely, of being tender, caring, considerate to his needs and desires, she was hard to like once more. Now it was back to business.

King respected that, but her switch in character confused and infuriated him.

He hurried light-footed down the wide staircase, making little noise as he rapidly descended to the deserted foyer. He could see from the gripper fixings that the staircase had once been carpeted but had been hastily ripped up. In fact, much of the fixtures and fittings were absent throughout the foyer. He could see Akmed Faisal outside, his back towards him, as he talked to Rocky, who was standing in the dusty street below. He walked silently across the foyer, then stopped at the glazed double doors and watched the two men. He listened, only picking up the few words he knew, but could make out the gist of the conversation all the same. The two men were concerned that both he and the American woman had left. King caught a movement out of the corner of his eye, then noticed the bulky frame of Shameel Faisal walking across the square. The man walked somewhat nonchalantly towards his two companions, his AK47 held casually in his right hand.

As he observed the three Kurds from the anonymity of his position, King had a sudden change of mind. Taking them out at this range would be easy, especially with all three clearly off guard. He didn't want to do it, but that was why he was here. He could always say no and leave the service, but his sense of duty to his country and the fact that he saw his work now as penance for his past life meant that he had no choice but to do what was ordered. He flicked off the pistol's safety catch, then slipped his finger carefully through the guard and rested it gently on the sensitive trigger. He kept his eyes on the three men outside. Rocky and Akmed had their backs to him and Shameel was staring down the street at the row of buildings on the outskirts of the village. King's breathing slowed, and his right arm tensed, as he raised the weapon. He would have to be quick, if he fired on

Shameel first, then he should have enough time to take out Akmed and Rocky as they turned around in the confusion. Thirteen rounds in the pistol, twenty feet to his targets. Should he use the rifle? Almost certainly, but they would hear him unsling it – those damned sling clips - also the safety made a desperately loud *click* as it was flicked downwards. King calculated quickly. Shameel would only need one shot. He would be aimed for; he would take it in the head. Double tap for Akmed, he was closest, best to get him down next. Rocky would have the most time to react and King had already seen that Rocky was twitchy and alert. Whether the Kurd could react in the two seconds that it would take to down the two brothers must remain to be seen. King studied the man's poise and stance, the way his weapon hung carelessly from his shoulder and knew that he could make the third target as easily as the first and second. This was his worst assignment. He loathed himself at this point. He steadied his aim, then tensed. His senses were honed to perfection, the apprehension of the moment always brought them out.

Which was why he hesitated.

The movement was slight, but he knew that he was not alone. Someone was near him and that someone was desperately trying to be quiet. He dropped down to a crouch and swung the pistol around in a wide arc. His focus stopped on Juliet Kalver's chest, the sights of the Browning levelling on her heart, as she knelt halfway down the stairs. She was using the bend in the staircase to take cover behind the wooden bannister.

She took her right hand off the Uzi's grip, and raised it submissively in the air, emphasizing that her finger was nowhere near the trigger. "Don't shoot!" she called softly.

King kept the pistol trained on her, then frowned as she rose to her feet. "What the hell are you doing?"

"Backing you up!" She slung the machine pistol over her shoulder and walked down the stairs.

"Ah! Mista English!" King turned around as he heard Akmed Faisal's unmistakable voice boom into the foyer. "You come to help us again?" the thin Kurd walked towards the double doors, his hands held out to embrace. "We kill many insurgents again!"

King quickly made the Browning safe and slipped it into the waistband of his trousers, returning the Kurd's smile. He felt uncomfortable, a fraud. He had been mere seconds from taking their lives.

Juliet Kalver stepped down the last few stairs and nodded a greeting to the two brothers, then stood aside and beckoned them into the foyer. The three men stepped in, then looked around expectantly.

"Empty?" Akmed Faisal asked, as he stared around the reception area.

"Deserted." King nodded. "I'm sorry about your brother. I didn't really get time to say..."

The Kurd shrugged. "There is much killing, much loss. It is not easy, but..." He shook his head in dismay, then motioned around the foyer, a watery glint to his eye. "I knew the owners well. Every day people leave. Only the old and the determined remain and I could not blame them if they decided to leave very soon." He looked around the foyer, taking it in. "During the time of Saddam many Iraqis took holidays here. The owners would roast whole goats and the rest of the people living here would bring dishes and we would have a celebration each spring. Winters can be harsh here. Then with the war this place was always full of journalists. Then, after Saddam it slowly became quieter. Now the insurgents are near, no journalists take the chance being here. If they are captured, they are filmed being beheaded and put on the internet. Now there is no trade for hotels."

Juliet Kalver started to walk up the large staircase, then turned around. "This way gentlemen, if you don't mind?" she said curtly. "We have some matters to discuss and very little time in which to do it."

The three Kurds followed her closely, all eyes fixed on her shapely behind, as she led the way up the stairs. King brought up the rear. As he reached the midway point he turned and looked down at the foyer towards the double glass doors below. From his position he was unable to see the doors. He dropped down onto his haunches, a similar height to Kalver when she was kneeling. Still he could not see the doorway. He thought of Kalver and the Uzi, and what she would have seen through the sights. He suddenly felt uneasy, his mind now full of nagging doubt.

CHAPTER FIFTY

"Is that it?" Stewart studied the building and frowned. "But it's tiny."

Holmwood checked the piece of paper in his hand, then nodded. "Yeah, that's the place. Callington and Co. Solicitors," he paused then watched, as an attractive woman walked out of the front door and unlocked a silver Mini Cooper S, parked directly outside the building. "I guess he thought that a small legal firm would be less obvious."

Pryce leaned between them, resting his arms somewhat annoyingly on the back of their seats. He watched the woman open the door, then hitch her tight skirt high up her shapely legs, before sliding gracefully into the driver's seat. "I couldn't half give her one!" he said, grinning wolfishly. He glanced back at the two men, then frowned when he noticed their expressions. "What?" he asked dejectedly. "Wouldn't you?"

Stewart smiled. "Margaret would kill me..." he paused, then pointed to a yellow alarm cover on the side of the building. "They have some security measures, which is to be expected." He craned his neck to see, then rested back against his seat. "Doesn't look like much though."

"Don't worry Sir, we have all the equipment we need to do a small place like this." Holmwood started the engine, then eased the car up the slope. "We'd better park, we don't want to look too obvious."

Stewart nodded. "All right, but before we look, we'll stop off and have a wee bite to eat. Falmouth looks as if it has a good few pubs, one on every corner at least."

"Shouldn't we do a thorough stake out instead?" Pryce suggested from the rear seat. "We could grab a Cornish pasty each and watch from the car."

"You grab a bloody Cornish pasty! I'm having steak and chips, this *is* on expenses after all." Stewart turned towards Holmwood, who was busy manoeuvring the car around a delivery van. "Your partner has a lot to learn, doesn't he?" He chuckled loudly, then took a thick Churchill cigar from his pocket and searched himself for matches.

Holmwood took a matchbook from his jacket and handed it across to Stewart, before glancing at Pryce in the rear-view mirror. "He certainly does Sir, he certainly does."

———

Stewart had tried several pubs but could not find what he was looking for. Many had given over to the student scene with cheap drinks and sharing platters of nachos or tapas. Others were chain pubs and Stewart took extra care not to patronise these. After almost an hour of searching, both he and Holmwood had eaten an agreeable lunch at a modern bistro bar furnished with distressed wooden tables and a great deal of modern contemporary Cornish art adorning the whitewashed walls. Stewart had indeed got his steak; a ribeye served rare and topped with a bone marrow, clotted cream and goat's cheese butter. A basket of twice cooked fries nestled beside the plate, which as was almost always the case, was not a plate at all but a plank of wood. Holmwood had opted for a double cheeseburger with the same fries, which again had arrived on another plank of wood. The cheeseburger had come in a toasted brioche bun and on a peppery rocket salad. The food had been excellent but came at London celebrity chef prices. Stewart had no idea how the Cornish could afford to eat out these days. Pryce, who had been given the task of staying with the car and watching the law firm, had indeed got his pasty; a giant pastry wrapped affair of beef, swede, potato and onion. Stewart had given him the steaming feast and Pryce could not have seemed happier as he tucked in and Holmwood had taken over the watch. There had been no movements and nothing to report.

Stewart ambled across the street and opened the door to the law firm's offices. The bell above the door frame sounded a brief, intermittent chime and he glanced automatically at the electronic bell as he stepped through the doorway, then closed the door behind him.

The alarm panel was fixed to the wall on his left and he quickly noted the set up. Key operated, with a push button panel and a digital display. No wires visible, most probably entered the panel from within the wall. He peered up the narrow staircase, then smiled when a pretty blonde secretary appeared at the top of the stairs.

"Can I help you, Sir?" she asked politely, yet with an underlying hint of concern. "Do you have an appointment?"

Stewart walked purposefully up the stairs and smiled. "I was wondering if I could have a word with one of your solicitors. Mister Callington perhaps?" The young woman stood aside as he stepped up the last narrow riser and entered the cramped office. "Forgive me if I don't have an appointment," he smiled. "But I was caught on a whim, I've been putting it off for years, you see."

The woman returned to her cluttered desk and frowned. "Putting off what?"

"Making my will, my dear."

She looked at him strangely, then turned as the telephone rang. She sat down behind her desk and pointed to a comfortable looking chair near the window. "Err, sorry, I must get that. Would you mind taking a seat?" She picked up the receiver and put on her professional secretary's voice. "Good afternoon, Callington and Co. Solicitors, how may I help you?"

Stewart looked around the office and quickly scanned the walls. There was a movement sensor, or Passive Infrared (PIR), in the far right-hand corner, just behind the woman's desk. This would be controlled from the panel below. He decided to stand up and look out of the window at the traffic in the street below. To the young woman he simply looked bored and impatient, yet Stewart was really assessing every detail. Years of training and experience was telling him what would be needed. He stretched, then glanced at the ceiling. Another movement sensor fixed to the side of the entrance. Any intruder who defeated the first sensor with the panel below would be caught off guard by the second. This meant that the second sensor had its own power supply. Stewart glanced around the office as the secretary spoke to the person on the telephone, who judging from her answers seemed to be asking a lot of questions about probate. The young woman clearly relished the chance to answer the questions and was taking no notice as Stewart continued to survey the office.

He paced around the room, then glanced at the three doors which obviously led to other offices. The nearest two were brass-handled with scratches around the keyholes indicating that the doors were frequently locked. The third door showed no lock, and Stewart guessed that either this was a cloak cupboard, or it led to staff amenities.

The woman said thank you, then put down the receiver and looked up at Stewart. Her expression had hardened, and she stared at him coolly. "I'm afraid that both Mister Callington and Ms. Baker are unavailable. Mister Callington has a client with him now and a consultation directly afterwards." She glanced down at her appointment book, then looked up apparently unconcerned. "And Ms. Baker is in Truro at the court and will be out of the office for the rest of the afternoon."

"Oh dear," Stewart shrugged haplessly. "Perhaps I can come back later?"

"You will have to make an appointment, both Mister Callington and Ms. Baker are extremely busy people."

"I dare say they are," he paused, then smiled. "I tell you what, I'll check my diary, then telephone a little later How's that?"

"Fine." The woman looked back at the paperwork on her desk, then spoke without raising her head. "Goodbye, please be good enough to close the door at the bottom."

Stewart walked down the staircase, apparently unhurried. When he reached the bottom, he looked over the control panel once more, then opened the door and stepped into the deserted side street. He walked casually down the quiet road, turned left at the bottom then walked over to the Vauxhall Insignia, where Pryce and Holmwood waited patiently. Stewart opened the door and dropped into the passenger seat.

"Any luck?" Holmwood asked, immediately starting the engine.

"Plenty. The place is a doddle, just a few points to outline, but it should be a breeze." He turned to Pryce and grinned. "What the hell were you asking her?"

Pryce chuckled out loud. "I was chatting her up half the time! She's bloody desperate, well in need of a right good seeing-to!" He reached forwards and slipped the mobile tele-phone into the dashboard holder. "I just asked her a few ques-tions about inheritance tax; flirted a bit as well. I could hardly get away from her."

"Not that you tried," Holmwood interjected.

Stewart settled back into the seat and smiled at the jovial banter. It had been a while since he had worked in the field and he was starting to enjoy it once more.

CHAPTER FIFTY-ONE

Alex King closed the door, then paced over to the window. He peered out, waiting for the three men to reappear below. The sun hung low in the cloudless sky, and a sudden chill was starting to bite at his bare arms. He bent to pick up the military jacket and pulled it on, as he watched the street for any sign of the three Kurds.

"Do you think they'll go for it?" Juliet Kalver walked across the room and stood at his shoulder, her arms folded tightly across her chest. "You don't think it sounds too suspicious, do you?"

King watched Rocky walk out of the foyer and pause on the wooden veranda, as Akhim and Shameel jostled playfully to be the first in line for the wooden steps. The three men laughed, then walked across the square towards a large house by what used to be a fountain, now a mere pile of rubble towards the corner of the square. He watched the two men, knowing they had buried much of their family these past few months, their younger brother last week.

King kept his eyes on the men and shook his head. "No,"

he paused, then glared at her contemptuously. "They're loyal men, why should they suspect a thing?"

There was an atmosphere between the two of them, and tension filled the air. Neither mentioned what had happened before, but it was more than that. King couldn't help thinking about Kalver taking up her firing position on the stairs. The arc of fire made no sense. The thought of her there with the Uzi made him shiver. He glanced at the luminous dials of his Rolex in the dull light. His eyes were accustomed to the gloom, he had been in darkness ever since sunset. The old hotel was still structurally intact, but the electricity had been terminated for some time. He looked over at Juliet Kalver as he bent down and picked up the Galil ARM rifle. "Just getting some air, I won't be long."

"Air?" she frowned. "It's as cold as a witch's tit in here, what do you want air for? Just wait, we go in just over an hour."

King shook his head. "Okay, let me put it another way..." he paused. "In approximately an hour's time, two four-wheel-drive vehicles are going to go charging out of this village. It wouldn't be a bad idea for someone to check that half the Iraqi army aren't nearby or that ISIS aren't circling for a raid."

Kalver nodded from her chair. "All right, go for it." She watched him walk towards her, then suddenly raised both legs, resting her feet on the bed, blocking his passage. "On second thoughts, why don't you stay? The Faisal brothers reported no soldiers in the region and their intelligence is rarely incorrect." She crossed her legs elegantly, then smiled at him, her white teeth clearly visible through the darkness. "We could always do something else together, we have enough time."

King smiled at her. "I thought you were recently widowed?"

Her expression hardened, and for a second, King saw a

hatred and anger that threatened to cut through him, sending a shiver down his spine. She seemed to realise what he thought, and her expression softened, albeit ever so slightly. "What has that got to do with it? My husband died and left me all on my own," she paused, took her feet off the bed and rose to her feet. "I love him and miss him every day. If he was alive, I wouldn't look at you twice. But he's not and I have needs. I was only suggesting sex, what's the big deal? It didn't bother you before..." She cocked her head to one side and smiled.

King thought her an anomaly. When she smiled, she was more attractive. When she was angered, she sneered and became ugly. He looked at her, found himself wanting her again. He wavered, but thought of the arc of fire... the Uzi... "I don't think so," he said. "We need clear heads now. I'm going to do a quick security sweep. Get yourself ready. We'll leave when I get back."

"Fine!" she got out of the chair so quickly that it shifted backwards across the wooden floorboards. She strode towards the bathroom and spoke over her shoulder. "You're not half the fuck my husband was anyway..."

CHAPTER FIFTY-TWO

The night-chill was bitingly cold, and the stillness was unsettling. Only the thinnest slice of moon lit the dark sky, and the hard ground made far too much noise for King's liking. He continued to run all the same; there wasn't time to survey the whole perimeter of the village without breaking into a sweat. He covered the ground quickly, running a hundred metres at a time, then pausing behind pieces of natural cover to gaze into the night. He would naturally have preferred some night vision equipment, but he would have to do with the next best thing, besides, his eyes were well accustomed to the dark and the terrain around the village of Kalsagir was largely flat, with only the odd hillock to break the monotony.

He listened intently, slowing his breathing as he strained for any sound that might be out of keeping with the desert night. His vigil caught only the faintest sound, unrecognisable, but nevertheless he was convinced that it belonged to an animal. He waited, then heard it again. Most definitely an animal's call. There was no way that any soldiers could be nearby, desert wildlife tends to be the most sensitive and almost always nocturnal. Convinced that Kalsagir was not under any threat from Iraqi troops or ISIS insurgents, King walked along the rear of a row of empty shops, then turned down a narrow side street and made his way back to the edge of the square. As he walked along the hard, dusty ground, he heard a sound to his right, a sound which suddenly carried on the night air. He paused for a moment, straining to see in the dark, then cautiously made his way towards it. Again, he heard it. This time, he recognised the source – the booming voice of Shameel.

King realised that the three men had taken a house on the other side of the square and were obviously talking quietly amongst themselves; but in the silence of the desert, the faintest sound can carry for hundreds of metres. He stopped in his tracks as the voices ceased. He closed his eyes and slowed his breathing, heightening his hearing, which predominated in the darkness. The voices wafted eerily through the air again and King continued directly towards them. As he reached the front of the large building, he listened intently to the men's conversation, then felt another overwhelming pang of guilt, as he suddenly understood that Shameel had been praising him.

He made his way back to the hotel and climbed the stairs to their room. Juliet Kalver looked up at him venomously as he entered.

King smiled amiably, deciding it would either cool her a little, or fuel her fiery temper completely and at that moment he didn't particularly care which. He placed the assault rifle on the chair and walked over to her. "The perimeter is clear, I don't think there's anybody for ten miles." He glanced at his watch then nodded towards the door. "We'd better get going, I heard the others up and about from across the street."

"Fine." She turned away from the window and walked over to the bag, picked it up, then dropped it onto the bed.

"You can be responsible for that." She picked up the loaded Uzi submachine pistol and the two spare magazines, then walked towards the door. "Come on then, are you coming or not?" she asked curtly, not looking him in the eye.

King walked over to the bed, picked up the bag with the radio and interlocking aerials, swung it over his shoulder and then picked up his rifle. "Sure." He followed her out of the room, then reached out and touched her gently on the left shoulder. "Hey..."

She spun around and knocked his hand away. "Don't fucking touch me!"

"I was just seeing if you were okay," he shrugged apologetically. "I'm sorry about earlier..."

"Don't apologise to me." She shook her head and turned away. "Just get the job done and leave me alone." She walked ahead of him, swaying her shapely hips as she hurried down the stairs.

Rocky was waiting outside, his AK47 assault rifle hanging from his shoulder in his characteristically casual manner. Akmed Faisal stood a few paces to the right, smoking an extremely rough smelling cigarette.

"Ah! Mista English! We kill some ISIS bastards now, okay?"

King nodded. "But if we see Iraqi soldiers, we avoid them at all costs. We don't fire on them. Got that?" He knew that Iraqi soldiers had used the ISIS situation to settle some old scores with the Kurds, but Iraq was Britain's ally these days and he had to keep the Kurdish fighters in check. At best they were trigger happy, at worst they were bloodthirsty.

The Kurd nodded, as if he were a small child having just been reprimanded. "I remember. But I don't have to like it!"

Rocky laughed heartily, then looked up as Shameel raced the Land Rover around the corner and into the square.

"Right, everybody get in," Juliet ordered quietly, then

looked at Shameel as he pulled the vehicle to a halt. "You can give us a lift to my vehicle."

"Lift?" the Kurd asked, somewhat puzzled at the term.

"Yes, a lift. You know, a ride!" she snapped, opening the rear door. She sat down and glared at Alex King who was talking to Akmed at the foot of the hotel steps. "Move your ass will you!" she shouted. King walked towards her and placed the bag carefully on the rear bench seat. "We'll be late for sending the message."

Sending a scrambled message on a dedicated frequency was only a pretence. Kalver had convinced the three Kurds that they were there acting as their bodyguards and all three men had liked the description, especially Rocky, who had seen a bootlegged copy of *The Bodyguard* starring Kevin Costner. Now, as they travelled through the deserted streets, Rocky insisted on singing the Whitney Houston version of the accompanying theme song. It sounded dreadful. What puzzled King was why Kalver was being so aggressive. He had turned her down in the room, but he couldn't imagine that it would have such an effect.

Shameel pulled the Land Rover to an abrupt halt to the side of Kalver's Toyota. King opened the rear door and grabbed the bag, then jumped to the hard ground. Kalver followed, ignored his proffered hand, walked straight around the vehicle and unlocked the driver's door. "Come on then," she said to him curtly. "It's central locking, you *can* get in."

King opened his door, threw the bag onto the rear seat then got into the cab without a word. He stared straight ahead as she started the engine and drove erratically round the parked Land Rover. She raced up through the gears, misjudging the engine's revs at every change, then settled at around eighty kilometres an hour, which seemed to be more than enough for the potholed road. The two-vehicle convoy travelled for about an hour, with the three Kurds in the much slower Land Rover struggling to keep up for much of the time. Every now and then, Kalver would curse loudly, releasing a mouthful of four-lettered expletives, then ram her foot hard on the brake. The Land Rover would close the gap a little, but soon enough, she would repeat the process, much to King's silent amusement.

Before long she pulled off the main highway and onto a narrower, bumpier side road. The potholes were worse and at the speed that they were travelling it physically hurt when the vehicle's axle ground on the rocky ground. King could only imagine what discomfort the three Kurds were feeling inside the older and far less luxurious Land Rover.

After an unusually excessive grounding, King broke his silence. "Come on, ease up. I know you're mad at me, but if you're not careful you're going to snap the drive shaft in a minute. Then we'll be in real trouble."

"Mad at you?" she tossed her head back and laughed. "Mad at you? You have no idea!"

"What?" King frowned.

"I'm mad at myself!" She shook her head in dismay. "The first time I feel the desire to go with another man since my husband's death and he makes a fool out of me! Gets what he wants, satisfies himself, then turns me down..."

"It wasn't like that..." He rested his hand on her knee, she flinched but he left it there and he felt her relax a little. "It's just the mission. I never usually mix business and pleasure. I didn't realise I was your first since your husband..."

"You were there, weren't you?" She smiled. "That wasn't everyday sex..."

King gave her knee a squeeze, then took his hand away. Juliet Kalver was an enigma. Either that or bipolar. She made him uneasy. Maybe it had to do with shutting down the American operation here. Maybe it had something to do with her. She struck him as desperately unstable.

He watched the line of hills draw closer, then spoke without taking his eyes off the night sky. "Slow down, this looks about perfect..."

The silence in the desert at night was eerie. It was cold also and King shivered slightly as he scanned the night sky, watching the horizon to the east and the line of distant hillocks to the south, beyond which lay the deserted village of Kalsagir. He turned back to the others, who were waiting for his signal to follow and waved them towards him.

King had taken point and was making his way up the series of rocky ledges and inclines, approximately fifty metres ahead of the others. Now that he had finally reached the top of the hillock, he waved for them to follow the rest of the way. He kept his eyes on the horizon, then looked down at the two vehicles parked below. He was only around a hundred feet above them, but the incline varied in gradient and in the dark the walk had taken almost twenty minutes. He watched them approach him and realised why Kalver had chosen this spot. It was far enough off the beaten track, yet easily accessible. Moreover, it was only a few miles from the border. After he had killed the Faisal brothers and Rocky, he could be over it very quickly.

He turned around just in time to hear Kalver order Rocky to be gentle with the radio. She stood with her hands on her hips watching the Kurd carefully place the bag on the ground, then looked up at King, unsure of what to do next.

It was *his* time now, time for him to go to work. She had come up with the story of having to send a special high-tech radio message, a burst or squirt signal, which would need a higher altitude to avoid atmospherics and the three Kurds had swallowed it.

King breathed steadily, he put the rifle down carefully on the ground, keeping the weapon's breech and cocking lever facing upwards and out of the dirt. He methodically flexed his fists, loosening his muscles, calming the adrenalin. He was ready. He stepped down from the rocky ledge and walked towards the group, then shook his head at Kalver. "Sorry," he said and caught hold of the barrel of her Uzi with his left hand and pointed the muzzle down to the ground. He had the Browning pistol held firmly in his right hand and aimed at her head. She seemed to weigh her options for a moment and released her grip on the machine pistol.

"What? What are you doing?" she asked, looking at him in bewilderment. "For Christ's sake, do what you're here to do!"

King kept his weapon trained on her forehead as he dropped the Uzi a few feet away. "I had my doubts about this mission, but I would still have done my job." He nodded towards Akmed Faisal, who in turn picked up the radio and beckoned the other two men to follow him back down the hill. King had briefed him at the steps of the hotel. Akmed had in turn briefed his two companions on the way. King shook his head at Kalver. "I'm an assassin, I do what I'm paid to do all the same. Even if it's a bullshit job like this one."

The woman shook her head in disbelief. "What's going down then? Why the hell are you pointing the gun at me?" she looked at him tearfully. "Don't kill them, let them go. See if I care!"

King backed up a couple of paces, lowered the pistol, but kept it pointed in her direction. "It's not as simple as that, is it..." he said flatly. "Although this mission stinks, and although the CIA duped my service into performing a cleaning job, I would still have followed orders and killed the Faisal brothers. The trouble is, in being super-efficient, you ruined things for yourself," he paused. "You see, I checked your position on the stairway back at the hotel. You said that you were backing me up. Well, that wasn't the case, was it?"

"Of course, it was!" She looked at him pleadingly. "Please, you've got this all wrong!"

King shook his head. "From the stairway, you cannot see any further than the double doors. You weren't aiming at the Kurds, you had the Uzi aimed at my back. The moment I ceased firing, you would have sprayed me all over the reception desk. You're pulling out of the area *and* the operation, and you don't want a single loose end to trip up on. Your orders are to have me killed..."

Her shoulders sagged, and she looked forlornly at the ground. "So, what happens now?" She chuckled morosely. "Do I have a last request? Will you administer the *coup de grace?*"

"I don't do last requests, never have done," King said flippantly. "But so far, nobody has got hurt. Let's leave it that way." He pointed to a clump of rocks on the opposite side of the hillock's summit. "Sit down over there and wait until dawn. You have the keys to your own vehicle, just ride it out and go home unscathed. Leave somebody else to sort this shit pit out..." He holstered the pistol, bent down and picked up the Uzi and walked to the edge of the first shallow ledge.

"Just answer me this..." Juliet Kalver called out. "Why go to the trouble of bringing me up here?" King frowned. He heard her question, but also a familiar sound, a metallic sound which her voice had all but muffled. He threw himself to the ground on his left, rolled onto his shoulder, then brought the Uzi up to aim. He was aware of a blinding flash in the dark, it illuminated the ground between them. There were two quiet, suppressed shots in the silence of the night and the sensation of a breeze near his head where the bullets passed inches away. He squeezed the Uzi's trigger twice, releasing two short bursts of approximately five rounds each. The muzzle flashes lit up Kalver's face, the ground and the rocks behind her. The sharp roar of the machine pistol echoed off the rocks around them.

The woman fell backwards onto the rocky ground, her hand releasing the grip on the tiny silenced 9mm Glock pistol, supposedly lost when King had made the drop.

King walked over to her, keeping the Uzi's crude open sights trained on her. She looked up at him, her eyes wide and panicked, her breathing erratic and rasping. Most of the bullets had found their mark and the holes were now indistinguishable by the amount of blood soaking her chest and stomach. There was blood on the ground also and King could tell that she did not have long left. The ground would soak up the blood quickly, so to look like a large quantity in the dirt she was bleeding out fast. "Why bring you up here?" He crouched down, put the Uzi on the ground and picked up her hand in his. "In case you tried something stupid like that, that's why." He kissed the back of her hand and looked into her eyes. She breathed shallow and hard breaths, her limbs shaking. "Relax, don't fight it, let it find you," he said. "Close your eyes and think of your husband. Picture his face..."

She did just that and started to smile, squeezing King's hand tightly, until after a minute or so she let go and lay still.

King watched her for a while. She was still and at peace. There was no pain for her now. He had tears in his eyes and an ache in his belly. He had only been with, comforted, a dying person like this once before. The night he had been widowed.

Akmed Faisal looked up expectantly as King walked back to the Land Rover. "We heard gunshots, is it done?" the Kurd asked.

King nodded. "Unfortunately. She had a choice and she made it." He opened the passenger door, then slipped inside and rested the rifle and Uzi beside him, with the muzzles of both weapons pointed at the floor.

"We go now?" Shameel asked hesitantly as he sat down behind the steering wheel.

King nodded. "Yeah, we go."

"What is his name?" Akmed asked, leaning curiously between the two front seats.

King stared straight ahead into the night. "His name..." he paused, trying to push the sight of Juliet Kalver's dead body out of his mind. "His name is Osman Emre. He's a Turkish pilot who works for my government. He has been helping in the fight against Islamic State extremists and he is being held prisoner at the military installation near Zakho," King said. "And we are going to get him out."

CHAPTER FIFTY-THREE

The sea mist hung close to the narrow road, and the car's headlights merely reflected off the impenetrable barrier, creating the illusion of oncoming traffic. He eased his foot off the accelerator and the vehicle's pace slowed considerably, as he negotiated the next sharp bend.

"For Christ's sake!" Stewart shook his head. "We'll never get there at this rate!"

Holmwood kept his eyes on the narrow country road as he strained to see through the barrier of fog. "I can't help it Sir, I can hardly see the road."

"What the hell did you bring us in this way for?" Stewart asked abruptly. "We'll end up in a bloody farmyard in a minute!"

Holmwood bit his lip in frustration, then readied himself for the next blind corner. "This *is* a main road Sir, it's just a bit narrower than we are used to, that's all." He shrugged submissively. "It looked quicker on the map."

"Oh, I see! Quicker than a main road littered with dual-carriageways and nice gentle bends," Stewart replied sarcastically. "I'll have to remember that next time I plan a route."

He settled back in his seat, then pointed straight ahead. "Watch it!"

Holmwood saw the mini-roundabout just in time and hit the brake. The car skidded slightly, then came back under control as the ABS system cut in.

"Didn't you see the sign?" Pryce asked from the rear seat.

"Did you?" Holmwood paused, as he steered the car around the obstruction, then turned onto the road, which was simply signposted 'Penryn'. "I can hardly see a thing the fog is so bloody thick!"

After a few miles the mist had largely given way to a curtain of drizzle which annoyingly covered the windscreen in a thin film of water yet proved to be too small a quantity for the windscreen wipers, even when turned on to the intermittent setting. The wiper blades streaked the sheen of drizzle away, then smeared the windscreen with the return stroke, creating a reflective sheen in front of them under the orange glow of the street lamps.

Holmwood steered the vehicle down the steep hill, paused at the junction and turned left into High Street. He drove the Insignia steadily, then slowed almost to a stop when a group of men staggered across the road ahead of them.

"What the hell's this?" Stewart leant forward in his seat and stared at the men in front of them. Each of them carried a plastic carrier bag, stuffed full to bursting, and several carried either bottles of wine or cans of lager.

Holmwood watched as one of the men gave them a hand gesture, then continued to walk unhurriedly across the road. "Down-and-outs," he commented, then drove the car steadily onwards. "It looks as if Falmouth has a homeless problem as well."

The group stepped onto the pavement, then continued down a paved walkway towards a series of shelters at the end of a long pier.

"Prince of Wales Pier," Stewart read the sign, then shrugged. "Must be a hangout for the local bums."

Holmwood watched the wiper remove the thin sheen of drizzle from the windscreen and shivered involuntarily at the thought of being left with no alternative but to sleep rough on the end of the pier. He turned to the left and joined the bumpy cobbles of Market Street, with its rows of shop fronts and public houses. The street was deserted, the pubs long since closed. He presumed they opened later in the summer months. The swirling mist created an eerie feeling, as if they were driving through a ghost town.

Stewart bent forwards and pointed at the side street on the right. "That's it, isn't it?"

Holmwood glanced down at his own handwritten route plan, which was resting on the central console, then looked up at the tiny side road. "Certainly, looks like it, seems different in the dark though," he paused, then noted the tiny bakery further down the street where they had bought Pryce his Cornish pasty. "Yes, that's the one." He eased the car across the narrow road, then turned to the right and carried on up the steep hill for approximately fifty metres, where he found a pull-in on the left. "This ought to do, there's nobody about anyway."

Stewart nodded. "OK, lads, you know the score. We are to locate Alex King's security blanket, that's all. Photograph, confirm and then get the hell out. All right?" The two men nodded in unison, and Stewart smiled. "Right then, let's get to it..."

The door was opened with consummate ease, but it was the alarm control panel which caused the problems. No wires fed into the unit from outside, all connections were made from within the stud-partition wall.

Holmwood worked quickly, urgently. The door was coupled to a silent sensor, with a time delay to allow for the disarming of the alarm and as he did not know the exact duration of the delay, it was imperative to remove the control panel as quickly as possible. Pryce stood at his shoulder, holding all the necessary tools at the ready, like a surgeon's assistant in a life-threatening emergency operation. Knowing the procedures himself, he had the appropriate tool in Holmwood's hand before the man had need to ask.

"That's twenty seconds..." Pryce whispered, glancing at the luminous dials of his watch. "My guess is another twenty, but no more."

Holmwood remained silent, working his way through the pattern of wires and the series of connectors which lined the inside of the control panel. Satisfied that he had located both the 'in' and 'out' routes, he snapped the crocodile-clips of the circuit-breaker around the entrance and exit wires, then flicked on the device's power switch. He glanced down at the connected fascia, which dangled down from the panel, carelessly abandoned less than a minute ago and breathed a sigh of relief when he saw the 'disarmed' light flash for three seconds. He stepped away from the wall and turned towards Pryce. "All right, go and get the old man, and tell him, we're in."

CHAPTER FIFTY-FOUR

He lay as flat to the cold ground as he could, keeping his movements deliberately slow as he crawled along the ridge until he found the ideal vantage-point. The moon was barely a glimmer in the dark night sky, yet the whole plateau seemed to be floodlit. The sky was so clear that the starlight alone gave enough light to see by. As he eased himself into the shallow, dried-up wadi, he glanced back and cringed when he saw the unmistakable silhouette of Shameel streak across the brow of the tiny hillock and dive behind the first of a series of boulders which lay scattered across the narrow ridge.

Alex King returned his attention to the military outpost below and the mass of troops who were boarding the endless stream of trucks and armoured personnel carriers. The base was a hive of activity and King guessed that the army was mounting a full-scale search for him, as well as hunting the Faisal brothers for their poorly placed IED. Osman Emrie had no doubt talked by now. King could not blame him for that, but he realised that whatever details Ozzy knew were surely known to the Iraqi Secret Police and Army Intelligence by now. Their methods were brutal at best and in 'peacetime', they would not show the same clemency as they would to a captured soldier or downed pilot in time of open war.

Shameel rolled into the shallow wadi, puffing breathlessly as he eased his head above the gully and peered down on the military compound. "Ah, much action going on! They go look for ISIS, no?"

"No. Me, I expect. And you and your brother." King said, matter-of-fact.

"Good!" Shameel laughed. "They will not have far to search!"

King chuckled and looked past him and saw Akmed ease himself over the nearby ridge, taking a considerably more careful approach than his brother. He turned back to the show below them, then started to count the vehicles, which were now starting to drive towards the huge metal blast gates on the other side of the base.

"How many?" Shameel asked, straining his eyes. "I not so good at long distances," he added apologetically.

"Twenty-seven." King did a few multiplications in his head, then looked up as Akmed slid silently and gracefully into the gully. "That's anything up to three hundred troops, if they fill them all." He turned his eyes back to the last of the vehicles which were exiting the base. "That's one hell of a patrol!"

Akmed studied the buildings towards the eastern perimeter of the compound, then looked across at King. "The third building on the right. It looks more like a hut, but it is where the prisoners are interrogated. After that, they are spread between the fifth, sixth and seventh buildings in the row."

"Are you sure?"

Akmed nodded positively. "Yes. I knew someone who was interrogated then escaped," he paused, staring at him with great intensity. "It doesn't happen often. She was captured and held for six days, she escaped after seducing one of the guards. After he had finished using her, she took a knife from his belt and cut his throat."

"Quite a girl," King commented flatly.

"She was, but she was killed soon afterwards. A revenge raid. Many lives lost," Akmed looked away, his eyes glistening moistly in the moonlight. "She was my wife..."

The two men made their way down the steep slope, taking great care not to dislodge the shingle or the small rocks which made up most of the hill's surface. King led the way, followed by Shameel, with Akmed covering their progress through the sights of a PKM machine gun. It was a belt-fed weapon with a range of up to one thousand metres and a rate of fire of twelve rounds per second. American soldiers serving in Vietnam and facing the business end of it had named it *The Meat Chopper*...

As King reached the sanctuary of a large boulder, he crouched down on one knee, waved Shameel past his position and signalled up the slope for Akmed to advance.

The Kurd got to his feet and made his way gingerly but sure-footedly down the steep hill. He clutched the weapon to his chest with his right hand and kept his left hand outstretched, pushing himself away from the slope as he half slid, half ran down the rocky hillside. As he neared King's position, he slowed up and looked uncertainly at the English-man. King waved him past, then waited for the man to take cover behind a large boulder, thirty metres further downslope.

The system worked well; two men moving, one weapon covering. King watched the two men, then made his move and broke into a semi-jog, keeping the rifle in his right hand with his finger resting safely alongside the trigger guard.

Akmed looked up at him expectantly, as he slowed his

pace and took cover behind the same boulder. "What now, do we go in?"

King studied the perimeter fence for a moment, then turned to the Kurd and nodded. "Yes, but not here," he paused and looked up at the moon, which was nearing their left. "The moon is casting a bloody beam of light along the fence, it's standing out like a bulldog's bollocks!" He turned his back to the boulder and watched an area of fence approximately one hundred metres to their right. "Over there," he pointed for the Kurd to see. "Where the fence starts to deviate from that rocky outcrop."

Akmed nodded. "Yes, I would agree." He motioned towards his brother, then looked back at King. "Shameel has volunteered to stay outside the fence and give covering fire." The Kurd smiled, "Besides, he is not the fastest of runners..."

King smiled, realising that the job to do inside the compound was probably best done only by two. He looked at the overweight Kurd and nodded approvingly. It was imperative that someone give covering fire if anything went wrong and he knew that when the bullets started to fly, the Iraqi soldiers would give their full attention to the muzzle flashes outside the compound. Shameel's task might well prove to be the least desirable of all, if it came to a fire-fight. The big Kurd took the PKM from his brother and walked back to the cover of boulders higher up the slope.

"I shall lead the way to the interrogation building," Akmed paused, then looked up at King. "After that, you take over and I shall follow you. Whatever you shoot at, I shall shoot at as well."

King nodded. "Sounds about right." He checked the breech of his weapon, then placed it against the boulder while he checked over the Browning. "If Osman Emrie is not in the first block, then we'll head for the next three buildings. Fifth, sixth and seventh, right?"

The Kurd nodded. "That was how it was four months ago."

King looked at him, wondering if it had only been four months since the death of his wife. He had had no idea of this when he had last been here; the man had hidden his grief well. "All right, we'll go in now. There's no sense in delaying. Besides, it looks as if almost every soldier in the compound has left with that patrol." He rose slowly to his feet and jogged in front of Shameel's position towards the outcrop of rocks and boulders which extended across the plateau, almost touching the bottom of the twelve-foot-high wire fence.

He slowed his pace as he reached the rocks, then walked carefully forwards, keeping the butt of the Galil assault rifle pressed firmly against his shoulder and the weapon slightly lowered so it was quick and fluid to bring to aim. He crouched down, then knelt on one knee and waited for Akmed to run across the open ground towards him. The Kurd ran quickly, although he had not paced himself as well as King and arrived at the outcrop a little breathless, though breathing with much less labour than his brother would have been able to manage.

King beckoned him closer, then spoke quietly into his ear. "Stay here and keep me covered. If you have to fire for any reason, I will roll to the right. Make sure you don't hit me."

The Kurd smiled. "I am sure that you would come back and haunt me if I did."

"You can count on it." King returned the smile, then crawled towards the fence on his stomach and elbows, keeping his rifle resting across both forearms, as he propelled himself across the desert ground. His progress was slow yet silent and he reached the fence in less than a minute, keeping his eyes on the camp and the first set of buildings to his right. He studied the wire, looking at the weave of strands that gave the appearance of diamond shaped gaps in the mesh. On top of the fence, pitched out on both sides, were two strands of razor wire, which King knew to be impenetrable – in cold blood, at least. He eased his weapon forwards, then made sure that he touched only the wooden stock, as he rested the barrel against the wire mesh. He felt no mild tingle through the wood, which told him there was no electric current running through the wire. With the status of the fence determined, he pulled down the bipod on the barrel of the Galil and started to use one of the weapon's valuable extras – the standard issue wire cutter.

Progress through the toughened wire was slow, but the wire cutter sliced cleanly through as King squeezed the prongs tightly together. The cutters were sharp, but it was the barrel of the weapon which slowed matters considerably, as with each cut, King had to slide the barrel through the fence so that the jaws of the wire cutter could cut a clean line through the wire mesh. With a perfect 'C' cut into the wire, King pulled the loop round and fastened it back against the fence, creating a hole large enough for them to crawl through. He turned to wave Akmed forward, then returned his attention to the compound and the small group of buildings close by.

A light flickered for a second or two in one of the buildings, then suddenly shone bright. King ducked, keeping the weapon tight to his shoulder, the sights trained on the brightly lit window. Akmed reached him, but remained on his stomach, choosing to train the AK47's sights on the door of the wooden building. Both men held their breaths in anticipation of being compromised, but relaxed when they heard the familiar sound of a toilet flushing. Less than a minute later, the light switched off and the base returned to a starlit half-light.

King nodded to Akmed, indicating that they were ready, and the man pushed himself to his feet and trotted quietly ahead, past the nearby buildings and towards the row of wooden huts further up the compound. King waited until there was approximately forty metres between them, then rose to his feet and jogged quietly after him. With a decent distance between the two men, the enemy would be presented with a tougher target, at least both men would not be mown down with the first burst of fire.

Akmed slowed his pace, eased himself behind one of the buildings and waited in the shadows for King to join him.

King cursed under his breath, but he had no choice and deviated towards the shed-like building, taking sudden advantage of the welcoming shadows. "What is it?" he asked quietly, choosing not to whisper. Whispering often carried further on the air than a softly spoken voice.

"A guard," Akmed stated flatly. "Between us and the interrogation block."

King felt deflated, knowing that it was imperative to reach their first objective silently and without being compromised. "Let me see." He eased himself past the Kurd and crouched low to the ground, edging his head tentatively around the corner of the wooden building.

The guard was young, most likely still in his mid-teens. King guessed him to be around seventeen, although he was aware that Iraqi troops often looked younger than their age. The guard carried a standard issue M16A4 assault rifle. Part of Uncle Sam's legacy to rearm and retrain the army after it pulled out. King wondered if part of that legacy was turning a blind eye to the treatment of the Kurds in the north. He hoped not, but how this camp got away with what it did gave him more than a few doubts. The soldier held the weapon casually over his shoulder, the last few inches of the barrel in his left hand. He not only lacked enthusiasm for his duty but seemed to lack the ability to walk in a straight line, taking ambling steps, then pausing whilst he looked around, obviously wondering whether it was worth patrolling an empty camp.

King looked at the building beyond the guard and knew that it must be the interrogation block. There was no other way for them to go but straight ahead and that meant confronting the guard. At this range a rifle shot would be the best bet, but the isolated sound would be enough to wake the dead. The 9mm Browning would be a little quieter, but only in relative terms and the sound would have a similar effect, as soon as he pulled the trigger, all hell would break loose. That left his silenced Glock, taken from Juliet Kalver earlier. However, at this range the tiny weapon would most probably not prove accurate enough for a one-shot silenced kill. One mistake, one scream from the guard, and their presence would be apparent.

Akmed tapped him gently on the shoulder and spoke quietly into his left ear. "Here, take my gun, I will do it."

King turned around and saw the Kurdish khanjar in the man's hand. It was a wicked looking curved Arabian dagger with a needle tip and a razor-sharp blade. The browned-steel was dark, almost as if rusted, but for a shiny silver edge that ran from the tip to the hilt. King saw the conviction in the man's eyes and decided to let him take the chance. The Kurd had personal history with this camp. Perhaps it was the local emotion which had led the CIA to shut down the operation against ISIS. The Kurds had history with everyone in these parts.

He took the rifle from him, then eased himself against the wall of the building to allow the Kurd to pass.

Akmed held the dagger in his right hand, keeping the blade pointing downwards. He watched the youth intently, then waited for the ambling soldier to turn his back on them. It didn't take long. The youth casually turned around, took another two or three steps, then looked up and stared complacently at the hillside.

Akmed moved with lightning speed, sprinting from a crouch and gaining fearsome momentum as he ran across the open ground towards the unsuspecting Iraqi soldier. As he drew near, the guard heard rushing footsteps and turned around, but too late to stand any chance of defending himself. Akmed lashed out with his right hand and drew the blade savagely across the soldier's throat. There was a clearly audible sound as the razor-sharp blade slashed cleanly through the windpipe and grated against the man's spine. The young soldier fell forward onto his knees, clutching at his throat and attempting to breathe, but he was dying quickly and by the time Akmed caught hold of him by his belt and collar and started to drag him towards the edge of the interrogation block he was already unconscious.

King rushed out from the shadows of the small building and passed the rifle to the Kurd, then caught hold of the soldier's belt and helped to drag him across the dusty ground. Progress was quicker with two and it only took seconds to reach the side of the building. He went back for the soldier's weapon, then dropped it on top of the body. He looked at Akmed, who was wiping the blade of his dagger clean against his sleeve. King nodded at him, then turned around and climbed the rest of the wooden steps. He motioned towards the door, then waited for his companion to get into position. Akmed mounted the steps, paused at the side of the door, keeping the muzzle of his weapon trained on the jamb and nodded that he was ready.

King tried the door handle cautiously, then sighed with relief when it opened quietly. He eased the door inwards, then waited for a moment. Satisfied that the entrance was clear, he stepped inside and walked carefully towards the first door on the right.

Again, the two men repeated the process; King opening the door, Akmed covering. The door was made from steel, painted grey and bolted. King knew the purpose of the outside bolt, but as soon as he stepped inside the room, he knew its sole purpose only too well.

The floor was made from rubber compound, easy to clean, and in the very centre a grate covered a drain. A single wooden chair stood alone in the middle, above the grate. The room was windowless and at one end stood a table with a strange-looking box with a number of wires emerging from the top. Each wire was tipped with a crocodile clip and although King had never seen such a contraption in action, he knew what it was meant to do. A circuit-breaker fed high voltage into the wires, but at negligible ampere. With the life-threatening amps out of the equation, the torturer knew that they could inflict agonising pain with minimal risk of killing the recipient.

King walked around the room, then glanced down at the wooden chair and noticed that the seat was horribly stained. He looked up at Akmed and shook his head in disgust. Akmed nodded knowingly, breathing through his mouth to avoid the room's fetid smell. "Recently used," he commented flatly. King noticed the man's eyes were moist. Akmed's wife had been in this room, had seen and been subject to its horrors.

King nodded as he walked to the door. "Come on, there's nobody here. My guess is they've finished with him for the time being and he's in one of the other huts."

Akmed nodded. "OK, I'll lead the way."

———

From his raised position and with a clear view for one hundred and eighty degrees Shameel scanned the compound through the open sights of the PKM machine gun, then allowed the weapon to rest on its folding bipod. He had watched his brother and the Englishman make their way from the interrogation block to the fifth building in the row, taking turns to cover one another as they cautiously penetrated deeper into the deserted compound. He had witnessed the killing of the guard but had not been able to see it in detail, as his position was almost two hundred metres away from the compound and a further fifty metres from the interrogation block. He wished the weapon had been equipped with a scope. It struck him that at this distance and with his weak eyesight he may well not be able to pick out his brother and the Englishman if the alarm was raised.

The night air was now icy and with the cloudless sky, it looked as if it may well freeze. He pulled the collar of his greatcoat up around his ears, then blew warm air onto his cold hands, before rubbing them together vigorously. It seemed to help a little, if only to take his mind off the cold. He looked back at the compound, then froze as he saw a convoy of headlights in the distance.

———

King paused outside the wooden building. He could hear the muffled sound of music and people talking, then came the louder sound of a man laughing. He strained to hear through the wall of the prison block, then suddenly gathered that it was the sound of a television set. Someone inside the building was clearly awake and watching the box. King took out the silenced Glock, checked the chamber then turned to Akmed, who was already holding his khanjar at the ready. "Cover me Akmed, I'm going in..."

The Kurd caught his arm and frowned. "Let me, *I* have the knife."

King thought of the grisly scene back at the interrogation block, then shook his head. "No, I'll see to it, just stay behind me and be ready to give me cover." He passed his rifle to Akmed and cautiously climbed the six wooden steps to the door.

The door was unlocked and as King gingerly eased it inwards, he was engulfed in a bright light, which was momentarily painful to his sensitive eyes. He cursed under his breath, knowing that his night vision was now ruined. It would now take a full twenty minutes to return, rendering the escape back to the fence even more hazardous.

The sound of the television grew louder as he stepped inside, straining his eyes against the bright light. He could smell pungent cigarette smoke wafting closer to him. He turned back towards Akmed, but the Kurd was already at his side, his own rifle slung over his shoulder by its sling-strap and King's Galil assault rifle clasped firmly in his hands. King relaxed a little. Akmed Faisal was not a professionally trained soldier, but he was loyal and fearless. He had also served his apprenticeship on the battlefield, handed a gun as a child and forced to learn merely by watching what actions had killed his comrades. If that didn't make him a professional, then King did not know what else would. As he edged his way down the narrow corridor, King felt quite safe with the Kurd covering his every move.

He stopped suddenly, as he neared the first door on his left, which was fitted with a wire mesh reinforced glass panel in its upper half. It was the guards' room, fully equipped with a rack of keys hanging from the wall, a two-way radio on a nearby shelf and a weapon rack on the adjacent wall stacked with American made M16A4 rifles, some with underslung M203 grenade launchers and some battered AK47 and AK74 rifles. The guard was in his mid-forties and going to seed. His shirt strained under his immense stomach, and he was sporting a crafty comb-over across his largely bald scalp. He wore a shoulder holster with an automatic pistol under his left armpit and spare magazines in pouches under his right. He was slouched in a plain wooden swivel office chair, his feet resting on the desk, as he chuckled to a dubbed episode of the British 70's hit: *The Benny Hill Show*. It seemed that Iraqi comedy had a long way to come.

King nodded to Akmed, then placed his left hand gently on the door handle. The guard erupted into a roar of laughter, throwing his head back at the sight of Benny Hill dressed as a woman. King took the opportunity and tucked the pistol into his belt and opened the door quietly. He rushed into the room and wrapped his left arm around the Iraqi's throat. Then he brought his other arm around the back of the man's neck and locked his left hand into his right elbow, the well-practiced procedure taking less than a second. The guard struggled frantically for a moment, then sensibly came to terms that he was no match for King's strength and experience.

Akmed rushed over and took the man's pistol out from his shoulder holster and stood back. King turned to him and scowled. "Tell him that I shall only ask once and that if he lies, I will choke him to death..."

Akmed bent down and spoke quietly into the man's ear. The Iraqi tried to nod, then thought better of it, King's grip did not allow much in the way of movement.

King released his grip a little and looked at Akmed. "Ask him where the Turkish pilot is being held."

Akmed bent down again and spoke quietly. The Iraqi nodded, then patted King's arm gently, by way of asking permission to speak. He looked up at the Kurd and started to chatter frenetically.

"What's he saying?" King glared at Akmed. He knew enough Arabic to get by, but the northern dialect with mostly

Kurdish spoken or interspersed left him at a loss when spoken quickly. "Does he know where the pilot is?"

Akmed shrugged. "He says that he has a family and that he does not want to be a soldier anymore. He says they should be fighting Islamic State and not settling old scores with the Kurdish..."

"I don't want to know that!" King released his grip, spun the man around and took the silenced Glock from his belt. He forced the muzzle into the guard's crotch. "Tell him to answer my question, or I swear I will blow his fucking dick off!"

Akmed started to ask the man again, but the Iraqi had caught King's drift and was starting to chatter away uncontrollably. Akmed looked up and smiled. "Cell four. It's the fifth door on the right."

"All right." King took the pistol away from the man's pride and joy, then looked up at the selection of keys which hung from the row of hooks. "Tell him to get the key and lead the way for us," he paused, then added. "And tell him that if he tries anything, he's dead..."

———

Shameel Faisal's heart pounded as he half ran, half climbed his way up the steep hill. His hands bled as he scrabbled frantically for purchase against the cold rock and his heart pounded so fast and hard, it seemed about to rip through his chest. The machine gun was heavy and awkward and both the two-hundred and fifty round ammunition belts he carried weighed him down further still. He contemplated discarding the weapon, but it looked like he'd be needing it soon...

He had watched the convoy of vehicles head towards the base and knew that if he did not at least attempt to do something, he would be forced to watch his brother's capture no doubt resulting in certain death. The Faisals were not big on surrender. He fought for breath as he climbed, but he knew that there was no time to rest or falter as he scrambled up the steep slope. As he reached the ridge, he turned around to look down at the compound and to his horror saw the first vehicle drive through the main gate.

———

King stared at the man in front of him and shook his head in disbelief. Osman Emrie was barely recognisable. His clothes were reduced to rags and his face had sustained a ferocious beating. The fingers of both hands had been bound together with makeshift bandages and his feet had taken a similar beating, probably with the heel of a boot or a rifle butt.

King bent down and spoke softly into the man's bloodied ear. "Ozzy? Ozzy?" he paused, then shook his shoulder gently. "Ozzy, wake up man!"

Osman let out a groan and raised his hands above his head in a desperate bid to protect his face from further punishment.

King shook his head. "No Ozzy, it's me, Alex King." He eased the man's legs off the single wooden bunk, then looked him in the eyes. "See? It's me, I've come to get you out."

The man sobbed quietly, then attempted to push himself up, but the effort proved too much, and he collapsed back down onto the hard, shelf-like bunk.

King turned back to the Iraqi guard, who was standing in front of Akmed. He caught hold of him by his shirt and pulled him close, then without a word, he lashed out with a fearsomely powerful blow to the nose using the point of his elbow. The Iraqi sprawled backwards and landed in an unconscious heap at the rear of the cell, his nose a bloodied mess.

King turned back to Akmed, then beckoned him over to

help. "Here, help him over my shoulders, then pass me my weapon."

The Kurd did as he was ordered, then picked up his own assault rifle and led the way out of the cell. King struggled at first. Osman Emrie was well muscled and a fair weight for any man to carry. He eased the Turk over his shoulder a little more, so that most of the man's torso hung across his back and felt better for the slight adjustment. He followed Akmed down the corridor, then hesitated as he heard the sound of approaching vehicles.

Akmed stood at the door peering through the slight gap, then turned around, a look of horror upon his face. "They've come back!" He shook his head despondently. "We are dead men..."

"Shut up!" King stepped forward, cold determination in his eyes. "You're not dead until you take your last breath!" He pushed past the Kurd and stared out into the compound. From his position, he could not make out the exact location of the vehicles, but he knew that they were near, by the way parts of the compound were brightly lit from their headlights.

"What do we do?" the Kurd asked, a little more composed than before.

King turned and shrugged. "Brass it out I suppose..." He thought for a moment, then looked at Akmed. "We head straight for the hole in the fence. Don't stop for anything, just keep running!"

The Kurd nodded, then gripped the AK47 firmly between both hands. He looked determined, resolute. "I will lead my friend, you follow Akmed Faisal!" He caught hold of the door and flung it wide open, then stepped into the night.

Shameel slid most of the way down the other side of the steep slope, using the butt of the large machine gun as a makeshift brake. He had tripped and fallen several times, but he was feeling no pain yet. Only one thought dominated his mind, and that was to be at his brother's side. Alive or dead, it was the only place for him. They were the only Faisals left now.

Rocky looked up at the overweight Kurd as he took yet another tumble on the hard ground. Sensing that something was amiss, he opened the door of the Land Rover and looked expectantly at his old friend.

"They are in trouble!" Shameel cried out in anguish. "The troops left in a convoy before they went in but now the troops are back!" he paused, gasping for breath. "They will be either killed or captured if we do not do something!"

————

Akmed Faisal ran across the open ground, bolting like a freshly flushed hare as he led the way for Alex King to follow. King had cursed him at first but felt a pang of relief when he saw the Kurd stop in the shadows with his weapon trained on the Iraqi troops, who were gathering around the entrance to the most distant building in the row.

He made his way as best he could, hampered less by the weight of his heavy load than by the struggle to keep his balance as he lengthened his stride to a run. He heard the shout from behind him and his heart sank, knowing that it was too late. Then a burst of gunfire erupted and the chaos that arose in its wake.

Akmed had taken the initiative as soon as the young soldier had shouted. He had stepped from the shadows and released a sustained burst of automatic fire at the group of soldiers and was now reloading as King reached him in the shadows.

"Okay Akmed, balls out all the way!" He readied himself for the run, then bolted out of the shadows and into the vulnerable open ground. "Go! Go! Go!"

The mass of troops were still wondering what all the gunfire was about when King ran out in front of them. Most of them looked up in surprise, some even went for their weapons, but King was already firing. He wielded the weapon in one hand keeping the butt tight to his hip to absorb the recoil, firing steady single rounds of fire at each of his targets as he kept a firm hold on Ozzy's shoulder with his left hand. The men fell one by one, then even quicker as Akmed started to fire short bursts aimed carefully from his shoulder. Bullets sailed past King's head, but he knew the first and only rule of a fire fight; keep moving and keep firing. He was halfway towards them when he felt the 'dead man's click', the terrifying signal that he had run out of ammunition. He quickly dropped to one knee, to present himself as a smaller target and hastily tried to insert a new magazine. He was hampered by Ozzy's weight, but managed to get a magazine in and charged the cocking lever. He fired a couple of rounds at the closest soldier, then stood up and caught hold of Ozzy's arm and got the man's leg under his armpit in a fireman's lift. He started to run and leapt over the dead soldier's body as he gained momentum.

Akmed kept firing but the soldiers were massing, and gunfire was erupting all over the camp. The increasing opposition caused the Kurd to start firing with wild abandon, but it still had the desired effect, dropping more soldiers as he followed close behind King. The few remaining soldiers realised that the two men were not about to stop for anything, and suddenly decided to turn tail and run. This presented them both with easy targets and they continued to fire at the running soldiers as they made their way across the remaining open ground.

King darted into the shadows of a nearby building and swiftly changed to another magazine. Akmed followed, walking backwards and firing at the struggling wounded on the ground. King tapped him on the shoulder and readied himself for the next stretch of open ground. "Come on, Akmed!" he paused, fighting to get the icy air into his aching lungs. "Only another sixty metres to the fence... But if we aren't out of here before they get the heavy guns mounted on the vehicles onto us, then we're fucked!" He looked up at the hillside, suddenly aware that there had been no covering fire from Shameel up on the hillside.

Akmed realised what King was thinking and drew the same conclusion. He looked tearfully at him. "They have killed my brother!"

"We don't know that for sure. Come on man, move your arse!" King stepped out into the moonlight, then felt a wave of heat near him as bullets shot by barely inches from his face and peppered the building with tiny holes. Some were tracer rounds and the shots that missed fizzled off into the night dropping to the ground a quarter of a mile away. He darted back behind the building, then peered back around just in time to see the muzzle flashes subsiding. He turned back to the Kurd and shook his head. "It's no good, we're cut off!" he paused trying desperately to gather his thoughts and make some sense of the situation. "Our only way is back the way we've come. Either that or chance the guns ahead." He peered back around the corner of the building, then frowned as he saw headlights coming straight towards the fence. There was the sound of a heavy impact, then the screams of injured men caught in its path, but still the headlights advanced. King watched, fascinated as the vehicle drove through the compound with the fence wrapped round its axle. An eruption of sustained automatic gunfire came from the passenger seat, the muzzle flashes lighting up the compound enough to see the Iraqi soldier's faces as they turned to face the onslaught.

"Akmed! It's Shameel! He's come to get us..." King sensed that Akmed was not beside him. He turned to see the Kurd standing at the end of the alley between the two buildings. He was steeling himself, then without warning he disappeared. King heard Akmed shout some sort of shrill battle cry and the gunfire started up immediately.

King looked back at the Land Rover. Muzzle flashes appeared from the driver's seat, followed by the familiar figure of Rocky as he got out and fired more carefully aimed shots. He bent down briefly using the open door as cover then reappeared with a rocket launcher. He fired at a fuel tanker some eighty or so metres away and about a hundred Iraqi soldiers fled in all directions. The explosion was terrific, and the entire compound was lit up like daylight. King ran out from the cover of the building and made for the Land Rover. He looked to his right and saw Akmed on his knees. He had the guard's pistol in his hand and was firing at an advancing group of soldiers. King turned toward the Land Rover as he neared. Shameel had put down the PKM and rushed forward to help King with Ozzy. King was glad of the help and felt the weight halve as the big Kurd dragged the Turkish pilot off his shoulder and helped to heave him into the pickup bed of the Land Rover. When King looked back at Akmed he could see the group of soldiers standing over his body, bayonetting his corpse relentlessly. King raised his rifle and picked off the group of five men with eight carefully aimed single shots. Shameel looked towards his brother and screamed. He rushed out from the cover of the Land Rover and ran towards Akmed. He almost made it too. And then he took a bullet in the chest and went down hard. He crawled slowly, his hand outstretched, his fingers reaching until they took hold of his brother's hand. A second later a bullet smashed into his head and the Kurd lay still, his hand still holding his brother's. King looked at Rocky, who seemed to read his mind and threw down the RPG to get into the driver's seat. King was already in the bed of the truck and had the PKM rattling off steadily as they moved off. The fuel tanker was engulfed in flames and the fire was spreading rapidly as the fuel leaked and boiled, taking the first three huts with it. There was so much light to see by King had almost forgotten that it was night time. He knew that if the remainder of fuel reached a high enough temperature to detonate rather than ignite then it would obliterate everything within half a mile.

Rocky got the Land Rover up to about thirty miles per hour and drove over both casualties and dead bodies alike. King was getting low on ammunition and started to rattle off three round bursts at anything that moved. It was difficult standing in the tiny loading bed of the pickup as he had to step over Ozzy and balance as best he could as Rocky drove erratically towards the jagged hole in the fence. Bodies lay strewn everywhere, but soldiers were massing and regrouping quickly. Many of the soldiers had unloaded and made their weapons safe after arriving back to the compound. They had been surprised, but it wouldn't last long. King could see weapons and magazines being distributed and with every yard they drove more and more shots pinged past them or hit the ground around them throwing up dust and gravel. They would soon find their mark or give pursuit and would be on top of them. They had overwhelming numbers.

King sat down and pushed up against the rear window of the cab. "Get us out of here Rocky!" he shouted through the glass. He put down the empty PKM and picked up Shameel's AK47. The soldiers were almost one hundred and fifty metres away, but bullets were starting to get close to them as they fled. Some were hitting the tailgate and both wing mirrors were shattered. King fired single shots at the regrouping men, he wasn't sure if he hit, nor was he really trying to. He just wanted them to keep their heads down and make them reconsider fighting. Most soldiers when faced with a surprise attack and without clear objectives or orders set out for them will concentrate on keeping their heads down and getting through the battle unscathed.

Rocky drove through the hole in the fence with King ducking down to avoid the shredded and twisted wire, and they were soon out of range, both by a combination of distance and the bend in the road which took the camp from view. The great orange glow from the fire still lit the night sky and as they approached a mile and a half distance from the compound a tremendous explosion detonated, and the ground shook the Land Rover momentarily off the road. King felt a wave of heat envelop him like opening an oven door. The entire southern sky lit up as bright as day and a mushroom cloud plumed skywards throwing up an enormous ball of black, acrid smoke. Slowly the light dissipated leaving a bright orange glow which pulsated like a distant strobe.

King knocked on the window and signalled for Rocky to stop. The Kurd pulled the Land Rover to the side of the potholed road and King stood up. Ozzy was stirring and groaned. King leapt over the side and opened the passenger door. "Right, nobody's going to follow us with that tanker going off like that. Let's get going but take it steady. Ozzy needs to see a doctor. Over the border is the best bet," he paused. "About twenty miles north east will give us a few options." He changed over magazines on the AK47 and put it muzzle downwards in the foot well. He did the same with Rocky's weapon. They were going to go through the heart of

Islamic State held territory, but at least the border would be unguarded on the Iraqi side.

Rocky nodded and pulled away. "Is your friend okay?"

King glanced back at Ozzy. He didn't have any friends. Never needed them. He was stronger on his own. He'd loved and lost, and he'd promised himself no more ties. But then why in hell's name had he risked his life to get a man back? A man he'd known for only one night? He looked back at Rocky. "He's injured from the crash and they've beaten him up pretty well, but I think he'll be all right." He looked out of the window, thinking about Shameel and Akmed. "I'm sorry about your friends. They were brave men."

Rocky looked tearful as he drove. "They were lucky," he smiled. "They got to die like lions. Not like lambs..."

CHAPTER FIFTY-FIVE

Charles Bryant closed his eyes and rested his head against the corner of the wall. His mind was buzzing, and the musician's bad rendition of Barry Manilo's *Copacabana* only made matters worse. He was sure that the man had only recently seen a sheet of the words and his timing was that of a drunken karaoke contestant. Perhaps there was an ironic comedy angle that he was failing to appreciate.

Bryant opened his eyes and reached forward for his gin and tonic, taking a deep, refreshing mouthful as he looked around the quiet bar and studied the clientele. He had not even known of the establishment's existence, let alone visited the place and was surprised by the number of attractive women lining the bar. They were mainly Indonesian or Filipino, although there were plenty of western women, dressed to the nines, perched elegantly on raised barstools, sipping elaborately decorated cocktails. Bryant listened to the chatter which was suddenly audible, as *Copacabana* came to an end, and he quickly realised that one of the women was speaking to an Indonesian man in English with a heavy Germanic accent. He listened intently, but the snippet of conversation was soon drowned out by the adaptation of *New York, New York*. Frank Sinatra was not being given justice either. He wondered if the playlist contained anything from the past three decades.

Bryant sipped another mouthful of his drink then noticed Junus Kutu walk into the bar and glance casually around. His eyes suddenly met Kutu's and the little Indonesian smiled as he walked hastily over to the quiet corner table.

"My good friend, how are you?" Junus Kutu sat down and smiled at the Englishman. "Pleasant journey? You are back so soon..."

Bryant shrugged. "What can I say? I have only just stepped off a plane, why could we not talk somewhere a little quieter?" he asked, rubbing his temples with both index fingers. "Frankly, I feel like warmed up shit..."

Kutu signalled to a waiter at the bar, then turned to his companion. "You don't look so hot either..." He smiled, then glanced up at the little Indonesian who stood at his shoulder. "Bintang, terima kasih." He glanced at Bryant, who simply held up his half-empty glass and nodded. The waiter ambled his way back to the bar and Kutu looked at Bryant and smiled. "I trust London was a success? You seemed in the best of spirits when you telephoned."

Bryant leaned back against the wall and rested his elbow on the back of the next booth's seat, then smiled wryly. "A positive result. My contact will call me when the arrangements are definite."

The little Indonesian smiled triumphantly. "Excellent!"

"One minor hitch though."

"Which is?"

"He wanted more money," Bryant paused, watching Kutu's eyes for any sign of doubt. "I agreed to one and a half million for his cut. I trust that will be acceptable?"

Junus Kutu stared at him coldly then smiled. "I think we

can meet his demands," he said, keeping his small, piercing eyes firmly locked on the Englishman's. "I suppose it was only to be expected..."

Bryant knew that the Indonesian was aware of his little ploy but had no choice but to continue with the charade. Cutting his contact out of half a million pounds was one thing but cutting Junus Kutu out of a further half a million was quite another. He shook his head theatrically and shrugged his shoulders. "I tried my hardest, but he was most insistent, he made it quite clear that unless I bumped up the fee, there would be no deal."

"Of course, he did..." Kutu seemed uninterested as the young waiter arrived with a bottle of cold beer and another gin and tonic. He took a long pull from the neck, then looked coldly at Bryant. "So, what are the arrangements?"

Bryant glanced at a pretty blonde at the bar, then looked back at Junus Kutu. "It will go ahead, simple as that," he paused, unable to look his friend in the eye. "Payment will be made in two instalments, half *before* the hit and half when the job is done."

"And what are the payment arrangements?" Kutu asked curiously, although he felt that he already knew the answer.

"Cash. I have to make the payment in person." He looked away again, turning his attention back to the good-looking blonde, who was now talking to another Indonesian businessman.

"You have to take two instalments of seven hundred and fifty thousand pounds to England," Kutu stated dubiously.

"I have to *pay* him in cash. I plan to wire it from here through my accounts and draw it in Britain in dollars, pounds and euros."

"I trust the money will arrive as planned?"

Bryant looked back at him and frowned. "What the hell do you mean?"

The little Indonesian smiled. "Oh, come now, you don't think you can play your little games with me, do you?" he paused, staring coldly into Bryant's eyes. "What's half a million between friends? I'll tell you, it's peanuts to men like you and me." Kutu took another sip, then placed the bottle on the cardboard place mat. "We both play with the figures from time to time. I'm making more out of this deal than you are, even with the half a million you fleeced from both ends." He smiled knowingly, then shook his head slowly. "But if the money does not arrive, or if this deal does not come off, I will see to it that you do not reach your next birthday. Believe me Charles, you will discover that my reach, particularly in Indonesia, is very long indeed..."

———

"But I don't understand why I was called back," Stewart protested. "Surely locating the final segment of King's security blanket means that we can go forward and put the retrieval stage of the operation into action?"

McCullum nodded. "Of course, it does, old man. However, we are faced with a somewhat unexpected problem..." he paused and smiled wryly. "But what's more, an unexpected solution."

Stewart leaned forward in his seat and looked at Donald McCullum intently. "And what is that?"

"The problem or the solution?" the Deputy Director smiled. "I think I should explain a little more about the problem first." He glanced across at Arnott, then looked back at Stewart. "I called you as soon as we found out. King's insertion into Iraq had not gone quite according to plan..."

"Now *there's* a surprise," Arnott mused.

"Quite," McCullum nodded. "There was a problem when

he made the jump, and to cut a long story short, the plane crashed."

Stewart sat up in his seat, a look of concern on his haggard face. "Did King make it?"

"He would seem to possess an annoying penchant for survival," Arnott commented flatly.

"Yes, he did." McCullum nodded. "But the Turkish pilot was captured by the Iraqi army. Fortunately, he was not privy to the operation, he only knew about the insertion aspect."

"So, what's the problem?" Stewart asked, dividing his stare between the two men. "Did King do the job or not?"

"Yes, it would appear so," Arnott nodded. "Osman Emrie, the Turkish pilot, verified that both brothers were killed."

Stewart frowned. "But he was..."

"Captured, I know," McCullum nodded. "King rescued him from the military compound at Zakho, used the two Kurds to help him but they were both killed in the rescue. The Turk has filed out an extensive report on the whole affair."

"Incredible. That compound is a forward operating base for the region. Very well equipped and heavy on personnel." Stewart mused. "So, what's the problem?"

"King is on his way back," McCullum paused, glancing at the brass wall clock to his right. "He's in the air as we speak. If he were to arrive back to discover that his security blanket had been raided, well you know how he would react..."

Stewart nodded, knowing full well that King would be more than a little put out. "I see, you're right, that *is* a problem."

McCullum looked at Arnott and smiled wryly before turning his attention back to Stewart. "A problem indeed," he commented flatly. "Now old chap, would you like to hear our little solution?"

"So, you need the money immediately?" Kutu sipped a mouthful of the warming beer, then held the bottle on the arm of the chair and studied his colleague's expression. He turned his eyes to a smart-looking businessman, who was sitting down with an Indonesian woman at the next booth, then looked back at Bryant. "Let's not play games with each other Charles, we both know that you have played with the figures at both ends, but just tell me how much you will need and when you will need it by. I am assuming you've added some on to your initial fee and trimmed a little off your contact's fee? So, where are we? How much do you need? Let's call your fee two million. That's safe. What do you need for your contact's first instalment?"

Bryant looked at him with contempt, then sipped some more of his gin and tonic. He placed the glass on the placemat with somewhat exaggerated precision, then looked back at the little man. "I will need seven hundred and fifty thousand for the first instalment, and the same again for the second," he stated flatly. To hell with Junus Kutu, the arrogant little man. He'd upped his fee and he'd have the half a million on top. "But he wants the first instalment in his hand before he sends someone to do for General Soto."

Kutu looked up at the man in the next booth, then glared venomously at Bryant. He leaned across the table conspiratorially and spoke quietly. "No more names, we cannot afford to get sloppy! And I don't believe a word of it! But you'll get it, and your renegotiated fee..."

The Englishman turned around and looked at the Indonesian couple sitting in the booth behind him. The man was sipping from a glass, while the woman rested her head against his shoulder and stroked his crotch tenderly with her fingertips, talking to him softly in their own tongue.

Bryant looked back at Junus Kutu and shrugged. "All right, I'll be more careful," he agreed, and grinned at his companion. "I shouldn't worry about those two, he's about to ask how much a blow job will be any minute now..."

The Indonesian smiled and glanced across at the good-looking blonde at the bar, then turned his eyes back to Bryant. "It's usually about thirty American dollars," he paused, breaking into a wolfish grin. "Most of the western girls charge a little more though."

"You mean she's a..." Bryant stared at the blonde in disbelief, then looked back at Kutu. "I had no idea that there were western women working here!"

Junus Kutu smiled and sipped another mouthful of *Bintang*. "Why not? I mean, you like to come to my country and do more than your fair share of novelty fucking, why shouldn't Indonesian men want the same?" he paused, glancing briefly at the blonde woman. "There are a few establishments in Jakarta with western working girls and the ladies are kept extremely busy indeed. I like to come every two or three weeks," he smiled. "If you'll pardon the expression?"

Bryant remained silent, choosing to stare lecherously at the woman in question. He picked up his glass, downed the remnants, then turned to the Indonesian. "Another drink?"

"No, thank you," Kutu paused and stared at him. "So, when do you need the money?"

Bryant shrugged. "When do you want business to commence?"

Junus Kutu nibbled at the inside of his cheek while he thought, then looked at Bryant coldly. "As soon as possible," he paused and rose to his feet. "I will make the arrangements first thing in the morning. Come to my house at around lunchtime, I shall have the money by then. I want things to get underway immediately." He took out his wallet and dropped a handful of one thousand-rupiah notes onto the table. "You had better book yourself onto another flight." He slipped the wallet back into his jacket pocket and grinned at the Englishman. "I trust you can spare the money for the fare out of your little... *bonus?*"

———

Stewart studied the photograph carefully, taking note of the subject's features and the way that he carried himself. Stewart knew that you could often tell a great deal about a person from the way they carried themselves. Judging from the man's poise, he was prepared to bet that he was immensely powerful and self-disciplined. His uniform was well pressed, with blade-like creases ironed into his shirt and trousers and his flat stomach, straight back and broad shoulders indicated that he was in exceptional physical condition. Stewart reached forwards and placed the photograph on McCullum's spacious desk. "Quite a memorable man."

"His name is General Madi Soto," McCullum replied. "A thorn in the proverbial flesh, both to Britain *and* Indonesia."

"And if we are not careful, to the rest of the western world," Marcus Arnott interjected. "At the moment, he has his hand on China's arse and he is stroking it very softly indeed."

"I've heard the name," Stewart pontificated. "But until now, I have never seen a picture," he paused, glancing at the two men. "So, what has he got to do with solving our current problem?"

"The Indonesian government want him assassinated. The directive landed on my desk this morning," McCullum paused, glancing at Arnott. "It looks as if the British government has sanctioned our department to do the dirty work. We do a great deal of business with Indonesia, we need stability problems out there about as much as they do."

"And the Foreign Office has granted General Soto an Executive Order?" Stewart shook his head. "That is extremely unusual, Sir."

"What do you want? Would you like to see the bloody directive?" McCullum opened the drawer of his desk and snatched out a typewritten sheet. He dropped the sheet just short of Stewart's hand, forcing the man to lean across the large mahogany desk. "First, I have Alex *bloody* King questioning a legitimate operation, now I have *you* doubting an order from the bloody top!" he paused as he watched the Scotsman read the Executive Order. "Should we be watching out for your security blanket as well?"

Stewart calmly replaced the paper and smiled. "I was merely intrigued that there should be an order on such a prominent figure." He shook his head and stared at both men suspiciously. "The last one I saw for such a figure was Saddam Hussein. Bin Laden's was different, he was a terrorist. I take it that Alex King will soon be on a little trip to warmer parts?"

"You guess correctly," Arnott said. "That should give you enough time to seize all the components of his security blanket, shouldn't it?"

"I should think so," the Scotsman stared at him coldly, then turned to the Deputy Director General. "You obviously want me to brief King on the mission. When do you want him to go?"

"We'll give him a day to recover, then send him on his way. He can stay in service accommodation. I don't want him traipsing down to Cornwall and chancing him knowing someone's been eating his porridge and sleeping in his bed..." McCullum replied, smiling at his own wit. He turned his attention to another sheet of paper. "Oh yes, before I forget..." He rummaged through a pile of paper files on the edge of his desk, then smiled when he found the relevant folder. "We have a suitable liaison officer for him, it should enable him to find his way around a little easier." He opened the folder and extracted a large photograph and two typed sheets. "This is his dossier, it's slim, but we have used the man on several occasions, and he is extremely reliable."

Stewart picked up the photograph and briefly studied the man's nondescript face, then turned his attention to the two typewritten sheets.

"He serves with Indonesian Internal Security, but also keeps us in the know for a retainer. Barely enough to live on, but he's an idealist. Anti-communist to the core so doesn't have a problem helping us out, as long as Indonesia stays a democracy and we help maintain the status quo..." McCullum smiled wryly.

Marcus Arnott craned his neck to see the photograph of the man, then turned to Donald McCullum. "What's the chap's name?" he asked casually, as he inspected an imaginary blemish on his well-manicured fingernail.

"His name?" McCullum frowned. "His name is Abdul Tembarak."

CHAPTER FIFTY-SIX

The night air was stiflingly hot, and the mosquitoes gathered around the single dim light bulb in the middle of the ceiling, as if taking a well-earned rest before preparing for another relentless attack on his neck.

The room was much as it had been left and even now, two days after he had returned, he could not bring himself to tidy up and put his life back into some sort of order. What would be the point? The two most crucial details, the only details which really mattered, were missing. How could he put his life into order without the two people who had made his life complete?

Abdul Tembarak walked through the lounge and into the small bedroom. He stared at the motionless mobile which hung directly above the empty cot. It was made from Javanese shadow puppets, the guardians of family and loved ones. A present from Abdul's mother. He watched it hang still, then felt a sudden eruption of bile in the pit of his stomach. He turned and ran, hobbling as best he could on his bandaged knee, into the adjoining bathroom, where he vomited violently into the sink, heaving uncontrollably as he strained the very last of it out. He panted, gripping the edge of the basin, then looked up and stared at himself in the mirror. He was dead. There was no other description more fitting, or better suited to his appearance. His eyes were deeply sunken in their sockets, and his hair was matted with sweat, blood and his own vomit. He turned on the cold tap and washed the vile, fetid smelling liquid away then bent down and splashed the refreshing water over his face. It felt cool and pure and he took large mouthfuls to rid his taste buds of the burning taste of bile in his mouth. The cool water stung at the ulcers at first but soothed his throat of the dryness which had stayed with him since he had been released from the military compound.

It was almost too easy to forget. To push the whole trauma from his mind and forget that it ever happened, forget to do as he was ordered. To go on with his life, safe and never fearing the fate which was so forcefully promised. But then there was Wyan and their little baby son, Numan. He thought of his wife and of the terrible treatment she had suffered at the hands of General Soto and that hideous monster Sergeant Grogol. How could two men be so fundamentally evil? He stared into the mirror and felt himself drifting back to the compound, and to his wife. His beautiful young wife. The mere thought of her, spread out for the soldiers to feast their eyes on her most intimate nakedness, made him want to vomit again. He suppressed the feeling and limped out to the narrow hallway and into their bedroom, his knee was bandaged well, the wounds expertly tended to, but still the joint was stiff and painful. Two shattered teeth had been pulled, and two more filed and filled. His lips were cut and swollen.

The bedcovers had been ripped and the mattress had been overturned, slashed open and discarded against the wall. Everything that the couple owned had been discarded on the floor and most of their valuables had found their way into the soldiers' pockets. Tembarak stared around the room then stopped when something caught his eye. He looked at the frame, then walked over to crouch on the floor beside it. The glass had been shattered, but the photograph was blissfully still in one piece. He clutched the frame to his chest then looked down at the picture and stared tearfully at his wife. She had been so beautiful on their wedding day and had worn the long flowing dress that her mother had bought for her especially. She had been so pleased, especially as her family was so poor. Tembarak looked at her; young, innocent and beautiful. How easily innocence could be violated and had been.

Tembarak walked tearfully out of the room. He had no idea where he wanted to go, nor would he feel any better once he got there, but anywhere would be better than the couple's bedroom, where so much love and intimacy had passed between them. He stood in the middle of the room, then decided to sit on the bare floorboards. He could not sit in comfort, not while his wife and child were incarcerated. To do so would be disrespectful of Wyan's suffering, and she deserved so much more.

The announcement had caused him a great deal of confusion at first and almost as much confusion later. General Soto was not only cunning, his idea of irony was certainly well honed. The Indonesian General had cut Tembarak's bonds, given him his clothes and told him that he was free to go. Of course, Abdul Tembarak had regarded this as a trick; after all, it was standard procedure to keep a prisoner off balance, and Tembarak was certainly learning fast.

Then came the bombshell. Wyan Tembarak would not be leaving with him. She would be staying as General Soto's personal guest. She would be extended every courtesy but would not be able to leave until the Indonesian intelligence agent had completed certain tasks. If he did not perform these tasks, she would become the camp whore and he would never see her again. Unless he did as he was ordered. His son would be sold to a childless couple and he would never see him again. Unless he did as he was ordered...

Tembarak would have to return to Yogyakarta and go back to work at the MB&C Bank as usual. He would then have to contact his control in Jakarta and report back in, after which he would start to send back information. However, this information would be different. This information would come direct from the mouth of General Soto.

Disinformation.

————

The woman continued to whisper softly into the man's ear, but the intimate erotic desires to which she laid claim did nothing for him; nor for that matter, did her gentle, experienced touch. He sipped another mouthful of his drink, then turned his head casually and watched the westerner leave. The man was tall, fit-looking and had an air of authority about him, quite frankly more his type than the woman who paid close attention to waking his flaccid manhood.

He set his glass back on the glass table, then took out a thick wad of American five and ten-dollar bills and dropped them into the young woman's lap. She looked up in surprise, then pocketed the money before any of the other girls at the bar had chance to see. Then she turned her eyes back to the somewhat effeminate-looking man and smiled, before leaning forwards and whispering into his ear. The man listened to her suggestion, humouring her at least, then shook his head and silently rose to his feet.

————

Charles Bryant stepped out of the air-conditioned building and into the stifling heat of Jakarta's rush-hour, which, for reasons best known to the locals, seems to last from midmorning to sometime just before dawn. He walked down the concrete steps, then dodged his way through the hordes of pedestrians and stood at the side of the road with his hand outstretched to signal for a taxi. Within seconds, a blue Toyota Corolla pulled across the road, cutting in front of a bus and narrowly missing a collision. As the taxi characteristically held up the rest of the traffic in the lane behind. Bryant opened the car's rear door and dropped down heavily onto the seat, which for reasons he would rather not know, was covered with a hot, damp plastic sheet.

———

The effeminate-looking man casually stepped out from the air-conditioned foyer and like so many Indonesians, paid no heed to the dramatic change in temperature. He watched Charles Bryant get into the rear of the taxi, then looked further down the busy street and signalled to the scruffy-looking Javanese, who was seated on a motor scooter smoking a cigarette. The man held up his right hand in acknowledgement, then started the scooter's tiny engine. He casually flicked the cigarette onto the pavement, then rode off slowly, weaving his way erratically through the traffic, until he was only two car lengths away from the blue taxi.

CHAPTER FIFTY-SEVEN

"So, Donald…" Martin Andrews looked across the desk at his opposite number and smiled. "When on earth are you going to get some decent brandy in?"

McCullum sipped from the crystal tumbler and frowned. "What's wrong with this?"

"Where did you get it?"

McCullum continued to frown, a little perplexed. "At a local off license. Why?"

"An off license!" The man's angular features gave way to surprise and he chuckled out loud. "One would assume that a man about to take the service's helm and mix with a whole new social circle, could tell a good brandy from off license rotgut, would one not?" Andrews sipped another mouthful of the disagreeable spirit and looked at him seriously. "Come over to the house for some supper one evening next week and I'll treat you to a guided tour of my cellars. I'll even put you in touch with my wine merchant."

McCullum nodded politely and smiled. "I'd like that very much; shall I bring the wife?"

Andrews thought for a moment, then nodded. "Why not,

indeed? Carol has recently had the decorators in and she's simply dying to show off to someone. We'll leave them to it, while I take you on the boys' tour," he paused and smiled excitedly. "Just bought myself a rather attractive Holland and Holland, side by side, with fully engraved side plates. What say we dust a few clays with it before supper? Providing there's enough light, of course."

McCullum hid his thoughts as best he could behind a fixed smile. He made a mental note to arrive late, in the dark maybe. He had never been into guns or shooting and the prospect of clay pigeon shooting with a marksman as skilled as Martin Andrews filled him with dread. He knew that Andrews always took August the twelfth off to go to Scotland for the start of the grouse season. He also took off the first and last days of the pheasant and partridge season, but he couldn't recall the dates. There was also deer stalking around Christmas with some Lord and Lady somewhere or other, who always held a Boxing Day pheasant shoot. "Sounds marvellous," he replied emphatically. "Can't wait."

Andrews leaned back into the comfortable leather chair and smiled. "That's settled then," he paused, then added in a concerned tone. "How's the *delicate* situation going? Can't say I've heard any whispers about our American cousins along the corridors."

McCullum stared at him for a moment, then took another sip of cognac. "It's quietened down. The whole business seems to have sorted itself out."

Andrews nodded. "Good. I take it Iraq was a success then?"

"Yes, it was." McCullum picked up a copy of *The Times* from the desk in front of him and waved it triumphantly. "Nothing in there, for the first time in over a fortnight!"

Andrews smiled. "Old news then?"

"It would appear so, yes."

Andrews smiled. "Of course not, but I *have* heard something on the wind. Voices tend to carry a little further at my end of the building."

"And what would these voices be saying?" McCullum smiled. "Or were they not awfully clear?"

"The CIA are missing a prized agent," Andrews shrugged. "It was only a whisper, but they tend to carry the furthest of the lot."

"That's why they're always more dangerous..."

"Word is, Alex King arrived back, safe and sound," Andrews paused, picking up his glass. "An American contact is asking a couple of questions already. 'Where is their missing agent?' is one question. 'Where is the confirmation of the Faisal hits?' is another..."

McCullum leaned across the desk, placing his elbows down carefully on the polished wood as he stared at him. "The Faisal brothers died in a raid on the nearby military base to liberate an agent of ours captured when King's plane went down. I haven't had the chance to debrief King yet, but one of our top agents in Turkey, the downed pilot himself, has verified the Faisal deaths," he frowned as he watched the man's beady, penetrating eyes. "Peter Stewart is on his way to meet King as we speak. King trusts him and fortunately for us, Stewart is batting on the same team. *Our* team. Any impropriety on King's part will soon reach our ears."

"Only too glad to hear it," Andrews stated flatly. He sighed and shook his head in deliberation. "Who gave King the order to mount a rescue mission?"

"Nobody," McCullum paused. "He acted on his own."

"Interesting. Overall though, Alex King is fast becoming a liability," Andrews sighed. "If agents just act on their own making key decisions, then what is to become of people like us?"

McCullum nodded. "The feeling's mutual." He looked at

the man carefully, deciding just how much he should to know. It always paid to play one's hand close to one's chest, but certain matters were often worth another's input. However, this *was* the SIS and sometimes it paid to keep even the most trusted ally in the dark. He smiled wryly at his opposite number and held up his hand as if to silence him before going any further with the subject. "Alex King's operational future is soon to come to an end. He's too much of a liability..."

Andrews nodded, understanding that McCullum's reply meant that his point had been noted, but the matter was already in hand. "Just thought I'd add my two pennies." He drained the remnants of his cognac and replaced the crystal tumbler on the mahogany desk. "Retiring, is he?"

"Yes," McCullum nodded. "Something along those lines."

CHAPTER FIFTY-EIGHT

"Take a seat." Stewart waved towards the three-piece suite in the middle of the cosy lounge. "I'll get us some coffee. Black with two sugars, right?"

King nodded silently as his host walked out to the kitchen, but declined the man's offer of a seat, preferring to stand and pace casually round the room, admiring the series of water colours which lined the pale magnolia walls. He appreciated a wide range of art, landscapes in particular, but did not recognise the style as that of an established painter. He looked closer, noted the name, but could not recall having ever heard of the artist.

"Adrian B. Pollock." Stewart walked into the room and leaned against the back of the tan leather sofa. "He's a local chap, lives near Guildford. Margaret knows his sister well and bought one of the chap's paintings as a token gesture when he started working commercially. She liked it and has been collecting them ever since."

King nodded and studied the second painting. "Nice. Simplistic at first blush, yet with some delicate details at a second glance. Rewarding." He turned around to smile at the Scotsman. "Where's the coffee?"

"Give us a bloody chance, the kettle hasn't even boiled yet!" He pointed to the nearest seat and grinned. "Now take a seat, you're making me nervous." He walked out into the kitchen, then shouted back through the open doorway. "Pull the chair round to face the sofa if you want. It's Margaret, she's into all this *Feng Shui* bollocks! The chairs have to face the compass points to be in line with your 'spiritual self', or some shit like that..."

King looked at the seating arrangements and smiled. He had known Margaret Stewart for almost as long as he had known her husband and had given up counting how many fads and phases she had been through. *Feng Shui* was obviously the latest and would no doubt last until the next weird and wonderful life-enhancing revelation.

"Here, take this..." Stewart handed him the steaming mug of coffee and smiled. "See what I mean? We have four chairs and a sofa. The chairs face the four compass points, with the sofa in the middle. The idea is that you can choose the direction you face, depending on the mood you are in, or the mood you may turn to. I just want them to face the bloody TV."

"What about the sofa?" King looked at the large leather sofa in the middle of the configuration and frowned. "What happens with that?"

"Ah!" Stewart raised his eyebrows and smiled. "When one has found one's spiritual self, one moves the goddamn sofa and faces it in the same bloody direction!"

"Should help keep you fit," King commented flatly, as he sipped the steaming liquid.

"Frankly, I think she's reading the bloody book wrong, but you know what Margaret is like, she can't be told anything."

King nodded reminiscently. He had once been present

when the couple had argued, and it had been quite an experience. He looked over to the corner of the room and noticed the large chess set resting on an expensive-looking and heavily decorated Queen Anne table. He looked back at Stewart, surprised. "Didn't know you were into chess."

Stewart smiled. "I wasn't, but Margaret thought that it would be a relaxing hobby for me."

"Just for you?"

Stewart grinned. "*You* realise that, *I* realise that. But Margaret, bless her, did not reach the same conclusion," he paused, looking at the ornate chessboard and hand-carved pieces. "The board is solid mahogany, with ivory and ebony inlays, shrouded in woven silver thread and the pieces are both ebony and ivory. She bought it for me as a surprise. The biggest surprise was how much it bloody cost me!"

"It's a brilliant discipline for enhancing your concentration and tactical thinking. Ever learn to play?" King smirked, suspecting just how miffed the man must have been.

"Yeah, but I play against the computer now. Either that, or on the net with some anonymous enthusiast. The set's really only for show." He turned back to Alex King and sighed, his mood changing dramatically. "You know what comes next, don't you?" he said flatly. "Our days of happy banter are all but over. The service seems only to allow time for formality and regulation."

King sipped another mouthful of coffee and smiled. "You want to know how it went." He leaned forwards and placed the mug down onto a silver coaster. "So, I had better tell you," he paused and shook his head. "As you are probably aware, things did not get off to the best of starts..."

CHAPTER FIFTY-NINE

Charles Bryant watched as Junus Kutu chipped the ball gently onto the green. The ball rolled steadily towards the pin, but gradually veered to the left and came up just a few inches short. "Oh, bad luck old boy!" He jogged down the remainder of the slate steps, then walked purposefully towards him. "Want me to show you how?" He called out jovially as he watched the little Indonesian line up the putter for his final shot.

Junus Kutu tapped the ball gently, sinking it decisively into the cup. He turned around, glaring contemptuously at the Englishman. "There will be no need. I have asked you here today for a purpose, as you know well enough. Let's not confuse the issue." He bent to pick up the ball, then walked past him towards the swimming pool and patio area. "I have the money, I trust you have made the necessary travel arrangements?"

Bryant looked surprised, but he quickly regained his composure and walked casually after the Indonesian. "All sorted, I fly out at two this afternoon."

"Good." Kutu dropped the sand wedge and putter beside

his chair, then bent to pick up a brown leather case. "It's all there, in American dollars. The equivalent of one and a half million pounds sterling."

Bryant frowned. "But..."

Kutu held up a hand to silence him. "I know, you only need half the money. Frankly, I think you had better stay in England until the hit has been completed. That way you can then pay your contact his other instalment after the hit has taken place. Besides, I don't want you making anyone suspicious with so many comings and goings," he paused, gazing distantly towards the horizon, watching the heat-haze waft skywards. "As for the other five hundred thousand? Well; disgruntled partners do not good bedfellows make. I hope you find it was worth it..."

Charles Bryant nodded gratefully, although a little subdued. He knew he'd pushed it too far fiddling the fees at both ends. He looked at the man with concern. "There are other arrangements to make. I had to bring a photograph of the assassin back with me, it was part of the deal for him to take a fall."

"Send it, along with any other information, via e-mail. I can make all the necessary arrangements from here. There are some people I know who will be able to deal with him, for a small price. It's not like getting to a military leader. The man will have no protection, no resources. The people I know will make it look like just another tourist robbery or hit and run vehicle accident..." he paused, looking intently at the Englishman. "You have my email address, don't you?"

"Yes."

"Good," he paused. "The rest of your fee will be put into your business account via internet transfer. If I were you, I'd bank that money here before you go and withdraw in England or do a bank transfer. Cash money is always likely to arouse suspicion. Well, that would appear to conclude our business," he said curtly and picked up his two golf clubs and took the ball out of his trouser pocket. "Good luck…"

Bryant picked up the leather case and nodded an acknowledgment. As he walked casually towards the steps, he knew that he had lost the Indonesian's trust and could tell from the man's manner that any future business with him wasn't merely in doubt. It was finished. However, Bryant couldn't help smiling. He was making so much money for his troubles that for now it didn't seem to matter.

CHAPTER SIXTY

"How are you going to do it?" Stewart reached for his coffee mug. "Near or far?"

King put the file down in his lap and shrugged. "Your guess is as good as mine. There are a lot of potential issues to consider. Senior military personnel are not the easiest of targets. A controversial man of Soto's standing will be harder still. I don't know what the terrain is like, whether a long shot will even be feasible. I doubt it though. And I don't know the resource situation yet."

"Oh, don't worry about that," Stewart paused. "It's Indonesia after all. There will be the best possible equipment at your disposal. Christ, we sold most of it to them. Our man Abdul Tembarak should be able to get whatever you want."

"What's he like?"

"No idea."

"Great."

"He's an asset," Stewart shrugged. "That's all I know. He's Indonesian Intelligence, but he was recruited as a British asset because of his deep-seated hatred of communism. Indonesia has veered left and right but given enough push

Tembarak was aware that it could go left and further still. The South-East Asia desk has had Tembarak on its books for over five years. I've read up on him and he seems a favourable chap."

"Untested though."

"He's dropped a few things on our desk. Doesn't take too big a retainer. Loves his country for sure."

King nodded. Dropped the hastily put together file onto the coffee table. "I need to do a thorough recce. I'll have to keep things loose until I know more," he paused thoughtfully. "A hell of a lot more..."

"True." Stewart glanced at his watch, then looked up at him. "Not long before you have to leave. Anything else you want to know?"

King smirked. "About a million things, if the truth be known..." He opened the file again and memorised the last few details. Addresses, names and numbers were easily remembered, advanced training techniques had taught him that. He looked up at Stewart and frowned. "This is more than just a bit rushed. This is outrageous. Why so sudden?"

Stewart looked at the man who regarded him as a friend and felt a wave of guilt wash over him. The man trusted him, the man confided in him, yet he was conspiring behind his back. Why? To keep his job and save his pension. When it came down to it, it was as simple as that. Simply to make it a few more years to retirement age and get out with his dues. Not the most admirable of motives, but practical, none-theless. He shrugged, his expression neutral. "General Soto is in league with China, and something big is about to happen. Not an invasion, more of a franchise with zero possibility of other countries getting a look in. We do hundreds of millions trading with Indonesia, so we can't be having that. Time was not on our side for this one."

"It seldom is, is it?" King looked at his watch. "I take it

you're driving me to the airport? Better get going, I want to spend some of the company's money in the duty free."

Stewart reached into his jacket pocket and retrieved a brown envelope which he dropped on the table. "False passport – study the legend card then destroy before checking in – twenty grand sterling and your tickets." He smiled. "The exfiltration will be through Bali, at Denpasar airport. The ticket is open-ended, instructions about booking your return flight are with the tickets."

"Don't I just do it at the airport booking office or phone the confirmation line?" King frowned.

"No. You are flying with Qantas, they have an office in a hotel at Sanur. Bit of a daft arrangement, but that's the way it is," he paused, guilt starting to get the better of him. "Hey, after the hit, take it easy for a bit. Act like a tourist and work your exfiltration at your own leisure, after all, it's the company's time and money," he paused. "You go back through Thailand, stop off in Bangkok for a while and see the sights."

King smiled. "Thanks, but Madam Woo's isn't my style."

Stewart returned the smile, sharing his friend's humour for what might be the last time. Frankly, he couldn't see a way of King pulling off such an audacious assassination and making it out of Indonesia. Not with a man like Soto, not with the resources to hand. "You haven't got any style King, you know that!"

———

The Airbus A-380 gained momentum, its Rolls Royce engines roaring aggressively as it neared take-off speed. Then, as the mighty jets reached crescendo, the nose lifted, and the giant aircraft parted company with the runway, lifting gracefully into the sky. Within seconds the leviathan was engulfed in the pitch of night, its only visible trace, the red light flashing intermittently on the port-side wing.

Stewart took the mobile phone from his pocket. It was a cheap, durable and basic phone which could be thrown away if necessary. The memory was empty, as was the address book. Stewart knew the numbers he needed to dial and always erased the call list the moment he hung up. He glanced up at the night sky but had already lost sight of the Jakarta bound Airbus, which could by now be any of the myriad lights which glinted in the sky. He turned his attention back to the telephone's brightly-lit keypad and dialled the number from memory.

———

Donald McCullum looked up suddenly as the telephone rang beside him. The telephone was on a different circuit from those in the rest of the house and was dedicated to a secure number, coded and for work-related matters only. He sighed apprehensively, knowing that this telephone was usually the bearer of unwelcome news and often announced a crisis of some description. He folded his newspaper and dropped it dispassionately onto the desk, before reaching for the receiver.

"Hello, Donald McCullum speaking."

"Sir, this is Stewart. Just thought I'd let you know, King is on route."

McCullum leaned back in his comfortable leather chair and smiled. "Not suspicious, was he?"

"No, Sir," Stewart said. "He bought the whole affair on face value."

"Jolly good," McCullum paused. "All right best get the operation underway. I want it coordinated precisely, all three offices hit simultaneously. You'd better get the men and resources to hand."

"Yes, Sir."

"And Stewart," McCullum paused. "You are batting for the right team, aren't you?"

"Of course, Sir."

"Glad to hear it." McCullum replaced the receiver on the cradle, then picked up his newspaper. He knew that he had ended the conversation abruptly, but he also knew how to keep his agents on their toes. It was all in Stewart's hands now, and soon King's damning security blanket and any potential hold over the Secret Intelligence Service would be only a frustrating memory.

CHAPTER SIXTY-ONE

Peter Stewart had put the order out to his teams to get in place to lift the information while King's Airbus was still climbing into the sky above London. He had a team in Norfolk and Hereford waiting. Pryce and Holmwood were staying at a hotel in Falmouth awaiting further instructions. He drove down the M3, A303, M5 and A30 meeting little traffic and had even managed to stop for light refreshment at Taunton. He arrived at the hotel at around midnight and loaded up on coffee while he briefed the two men. It was now approaching three in the morning as he watched the street intently. There had been no traffic for the past half hour and the last of the late-night revellers had dragged themselves off the streets, presumably to continue their weekend celebrations at private parties.

The weather was mild for the time of year, but the sea was icy cold, causing a barrage of thick sea mist which wafted eerily down the deserted streets and sprayed a continuous drizzle on the windscreen of the car relentlessly. Stewart glanced at his wristwatch, then turned around in his seat and stared at Pryce, who had spread himself across the back seat and seemed to be asleep. "Wake up man!" he paused, shaking his head in exasperation. "We go in a few minutes."

"I was just resting my eyes," Pryce smiled.

"Whatever." Stewart took his mobile telephone from his jacket pocket, then opened the tiny notebook resting on the central console. He keyed in the digits, then waited for his call to be answered.

"Hello?" Came the calm reply.

"Mike, this is Stewart," he paused, double-checking his wristwatch against the digital clock on the dashboard. "We go in two minutes, that's zero three hundred Zulu..."

"Roger that, zero three hundred Zulu," the voice paused. "Anything else?"

"No, good luck." Stewart ended the call, then returned his eyes to the tiny notebook. He dialled another number and waited patiently.

"Hello?"

"Harrison, this is Stewart, everything set?"

"All set and ready for the word."

"Good. The word is *go,* the time, zero three hundred Zulu. Good luck." Stewart deleted both calls from the call list then switched off the mobile telephone and returned it to his jacket. He looked across at Holmwood in the driver's seat. "Ready?"

"As I ever am Boss," he paused. "Or ever will be."

"Good." Stewart looked down the street at the deserted building, then reached for the door handle. "Let's do it..."

CHAPTER SIXTY-TWO

Jakarta, Indonesia's capital, is like no other place on earth. The largest city in the southern hemisphere, it not only boasts the highest human population per square mile, but possibly the highest density of taxi drivers anywhere. Alex King had become acutely aware of this as he stood outside the airport terminal, desperately searching for his contact.

The humidity was almost intolerable, and within seconds of exiting the cool, air-conditioned building, he had become drenched in his own perspiration. Having visited Indonesia once before, he knew what doubtless lay ahead, but the reality of the stifling heat and the closeness of the air had been easily forgotten. He also knew that he would be hassled beyond belief, but the difference between the country's principality of Bali, which he had visited on the previous occasion, and the capital of Java was no comparison. The people took on an entirely more hostile, somewhat aggressive manner here and as he waited at the pre-arranged rendezvous point, it seemed that none of the taxi drivers, drug dealers or prostitutes could take no for an answer.

King continued to shake his head politely to every proposition, be it for a ride in a taxi, a trip, or ride of an entirely different nature, or the three combined, but as his brittle calm was tested to destruction, he adopted a more hostile manner. It was easy to see why many visitors to the country come to adopt a rude, arrogant manner towards the people, and it also became clear why the locals chose to hustle them so insistently. They were mostly poverty-stricken and no doubt desperate for the business. The whole situation had become counterproductive, with the locals hassling, the travellers retaliating, and such good will as there might once have been getting mown down in the crossfire.

He had become aware of a man to his right, who seemed to be loitering. He was tall for a native Indonesian, with hair held down either by gel or natural grease and styled backwards like a sixties rocker. His fashion sense displayed many features from the same era and looked laughably out of place here among mainly shorts and T-shirts.

As King looked at him the man turned his gaze away, a little too quickly for his liking. And now, as he observed his admirer, he was very much aware of the man's uneasiness. King looked away, returning his attention to the crowd to spot his contact. He could not afford to wait too long; either Abdul Tembarak would show, and he would have the help of a liaison officer, or he would have to make his own arrangements on a make-do-and-mend basis. He glanced at his watch, then continued to scan the crowd. It was ten-past eight, he would give his contact another ten minutes and then he would take care of matters on his own. It wouldn't be the first time...

———

Abdul Tembarak watched from his car, not daring to take his eyes off the westerner. His orders were clear, he was to assist him with whatever he needed and oversee the finer details of the mission. King would have the decision-making authority, but he was to make sure that the westerner's getaway went without a hitch, and that meant making the man's travel arrangements across to the island of Bali and supplying him with such equipment as he would require. Of course, there was also the second, parallel set of orders, which had been issued by General Soto, upon hearing of the audacious plan from Tembarak. The order was more forceful and offered a higher payment than the British could ever match. The scenario was almost risible. There was only one set of orders which he could follow, only one payment which he could realistically accept, and that payment was that his family would be allowed to live.

Abdul Tembarak studied the unsuspecting westerner and sighed deeply. He ached inside at the inevitability of the poor man's fate, but that ache panged more at the thought of his family. He had never killed before, nor would he, yet his actions would doubtless end the stranger's life. He reached for the door handle, breathing deep, calming breaths as he readied himself for what lay ahead. What was the price? What choice did he have? He did not even know the man, would never know him, yet the man's death would reunite him with his wife and son. It was no price to pay and Abdul resigned himself to the fact that he would be able to live with it.

———

King watched the sixties rocker with apparent indifference using his peripheral vision. Unsuspecting, the man continued to look at him. King turned and stared at him and was not surprised when the man averted his eyes and looked decidedly uncomfortable. It could have been innocent, merely a homosexual on the make, waiting until he received some tell-tale recognition signal, but the guy's 'gaydar' would have to be offset somewhat to home in on King. He did not convey an aura of homosexual orientation. Perhaps the man was marking him out to steal his wallet or his bag? But King was extremely physical. Tall, broad and strong looking. He also carried himself well, loosely. There were far softer targets on the pavement. He decided that there was more to the man and felt the need to test his theory.

He swung his sports bag over his shoulder and casually started towards the taxi rank, letting himself in for the tirade of shouts and propositions from the mass of people, all trying to lower the next person's bid. As he stood in the middle of the crowd, a clear head above all others, he turned around and looked for the sixties rocker, then smiled when he noticed him studying a group of young backpackers. The man clearly preferred the younger, blond surfer type. With the threat of the sixties rocker behind him, King walked to a nearby pillar and started to watch the crowd for his contact. Abdul Tembarak could have five more minutes, then King would cut the ties. If the man couldn't even get himself to a rendezvous within the required time frame, then King was not overly bothered about losing his liaison officer.

As King scanned the crowd again, he found a certain familiarity in one man and relaxed a little. He was thinner than he had been in his photograph, but weight is never the best feature to observe, it can go up and down so quickly that it's almost pointless noting it. Features are the key; bone structure, the nose, the mouth and the eyes. A lot could be gleaned from a person's eyes, and Abdul Tembarak was no exception. King studied the man's eyes, noting not only a great sadness, but also an extreme uneasiness. Neither had been apparent in the dossier photograph, but a great deal can often happen in a brief time. The man looked stressed, harassed.

Abdul Tembarak stepped forwards and held out his hand. "Mister King, I'm..."

"Forget it," King glanced around, then handed the man his bag. "Make out like you're a taxi driver. I don't want to draw attention to myself. You should have had my legend details sent to you. It's Anderson. Thomas Anderson. Don't use the name King again..." He thrust the bag into the man's hand, then beckoned him to lead the way. Tembarak dutifully followed the order and pushed his way through the manic crowd, turning around every so often to check that King was behind him. Once through, he stepped into the relatively uncrowded road.

The road at Jakarta International Airport separates the carpark from the terminal and with those few steps, the scene changes dramatically. The hordes of people, the uncertain travellers and the noise of incessant shouting and hassling become almost like distant memories.

King breathed a sigh of relief as his mind gratefully stopped buzzing enough for him to think normally. He quickened his pace and caught up with the Indonesian "A bit hectic, don't you think?"

"That is Jakarta, you will have to get used to it," he paused. "Did you have a good flight?"

King smiled. "We took off, flew and landed safely," he paused. "That's plenty good enough for me. What's wrong with your leg?"

Tembarak hesitated. "I slipped in the shower."

"Careless."

"It was soapy."

"What did you do? Crack the bone?"

"I'm not sure," the Indonesian said.

"Should get it looked at. That's quite a limp..."

Abdul Tembarak nodded, then pointed to a nearby Toyota Corolla. "This is my car."

King looked at the blue and yellow taxi and frowned. "I take it that this is a cover?" He smirked. "You don't moonlight on the company's time, do you?"

Tembarak laughed, although it sounded rather forced. He unlocked the driver's side, then reached behind the seat to unlock the rear door and motion towards it. "It's good cover. Best keep to the illusion, ride in the back until we are outside the airport, then I will stop, and you can sit in the front for the rest of the way."

King nodded. "Sounds good." He opened the rear door and dropped onto the seat, the air so hot and thick in the rear of the car that he felt he could touch it. Tembarak's cover was well thought out, perhaps he would be all right to work with after all. He relaxed as best he could against the headrest, willing the Indonesian to get the car started and the air conditioning on. He had already decided that Indonesia was not his favourite nation and the sooner he finished the assignment, the better.

Tembarak started the engine and the car coughed and spluttered for a few moments before resting into a noisy idle. He crunched the gearbox into first, then drove steadily out of the car park and into the one-way system, past the hordes at the terminal. Indonesia drives on the left so King did not feel uneasy at first, as he so often did when getting into a vehicle in another country. The roundabout was negotiated in the same manner, albeit with nobody giving way to anyone else, yet it still felt comforting to be instinctively aware of where the traffic was. He settled into his seat and closed his eyes, suddenly feeling tired. Flying from west to east always brings on jet lag and it was difficult to remember what time it was. The airline meals had already disrupted his body clock and he had found himself eating at all sorts of times and sleeping when he should have been eating. He was now eight hours ahead of Britain and would have to sort himself out if he was to operate effectively. A cold, refreshing shower should go a long way to reviving mind and body.

Tembarak eased the taxi to a halt and King opened his eyes, but too late. All three doors were open in a flash, and the pistol was pointed at him before he had time to react. Sixties Rocker smiled coldly at him from the front passenger seat, keeping the tiny Rohrbaugh R9 Stealth pocket pistol steady on the centre of his chest.

King cursed inwardly, but cooperated, easing himself into the middle of the rear seat, as the other two men slipped silently to either side of him.

CHAPTER SIXTY-THREE

The humidity was stifling, thick and oppressive. The air temperature was at least forty degrees centigrade and would undoubtedly get hotter as the day went on. The vehicle's windows were open, and a waft of warm air drifted into the rear of the car but did nothing to ease the heaviness around the inside of the vehicle.

King looked into the rear-view mirror and stared at the man behind the wheel. His features were like those of the photograph, and he had been sure that the man *was* Abdul Tembarak, although the man looked tired and stressed to the point of sickness, so why the double cross? There was bruising on his chin, a slight split in his lip and his left eye was swollen. Maybe that had something to do with it. King was certain of it. So much for slipping in the shower... He turned to the man on his left, who was heavily built and wore his black silk shirt unbuttoned to the waist. He was big for an Indonesian, at a shade under six feet tall and at least fourteen or fifteen stone in weight. The size of his muscular chest and six pack stomach showing through the open shirt were evidence that this man liked to work out with weights and was extremely strong. He also wore his sleeves rolled up high, his biceps treating everybody to a 'gun show'. The man to his right on the other hand was slightly built and wore a cheap-looking white linen suit with a black T-shirt. King guessed he'd seen the eighties TV show *Miami Vice*. He was half the size of his companion, yet King was more worried about him, or more accurately the knife which remained firmly in his hand, and occasionally reminded King of its presence by prodding into his side at every pothole.

Sixties Rocker, on the other hand, had settled comfortably into the passenger seat and gave brusque directions to Tembarak, who drove calmly through the light traffic. King could no longer see the passenger's pistol, but he knew that it would be close to hand. Any attempt to overpower his captors while the vehicle was on the move, would result in certain disaster.

King settled back into his seat and watched the road ahead. They were making timely progress, not that he knew their destination, but the speed which they were doing felt extremely rapid for the potholed road. It seemed that they would skid off the tarmac and crash into the irrigation ditches at every corner.

The airport lay approximately ten miles behind them and now that he knew that his captors were not going to do anything, at least until they stopped driving, King decided to chance talking for the first time. He looked at the man in the passenger seat, whom he guessed to be in charge. "Who are you?"

The man turned in his seat and scowled. "That is not of your concern," Sixties· Rocker replied in a thick Javanese accent. "If you know what is good for you, you will keep quiet." He pointed the tiny pistol at him and mouthed a silent 'bang' with his lips.

"Bullshit!" King snapped. "If you were going to do it yourself, you'd have done it by now. Where are you taking me?"

He felt a sharp jab in his side, as the tip of the knife eased through his shirt and threatened to break the skin. He turned to the smallest of the three, who smirked at him in return.

"My friend there wants to gut you like a pig." Sixties Rocker smiled menacingly at him. "If you continue to ask pointless questions, he will slice you into tiny pieces."

The little Indonesian in the cheap suit nodded enthusiastically, giving the knife a vicious little twist. King felt the needle-like point ease into his flesh but refrained from showing any emotion. Years of training and hardship had taught him to ignore all but the most agonising pain and calming respiratory techniques and martial arts meditation had further hardened his pain threshold.

Sixties Rocker looked at King's side and smiled as he saw a small stain of red soak through the man's shirt. "You are a real tough guy," he commented. "But General Soto can take that out of you as easily as the next man." He gave a sadistic little chuckle, then stared coldly at him. "He is not amused. He does not take kindly to westerners who come to assassinate him. He will make you pay, and he will make your government pay too."

King remained silent. So that was it, the security surrounding the whole operation had been breached, and he did not need three guesses to know *who* had double-crossed him. He looked into the rear-view mirror and stared coldly at the traitor behind the wheel.

Abdul Tembarak took his eyes off the road and glanced back at him momentarily. There was no emotion in the Indonesian's eyes, but he could not even attempt to hold King's stare and quickly looked away.

As with all roads in Indonesia, the further they drove from the city, the worse the road surface became. With the city and outer suburbs some twenty miles behind them, the road had become more of a track than anything else and it was a rough ride inside the humid vehicle, especially with his new-found companions sitting to either side of him. Oncoming overtaking vehicles, especially heavily laden trucks and buses drove with reckless abandon and Tembarak regularly took the car on to the scrub grass verge to avoid collision.

King watched the road intently, noting the road signs at every opportunity. There had been a few, mainly indicating speed limits, which every vehicle seemed to ignore, and a couple of small villages which had taken them no time at all to drive through. The next sign however, looked more promising; Karawang.

King concentrated hard, noting the corners and turnings, and the buildings which had started to appear more frequently on either side of the road. He stared down the road ahead, then noticed the sign for a railway station. The car slowed down considerably, then pulled into a small gravelled carpark and eased to a halt.

"You like to ride on trains, Mister King?" Sixties Rocker had turned around in his seat and was staring intently at him. "It will give you a chance to see our fine country before you meet General Soto. After that, your life will not be worth living, and you will beg for him to kill you," he paused, grinning sadistically. "*I* know, *I* have seen it before, on many occasions."

"I bet you got off on that," King smiled sardonically.

"Oh, I did!" he smiled. "And I will enjoy watching him make you scream."

King turned away, assessing his situation. The man to his right was not physically imposing, but he did have an extremely nasty looking knife. Sixties Rocker carried a pistol, which King had identified as a Rohrbaugh 9mm. The weapon was tiny but packed a punch and at this range nobody could miss. This determined the pecking order among the opposition. To date, the hulk beside him had not spoken, and had certainly not shown any signs of carrying a weapon. Nor, in fact, had Abdul Tembarak, who was sitting patiently behind the wheel as if awaiting orders.

King knew that it was just a matter of time, and the longer he left it, the closer they would get to their destination. He certainly wouldn't be able to attempt anything on a fast-moving train packed with passengers, and once he was inside the military base, he wouldn't be getting out.

He looked to his right and noticed the gathering of people on the station's dilapidated platform. They were waiting patiently, but unless there was a train arriving soon, it would make more sense for the people to wait inside the station, where the air conditioning would doubtless make the wait a little more comfortable. He breathed deeply a couple of times, filling his lungs with as much air as he could. A fight inside the vehicle would have to be quick and would certainly be frantic. This was not a pointless scrap outside a pub or nightclub, this was survival. Each blow would have to be landed with the utmost precision, and it would ultimately end in death; if not theirs, then his own. He had decided there was no way he would become a prisoner at the hands of General Soto.

He clenched both hands into tight fists for a second or two, then consciously tensed the muscles in both arms. This would make any blow more powerful, creating a harder weapon to strike with. He breathed in deeply again, then suddenly forced his right elbow back into the smaller man's throat. The man cried out silently through his crushed windpipe, dropping the knife and reaching up to his own throat as he found it impossible to breathe.

It was too late now, King had made his move and the only way to go was forward. He elbowed the larger man, catching him full in the face, then punched out at the man in the passenger seat. The blow was not as effective as he had hoped, and Sixties Rocker let out a cry of pain as he struggled to aim his weapon. King struck the man's forearm with his own, but King's forearm was heavily muscled and conditioned to martial arts blocking and striking. The man's forearm practically snapped like a piece of two by two and the pistol dropped out of his clasp as he let out wail in pain.

The large muscular Indonesian clutched at his broken nose, then came to his senses and flailed wildly at King. The vicious onslaught was hard to avoid, and King grit his teeth as the man rained blows on his face and the side of his head. He dodged as best he could, then saw an opening and went for it. He thrust out his hand, his fingers spread into prongs, which caught the man in both eyes. He cried out in agony, but King was already thrusting them deeper, cupping the back of the man's head with his other hand and pulling him onto his rigid outstretched fingers. King pushed and pulled at the same time until blood and a sticky, milky white fluid oozed out onto the back of his hand. The man's screaming was feral, animal-like. King pulled his hand free and aimed a savage punch into the middle of Sixties Rocker's face. The man's nose flattened, and King pushed forwards, caught hold of his head with both hands and twisted until the man's jaw jutted at an absurdly, impossibly upward angle, then snapped and his head flopped forwards. King was on to the large man again, this time chopping his throat repeatedly as the man continued to scream in agony and shock, holding his hands to both empty eye sockets. There was a crunching sound with each blow, and the big man went limp. Tembarak was struggling to remove his seatbelt and King hooked him in the ear with his left fist sending the man sprawling into the steering wheel. The smaller man was dying noisily in his seat, still unable to breathe. King picked up the knife from the foot well and pulled the man's head forward. He put the tip of the blade on the back of the man's neck, searched momentarily for the gap between vertebrae and jabbed the top of the handle with his other hand. The blade slipped in about an inch slicing the spinal cord and the man simply flopped and went silent. There was little blood, but King wiped the blade on the man's shoulder and turned his attention to Tembarak, who was stirring and holding the steering wheel with one hand and his thick and swelling ear with the other. King picked up Sixties Rocker's pistol and held it firmly against Abdul Tembarak's temple. "Stay still," he commanded breathlessly through gritted teeth. "One move and you're a dead man."

The Indonesian froze, closing his eyes in terror. The attack had been so swift, so violently decisive, he had barely time to react. He started to tremble, then took the chance and opened his eyes. "Please, don't kill me…"

"Why shouldn't I?" King transferred the pistol into his left hand, then caught hold of the dead man in the cheap suit and pulled him into the middle of the seat, before easing himself closer to the door. "Give me one good reason."

Tembarak shook his head. "I… I can't, I'm sorry I betrayed you!" He started to sob but stopped suddenly as King clipped him harshly on the side of the head with the muzzle of the pistol. "It's not like you think!" He wailed. "I had no choice!"

"Bollocks! There is always a choice," King paused. "You just made the wrong one, that's all."

Tembarak shook his head pleadingly. "They took me prisoner, they are holding my wife and son captive," he sobbed. "Who knows what they will do to them? They have already cut off one of her toes, I can't even think about it without feeling sick!" He shook his head. "They have violated her, molested her…" He cupped his head with his hands. "I'm so sorry. I was caught investigating him at the bank... They came for us in the night... My wife, my son... He let me go to report back to him. He had no idea I also help MI6 from time to time, when I was informed of you coming to do your job, well, it was like striking gold and oil all at once. I felt for sure he would repay me with letting my wife and child go..."

King looked up as a silver train thundered past them, then slowed suddenly for the platform, a squeal of brakes and sparks showering upwards from its wheels. He looked back at Tembarak and frowned. "Where is the train going?"

"To Yogyakarta," the Indonesian replied hesitantly.

"What time is the next one?"

Tembarak glanced at his watch, then looked at him in the rear-view mirror. "There is only one more today, and that is at seven o'clock tonight."

King quickly slipped the pistol into the waistband of his trousers and opened the door. "All right Tembarak, there's bugger-all time to waste sitting here," he paused, catching hold of him by the shoulder. "We're boarding that train."

"You're crazy!" He shook his head belligerently. "Soto's men will be at the station to meet us!"

"That they might, but maybe they'll have a long wait," he said. "There is more than one town between here and Yogyakarta. We can get off at another station." He shepherded the Indonesian across the carpark, then clenched his shoulder firmly. "Maybe you had a reason for setting me up." He glared at him menacingly. "But you have been given a second chance. A chance to redeem yourself and save your wife and child, like a man." He pulled his shirt tails out from the waistband of his trousers, to let them hang casually over the butt of the pistol, then released his grip on the man's shoulder as they neared the building. "However, I'm telling you one thing, Tembarak, cross me again and I'll kill you before you have chance to blink."

CHAPTER SIXTY-FOUR

The train's carriages were basic in design, with none of the creature comforts which Alex King was used to. He was not an experienced train traveller, taking the train occasionally from Paddington to Truro and occasionally on to Falmouth. More often than not he drove, much preferring the control and freedom it gave him. The handful of trains he had taken around the world could not compare to this. The seats were wooden slatted without tables. In fact, the only concession to modern comforts was a propeller fan at each end of the carriage, which took a little off the inside temperature. With the addition of the open windows, it was a lot less stifling than it had been inside the taxi, though still very humid.

Progress was slow, with the train travelling at a maximum of sixty miles per hour, with a seemingly endless series of stops along the way. These brought aboard a continuous stream of men and women trying to sell the passengers everything from bottled water to cigarette lighters which played a tune when the flame was lit. Every stop was identical to the last, and the products much the same.

At midday, with the heat and humidity approaching its

peak, King conceded and bought a large bottle of water and a packet of peanut brittle. After the woman had taken his money and bid him farewell and the train had started to move again, he noticed that the seal of the bottle had been broken, and the label was badly worn at the edges. Tembarak dutifully informed him that each bottle was subsequently collected by other traders and refilled from a tap in the station toilets, to be sold time and time again. With the heat doing its best to dehydrate him, King decided to risk drinking the tepid liquid, vowing that from now on, he would drink only from cans or shop-bought bottles. He bent forwards to pick up the bottle of water from between his feet, then looked at Tembarak once more. "So, they came for you in the night, and took you straight to the base at Yogyakarta?" he asked, pausing to unscrew the well-worn bottle cap. "How long were you there?"

"Three days, but it felt like a lifetime. There is great evil there. Like no place I could ever imagine. It is a base within our country's own military, yet it is separate, a place beyond control," said Tembarak. "My wife is still there. General Soto ordered a soldier to rape her, to get me to talk." He looked away, a lone tear trickling its way down his cheek. "I had no choice, I *had* to cooperate. I held off for as long as I could, but when they cut off her toe, I gave in completely. I'm sorry..."

King nodded understandingly. He had known the toughest of men crumple under interrogation, it was just one of those things. Once the captors have discovered your weakness, and everybody has one, they would exploit it to the full. He lifted the plastic bottle to his lips and drank some more of the water, then held it out for Tembarak. "Here, drink some."

Tembarak smiled gratefully and took hold of the bottle. "Thank you," he paused. "What happens to me now?"

King shrugged. "You're back on the right team now, aren't you?"

Tembarak nodded hastily. "Of course, I am! I want nothing more than for General Soto to take a bullet, but I had no choice, it was the only way that I could get my wife and child out safely."

"It wasn't, and it still isn't." King took the bottle from him and screwed the cap back on. "Soto knew that he would have you in his pocket, it's how the man's mind operates. When his men fail to show up at the station, he will not accept that you have double crossed him. He is a powerful and egotistical man. He will assume that there has been a minor hitch."

"But he will find out what happened eventually," Tembarak protested. "What will happen then? He will kill my wife and child for sure!"

"No, he won't," King replied. "He will hold on to them, because they are *still* a valuable bargaining chip, and he needs them alive to force you to spread disinformation back to your superiors at Intelligence." King set the bottle back on the floor and broke off a piece of the peanut brittle. He snapped it in two and handed a piece to Tembarak. "He fears an assassination attempt. So scared, that he met the threat head-on and sent a team to deal with it. That was his first mistake. He wanted to know more, he wanted to interrogate me and find out *everything*. He should have sent the team to eliminate the threat," King paused. "But now he has a problem. We have a distinct advantage. We are on the loose, we have surprise on our side, and we know where he is."

CHAPTER SIXTY-FIVE

The waiter flounced over to the table, a little too camp and with a little too much attitude for Charles Bryant's liking, but then he didn't have to like it. He didn't have to leave a tip either.

"Eggs Benedict?" The waiter hovered briefly, waiting for one of the men to answer and then lost patience before either of them could muster a response. "Full English with extra black pudding then?"

Bryant nodded. "Yes."

"Which?" The waiter asked tersely.

"The one you just said, full English with extra black pudding," he paused, glaring at the balding man in his thirties. "Sorry for the confusion..." The waiter nodded, graciously accepting his customer's apology. "It's just that I am used to dining in the type of establishment where it is the waiter's job to remember what the customer has ordered, not just move plates around," he paused, picking up his cutlery and studying a speck on the blade of the knife. "I understand that it must be very taxing on the mind; writing orders in a little book, walking out to the kitchen, then walking back into the restaurant, there must be so much to forget..." He glanced momentarily at the laminated menu card, then looked back at the flabbergasted waiter. "I'll have some milk please. To drink. So, it will need to go in a glass. And you'll find that the milk is the white stuff in the fridge, next to the butter..." He waved the man away and looked back to his companion. "Can't beat the stuff, I always make sure to drink some when I'm back in England, the UHT rubbish you get in Jakarta tastes like medicine."

"The milk here won't taste so good after he gets all the kitchen staff to spit in it."

Bryant looked shocked at the very idea. "You don't think he will, do you?"

"He might after you spoke to him like that," he paused.

Bryant shook his head. "Why on earth would they do that?"

The man smiled. "I don't know, maybe it could have something to do with you treating him like an amoeba. The man was busy, this isn't the bloody tropics, you can't speak to the waiters like that and not expect to get the sticky stuff at the back of their throat in your food..." He shook his head and smiled. "Sometimes, Charles, I think you have spent too much time in the third world." He picked up his fork and carefully broke the yolk of his lightly poached egg. "Frankly, it's beginning to show..."

"Nonsense!" Bryant exclaimed. "He just needed a kick up the backside, that's all." He looked up as the waiter walked out from the kitchen carrying a lone glass of milk on a small stainless-steel salver. The man was in his mid-thirties and slightly pear-shaped, with womanly hips. Bryant watched him, wondering how well-founded Sandy's comment was about spitting in his glass. "Anyway, I'm not always in the third world. I spend half my time in Texas and Louisiana. And Aberdeen..."

"I rest my case..." Sandy smirked.

"Here you are, Sir," the waiter paused, forcing a smile to his lips. "Will there be anything else?"

Bryant did not look at him, but simply shook his head and returned to his breakfast. "I don't know about a kick up the backside," he remarked to his companion. "But he's probably had something up there recently! What a fag..."

Sandy screwed his face *up* in disgust. "Oh, for Christ's sake, Charles, leave the poor fellow alone!" He dipped a piece of toast into the soft yolk, then smeared it lavishly with hollandaise sauce, before taking a mouthful. "If the dear fellow wants to do some shirt-lifting, leave him to it. He's not hurting you, is he?"

Bryant shovelled a large piece of black pudding into his mouth and stared at his friend in surprise. "That's awfully *lefty* of you, Sands," he smiled wryly. "I remember you teaching that queer a lesson with the handle of your cricket bat when he brushed against you in the showers. Oh, what was his name? Asher... Ashworth? Something like that. Didn't half struggle! You taught him good and proper! What did it take, four, five of us to hold the little bum-boy down? God, I didn't think you'd ever get the handle in! Priceless! Must say, did you ever wash the handle? Can't say I'd have liked to bat with it after that!"

"Ashdown," Sandy commented flatly. "And that was a long time ago..."

"That was it! Ashdown!" Bryant smiled. *"Never take your pants down in front of Ashdown!"* He chanted loudly, much to his companion's embarrassment. "Marvellous fun! It was just after we whipped Harrow for the cup. Gosh those were the days!" He stabbed another piece of black pudding with his fork, then thrust it voraciously into his mouth.

Sandy forced a smile, not so keen to remember the incident. He watched Bryant chew his black pudding, then pulled a face of distaste. "I really don't know how you can put that stuff in your mouth," he paused, delicately smothering another piece of toast with warm hollandaise. "For God's sake, it's dried pig's blood!"

"Amongst other things, old chap," Bryant smiled. "That egg you're eating isn't so damn great, it entered this world out of a chicken's arsehole you know!"

The man smiled, then casually reached into the inside pocket of his well-tailored, Savile Row suit jacket and took out a plain brown envelope. "Here, take this." He passed it casually across the table and smiled. "Just a photograph of our man. His legend details are on the back. He entered the country under the name Thomas Anderson." he paused. "I take it you're flying back to Java? Our man is already there."

Bryant smiled wryly. "All in hand, old chap, all in hand." He waved breezily. "I'll take a picture of it on my iPhone and email it to my Indonesian contact. After that, it's all up to him. He is making the necessary arrangements."

"But he will make sure that our man never gets back onto an airplane?" Sandy looked at him warily. "It's non-negotiable Charles, those were the terms. He doesn't leave Indonesia alive..."

"Indeed," Bryant nodded emphatically. "He's dead. He's a doornail, he just doesn't know it yet," he paused. "I have half your payment with me." He bent down and patted the leather briefcase beside him. "Two hundred and fifty thousand pounds, as agreed. The other half will be paid when I hear confirmation of General Soto's assassination."

"Of course, perfectly acceptable," Sandy smiled. "American Dollars?"

"It's dollars, euros and sterling. I drew it out this side." He bent down and casually slid the briefcase towards his companion. "Here, keep it. Take it to work afterwards, it's from *Aspinal*. Jolly smart for the office. My mistress bought it for me last Christmas, I've been trying to lose it ever since. I thought it would suit your· image better than a plastic carrier bag."

"I'm glad of the vote of confidence!" Sandy chuckled, then looked at Bryant seriously. "Don't let your contact underestimate Alex King."

"What do you mean?"

"Not just anyone would have the skills to go after a man like Soto. Let alone do the job. We're talking about an army general, surrounded by military personnel and a following that would support him as leader, or at least as instigator of a military coup. But if it can be done, King will do it. Your contact can't just hire some thug and hope King is taken out of the picture. He will have to be utterly surprised and overwhelmed."

"Oh, I think he will get enough people."

"Just remember..." Sandy looked coldly at Bryant. "A wolf is a wolf and no amount of sheep will bring one down..."

CHAPTER SIXTY-SIX

The uniformed steward made his way slowly along the aisle, stepping over the outstretched bodies of the people who had decided to sleep on the hard-wooden floor. King watched him, slightly bemused at the scene, but then again, this *was* Indonesia; if the people wanted to sleep, then they simply took to the floor and slept. Life really was that simple.

The steward looked at the seat number as he drew near, then cross-checked his reference card accordingly before handing them the two white plates heaped with steaming fried rice and topped with a fried egg. "Nasi Goreng?" he asked, apparently uncertain of their choice. Abdul Tembarak nodded eagerly and took one of the plates from him, then sniffed the pungent aroma of the fried rice before shovelling a huge quantity onto his spoon. King, a little less excited about the prospect of eating food cooked aboard the train, thanked the steward as he took the plate, then eyed the food warily.

"Is there something wrong?" Tembarak asked, losing some rice out of the corner of his mouth as he went on chewing. "You do not look pleased..."

King wiped the tarnished fork on his trouser leg, then

dipped it into the greasy-looking rice. "No, I'm not familiar with Indonesian cooking, that's all."

Tembarak finished his mouthful and smiled. "Let me familiarise you then." He pointed to a small parcel in the centre of the plate, which appeared to have been made from a dark green leaf of some kind. "That is steamed rice, wrapped in banana leaf. It is steamed for two or three hours and turns sweet as a result." He cut his own parcel open with his spoon, then poked at the solid block of rice. "It looks like boiled potato, no?" He smiled, then pointed at a pool of white sauce on the edge of King's plate. "That is creamed coconut. Next to that are sliced chilies fried in peanut oil, and the meat is probably chicken..."

King stared at the tiny bone, unfamiliar with both the size and shape, then frowned as he looked back at the Indonesian. "Probably?" he enquired uneasily.

"Probably," he reassured him. "The rice, the actual Nasi Goreng, is fried rice, with chilies, peanuts and spices and a few drops of fish sauce and soy sauce," he paused. "Oh, and Catsup."

"Catsup?"

"Yes, it's a thick soy sauce," he smiled. "Much thicker than the other types they use in the rest of Asia."

King nodded, then dubiously dipped his spoon into the rice and took his first mouthful. The rice was moist, and full of flavour, but there was a background taste of burnt nuts, which he was unsure of. Either it was part of the dish, or the chef had burnt the oil. Either way, Tembarak seemed to enjoy the offering, so King thought it best not to ask and simply took a mouthful of what was familiar; the fried egg which topped the mound of fried rice.

"You like?"

King decided that the food was the product of a basic, somewhat unimaginative cuisine. Fiery from the abundant chilies, and smothered with garlic, yet lacking in true layers of flavour, infinitely inferior to Thai, Malaysian or Chinese food. King was no gourmet or foodie snob, but he spent a lot of time abroad and generally ate the traditional food of that country. When he was staying in hotels on the company money, he experimented with the best dishes available. It had become a sort of game to amuse himself by. He looked across at Tembarak and nodded all the same, there was no point in offending the man who was here to help him. "Yes, it's very good." He cut off another piece of egg with his spoon, then scooped up a few pieces of chopped green beans. Only when he started chewing did he realise that the beans were in fact tiny green chilies. "Oh, dear God!" He picked up the bottle of water and drank most of it. His mouth burned and his eyes watered. His eyes seemed to have trouble focusing. "What was that?"

"Ah, bird's eye chilies," Tembarak smiled. "Very hot..."

"No shit," King looked down at the man's plate, surprised to see that he had almost finished. "Hungry?"

Tembarak replaced his spoon on the plate and picked up the highly dubious piece of chicken. "I haven't eaten since yesterday morning." He glanced down at the food on King's plate, then looked back at him. "Soto has cut off my funds, he's paying me an allowance, expenses only. But it's nothing..."

King passed the man his plate. "Here, have this," he paused. "My body doesn't think it's mealtime yet." He watched as Tembarak tucked hungrily into the food. "Of course, General Soto has cut off your funds. He wants to control you in every way that he can. He not only holds your wife and child as bargaining chips, he holds your wallet. In fact, the man owns you entirely..."

"Not any longer," Tembarak paused while he finished the mouthful of steamed rice. "He holds my wife and child, yes. But he does not own *me*. I am going to do everything to see that you succeed in your mission. Strap a bomb to me and I'll give the bastard a hug..."

King patted the man on the shoulder, then drank more water. His eyesight was back to normal, even if his mouth wasn't. "I'll do my best to see that your wife and child get out safely." He unscrewed the cap and took a tepid sip. "What we need is a plan."

"Well, obviously."

King smiled wryly. "All right," he watched the Indonesian scoop another prize-winning spoonful of fried rice. "Start at the beginning again. What do you remember of the military compound?"

CHAPTER SIXTY-SEVEN

Despite its appearance on the map, the island state of Java has no straight roads or railway lines. This fact is most evident between Bandung and Tasilanalaya, where the track twists and weaves its way through and around rainforest, mountainous regions and vast areas of swampland. However, as the track emerges from the wilds of deepest Java, the obstructions become even more apparent, with huge bends and many lesser diversions, to avoid the broad latifundium of rice paddy and in the higher and cooler regions, tea plantations.

The train lurched and bounced over the uneven track, but most of the people sleeping or resting haphazardly stretched on the floor to take advantage of the cool lengths of timber board and the occasional strip of linoleum, seemed oblivious to the discomfort. These people had paid a premium for the privilege of travelling in the spacious carriage. This was First Class, and First Class meant there was more space on the floor.

Alex King looked at his watch, then peered out of the window. The scene had remained unchanged for the past hour, with nothing but the seemingly endless expanse of flooded rice paddy, with the occasional strip of rainforest to break the monotony.

He glanced at Tembarak, who like every Indonesian, seemed to possess the ability to sleep when and wherever he wanted. The man had held his eyes firmly closed for the past hour and despite the carriage's voracious humidity and nauseous instability on the rickety track, had uttered not so much as a murmur. King nudged his arm, but he remained insensible. After several attempts he decided to leave him be. He rose unsteadily from his hard seat and carefully aimed his first step between the bodies of a young man and woman, then found a steadier footing with his second step, between the legs of another sleeping woman. Progress was slow; with so many recumbent people in the cluttered aisle, every step must be carefully taken to avoid crashing to the floor. King smiled at the thought; at least he would have something soft to break his fall. It was hard to imagine a similar scene on a British train - for that matter, it was hard to imagine a similar scene on a train anywhere else in the world, but as so often transpires when travelling in Indonesia, he was discovering that the place was truly unique.

For reasons best known to the train's conductor and two stewards, the adjoining carriage was deserted. The rows of hard-backed seats were empty and without a single person spread out on the floor, King quickly made his way through to the next section. The door was a stable type, which seemed a poor choice for a train; but then again, this *was* Indonesia. He rested his elbows on the bottom section and took advantage of the splendid, if somewhat over-familiar view. After the last hour King had decided that, though the fields were the product of the ancient and highly sophisti-cated science of irrigation, they possessed only so much visual appeal. As far as he was concerned; enough was enough.

As the train slowly trundled through the endless paddy, King watched the women working up to their thighs in the muddy water. Each wore a huge wicker basket on their back, which they slowly filled with their pickings. It looked like terrible work. He imagined sores and cuts becoming infected in the muddy water, which he'd read somewhere, were also full of rats and snakes, as well as eels, carp and perch which were added to provide the workers with a sustainable lunch.

King's thoughts were suddenly broken by a surge in the train's momentum and a dramatic tilting of the carriage. He pressed himself back from the door, feeling the force of inertia threaten to topple him over the door and out of the train completely. He braced his shoulder against the side of the carriage, expecting the train to derail at any moment. As the brakes squealed against the track, King glanced out of the nearby window and stared aghast at the sight beside the railway tracks. There, half on the embankment and half submerged in the flooded irrigation ditch, the remains of three wrecked train carriages lay strewn on their sides, large piles of gravel pushed up around them where they had slid along the sidings on their sides. King looked at the embankment, then noticed to his horror that there was a line of rotting corpses spread out, uncovered. Twisted, burnt and dismembered, they had been casually left to rot by the track. A flock of crows were picking at them, fighting one another for the best pickings. King shook his head in disbelief, then stared at the next horror. Beside the broken carriages, children played happily among the scattered debris. King turned around, sickened by the sight. He had seen such things in Afghanistan and Iraq, in Syria and Libya. Bodies were a regular sight in places like that. Many were booby trapped with IEDs so left well alone by the people living there. But Indonesia was not a country at war. Not in Java at least. There were places like Sumatra and East Timor where there were terrorist activities and civil unrest, but the country was not a war zone. How could something like this not have been dealt with? He stepped away from the window, then noticed the young steward walking down the aisle to the occupied carriages. The steward stared at him, apparently outraged to find him in the empty carriage.

King stared back, then pointed towards the scene on the embankment. "Why haven't the bodies been cleared from the crash?" The steward shrugged, apparently unconcerned and attempted to continue on his way. King grabbed the man by the shoulder. "Do you speak English?"

The steward nodded. "A little," he paused. "I very busy, I have to go."

"No." King tightened his grip and pulled the man towards the open door. "Look at that. Why hasn't somebody cleared the bodies away?"

The man shrugged. "Why you ask me? I work on train. I not do it." He pulled away from King's grasp but remained where he was. "Soldiers help the people who live, then they go. Nobody can help the dead. People come soon from government and move bodies. Next week."

King shook his head but said no more. There was nothing *to* say, the steward had said it all. King pushed past the young man and walked back towards the packed carriage. There was only one thing on his mind now; the sooner he could kill General Soto and get the hell out of Indonesia, the better.

CHAPTER SIXTY-EIGHT

Junus Kutu stepped into the blissful relief of the air-conditioned study and walked decisively over to the Chippendale sideboard. He placed the frosted glass of ice on a leather coaster, the outside of the glass dripping beads of condensation already. The day was oppressively hot, and the forecast showed little respite. He was used to varying temperatures now, it came with business meetings in expensive restaurants or international offices, luxury cars with fridge air conditioning. He was now far removed from his family's fishing hut where he grew up sleeping on hammocks made from fishing nets and the tin roof, which although thankfully water-tight, heated the hut like an oven by day.

Kutu opened the double glass doors, then paused as he noticed that a strip of rosewood veneer had started to peel at the edges of the sideboard. He shook his head regretfully and reached for the bottle of vodka.

He had purchased the teak and mahogany piece from one of Charles Bryant's contacts. He had been given the web address of the detailed site and had been at great pains to choose a piece of furniture which would complement his teak panelled study but would also proclaim both his opulence and his taste. What he had not known when purchasing such a period piece, was that within a matter of months, Indonesia's voracious humidity would age and devalue something which had merely mellowed under the gentle impact of over three centuries in England. The rosewood veneer, the satinwood beading and inlays, and the teak surrounds had almost parted company entirely with the mahogany structure, and the detailed marquetry of garden flowers and climbing ivy, embossed onto the sides, had bubbled and peeled, reducing the piece to a value which Junus Kutu quite happily carried in his back pocket.

He opened the vodka and poured a generous measure into the silver cocktail shaker, before reaching for a bottle of dry vermouth and adding a similar quantity. Kutu prided himself on his cocktail making skills and took the art very seriously indeed. He reached into the cabinet for the jar of green olives, then picked up the bottle of gin, and added a dash to the concoction. With one olive crushed and dropped casually into the cocktail shaker, and another placed in the tall glass, only the friction remained to blend and emulsify the ingredients perfectly. He screwed the lid down tightly and shook the mixture vigorously. Satisfied that the vodka martini had been expertly prepared, he opened the lid and poured the contents over a large pile of roughly crushed ice.

———

The snake's tongue flicked in and out of its mouth, tasting the air around it, feeling the presence of another being nearby. It paused, its head held perfectly motionless as it weighed up its options. The forked tongue flicked again, and the sinister looking oval eyes of the viper reflected in the bright sun as it concentrated on the potential threat.

Malik remained still as he watched the venomous snake flick its tongue just inches away from his face. He knew that the chances of being bitten were low if he remained still. The snake knew where he was and was probably scared too. The stand-off had begun.

Sweat trickled down his brow in rivulets and the salt stung at his eyes, but still he did not move. There was nothing he could do; one movement, and the snake would most probably strike. The viper's fangs would lance through his flesh and release a deadly measure of venom. His heart would slow considerably, his breathing would become laboured and the venom would start to dissolve his internal organs long before he lost consciousness. He would become disorientated, and the trek through the dense rainforest undergrowth would prove impossible. He would collapse to the ground, and slowly suffocate as the venom shut down his nervous system. The snake flicked its tongue again then moved its head to one side. Malik tensed involuntarily, and the snake coiled. There was no hiss, no baring of fangs, it simply eased itself backwards, then flashed back into the undergrowth.

The scruffy Indonesian let out a deep sigh and dropped his head to the ground in relief. He had been lying on his stomach, outstretched and his neck was aching from having to remain held back from the snake for so long. He raised his head from the damp earth then rubbed the sweat and mud away, circled his head a few times to relieve his neck before placing his eyes back to the rubber eyepieces of the binoculars. His heart pounded from the surge of adrenaline and before he caught sight of Junus Kutu, he felt the sudden powerful urge to vomit, which he barely suppressed by swallowing hard. He took a deep, calming breath, then raised the binoculars to his eyes once more.

———

Junus Kutu leaned back in the comfortable leather swivel chair and stared at the screen in front of him. He took a large mouthful of his drink, then rested the glass lazily on the armrest as he continued to stare at the image on the tiny screen of the laptop. The picture was of a man whose features were strong. Once seen, easily remembered. Kutu thought that odd for a man in his line of work. There was a distinct sadness in the steely grey-blue eyes and what Kutu could only think of as a cruel looking mouth. The man was ruggedly handsome, with a strong jaw-line and a pugilist's brow and his wide chest tapered towards a narrow waist, indicating that he was both strong and fit.

Kutu moved his finger across the mousepad and saved the picture before opening his email folder. He looked at his watch. It was about time. His contact knew the message would be sent soon. He leaned forwards, placed his drink on a coaster beside the laptop and started to type his message.

THE TRANSACTION DATE IS NEAR. YOUR SERVICES ARE REQUIRED IMMEDIATELY. I HAVE THE RELEVANT DETAILS FOR YOUR ATTENTION. AWAITING YOUR REPLY. K

He then directed the cursor into the send mail box and double clicked the left mouse button. Kutu picked up the glass and drained the contents in two large mouthfuls.

————

Malik watched the ground cautiously as he walked through the thick undergrowth. His mind had started to plague him with paranoia; every stick or twig became a poisonous viper, and every patch of earth, a spider or a scorpion. The tiny hairs on the back of his neck stood up and tingled, and every recollection of his encounter with the snake sent a shiver down to the base of his spine.

He stepped over some loose branches and was relieved as the undergrowth started to give way to brushy scrubland, and rice paddy appeared in the distance.

The car was parked on the side of the road, beyond the scrubland. It was a car which he could only ever own in his wildest, most unrealistic dreams. A Jaguar XJ, with everything that the Indonesian had always wanted. A big supercharged engine, air conditioning, sumptuous leather and a whole host of optional extras and in car entertainment. It cost more than he would earn in a dozen lifetimes, yet the owner purchased a new one, or something similar every year.

He eyed the irrigation ditch warily, knowing full well that such obstacles were always a favourite haunt for a host of snakes, especially in the afternoon heat. Even snakes had to drink sometime, but they fed mainly on the water rats or occasional careless fish feeding at the surface. Satisfied that it was safe, albeit after several shivers down his spine, he took a long stride to the short grass verge.

He watched the man who owned the Jaguar as he approached the car. The windows were closed so that the air conditioning could work more effectively and from the incessant thudding which came from within, he could tell that the car's owner was putting the two-thousand-watt music system through its paces.

The electric window lowered as he drew near and a sudden blast of eighties New Romantic burst into the outside world. The beat suddenly quietened as the man adjusted the volume and stuck his head out of the window. "Is he there?"

"Yes," Malik paused. "He's working on his computer."

With his habitual gesture the effeminate looking man

adjusted his tie, then smiled. "Good, once again, you have earned your money." He eyed him dubiously, then reached inside his jacket pocket and took out a small brown envelope. "Here," he paused. "Take it, you've earned it. Don't spend it in cheap brothels on cheap whores, save it and make something of yourself."

Malik stepped forward and took the envelope from the man's grasp. He opened it, peered inside and then tapped the envelope nervously with his fingertips. "I should have more," he paused. "I have helped you a great deal. I know many things..."

The effeminate looking man was silent for a moment. He eyed the scruffy Indonesian with indifference, then smiled. "Yes," he said. "Yes, you are right. You have been a great asset. I shall give you another hundred dollars when we get back to my office."

"Five."

"What?"

"Five hundred," the scruffy little man smoothed his hand over the roof of the Jaguar. "Maybe I can buy one of these one day. With more jobs from you..."

The effeminate looking man smiled. "Of course." He closed the window and opened the door, got out into the blistering heat. "You can stay to help me though, we'll add it to your considerable fee..."

———

PLEASED TO HEAR THAT YOU ARE READY FOR TRANSACTION. CREDIT CARD PAYMENT WILL GO OUT UNDER 'TRANS. OPTIMUM BUSINESS SERVICES, KUTA OFFICE, BALI' SEND CREDIT CARD DETAILS AND PHOTOGRAPH IMMEDIATELY. GOOD LUCK WITH YOUR OTHER PROJECT.

T.O.

Junus Kutu smiled at the email, then deleted the message and set about typing his reply. He had used the services of Trans. Optimum before, and was on friendly, occasionally social terms with the rather brash Australian and South African duo who owned and ran the company. Essentially private investigators, David Ross and Bernard Ottowi had set up business in the Indonesian archipelago some ten years before, and operated a highly lucrative, though somewhat dubious security operation. Trans. Optimum assisted businesses over their less reputable problems, which so often arose in Indonesia. Mainly, the company provided security, close protection and intelligence gathering. They also worked as muscle for large mineral excavation and mining companies bringing work disputes to an end far more quickly than negotiations ever could. Junus Kutu had used the company on several occasions and although they wanted nothing to do with the General Soto affair personally, reasoning that a hit on such a notorious figure would be outside their own remit, their skill set and far too close to home, they *had* agreed to keep the matter to themselves. Furthermore, they had agreed to source a few individuals who would jump at the chance of dispensing of the assassin afterwards. Trans. Optimum's services would not come cheap, but good help never did.

Having typed his credit card number into the box Trans. Optimum provided, he opened the relevant folder on the menu and the British MI6 agent's photograph appeared on the tiny screen. He attached the photo and typed out the documented description of Alex King from the original email. He copied in all the details of King's exfiltration that he had, then sent the email by way of return.

He stood up and walked over to the sideboard, fixed

another martini and took a sip as he walked back to the desk. His heart pounded at the enormity of it all. He had never killed anyone before and had certainly never paid somebody else to do so either, yet in the past few days, he had not only arranged the death of a prominent Indonesian figure but had just paid for the death of the very man who was about to help the nation he loved. The British assassin should have been hailed a hero if he was successful, instead, he had just signed the man's death warrant. He raised the cocktail to his lips again and drained the icy remnants in one huge gulp. He felt a little lightheaded as he set the glass back on the leather coaster. When he looked back at the screen, he noticed the mail folder flash in the top left-hand corner. He opened the email.

YOUR PAYMENT AND DETAILS HAVE BEEN ACCEPTED. TRANSACTION PROCESS COMPLETE. YOU WILL RECEIVE POSITIVE CONFIRMATION WHEN BUSINESS CONTRACT HAS BEEN COMPLETED.

T.O.

Junus Kutu's heart fluttered. The deal had been completed, there was no going back now. With the press of a button, he had sentenced a stranger to death. Strangely, he found the experience exhilarating.

He deleted all the emails, the document and photograph, then shut down the laptop and sat back in his chair. He looked out across his lawns and the rice paddies beyond. He saw a flash of light beyond the paddies from the bush and scrubland in the distance. It was the last thing he saw as the 7.62mm bullet travelled through the open French doors and

penetrated the centre of his forehead. The bullet had travelled in an arc and was on a downward trajectory. The biggest
percentage of its energy had been dissipated but as it travelled through Kutu's skull, brain and brain stem and through
the Chippendale sideboard and into the wall behind, it still
managed five hundred feet per second. Kutu kicked out both
feet in reflex to the sudden shutdown to his nervous system
and his chin slumped to his chest.

————

He kept the 3.5 x 60 wide-angle scope trained on the lifeless
figure behind the desk, keeping his right eye concentrated as
he readjusted his aim, compensating for the rifle's savage
recoil. He had seen Junus Kutu slump in his chair and knew
from experience that with a head shot from a high velocity
bullet, the victim always slumps lifelessly and never threw
itself wildly across the room as depicted on the screen.

He knew that the shot had been clean, and even at the
distance of approximately seven hundred metres, the 7.62mm
bullet would have hit with more force than any mainstream
handgun fired at point-blank range.

"Good shot!" Malik exclaimed excitedly. He took the
binoculars from his eyes and let them hang loosely from his
neck by the plastic strap. "Is he dead?"

The effeminate looking man nodded as he released the
magazine and ejected the chambered round. The SLR magazine held twenty, but he had only loaded it with three. He was
confident in his abilities and the scenario. He pushed himself
easily to his feet and dusted the loose pieces of earth and
foliage off his neatly pressed cotton suit. He had laid out a
ground sheet to protect his suit the best he could. He
reached out a hand and clicked his fingers for the binoculars.
"Here, let me see."

Malik caught hold of the strap and hooked it over his head, then held them out for him. He snatched the field glasses from the tiny Indonesian and raised them to his eyes.

There was no movement from the study, but the gardener was already walking around the terraced gardens, alerted by the sound of the gunshot. He was looking right at them but would not see them from their position ten feet back in the bush. The gardener was looking puzzled and then he turned and walked up the steps towards Kutu's study.

The effeminate looking man kept the study window in the wide-angle lens of the binoculars, then smiled as a distraught looking woman came running into the room. He turned to Malik and chuckled. "The maid is going to earn her money cleaning today!" he paused. "Be a good man and put the rifle back in the case. While you're down there you can fold up the sheet." He pointed to the customised match grade semi-auto FN SLR rifle on the ground, then kicked the leather carrying case a little closer.

The scruffy looking Indonesian did as he was ordered and bent down next to the high-powered rifle. "What happens now?" he paused as he carefully slipped the weapon inside, mindful not to touch the sights. "General Soto will promote you for sure."

"That he will," the effeminate looking man grinned as he carefully took the Walther PPK out of his jacket pocket. "He will probably make me a Colonel, maybe head of military intelligence operations..." He smiled, as he sighted the tiny pistol at the back of the man's head, and patiently waited for him to finish folding the groundsheet.

CHAPTER SIXTY-NINE

Alex King stared at the office of the car hire firm in disbelief, then turned slowly towards Abdul Tembarak with a raised eyebrow. "I thought you said this was a car hire company?" he said, his tone sarcastic. "You're not serious, are you?"

Tembarak shrugged. "We can hire vehicles here, what more do you want?"

King shook his head and slung his sports bag over his shoulder. "All right, you wait here, out of sight. If we're not seen together, then it will create less of a trail for General Soto when he finds out that three of his men didn't make the train," he paused, still looking at the building with trepidation. "I'll go and play the dumb tourist."

The building, if it could be honestly described as such, consisted of three bamboo walls, which had been woven into a fine mesh-like construction, and a palm thatch roof which, judging by its numerous tiny holes, served as a refuge for a host of small birds or large rodents. The building's entrance was simply a gap, where the builders had regarded a fourth wall as unnecessary.

The Indonesian man reclining against the back wall, his

legs crossed and resting upon the desk, eyed King curiously as he approached. He smoked a pungent smelling home rolled cigarette and made no effort to move, and by the look of the cigarette resting in one corner of his mouth, threatening to discard an inch-long plume of ash into his lap at any moment, King guessed that he had made no effort to move for quite some time.

King smiled politely as he reached the open fronted entrance, but still the man made no effort to greet the potential customer. "Hello," he said amiably. "Do you have any vehicles for hire?"

The man sighed deeply, then with significant effort, lifted a hand from his lap, took the cigarette out of his mouth and tapped it with his fingertip, sending the ash cascading to disintegrate on contact with the dry earth floor. "Depends..." the man smiled.

"On what?" King asked, his impatience growing suddenly.

The Indonesian shrugged, then took a long drag on the pungent cigarette. "On what you want."

"What have you got?"

The man smiled. "Whatever you need..."

King stared coldly at the man, then reached into his pocket and took out a wad of US dollars. Indonesian rupiahs were so low in denomination that he could have been a millionaire several times over and hold little hope of closing his wallet with basic expenses. He often found dollars were the best currency throughout the world, easily changeable and readily accepted. "I want a vehicle." He started to thumb through the thick wedge of notes, then stopped and smiled at him. "Now, do I get a vehicle from here? Or do I get a taxi into Yogyakarta and hire one from there?"

The Indonesian slid his feet off the desk, then stood up and beckoned King into his 'office', smiling profusely and offering him a seat. "Please, come in." He pulled a wooden chair out from the rickety looking desk and wiped the dust and dirt away with the edge of his hand. "We can do business. What would you like? A scooter? No, you look like the sort of man who likes to ride a motorbike..."

"I need a car," King paused, ignoring the proffered chair. "I am meeting some friends in Semarang, but want to do some sight-seeing along the way," he lied easily.

King had remembered the town of Semarang from the tourist map on the back cover of the in-flight magazine on the airplane. He had noted its position and remembered that it was indeed well north of Yogyakarta, on the northern coast of Central Java. Should General Soto initiate a search for Tembarak and himself, the testimony of this Indonesian might serve as a suitable diversion.

The man looked at him dubiously, then his expression changed to one of concern. "Where you go from Semarang?"

King frowned. "I'm not sure yet." He concentrated hard, desperately trying to remember the names and places on the basic map. "One of my friends is flying on to Lombok, we are taking him to the airport at Surakarta."

"Ah," the man nodded. "You come back here after?"

"Yes," King paused. "We may go into Yogyakarta, one of my friends is interested in silver and jewellery. I understand there is a major silver industry in Yogyakarta?"

The man shrugged, uninterested. He reached into one of the drawers behind the desk, then looked at a small chart. "I have two cars available, a Toyota Corolla or a Ford Focus," he thought for a moment, then smiled. "You need a jeep. A four by four."

King shrugged. "Why?"

"The roads are very steep and in poor condition and at this time of year there are many floods," he paused. "The roads to Semarang go through some of the highest mountains in all of Java."

King nodded, keeping up the charade. "I see. Well, a four by four it is then." He looked down at the man's chart. "Do you have something suitable?"

The man nodded, then looked concerned once more. "The roads through the mountains are dangerous, you must not stray off the main highway."

King knew what the man meant by dangerous but decided to maintain his persona as an innocent tourist. "Is that to do with the flooding?"

The Indonesian chuckled out loud, then slapped him on the shoulder. "You have much to learn about Java, my friend!" He laughed raucously and although King knew full well what the man was driving at, he couldn't help but think that he was overdoing the drama. "You not have news in Australia?" the man laughed.

King smiled inwardly. Australians made up the majority of western tourists, so the man had assumed that was King's nationality. A bonus, another diversion for any potential inquiries. He looked at the man vacantly, then smiled. "Of course, we do, what are you referring to, mate?" His new-found Aussie accent was subtle, but passable, nevertheless.

"We have many bandits in Central Java, many people are killed for their money on the small roads," he paused, shaking his head sombrely. "Bandits block main roads, then attack the vehicles when they drive on the small roads. Many people killed every month…"

King nodded. "I'll be careful." He looked around, then stared at the man inquisitively. "If it is so dangerous, do you know of a place that will sell me a gun?"

The man remained silent for a moment or two, then smiled. "Guns are expensive, my friend…"

———

The boy could not have been any older than twelve, yet he drove the white Suzuki Vitara with ease, reversing it off the bumpy dirt road, until the rear of the vehicle rested just inches away from the building.

King stared at the vehicle in surprise. At the very least he expected to see a few dents and scratches, maybe even the deep impact marks of a major collision with another vehicle. It was a facelifted model and although King had no idea how to date it from the Indonesian license plates, it looked new to him.

He had paid a premium for the vehicle. It is customary practice in Indonesia for vehicle hire companies to hold a person's passport as a security on the vehicle. King could hardly show him a British citizen passport having already played along when the man had mistaken him for an Australian, which could only help to cover his tracks should General Soto initiate a search. He had told the Indonesian that he did not have his passport with him, spinning the man a story about losing his passport whilst travelling in Sumatra and his friends delivering a replacement to him in Semarang. The man had been dubious at first but had relented - at a price. Having swiped one of King's credit cards to take a Visa guarantee for damages, King was now about to drive the most expensive hire car in the whole Indonesian archipelago.

He stepped out of the office and round to the front of the medium sized off-roader and looked closely at the gleaming bodywork.

"Something wrong?" the Indonesian asked.

King turned back to him and smiled. "Not a thing," he paused. "It looks brand new."

"It is." The Indonesian slipped a cigarette between his thick lips, then lit it with a silver Zippo lighter. "You surprised, no?"

"I expected something a little older, that's all."

"You pay good price!" the Indonesian smirked. "For good price, you get our best car!"

King smiled then reached into his pocket and took out a wad of banknotes allowing the man to see just how much he was holding. "My friends are in Java on business. They will be carrying rather a lot of money, and they will be purchasing a lot of silver and precious gem stones," he paused. "You said that guns are expensive. You didn't say that they were impossible to buy..."

The man remained silent for a moment, then broke into a wry smile and took a long drag on his pungent cigarette. He blew out a huge cloud of smoke before speaking. "You reporter?"

King shook his head. "No, just a tourist. But my friends are going to do a great deal of business."

"You are a mercenary," he stated flatly. "You here to make money out of other people's misery..."

"No."

"Why you want gun then?"

"You told me that the mountains are dangerous, full of bandits who will kill and rob. You have me worried now." King held the man's stare but did not look harshly at him. "Other people have told me the same..." He passed the wad of notes over to his other hand, forcing the Indonesian to look down at the considerable sum. "I'm just a tourist, but I guess you could say that I will be guarding my friends as a favour to them, for bringing me a replacement passport from the consulate in Jakarta."

"You know how to use guns?"

King nodded. "Yes, I was in the Australian army for a while, and then I worked on a game reserve in South Africa, protecting rich tourists from bandits and thieves," he paused, changing the money to his other hand. "So, do you know where I can buy a gun, or not?"

The man watched the money, transfixed on the thickness of the wad. He rubbed his chin thoughtfully for a moment, then smiled. "Yeah, I know where you can buy a gun."

————

Abdul Tembarak watched Alex King get into the vehicle, then frowned as the Indonesian climbed into the passenger seat and pointed to his left, directing him away from the building. King drove the Suzuki off the worn grass verge and onto the narrow road, then gently accelerated along the bumpy dirt track, moving swiftly through the low ratio gearbox, until the vehicle was suddenly out of Tembarak's view.

Tembarak unexpectedly found himself at a loss. King was to hire the vehicle, then pick him up at the railway station. This, however, was not part of the plan. He had no idea of what action he should take, or whether he should take any at all. The Indonesian had been smiling and King had certainly seemed comfortable with the arrangement.

Tembarak glanced around then decided to wait as he had been instructed. The light was getting low, darkness was a mere twenty minutes away and very soon he would find himself fighting off the attack of a thousand flesh-hungry mosquitoes, intent on vying for his blood. He shivered at the thought, then settled back against the knee-high wall which skirted the station, deciding to give the British agent the benefit of the doubt. After all, he had nowhere else to go and he would surely stand a much better chance with the Englishman accompanying him than taking off on his own. Whichever way he looked at it he was a fugitive. The Indonesian Intelligence Service would never forgive him for taking the easy option and siding with General Soto, and the Indonesian General would be hunting him down for the deaths of his agents. MI6 would certainly think twice about using him in the future for setting up King at the airport. As Abdul Tembarak thought of all this, and of his imprisoned wife and child, he was suddenly very much aware that the future had never looked bleaker. He closed his eyes and took a deep breath, trying to make sense of it all and find a solution.

He flinched as the warm metal of the pistol's muzzle pressed hard against the nape of his neck. He heard the weapon's hammer emit loud 'click' as it was cocked and then he realised that he had been wrong. *Now* the future had never looked bleaker.

————

"Take this left," the Indonesian pointed to the approaching track, then returned his hand to the handle on the dashboard in front of him.

King nodded, keeping both hands firmly on the steering wheel, but not wrapping his thumbs underneath. He knew all too well from experience driving off road that the deep potholes could twist the front wheels in an instant, and snap the steering wheel violently around, dislocating his thumbs savagely. He glanced at the Indonesian as he heaved the heavy wheel round and turned into the narrow dirt track. "How far?" he asked, his mind turning to thoughts of Tembarak, waiting at the station.

"Not far!" the man shouted above the noise of the wheels grinding on the uneven road surface. "Just another few minutes."

King frowned as he stared down the track in search for their destination. He could see nothing, and the Suzuki's headlights did little to cut through the darkness.

"Here!" the man shouted abruptly. "Pull in on the right."

King did as he was instructed and eased the little four by

four to a halt on the right-hand side of the dirt track. He looked around dubiously, then switched off the vehicle's headlights. "Where? I can't see a thing."

The Indonesian smiled, then opened his door. "Follow me, I'll lead the way," he paused. "Don't step on any snakes. The King Cobra is the worse, one bite and you're a dead man. We are too far from a decent hospital out here. Oh, and don't push branches out of your face before looking. It may be a temple viper hanging out of the tree..."

King nodded, undeterred by the man's pointless observations. He had worked in tropical territory many times and knew the odds of a snake biting someone. It was dark, so he wouldn't be able to see any snakes, even if he was about to step on one. If one bit him, he would just be unlucky. Anyway, the Indonesian was going to be ahead of him, so there should be little to worry about.

"We see my friend Todi now." The Indonesian pushed his way through a barrier of head-high bamboo, then held some of the leafy stems back for King to step through more easily. "He is a good man, but you must not offend him in any way. Supposing he offers you a drink, you *must* drink it. Otherwise, he will not do business at any price..."

King nodded but remained silent as he tuned in to his surroundings. The nearby jungle seemed to come alive at night, and the host of sounds which carried on the night air reminded him that they were far from alone.

They walked along the edge of the rainforest, across a piece of flat scrubland which separated the forest from the fields of sugarcane which dominated the mountainous region.

King placed his feet carefully, making certain to step as near as he could to the man's own footsteps. They were now skirting sugarcane fields, which were a prime habitat for deadly snakes such as the king cobra or the Malayan pit viper. Worse in King's mind was the spitting cobra which did exactly what the name suggested and blinded you by spitting venom before striking at your body. Even so, there was a whole host of nasties such as scorpions or spiders which could end their days with a single bite or sting, and the odds were extremely high that at least one of them was near.

Ahead of them a tiny light shone dimly at the edge of the forest and as they approached King could see that it was in fact a small bamboo house raised from the ground by stilts about three feet high.

"Good, he is home," the Indonesian turned around and smiled. "Our time has not been wasted."

King was suddenly aware of something behind him. A footstep extremely close to his own. In one smooth motion, he rolled forwards onto his shoulder, then came up looking back towards the threat, his left hand held up in a fighting guard, ready to defend himself, his right hand on the butt of the tiny pistol he'd taken off Sixties Rocker, which he'd tucked snugly in the waistband of his trousers.

There was a wail of laughter, as the threat lowered the large machete and stood facing the two men, his teeth gleaming brightly in the moonlight.

"Todi!" The Indonesian walked forwards and slapped the man on the shoulder. "I have brought someone here on business." He bent forwards and whispered something, too low for King to hear.

Todi nodded in reply to his friend then looked at King. "You heard me behind you," he paused. "You are very good. There is many a spirit who wishes that he had heard me." He smiled, making a cutting motion with the long machete. "But they can do nothing about it now!" He laughed out loud, then slapped King on the shoulder. "Come, follow me. I have much to offer you. At a price..."

Todi led the way and climbed the wooden steps. He held the door open for the two men to step inside. King shook his head and gestured them both ahead. He had the pistol in his hand behind his back. The situation had moved quickly, and he felt vulnerable. The pistol restored balance as it so often does.

The girl was beautiful and caught King completely by surprise as he followed the two men into the dimly lit bamboo hut. Her hair was the blackest that he had ever seen, long and straight, and hung down near to her pert, naked buttocks. King made a gesture of averting his eyes, but such was her beauty, he could not look away for long. She turned around, swept a hand through her blue-black mane and giggled childishly through her milky white teeth as she stood naked before them. Her breasts were small yet firm and seemed to defy gravity, in the way which only Southeast Asian women seem able to accomplish. Her skin was a light tan and the contrast with the dark tone of her hard nipples created an instant target for King's staring eyes. He turned towards the other two men, suddenly feeling uncomfortable in the man's home, then for the first time, saw Todi in the light of the house. The man was of average height, but extremely fit and wiry, with skin like tanned leather. His face was hard and weathered and his eyes had obviously seen a great deal of life. King estimated him to be in his late fifties, maybe older still, but the man's physique belonged to somebody much younger.

"You like?" Todi smiled wryly, almost proudly. "She is very beautiful. You like her, yes?"

King paused for a moment, watching as the girl covered herself with a silk robe. He thought about the man's question. If he seemed too eager, the man might well become jealous of another man's admiration for his woman. If he hesitated for too long, he could become angry at the inherent lack of respect. "She has beautiful eyes," King paused. "They denote an extreme kindness, and natural intelligence. You can tell a great deal from a person's eyes..."

"Hah!" Todi threw his head back and laughed. "You don't want to fuck her then?" He grinned at the Indonesian and shook his head. "Many men want to fuck her when we go to town, but they learn!" He made a gentle swinging motion with the machete, then pointed to a nearby doorway and the woman obediently exited the room. He walked over to a table at the other end of the small hut and picked up an unlabelled bottle. He turned around, staring King coldly in the eye. "You drink?"

King remembered what the Indonesian had said in the vehicle and nodded accordingly. "Please."

The man smiled then reached for three cups and brought the bottle back to them. "Jusi tell you about me?" He poured some of the liquid into one of the cups, then passed it to him. "Jusi tell you what I used to do?"

King shook his head, hearing the Indonesian's name for the first time. "No, he just said that we may be able to buy a gun, then directed me here."

Todi smiled and passed a cup to Jusi. "I kill Americans in Vietnam." He watched King closely but saw no sign of surprise.

I killed an American woman in Iraq, only a few days ago. So, what? King thought but kept his cool facade.

"That does not shock you?" Todi cocked his head to one side, and kept his eyes glued to King's.

"No."

Todi smiled. "I killed American soldiers in Vietnam. Then when Vietcong killed most of my family, most of my village because they took American food and medicine, I switched sides and hunted the Vietcong and killed them as well. For the CIA..." He stared hard at him. "What do you say to that?"

King held the man's stare, then smiled. "The Americans lost the war, I'd say you switched to the wrong side..."

"Ha! Maybe you right!" Todi grinned. "I am Vietnamese, I loved my country. I had to run for my life when the Americans pulled out of Saigon. I could never stay in Vietnam, not after I fought against the communists. They would have hunted me forever." He took a sip from the small cup, then eyed King warily. "I fled with my wife. It took us two years to reach Sumatra, but she died there from a fever. I came to Java alone but remarried ten years later. Most Indonesians do not like Vietnamese and life has been difficult..." He glanced at Jusi and smiled. "Most Indonesians at least..." He took another sip from the cup and looked at the ground solemnly. "My second wife died eight years ago, when my daughter was twelve years old. I have brought her up on my own, but she is a woman now, she wants to leave for the city and see the sights..."

King nodded, suddenly understanding the man's relationship with the young beauty. He had done mental math and had Todi down for mid-sixties at least. He had to be. But he was fit and wiry and could even have been a decade older. He raised the cup to his lips, then sipped some of the liquid. His lips pursed, and his throat burned as the whisky-like substance flowed down his throat like molten lava.

He looked calmly at the Vietnamese and smiled. "Very nice, make it yourself?"

Todi nodded, then replaced his cup on the table and stared coldly at him. "I have seen men like you before." His eyes glazed slightly, as his mind played back over the years. "American assassins, working for the CIA. Operation Phoenix. Or Project Phoenix, as most would say." The man's English was becoming more and more fluent, and King guessed that it had been some time since he had used the language. "You are a killer. You have killed before. Many times." He nodded knowingly at the Englishman, his eyes unwavering. "As you say, you can tell a great deal from a person's eyes…"

King stared into the man's eyes. They were familiar eyes. He knew them well. They were the eyes of a killer. The eyes he saw every time he looked in the mirror.

CHAPTER SEVENTY

When you stare into the barrel of a gun, two questions go through your mind. The first and foremost is: Am I going to live or die? The second is: Will it hurt? You find yourself praying that when the person pulls the trigger, the bullet will pass through cleanly. It will not smash into your jaw, it will not hit you in the eye, and you will not need another bullet to finish the job.

There were four men, all dressed in civilian clothing, but Abdul Tembarak knew that they were soldiers. Hard and trained and willing to kill. He looked at the man with the gun again then slowly raised a hand and wiped the trickle of blood away from his mouth. He could not stop shaking and the thoughts of how his life might end spiralled around his mind, pulling at his emotions and at his will to live.

"I will not ask you again," the man said adamantly. "Where is the British assassin?" Tembarak stared at the man who had degraded both his wife and himself and shook his head. "I don't know! I honestly don't know!"

Sergeant Grogol shrugged, then looked at the young

soldier who held the pistol. "If he does not answer next time, shoot him in the foot."

"No!" Tembarak pleaded. "I don't know where he has gone! For all I know, he has left me behind and gone to carry out his mission!" He stared at the ground, frustrated not only with Alex King for disappearing, but with himself for not remaining silent. He felt the guilt deep within him, like bile rising from the pit of his stomach.

Grogol growled. "Where... Is... The... British... Assassin?"

Tembarak stared at the man with the pistol, then looked back at the evil little sergeant, who was waiting for the soldier to follow his orders. "He has gone with the man who hires the cars." He looked up at Grogol pleadingly. "I don't know where they have gone, but they should come back soon. The Englishman was going to pick me up after he had paid for the vehicle." He bowed his head in shame, the tears flowing down his bloodied cheeks. "But he drove the other way. I honestly don't know where he has gone."

Grogol shook his head at the young soldier, then waved at the two men standing behind him. "Put him in the truck, I will work on him back at the base." He stared at Tembarak as the two men caught hold of him and bound his hands tightly behind his back with a roll of duct tape "Don't struggle Tembarak, it will not make any difference," he paused. "You have never really felt true pain, but I shall introduce you to it later."

"Please!" Tembarak struggled to stand as a wave of drowsiness washed over him. He felt faint, and he just wanted to die quickly, to be done with the whole ordeal as soon as possible. There was no fight left in him, and he knew it. What scared him most was that Grogol knew it too.

Sergeant Grogol caught hold of one of the soldier's arms, stopping him as they went to walk their prisoner forwards.

He smiled sadistically, then stared coldly into Tembarak's eyes. "Look at me, Tembarak. Look at me and remember everything that you hear." He pushed his face so close to him that the two men almost touched. "I have fucked your woman Tembarak. I have shown her what a *real* man can do. She loved it, Tembarak. She screamed with pleasure as I entered her, and she received me willingly. Time and time again," he paused, breaking into a cruel smile. "My seed swims inside your woman, Tembarak. I want you to remember that..."

Tembarak felt the life wrenched out of him. He tried to shout, tried to scream, but there was nothing left inside. He bowed his head in despair, then felt the weight lift from his feet as the two soldiers dragged his lifeless body towards the truck. It was all over, and he knew it. But with that realisation came something else, something indescribable. It was a new emotion, a relief. It warmed him, comforted him. He was going to die; he was sure of it. Nothing he could do would save him, his wife or the fate of their son. It was almost an out of body experience, making him a spectator to the events. He looked up and called out. "Grogol!" The stocky sergeant looked back, hesitated for a moment then strode arrogantly over. Tembarak muttered something incomprehensible and Grogol leaned in closer to hear. Tembarak lurched his head forwards savagely and connected with the bridge of the man's nose. There was a bone crunching sound and blood and mucus spurted out from his nostrils as the man reeled backwards and fell onto his backside in the dirt, his nose crushed flat to his face. His eyes flickered briefly, then he was out cold.

———

The box had remained untouched for quite some time. The dust and small pieces of debris were evidence of that. As Todi pulled it from under the single bed, a spider almost the size of King's hand scuttled quickly into the dimly lit room. The spider hesitated briefly as the three men blocked its escape, then reared up on its thick legs baring visible fangs, as if ready to pounce on some unsuspecting prey.

Seeing the large arachnid as a threat, or more likely an animal for which he had no compassion, King stepped forwards and raised his foot, ready to administer last rites with his size eleven walking boot. Todi sidestepped the spider, bumping into King and clearing a passage for the beast. Without further hesitation, the spider scurried on out of the doorway and out of view.

Todi looked up at King, who had been surprised at the man's actions. "Death is not always the answer," he smiled. "That spider is extremely poisonous and could kill you within a day or two if you didn't get medical attention, but it will only bite as a last resort. Sometimes it is better to give another option to something that we do not completely understand."

"Todi believes in Karma..." Jusi smiled wryly. "He thinks that if he spares the life of a humble spider, one day, a humble spider might well spare his own."

King remained silent. Killing was killing to him. If you were prepared to take the life of a human, how could you fret about taking the life of a creature at the bottom of the food chain? He looked at the long wooden chest, then glanced at the two men. "Shall we get on with it?" He glanced momentarily at his watch, then thought of Abdul Tembarak who was still waiting for him at the station. "I have to get going very soon."

Todi nodded, then bent and unlocked the box with a small key. He blew the dust away from the lid, then opened it carefully, until there was just enough room for him to squeeze his hand inside. He fiddled for a moment or two with something in the box, then opened the lid all the way. King watched, somewhat bemused at the man's actions, then noticed the British type L2A2 fragmentation grenade fastened to the lid with fuse wire, with a short length of string dangling from the ring-pin. He stepped forwards and sure enough he saw the loop in the end of the string and the nail sticking out from the side of the box, to which it had been attached. Given the confined space of the small bedroom and the considerable blast radius of the grenade, lifting the lid of the chest another inch would have meant certain death for all three men.

"My burglar alarm," Todi smiled. "Guaranteed to end a thief's career!" He reached into the box and pulled an oil-stained cotton sheet away, then beckoned King forward to take a closer look at the items for sale.

King looked at the assortment of spotlessly clean weapons. He squatted on his haunches, then delved deep into the pile and pulled out a familiar friend.

"Ah! You like communist reliability?" Todi smiled as King picked up the Kalashnikov AK47 assault rifle. "They lead the way in basic weapon design. That rifle has remained unchanged since I carried one in Vietnam, and twenty years before that even, but it would still be my choice every time. The Americans suffered many problems with their M16 rifles in Vietnam, the jungle ruined them in no time."

King knew what the man meant. During his extensive training he had gained experience of every military weapon in widespread use plus a fair range of exotics and had been made aware of every one of their faults, either in design or usage. But he had never found a fault with the AK47 sufficient to dissuade him from putting his trust in it. It wasn't as minutely accurate as the M16/AR15 derivatives for instance, but it was ten times as durable and reliable. In fact, what it was about the Kalashnikov that made it so effective was its averageness.

It was average in both weight and length, performed to average accuracy, and the 7.62mm x 39 mm bullet was average in both velocity and stopping power. The weapon was easy to strip and clean, operated almost entirely free from chamber stoppages and offered an all-round package that could not be bettered. There was no wonderful feature about it, but at the same time, there was no inherent fault with it either. With possibly the exception of its fire selector switch which went to fully automatic from safe. Nearly every other weapon went from safe to single fire to full-auto. King was aware of this but had become used to it and had grown to appreciate the rugged tool as a piece of equipment that he could rely on. He released the thirty-round magazine, then pulled back the cocking lever and inspected the chamber.

"All my guns are clean and work perfectly." Todi folded his arms defensively, then smiled. "I have ammunition as well, both full metal jacket and tracer."

King rested the weapon on the wooden floorboards, then reached back into the box. "I want five magazines, one hundred and thirty rounds of jacketed and twenty rounds of tracer." He pulled out the small Uzi 9 mm machine pistol, then quickly checked the weapon over. "I want some spare magazines for this as well, again, five in total and one hundred and fifty rounds of 9mm ball or full jacketed."

"I only have three clips for the UZI, Todi paused. "But there is an MGP-84 at the bottom of the box and I have five magazines for it. It is basically a copy of the Uzi."

"And it's a piece of shit!" King put the Israeli-made machine pistol down beside the AK47, then smiled at the man. "I'll take the Uzi and less ammo, over that Peruvian effort any day of the week. They are susceptible to feed problems when they get hot."

The Vietnamese smiled. "You know your weapons," he paused. "Who is your target?"

King shook his head. "I told you, I'm just a tourist," he smiled. "And you keep to that, all right?" He reached back into the chest, moved a couple of old British Army FN SLR rifles out of the way, then pulled out a Colt model 1911 .45 calibre pistol. He held the hefty handgun, feeling its weight as he looked it over, then frowned when he noticed an inch-long barrel extension, and a small additional lever on the side of the frame. He recognised the alteration but had not seen one on such a large calibre pistol, nor in fact had he seen anything so crude.

"I make adjustments." Todi announced proudly. He reached into the chest and rummaged his way to the bottom, then pulled out a foot-long cylindrical tube. "I use something similar in Vietnam and Laos, when I work for CIA." He took the Colt from King's clasp, then threaded the tube into the barrel extension. "I make improvements. This is the quietest silencer you will ever use." He reached back into the chest and retrieved a box of .45 ammunition, then proceeded to load two shells into the weapon's seven round magazine. "The lever on the side locks the slide, so no noise can escape out of the chamber. So, it is effectively a single shot piece..."

King watched the man load the pistol, knowing that the similar modification to the 9mm Browning HP35 used by the British SAS was formidable. However, even though the slide was locked in place and the slide had to be pulled back after every shot to chamber the next round, there was still an audible 'phut' to be heard as the bullet left the muzzle.

Todi walked across the room and lifted the bamboo flap, exposing the gap which acted as an open window. He cocked the weapon, then aimed the pistol out into the night and gently squeezed the trigger.

King listened intently but heard nothing, except for the hammer falling on the firing pin, as the cumbersome looking weapon rose gently in the man's hand. Thinking that the man was humouring him, he went to walk forwards, but stopped when the little Vietnamese pulled back the slide, ejecting the empty case and chambering the next round manually. He looked at the empty case on the floor in surprise, then held up his hand to halt him. "Wait, let me take a shot."

Todi smiled, knowing that the man had been impressed with his handiwork. He held out the pistol, keeping the muzzle pointed out of the window and waited for King to step in front of him. King felt the considerable weight of the weapon but was not interested in taking a shot at the dark. He looked out of the window and down to the sparse ground, which was illuminated slightly by the dim light from the bedroom. Amongst the pieces of scattered debris and dried leaves, he could see two beetles scurrying about in a frantic quest for food. He aimed the weapon carefully between the two, then gently squeezed the light trigger. There was a slight, almost lazy recoil aided by the sheer weight of the suppressor, and the section of earth between the two beetles exploded into a plume of dust. The beetles took a short flight, then landed a foot or two away, none the worse for the experience.

King looked back at Todi and grinned. "Just the ticket." He pulled back the slide and ejected the spent case, then placed the pistol beside the other two weapons. "All right Todi," he paused. "How much for the three?"

"How many bullets you want for the Colt?" the man asked, staring into the chest. "I only have one magazine."

King knew that the Colt was a specialist weapon and with the locking slide, would be good for no purpose except a calculated silent shot at an individual target. He thought for a moment, then looked at the Vietnamese. "Just seven."

Todi looked thoughtful, obviously performing mental calculations as he stared at the three weapons. "You have dollars?"

King nodded. "And British pounds."

"For three guns like that, then maybe fifteen hundred dollars would be about the normal price." He smiled wryly, then glanced briefly at Jusi. "But that would be unfair, wouldn't it?"

King remained silent. He was intrigued to know why the man had said, 'normal price'. Why should he regard fifteen hundred dollars as unfair? Why do him any favours?

"Come, let us drink some more before we talk of money." Todi bent down and closed the lid of the chest, then carefully refastened the hand grenade 'alarm'. He slipped the tiny key back into the lock, then looked up at King and smiled. "Maybe we can come to a more beneficial arrangement..."

––––––

The drink was strong and left a pungent scent at the back of the throat. King tried to work out what the drink was but decided to refrain from asking either of his companions. He took another sip, then replaced the cup on the table and stared at Todi dubiously. "I can pay the price in full," he paused. "I appreciate your hospitality, but I must be making a move very soon."

"You have no friends in Semarang." Todi said accusingly. "And you are not an Australian tourist."

King did not appreciate people doubting or exposing holes in his cover, it made him feel uneasy. It made him want to reach into his waistband, take out the small Rohrbaugh pistol and double tap the pair of them. He could take the guns, he could make his way back to the village and he could pick up Tembarak and finish what he had come to Indonesia to do. His patience was ebbing, and his survival instinct was rising to the surface. If he was not careful, it would take over and the two men would be dead. He breathed deeply, then looked calmly at them both. "I have hired a vehicle for at least double the standard rate and I am prepared to pay over the odds for the weapons." He took a thick wad of banknotes from his pocket and dropped it onto the table. "Take the money, please, and forget all about me."

Todi smiled. "I know you are a killer. I know that you are here to kill again." He held up his hand sensing that King was nearing his patience threshold. "I know, because I have killed, many times. I am Vietnamese. I could not stay in Indonesia, because I entered illegally, after the war. I was hassled, I was threatened and then I did the Indonesian Government a favour. A one-off favour for Golkar." He took another sip, then looked benevolently at his guest. "The PKI made a significant reappearance in this part of Java in the early eighties. They had been disbanded, but that is the thing about communism, it lies dormant, waiting for a suitable leader and a suitable following. It never dies and if anything, it grows stronger the longer it rests."

"Why tell me?" King stared at him, already planning which of the two should take the first bullet. "I'm just a tourist."

Todi smiled. "Golkar knew about my past, knew how much I wanted to stay in Java. They approached me with an ultimatum - put down the movement or be deported back to Vietnam. I was left with little choice. I would be disappeared as soon as I stepped off the plane. So, I returned to what I knew best," he paused. "I ended the attempted coup right here in Central Java. Now I am left alone to live my life."

King finished his drink, then placed the cup down and slid it forwards. "I'm happy for you. Now, I must be going..." He stood up, then looked at the Indonesian. "If you want a lift back to Purwodadi, then drink up and follow me."

"Communism merely sleeps, it only ever rests itself." Todi

stood up. "General Madi Soto is the country's threat, he can be the only reason that you are here..."

King stared at him in surprise, then shook his head. "Forget you ever saw me."

Todi caught hold of King's arm and glared at him. "I despised communism so much, that I turned on my fellow countrymen and fought on the side of a nation who eventually turned their back on me, and people like me. I had to leave my country, my family, and my friends. I dragged my wife away, then watched her die because I could not afford medical treatment for her cancer. *Her* cancer, which was given to her by the Americans. All that Agent Orange they sprayed on the river banks to kill off the jungle! She dies from a fever, but cancer ate her down to her bones..." He looked tearfully at the Englishman, then sighed deeply. "Keep the guns. Let me help you. I have seen what men like General Soto did to my country, I do not want it to happen here as well."

"What do you know of General Soto?" King asked. "How do you know what he has planned for Indonesia?"

Todi glanced at Jusi, then looked back at King. "Because we live here. Because the people of Yogyakarta all know but are too scared to mention it outside their own homes," he paused, shaking his head. "Because we all know that the coalition government is weak and that they are pretending that it will never happen. Just like in South Vietnam and South Korea. But it *does* happen, and it *will* happen again, if nobody makes a stand. And, I believe in Karma..." he smiled. "Why else are you here? Why ask my friend Jusi for a gun? Why a man who would bring you to my door? Karma..."

The moon was at its fullest, larger than King could ever remember seeing in his lifetime. Larger even, than it had seemed on the desolate plateau of Northern Iraq and larger than he had seen high in the rugged peaks of the Russian Urals. It seemed out of proportion with the rest of the sky, its craters fully visible and the light which it spread over the otherwise dark sky was considerable.

The small Suzuki bounced and scraped its way over the deep potholes, too light to hold the road and too low to avoid grinding the axle against the savage rocks and flood channels which made up the road's surface. King gripped the steering wheel tightly, feeling the uncertainty of the vehicle's traction.

Todi leant forwards between the two men, then pointed at the road ahead. "It is only another two hundred metres or so, then we take a right turn," he paused. "We will enter the village from the other direction, so Jusi's office will be on the left."

"Can't wait," King paused. "Don't you have highway maintenance in this part of the country?" He grit his teeth as another rock slammed against the rear axle, and the tail of the tiny vehicle jumped sideways. "This is appalling!"

"*This* is a river bed," Todi stated flatly. "The mining company changed the river's course to run into the silver mine and wash the ore. This only ever sees occasional flash flooding now, which is why the locals use it as a short cut down the mountain."

"And if it floods?" King asked, unsure of the reasoning behind using a river bed which flash floods as an alternative route. "What happens then?"

Todi grinned. "Then they get to the bottom of the mountain much quicker than expected..."

King steered the vehicle to the right, then drove up the steep slope of the worn riverbank and onto the relatively smooth highway. He felt himself relax a little, then caught sight of something to the rear of the railway station. He slowed the car to a halt, then looked at the Indonesian beside him. "Do you see that?"

Jusi frowned as he looked at the building ahead. "A truck," he paused. "A military truck!" He looked at the Vietnamese behind him, then turned back to King. "The army have no reason to be here. Purwodadi has nothing to offer them."

"Girls? Cheap alcohol? Drugs?" King asked, keeping his eyes on the green canvas sides of the military vehicle.

"Nothing like that!" Jusi shook his head. "They even prac-tice their war games to the east of Yogyakarta, the mining companies do not like the army on their land."

King stared at the truck, then shook his head. "It is parked out of sight of your office, *and* the road which we drove out of town on." He looked at the two men and frowned. "They can't be waiting for a train, no more are due until the morning. They must have caught up with my contact and are waiting to ambush me when I show up..."

Todi gave a little chuckle, then reached for his weapon. "Then we will just have to make a change to their plans." He eased back the cocking lever of the FN SLR and chambered the first of twenty 7.62mm NATO bullets. "I have an idea."

CHAPTER SEVENTY-ONE

Smoking is a dangerous habit at the best of times. However, when you are a lone sentry covering point at night, the habit becomes imminently life-threatening. King watched the bright orange light glow like the hot embers of a log fire. The light would brighten on each inhalation of breath, then disappear as the man withdrew the cigarette to exhale. He was standing deep in the building's shadows, taking refuge from the moon's bright illumination and maintaining a position where he could still observe the road.

King crouched low to the ground, squatting on his haunches as he kept his left shoulder tight against the timber building. There was little cover to take advantage of, but by using the shadows and by keeping below the enemy's eye level, he could remain virtually invisible. He rested the AK47 across his knees, then masticated a quantity of saliva, before spitting quietly onto the hard, dusty ground. He then worked the wet dust into a thick mud and scooped it up into his fingertips. Taking great care not to make a sound, he wiped the muddy paste onto his face, then worked it around his eyes and nose, until his face was virtually covered in the substance.

The moon was full and bright, and he needed to keep every advantage over his enemy. His training was coming into its own; now, to use it effectively was paramount.

Making sure not to drag his feet on the dry ground, King then edged his way along the side of the building until he was able to observe the ground ahead from the corner. The smoker was still in place, inhaling every twenty seconds or so. To the man's left, and King's right, a second sentry stepped momentarily from the shadows and peered down the road ahead. He turned around, stared straight at King but could not see through the dark shadows of the building. King tensed, holding his breath as his heartbeat started to pound and a shiver ran down to the base of his spine. He waited, his finger hovering near the weapon's trigger, then breathed a sigh of relief as the man walked casually back to the sanctuary of the vehicle's shadows. He studied the ground ahead, then squinted through the moonlight, concentrating on the sudden movement behind the military vehicle.

———

It had been a long time. More than twenty years and before that, it had been another ten, maybe more. Time did not register anymore. His heart raced, and his body shook with the sudden burst of adrenaline which surged through his veins like water through a high-pressure hose. There was no feeling which could touch it, not even come near. It was not simple to clarify, not simple to explain to those who could never understand. It was him against them; one mistake and he was dead. The feeling was everything.

Todi held the weapon close to his chest, his finger near the trigger with the weapon's safety catch in the off position. He had chosen, as always, semi-automatic on the weapon's selector switch, knowing full well that the heavy weapon, with the extreme power of the 7. 62 x51 mm NATO cartridge, was easier to control with one shot fired with each squeeze of the heavy trigger. This weapon was rare. Designated L2A1 by the British army it also operated in fully automatic mode. Designed as a light support weapon to give covering fire for the rest of the squad or platoon over their semi-auto L1A1 weapons. He placed his footsteps carefully, making sure not to step on a discarded tin can, or a twig, or anything else which might compromise his position. The truck was his objective, but nothing could be done without a thorough reconnaissance of the area. They had no idea of how many soldiers were in the vicinity and for all they knew, there could be a whole troop of up to thirty men inside the vehicle.

Todi crouched low and jogged over a strip of flat ground beside the railway lines. He caught sight of somebody smoking in the shadows of a building, then stopped and dropped down onto his stomach. There was a mere thirty-foot gap between himself and the large canvas sided military truck and as he started to crawl on his belly, he noticed a lone figure leaning against the side of the vehicle. His pulse raced. He had not seen the man as he approached, and his mind started to fill with the horrors of what might have happened, had he not noticed the enemy. He breathed deeply acknowledging that he was not as sharp as he had once been. That was an age ago, another lifetime. He was now an old man.

The dust wafted gently into his face as his elbows broke the hard crust of the sun-baked earth. The wet season was just around the corner, another week or so and the ground would be soaked for the next four months. He eased himself, snakelike on his belly, keeping the rifle resting on his outstretched forearms. There was not much distance in it now, and there was every chance that the sentry might turn around. Silence was the deciding factor and if he was to avoid a confrontation, he would have to be as silent as the grave.

The soldier stretched, arching his back as the monotony started to get to him. His joints ached as he rested against the canvas tarpaulin which covered the skeletal frame of the vehicle and as the night drew on, he was becoming more and more impatient at the delay. He stepped out from the shadows once more, then walked to the rear of the vehicle and lifted the canvas covering. Todi froze. The man had walked less than six feet in front of where he lay prone on the ground. He lifted his head slightly, then caught sight of the soldier, who was drinking water from a plastic bottle. The man drank thirstily, upending the bottle and downing all but a quarter of the contents, then lazily discarded the bottle back into the empty truck, before turning to look out over the waste ground and railway tracks beyond.

The blood surged to Todi's head, pounding in his ears as he remained stock still. One move, one twitch, and he might attract the soldier's attention and be left fighting for his life. He now knew that the vehicle was empty, but he did not know of the positions of the other soldiers. If he started firing his weapon, his muzzle flashes would soon expose him as an easy target. He kept his dark eyes firmly on the soldier, his hand near the rifle's grip and the comforting reassurance of the trigger. There was nothing he could do now but wait.

———

Alex King watched the soldier as he stood casually in the middle of the patch of waste ground, then fiddled with the front of his trousers for a moment, before urinating directly in front of him. He could not see the Vietnamese from his position but knew that he was not far away from the rear of the truck. He shouldered the AK47 and sighted the Indonesian soldier in the centre of the basic Vee & Pin sights. There was nothing more that he could do, but if Todi was indeed compromised, the Indonesian soldier would drop before he would have chance to draw his weapon. He kept his aim steady, his finger resting gently on the trigger, then watched and waited. The soldier zipped up when he was finished, turned around and walked back to the side of the truck and resumed his casual stance, leaning against the soft canvas tarpaulin. King watched intently, lowering the weapon and waiting for a movement. When it came, it was slight, as Todi gently edged his way back on his belly towards the railway tracks, then rose hesitantly to his feet and started to run in a crouched position. King watched the man move nimbly across the waste ground and through the long savannah grass, then disappear as he moved behind the nearby timber building. He returned his eyes to the smoker in the shadows, then relaxed a little when he saw the bright light of the cigarette tip glow in the darkness.

Todi appeared silently to the side of the building, crouched low to the ground. He eased his way along the wall until he rested just a pace or two away from King.

"Close one?" King whispered. "How many in the truck?"

The Vietnamese paused for a moment, fighting to regain his breath. He snatched a few lungsful of humid air and started to look a little calmer. "I don't think there are any soldiers in the vehicle," he paused. "But there is a man smoking in the shadows right in front of you."

"I've got him," King paused. "And I think I saw a movement towards the front of the truck, but I can't be sure. I was watching you at the time." He stared at the man, and could clearly smell the stench of urine, but chose not to mention it. From experience, he knew that the men of Southeast Asia could not stand to lose face. And besides, there was no point in telling the man that he had just been pissed on. King figured he already knew.

Todi nodded and glanced behind him, then looked back at

King. "I'll go back and signal Jusi, we have surprise on our side, we should not waste it any longer."

"Okay." King looked at the man gratefully, then smiled. "Let's do it."

———

He watched as the small Suzuki four by four vehicle drove steadily through the village, then performed a U-turn outside the front of the vehicle hire building. The car's dim head-lights shone on the ground ahead, but the moon was so bright they were hardly needed.

Sergeant Grogol pulled Abdul Tembarak close to him, then pointed at the slow-moving vehicle. "Is that it?" His voice was nasal. There was a long plaster stuck over it where the skin had been split. His grip tightened on the man's shoulder and he gritted his teeth savagely. "Is that the English assassin?"

"I... I can't be sure," Tembarak paused. He could barely see, for after Grogol had come around and recovered enough to stand, he had administered a terrible, sickening beating on him. Restraining himself just enough to avoid killing him. "It looks like the vehicle that he hired, but I can't identify the driver from here..." His voice was weak, speaking through swollen lips and shattered teeth.

Grogol glanced at the bright moon, then looked menac-ingly at him. "Don't play games with me Tembarak!" He looked up at the white Suzuki, which had cruised slowly past and was now stationary in the road outside the train station. "I will not spare your life if you try to double-cross me."

Tembarak bowed his head. "Fuck you. I don't care anymore..."

Grogol pushed the man on to his knees and drew the 9mm Browning from his leather hip holster. He cocked the hammer and placed the muzzle on the top of the man's head. He smiled as he watched him flinch. "Oh, I think you do care... Now stay still." He commanded in little more than a quiet whisper. He reached into his pocket with his left hand and pulled out a small ivory-handled flick-knife. "Try anything stupid, and you will be gunned down in an instant." He pressed the tiny button and a nasty looking stiletto blade shot out instantly. "You'll be dead, and I will be seeing that your widow spreads herself for me day and night." He sliced the blade easily through the parcel tape which bound his hands together, then reassured Tembarak of the pistol's presence by pushing the muzzle harder onto his head. "If that's not enough for you, then believe me when I tell you I will give your son to a paedophile... Understand?"

"All right!" Tembarak snapped. "What do you want me to do? You sick bastard..."

———

Alex King watched the Indonesian step calmly out from the shadows, then felt a sudden wave of heat come over him, as he realised that it was Abdul Tembarak. Had the Indonesian agent deliberately set him up? Or had he been forced into the betrayal? Either way King found it hard to decide on the appropriate action to take. If Tembarak had deliberately set an ambush, then he instantly became a legitimate target and remained a threat if he stayed alive. However, if the man had been captured, and been forced into a betrayal, then his life would be in danger as soon as he stepped out into the open. General Soto's men would simply have two easy targets in the road instead of one.

King turned his attention to the glowing tip of the soldier's cigarette. The bright light faded, dropping as the man lowered the cigarette and exhaled another lung full of smoke. King raised the heavy handgun and cantered the tiny sights in what he guessed to be the right area, praying that the soldier would indulge once more. The .45 Colt was extremely heavy, and he estimated that the suppressor, or silencer as it is often called, doubled the pistol's original weight. He kept his aim steady, glancing out of the corner of his left eye as he monitored Tembarak's slow progress across the railway yard. Suddenly, King saw what he had hoped for: the glowing tip of the man's cigarette. He lowered the pistol slightly, estimating the man's height from the tell-tale orange light, then gently squeezed the weapon's trigger. There was no sound, other than a faint 'whoosh' but as King kept his eyes on the shadows in front of him, he heard a loud, thud. Whether it was the sound of the heavy, slow-moving bullet impacting, or whether it was the sound of a dead man falling, he did not know, nor did he care. He quietly unlocked the weapon's crude bolt system, then chambered another .45 round into the breech.

————

Tembarak's heart raced as he traipsed slowly across the dusty ground. He felt lethargic, realising that there was no reason for Grogol not to fire on them both. General Soto's threat would simply have been fulfilled, and besides, what use was he to them now? They would have got what they wanted, it would be easier to kill him and be done with it. He looked up at the tiny four by four vehicle, then frowned as he noticed a much smaller man behind the steering wheel. Where was King? And what was he to do now?

Jusi reached across the passenger seat and carefully opened the door, not very wide. The window was open, and the man was staring straight at him. Tembarak hesitated for a moment, then decided to chance it, after all, the man was practically urging him to get into the vehicle. He walked more confidently, then frowned as stared into the barrel of a tiny pistol.

"Get in," the man spoke quietly, but firmly in their native tongue. "Quickly!"

Tembarak paused for a second, then shrugged. One gun in front of him, many guns behind him. There seemed to be little choice. He continued to walk forwards, then suddenly bolted towards the vehicle and flung the door wide open.

The gunfire erupted immediately, bursts of three or four rounds at a time, fired in concise patterns. The bullets hit the ground at first, then, as the experienced marksman corrected his aim with each burst, the bullets started to impact on the vehicle. Jusi rammed his foot to the floor, planting all his weight on the accelerator. The car protested at first, its wheels gaining too much traction, then lunged forwards, throwing up a thick cloud of dust as its wheels spun on the hard ground.

———

The first soldier to present himself was cut down in an instant. King held the AK47 firmly against his shoulder but did not engage the target. Todi had taken care of him with seven or eight rounds from the SLR. The soldier had thrown up his arms as he dropped to his knees with the first gunshot but Todi had simply kept on firing until the soldier lay prone and still.

King eased himself carefully out of the shadows, keeping the weapon aimed in front of him as he searched for a target. It was not long in coming as the soldier bolted out from the shadows of the truck brandishing a medium-sized semi-automatic pistol. King raised the weapon, but fired a short burst as he did so, if not to hit the target, then to give him more to think about. The tactic worked, and the soldier continued to run and take aim at the same time. King dropped to one knee, then fired a short, controlled burst into the man's torso. He folded instantly and stumbled to the ground. King quickly rose to his feet, ran past the man, then loosely aimed his weapon at the twitching body and squeezed the trigger twice more.

There was the sound of a small calibre weapon firing and King quickly took refuge in the shadow of the vehicle as he searched for the marksman's position. He eased himself around the bonnet of the large truck, then spied the soldier, who was still firing at the Suzuki, which by now, had sped off the road, and was resting stationary in the large irrigation ditch one hundred metres or so away from the station. The man stopped firing, ejected the empty magazine then searched his pockets for a spare.

King caught the man in the sights of the AK47, then lowered his aim when Todi stepped into the line of fire and dashed towards the unsuspecting soldier. King quickly side-stepped, attempting to take a clear shot, but it was too late. Todi tackled the man, taking him to the ground, but the man was fast, sweeping his right leg around in a wide arc as he fell and catching his opponent with a mighty blow to the head. The Vietnamese, smaller than his opponent, fell to the ground and dropped his rifle, but lashed out savagely at the Indonesian with a fist. Both men fell back but Todi was quicker, pushing himself to his feet in an instant and forcing home another attack on the soldier. Blow was met with counterblow and the two men were soon battling each other with an array of martial arts techniques in an impressive battle which King was covering in the sights of his weapon, unable to take a clear shot at the soldier.

Suddenly aware of the presence of others, King swung around bringing the weapon up to aim at the new threat. He relaxed when he saw Jusi escorting Abdul Tembarak towards them, keeping three paces behind his prisoner, the tiny Rohrbaugh 9mm pistol that King had given him aimed at the man's back. He turned and watched the two men fighting, then smiled to himself when the Vietnamese caught the Indonesian full in the groin with a savage kick. Quick to follow up the blow, Todi lunged forwards and punched him in the side of the face, then caught hold of the man round his head and pulled him down, at the same moment raising his knee to smash it into the man's nose.

The soldier fell backwards and sprawled lifelessly on the ground, but was allowed no mercy, as Abdul Tembarak suddenly bolted forwards and dived on top of him, administering a series of savage blows into the man's face and stomach. King stepped forward and pulled the Indonesian away, then aimed the AK47 into the surprised agent's face. "If you've set me up again, Tembarak, you're as good as dead!"

The Indonesian looked up at him tearfully. "I didn't! The bastards captured me when you left!" He shook his head, then stared at the man on the ground. "This bastard tortured my wife and made me watch!" He wiped away the tears, then shook his head despondently. "Now he said that if I didn't cooperate, he'd give my son to a pervert! He's evil, sick! Let me kill him, please!"

Sergeant Grogol looked up at his captors stubbornly, then wiped the blood from his mouth and nose. The plaster had come off and Todi had made an even bigger mess of his nose than Tembarak had. It looked like a squashed passion fruit. "You are all dead! General Soto will hunt you down for this, he will hunt you for the rest of your days!" He made to get to his feet but buckled and fell back onto his rear. "Surrender your weapons and I will see that you live."

King shook his head. "I have a better idea." He turned to Todi. "Search him, make sure he isn't carrying any more weapons," he paused. "Jusi! Look in the truck and find something to tie him up with."

Grogol looked up at him with contempt, then wiped some more blood away from his face. "And what is your *better* idea?"

King smiled, keeping the AK47 aimed at the man's chest. "I understand you are a torturer?" He smiled sadistically at the Indonesian sergeant, then stepped a little closer. "Good. Perhaps your pain threshold will be high?" He glanced across at Tembarak, then looked coldly back at his prisoner. "Personally, I think it will be extremely low. I think you're a tough guy when you are holding all the cards. But I think you are also a coward. And now you are not holding any cards at all. Whatever the case, we shall find out very soon."

CHAPTER SEVENTY-TWO

Most men of Sergeant Grogol's sadistic nature, men who live only to inflict pain and misery, are generally cowards who lack the resilience to withstand pain inflicted upon themselves. There was no disputing the man's physical strength, nor his proven ability as a soldier, but when it came to maintain his resolve under extreme duress, his ability as a torturer counted against him. Under the influence of his own imagination and experience, knowing how terrible torture interrogation could get, he crumpled and broke down in a manner which sickened King almost to the pit of his stomach.

King held the AK47 loosely at hip level, keeping the muzzle of the weapon trained on the soldier's chest. He stared at him icily, then shook his head contemptuously. "He hasn't even started yet," he paused. "But he soon will, if you don't tell me what I want to hear."

"I... I can't tell you!" The man looked up at him pleadingly, then swayed, almost falling forwards onto his stomach, unable to save himself with both hands bound tightly behind his back.

Todi caught hold of him, then pulled him back onto his

knees and pushed down on his shoulders, forcing extra weight onto his crossed ankles. He looked at King expectantly, then grinned as the Englishman simply nodded. The Vietnamese slipped his left arm under the soldier's left armpit, then lifted and wrapped his hand tight around the back of the man's neck. Then, without hesitation, he punched the man in the shoulder blade, dislocating the joint from its socket. Grogol screamed in agony, as the cartilage ground against the bone. His arm contorted in a sickening display, as the muscle contracted and seized itself into a severe cramp. He looked up at King, trying to regain some composure, but lost control and vomited pitifully down his front.

King stepped forwards and rammed the muzzle of his rifle into the man's sternum, glaring at him. "I'm an agent, *not* a torturer. Part of my job is to kill. I'm very good at it." He increased the pressure, pushing so hard, that Todi had to counter the force to keep the man on his knees. "That doesn't mean I enjoy it. I do not have a contract on you. I will not kill you, unless you get in my way. But I will count to three, and rest assured, there will not be a four..."

He rammed the rifle barrel into the man's chest with such force that he was toppled backwards, pushing the Vietnamese out of the way. King stepped over Grogol, placing a foot to either side of him, then pressed the muzzle up under the man's chin. The soldier was gasping for breath. "Start talking, or I'll pull the trigger." He looked up at Todi and pointed towards the railway station, some sixty or so metres away. "Get back there and see that Jusi and Tembarak have cleared the bodies away. Tell them to turn any residents around – we don't want the police here either. How far is the nearest police station?"

"Thirty minutes away," Todi said. "They may have cars patrolling nearer though..."

"Okay, we'll have to wing it... Save any weapons, take what

ammo you can then wait by the truck. We're moving out in five minutes." He turned back to the Indonesian and wrapped his finger around the trigger. "As I said, there will not be a four. One..." Grogol scowled at him defiantly and tried to wriggle away from the rifle. "Two..." King pressed the barrel even harder forcing the man's head backwards and shook his head regretfully. He lifted the rifle and pressed the butt firmly into his shoulder, then sighted his aim on the man's forehead. "Three..."

"Don't shoot!" Grogol cried out, then tried to speak, but could not get the words out in any comprehensible order.

King shook his head and tightened his finger on the trigger. "Are you going to talk?" He shouted. "Yes or no?"

Grogol nodded erratically. "Yes!" he blurted. "Of course, I will!"

CHAPTER SEVENTY-THREE

The heavy military truck bounced violently on the uneven road surface, its noisy diesel engine billowing a thick trail of black smoke from the exhaust with every change of gear. A dull orange light glowed in the centre of the roof emitting enough light to see by inside without ruining their night vision.

Tembarak closed his eyes for a moment, suddenly feeling exhausted after the adrenaline rush back in the village of Purwodadi. His mind raced with thoughts of what may lay ahead and when he opened his eyes, he thought of the last time that he was inside such a vehicle as this. Perhaps it had been in this very vehicle, his hands bound tightly together and the stifling hood blinding him from the outside world. He breathed deeply, trying to calm his nerves, then looked across at the two men sitting on the hard, wooden bench-seat opposite.

The Vietnamese, whom he had not so much as spoken to yet, was sitting upright with his eyes closed, the heavy rifle resting between his knees, its barrel pointing skywards. There was no sign of concern on the man's face and he seemed completely at ease with the situation.

Alex King also seemed at ease but was using the time to check over his weapons. He had stripped the tiny Rohrbaugh 9mm pistol down to its component parts, cleared the chamber of grease and the powdered residue of burnt Nitro gunpowder and was busy reassembling it. The man's face expressed inner calm, as well as extreme concentration and determination. He slipped the magazine back into the weapon's butt, then pulled back the slide and applied the safety catch, before looking up at Tembarak. "All right?"

The Indonesian nodded. "I think so," he paused. "Just a bit nervous, that's all."

"That is only to be expected." King slipped the tiny pistol back into the waistband of his trousers, then smiled. "Just think, you will soon see your wife and child," he paused. "What's a little nervousness compared to that?"

Tembarak smiled apprehensively, then glanced down at Sergeant Grogol, who was sitting on the floor, grinning smugly at him. "What's your problem?" He growled at him. "I wouldn't smile like that if I were you!" He tightened his grip on the AK47 which King had given him, then moved the barrel so that it lined up with Grogol's chest. "Just keep smiling, and I'll finish you right here and now you bastard!"

Grogol's expression dropped when he noticed the intensity in the man's eyes. He turned his attention to King, who merely stared at him coldly. "Stop this ridiculous charade Englishman. How long do you think you can keep it up?" He shook his head and grinned belligerently. "General Soto will hunt you down for this and kill you like animals."

"General Soto will be dead," King glared at him. "*You* still have a chance to live. Slim, but still a chance nonetheless..."

Grogol chuckled. "Do you seriously think that you can pull it off? You are quite mad!"

"Quite possibly," King stated flatly. "As for pulling it off, well that shouldn't be too much of a problem. After all, I've got you coming along to help me."

The soldier frowned. "What do you mean?" He shook his head, perplexed at the situation. "You are all insane! You cannot even expect to get near to General Soto!"

"No," King smiled wryly. "But you can."

————

After what seemed like hours in the stifling heat of the truck Jusi pulled the vehicle into a small side-turning off the narrow road, then switched off the headlights. He looked around at King, his expression showing concern. "The military base is about a mile ahead of us, after we drive around the next bend," he paused. "Are we still following the plan?"

"Right down to the last letter."

"This is never going to work... How the hell did I get into this? I have car hire business, I not soldier..." Jusi said, his hand shaking at the wheel.

"You can leave now my friend," King said. "You have been invaluable, and nobody will think less of you."

The Indonesian shook his head. "No. I owe it to Todi. He help plenty me in past. I help him now. He good man..."

King patted the man on his shoulder, then turned around and nudged the Vietnamese, whose eyes were tightly shut, as if meditating. "Wake up, we're near the base."

"I know," Todi answered, his eyes still firmly closed. "A mile ahead, after we drive around the next bend..." He smiled as he opened his eyes. "Which if I remember, is a long left-hand bend, which takes the road around a sugarcane plantation."

King looked down at the Indonesian sergeant, then caught hold of him by his shirt collar and pulled him abruptly to his feet. "All right, up!" He saw the soldier wince with pain, then remembered the previously dislocated shoulder. King had crudely put it back in place as they had got into the truck. "Still painful, is it?" Grogol grit his teeth but remained silent. King smiled. "Good. Give us any trouble and my Vietnamese friend will gladly dislocate it for you again." He dragged the soldier towards the rear of the truck, then lifted the canvas curtain and pushed him to the hard ground.

"No! Don't kill me!" Grogol spluttered as he stared up at the Englishman. "I am not to blame for anything, I just follow orders..."

"Good. Then, you should have no trouble following mine." He took the silenced .45 out from a leather shoulder holster Todi had supplied with the pistol and aimed it down at him. "As I said earlier, I do not have a contract on you, therefore you will be quite safe, *if* you help me." He stared coldly at the Indonesian, then pulled back the weapon's hammer with his thumb. "General Soto is going nowhere; he is merely China's glove puppet of the moment. Another footnote in communist history. Only he won't be, because he will be dead before he actually achieved a communist state..."

Grogol laughed out loud. "You are forgetting something! Communism is alive and well both in North Korea *and* Vietnam! And who is ever going to threaten China?" He stared at King defiantly. "Nobody, that's who!"

King shook his head. "Australia lies a few hundred miles south of Indonesia. New Zealand and Australia are peaceful nations, but do you think they will just sit by and watch as an overcrowded communist state is hatched on their borders? Two countries with more empty land than they know what to do with. Two countries with more sheep than people, for Christ's sake!" King paused. "They make a move and Britain will back them up. Britain makes a move, and America will follow. Before you know it, NATO is playing their card.

Chain reaction. You light the taper and there will be one big firework on the end of it."

"You know that you have lost," Grogol smiled. "You know that you have no chance of killing General Soto. You should have fled after you killed our intelligence agents in Karawang, but no... You still boarded the train and continued your mission. How very British, how very predictable of you."

"I'm not the one on my backside. I'm not the one with a gun to my head." King smiled belligerently. "And I'm not the one who cried for mercy..." He stepped down and caught Grogol by his hair, then pulled him harshly to his feet. "Turn around and face the vehicle."

"You're going to shoot me in the back!" Grogol blurted. "Please, don't kill me!"

"Don't tempt me." King took the flick knife, which he had taken from Grogol earlier, out from his pocket and pressed the small thumb button. The blade opened instantly, and he sliced quickly through the parcel tape binding the soldier's hands together. He pulled the man around to face him, then shoved the muzzle of the weapon up under his chin. "One move Grogol, one blink and I will make sure that you have nowhere to put your hat..." He caught hold of him by his collar, then moved him towards the front of the vehicle and motioned him to the passenger door of the cab. "Now get in, we've wasted enough time."

CHAPTER SEVENTY-FOUR

The LED floodlights illuminated the compound harshly, burning through the night air and almost turning it into day. Large buildings were clearly visible several hundred metres within the wire fenced boundary and a variety of military vehicles were parked near the gates, as if ready to leave in a convoy. From either side of the road to the main gates, bright orange streetlamps formed a glowing tunnel to direct their entrance, which was being noted by the three, armed guards beside the barrier.

King peered over Grogol's shoulder and surveyed the scene ahead. He studied the posture of the three guards, then noted a fourth in the security booth beside the barrier. The soldiers looked bored with their nocturnal duty and it was certainly not apparent that they had been ordered to be extra vigilant.

King nudged Jusi on the shoulder but continued to stare straight ahead. "Keep moving, don't hesitate. We are starting to look suspicious." He turned to Grogol, who was seated in the front passenger seat. "What is your entry procedure?"

Grogol hesitated for a moment too long and was duly

prodded in the ribs by the muzzle of Todi's rifle, from his crouched position in the flatbed behind. "Just drive in damn it!" He turned around in his seat and stared at King. "When they see me, they will open the barrier without question," he paused. "Just give yourself up, it will be easier in the long run..."

King shook his head. "I don't think so." He turned to Abdul Tembarak and nodded. "Okay, nice and tight now." He held out both hands patiently and waited as the Indonesian bound his wrists tightly with the roll of duct tape. "All right now keep Grogol covered, but don't let the guards see that Kalashnikov. If he tries anything, shoot him." He waited until the man had jammed the barrel into the soldier's back, then looked across to Todi and nodded. Todi moved across the truck and sat on the bench seat opposite him. He aimed the FN SLR rifle at King's chest but kept the weapon's frame hidden by his own body. If a guard peered inside the vehicle, he would not distinguish the weapon's barrel from the Heckler and Koch G3 assault rifles which were in widespread service on the Island.

"All right everyone, keep calm and brass it out," he paused. "That means be cool, bluff it like in a game of poker..." King looked over at Grogol threateningly through gritted teeth. "One slip-up from you and you take it in the back."

Jusi slowed the heavy military vehicle to a halt, then glanced at sergeant Grogol as the young soldier walked casually towards them. Abdul Tembarak pressed the barrel deeper into the man's back, then smiled to himself as he noticed him wince with pain.

The young soldier, like so many in the Indonesian army, appeared no older than fifteen or so, but swaggered with an overconfidence which was also typical of the nation's military and police. He stepped up to the driver's window, keeping his hand firmly on the butt of his pistol. "Registration and manifest!" He ordered abruptly. "Quickly!"

"Curb your tone, corporal!" Grogol snapped at the surly youngster. "Do you know who you are talking to?"

The youth seemed panic stricken as he realised who was sitting in the passenger seat. "I'm sorry Sergeant Grogol, I... I did not recognise you in civilian clothing. I thought it was C Company back from town..."

"If you had checked your log when you arrived on duty, you would know that I left with three other intelligence officers in this very vehicle! Try checking the registration plates from time to time, it might be of some use to your log!"

"Yes, Sergeant!" The youth looked thoroughly shaken, then glanced down at the register in his left hand. "Four men in total. All of them returning?"

"Try looking in the vehicle!" Grogol paused. "What's your number?"

"Seven... zero...one...two...one... nine... zero... one!" The youth stood to attention. "Gandok, Corporal!"

"Noted. Now continue your search, Corporal Gandok," he paused. "Quickly, I have a prisoner to interrogate!"

The young soldier hurried around to the rear of the vehicle and lifted the canvas curtain. He looked surprised as he saw the westerner, his hands bound together, and the barrel of the rifle pointed at his chest, but quickly added an entry to his register and closed the curtain at once. He stepped back a few paces, then signalled to the three guards and waited as the vehicle was waved through the gates and into the compound.

———

King craned his neck to watch the road ahead, then looked at the Indonesian sergeant. "How many guards will be at the entrance to the building?"

Grogol shrugged. "There aren't any, usually," he paused. "But General Soto has taken the threat of assassination seriously. He may have guards in place, he may not, I don't know."

"Come on! He's your commanding officer, you know what security measures are in place!" King looked across at Todi and held out his hands. "Here, cut me free."

The Vietnamese rested the heavy rifle across his lap, then sliced through the duct tape with Grogol's flick knife. King discarded the lengths of tape onto the seat, then held out his hand for the knife. Todi handed it to him and King rested the tip of the blade against Grogol's thigh. Grogol went to move but Todi clamped his wrists. The Vietnamese was surprisingly strong, and Grogol seemed helpless. "I am asking you for the last time, how many guards will be at the building?"

Grogol scowled, then relented when Abdul Tembarak prodded him in the back with the barrel of his assault rifle. "I don't know..."

King looked him in the eye, then pushed the blade deep into the man's flesh. Grogol screamed in agony and King twisted the knife as he pulled it clear. Todi let go of the soldier and Grogol held the wound tightly with both hands. Blood gushed between his fingers. He looked up at him and grit his teeth in a desperate bid to quell the pain. "You bastard!"

"That's what my mother called me," King said curtly. "I'll ask again; how many guards are at the building?"

Grogol closed his eyes and rocked backwards and forwards in his seat, as the muscle in his thigh started to spasm. "Two, both in his quarters. His own personal body-guards," Grogol forced a grin. "Part of a twenty-man team, sent to England to train with your SAS. Ironic, isn't it? The British government train his soldiers to keep him alive, then send an assassin to kill him..."

King knew that the British government earned good revenue from the Special Air Service Regiment in peacetime, making lucrative use of their expertise in training foreign Special Forces and diplomatic bodyguards. Part of their Third World Development Policy. Then, as times change, and the political landscape shifts, those specially trained soldiers may find themselves in the front line, taking up arms against Britain, knowing the most modern methods of warfare and how to implement their training. Irony always was a part of the British government's overseas programs, regardless of the political party in power. First, they sell the weapons, then they train the soldiers, then they go to war against them. *Ad infinitum.*

"What about placement?" King spun the knife in his hand, then eyed the man's other leg. "I want to know where they will be."

Grogol closed his eyes. "There will not be anybody on the door to his quarters, he doesn't want the other soldiers to know about the threat. He thinks he will lose face if he is seen to take further precautions." He shook his head despondently. "There will be a guard inside the front door and the other one will be nearer his bedroom. Or at least, should be."

King took his handkerchief from his trouser pocket and handed it to the Indonesian soldier, then watched as the man mopped the blood from his thigh. "See, that's better. You cooperate, and you will be all right."

"The hell he will!" Abdul Tembarak raised the rifle and pressed the muzzle against Grogol's temple. "Forget General Soto! I don't care whether he lives or dies!" His finger tightened on the trigger and his hands started to shake. "All I want is to get my wife and son back safely!" He looked at King and shook his head. "We are not going any further until they are freed! If you kill Soto are you really going to help me get back my family? What if it goes wrong? What if we are discovered? You'll all be trying to escape, and my family will be left here!"

King studied the determination in the man's face. He could tell the man was at his wits' end. And if he was honest, then he knew there would be little or no chance of going after Tembarak's family once they made a move on Soto. That's if they could even get near the man. He looked across at Grogol. "Take us to where they are being held," he paused, looking back at the Indonesian intelligence agent. "All right, Abdul, we'll get them out first. Just put the gun down. Grogol is my ticket to General Soto."

"Fuck General Soto! I don't care about your mission, I don't care about anybody, except my family!" Tembarak's index finger tightened on the trigger as he turned his attention back to the soldier. "Just direct us to where they are being held!"

Grogol seemed in a quandary. Tembarak was clearly not in charge, but he had the gun to his head and was now giving the orders. He also had reason to kill him and from the feel of the automatic weapon shaking in his hands he did not fancy his chances against an accidental discharge. "All right!" He shook with fear as he spoke. "I'll take you to them, just take the gun away from my head!"

King picked up the silenced Colt .45 pistol from the bench seat near Todi and aimed it at Tembarak's head. The man was oblivious and continued to look straight ahead as the vehicle crawled slowly through the compound, on route to the Interrogation Centre. There was so much at stake, so much to think about. Sergeant Grogol was King's ticket to General Soto. He was his eyes and ears, and a lot more besides. The man was cooperating, he knew the camp and he knew the security procedures. Not only that, it was quite possible that the man could help effect their escape. King's finger tightened on the weapon's heavy trigger as he took careful aim at Tembarak's temple. There would be no knee jerk reaction from Tembarak, no sudden reflex that would pull the trigger of the AK47. A shot to the temple at this range with the large calibre pistol would drop the man like a rag doll.

Todi stared at King intensely, shaking his head in bewilderment. King caught the reaction in his peripheral vision and suddenly felt ashamed with himself. Years of training, years of operating in the field had left its mark. He could kill. He could use death as an option and never look back. The man merely wanted to get back what was most precious to him and King had almost killed him for it. He lowered the weapon and breathed a deep sigh. There was more to life and he knew it. He wanted nothing more than to leave this life behind, find a good woman and settle down, finish the memoirs he had started, paint, live life to the full and never look back. He had grieved his own personal loss, but he was ready now. Ready to find some happiness again. He could do all this and more. He had finally realised it. He hoped now that it was not too late.

CHAPTER SEVENTY-FIVE

"There, straight ahead." Grogol grit his teeth as another violent spasm shot through his lower thigh. "That is the Interrogation Centre."

King studied the entrance to the building, noting the large metal doors and the camera and intercom system beside them. He looked back at sergeant Grogol and frowned. "No external security patrols?"

"No."

"What about inside?" King paused. "Give me the details."

Grogol removed the blood-soaked handkerchief from his wound, checked the bleeding and then pressed it back down onto the patch of blood, which had spread a few inches more. "I need a doctor..." he said feebly. "I'm going to bleed out..."

Abdul Tembarak rammed the barrel of the AK47 into the man's ribs and glared at him menacingly. "Hurts, doesn't it? Well, it's nothing compared with having your fucking toe cut off! That's what you did to my wife, you sick bastard!"

King gripped Tembarak's shoulder and pulled him gently away. He didn't understand a word Tembarak had shouted, but he got the gist. "Hey, keep calm, he's not worth it," he paused. "Your wife and child are behind those doors, just get your head together." He turned his attention back to Sergeant Grogol, placing the Colt .45 against the man's groin. "All right, time to get serious. The interior details, give them to me," he paused. "Bearing in mind that you will be walking ahead of me. One detail out of place and your brain takes a breath of fresh air..."

They maintained the charade. Getting out of the truck, but this time King pretended to have his hands bound, keeping them held tightly together behind his back, aided out of the vehicle by Todi. They walked as a group towards the large block-built building. Sergeant Grogol walked ahead, limping on his wounded limb, followed closely by King, who held his hands behind his back, as if restrained by handcuffs or bindings. Both the tiny 9mm and the heavy silenced Colt .45 tucked into the back of his waistband. Tembarak and Todi followed, weapons at the ready, aiming at the middle of the 'prisoner's' back.

Grogol played the game well. He knew that his slim chances of survival would fade to non-existent if he refused to cooperate and repeated the performance which he had given at the main gates. He strode confidently towards the large security doors, stared into the camera and pressed the intercom button. "Sergeant Grogol. Open the door immediately!"

There was no delay, no questions and no request for further identification. It seemed that Grogol was not a man to be crossed. King suspected that there was more to him than appeared. Soto had kept the man down-ranked to keep a finger on the NCO and enlisted soldiers' pulse. He would be like a one-man secret police. His role as interrogator would have been formidable.

The door clicked open and as instructed, the Indonesian sergeant stood to one side. King moved quickly, pulling the silenced Colt from his belt and stepping up to the door. He flicked the safety catch off, then held the weapon firmly in a two-handed grip before barging the door open with his left shoulder.

A single glance and he knew that Grogol had been as good as his word. The guard sat at a desk to his left, monitoring the security camera's view of the outside world. He may have seen the 'prisoner's' sudden hostile movement, or he may not; either way, he had not had time enough to react. He looked up, startled at the intruder and started to go for the pistol on his belt. He should have raised his hands instead. King raised the pistol, sighted the weapon's fixed sights on the man's forehead and squeezed the trigger once.

He cocked the weapon using the additional lever Todi had fitted as he stepped forwards. Checking the nearby office through the window in the top half of the door as he walked, he then turned back to the front entrance and opened the door casually. "Well done, Grogol," he paused. "Now, keep it up..." He swept his hand past him, indicating that the soldier should take the lead. "After you."

Grogol stepped hesitantly over the threshold, then stared at the growing pool of dark blood seeping from under the desk. He said nothing but glared his hatred at King as he walked past him.

"Lock the door, Todi," said King. He turned and followed Grogol down the dimly lit corridor, counting his paces as he went, extracting as much information as he could from his surroundings. Scenarios could vary enormously, it always paid to be ready for anything. One unexpected problem such as a power cut and the untrained or unfamiliar could find themselves lost in a world of darkness without an exit. Todi brought up the rear, walking backwards and keeping his weapon trained on the entrance.

Grogol hesitated at a set of double doors to his left, then

looked tentatively at Tembarak before turning his attention back to the Englishman. "That is where the children are held while their families are detained..."

Tembarak stepped forwards eagerly, but King caught hold of his arm and stopped him. "Wait!" He turned back to the soldier and frowned. "So, who looks after them?"

"We have a team of nurses, but there will only be one on duty tonight, the Tembarak boy is the only infant in the building."

King shook his head at Tembarak, then pushed him away from the door. "No, first we get your wife, then we get your son on the way out."

"It's not as simple as that..." Grogol hesitated. "Your wife is not being held here anymore..."

King lashed out and gripped the man's throat, then pushed him against the wall, knocking the wind out of him. "Don't fuck with me, Grogol!" He glared savagely at him and rested the muzzle of the silenced Colt under the man's chin. "You said that Tembarak's wife and child were in this building... I warned you not to mess me around!"

"I couldn't say where the woman was!" He glanced nervously at Tembarak then looked back at King. "That maniac would have shot me!"

"What do you mean?" Abdul Tembarak glared at him. "Tell me!"

The soldier shook his head despondently then started to shake. "Don't kill me, please!" He looked pleadingly at King. "Don't let him kill me! You *still* need me to get to General Soto, *and* to get away! You'll never get past the guards without me!"

King frowned. "Tell us, Grogol." He pressed the weapon harder against his throat. "Tell us now!"

"She is with General Soto." The man hung his head in despair, sure that Tembarak would shoot him or at least beat him with the rifle. "He has taken a liking to her and moved her into his private quarters earlier today."

"No!" Tembarak stepped forwards brandishing the rifle. "It isn't true!" He pointed the barrel into the soldier's face and fumbled his finger onto the trigger.

King lashed out, striking the Indonesian's neck with the side of his hand. Tembarak dropped to the floor, his rifle clattering on the hard, polished concrete.

Balls up! That was how his old friend and mentor Peter Stewart would have put it. *A complete and utter bloody balls-up!* King could hear the tough Scotsman's words ringing in the back of his mind. He had lost sight of the objective and was on a fool's errand. He kept the pistol trained on the soldier, then bent down carefully and picked up Tembarak's AK47. Using the weapon's canvas sling, he draped the rifle over his shoulder then stared at Sergeant Grogol. "All right, after you." He glanced down at Tembarak, who was unconscious, then looked at Todi. "Sort him out, will you?"

Grogol opened the door hesitantly and walked down the tiled corridor. King followed a few paces behind, keeping the cumbersome silenced pistol trained on the man's back. There was an overpowering reek of bleach and detergent, and he realised this was probably where the torture victims were taken for treatment after, or even during, their excruciating ordeal.

Ahead of them, the sound of pop music was clearly audible from what sounded like a cheap portable radio. King could see a faint flicker of a light under a door at the end of the corridor and noticed a shadow pass briefly across it. Someone was moving about in the room. Grogol knew this too and stopped several paces from the doorway.

"All right, nice and casual." King kept the weapon trained on him, then motioned him towards the door. "I'll be right behind you. Ask for Tembarak's child and tell whoever is in there not to try anything stupid."

Grogol nodded and walked over to the door, before knocking twice and opening it abruptly. He hesitated momentarily, then spoke rapidly in his native tongue and stood to one side as King entered, holding the pistol at waist level. The nurse stared up at the two men in surprise, her naked breasts squashed against the table, and her skirt pulled up over her waist. The young naked soldier was bent over her and stared in horror at the pistol in King's hand. He feebly raised both hands above his head in surrender.

Grogol barked the order once more and the nurse quickly pushed herself away from the table and fumbled for her scattered clothing, as the dumbfounded young soldier stood stock-still, his manhood rapidly flagging.

King ushered Grogol to one side and closed the door. Keeping his back to the wall, he edged cautiously towards the young soldier, the pistol still trained on him. He worked his way around until he was behind him but kept eye contact with Grogol. The young soldier did not see the blow coming, as King brought the butt of the pistol down onto the nape of his neck with terrific force. The soldier slumped forwards, instantly unconscious from the heavy blow, a little blood trickling from the wound. The nurse cried out as she watched her lover slump across the table but raised her hand to her mouth instinctively to silence herself. She quickly slipped the white blouse over herself and pulled her skirt back down, as she stared at the intruder with the gun.

Grogol snapped at her again and she dutifully turned around to hurry through an adjoining doorway. The Indonesian looked back at King and shook his head dispassionately. "Give this up. You can't seriously expect to escape, can you?"

King smiled wryly, confidently at the soldier. But he was starting to have his doubts. "You've helped me this far," he paused. "And you will help me to the very end. You don't want to die. You're a survivor. I can see that. You'd do anything to survive. He backed over towards the door and aimed the weapon at the opening. "If I don't succeed, then another will come in my place. This way, you have a chance to live."

The nurse hurried back into the room clutching the young boy close to her chest. The child was dressed in a sleep suit with a thin cotton sheet wrapped around him. He had stirred, but his eyes were opening and closing, like he was going back to sleep. The nurse was trembling. She could see the weapon with its big bulbous silencer was aimed at her head. She muttered under her breath and closed her eyes.

King glanced between her and Grogol and the unconscious soldier on the floor. Matters were becoming extremely complicated. Grogol moved slightly, and King turned the weapon on him. The man stood stock-still, his hands raised. King moved towards the nurse and took the child off her the best he could. He wasn't familiar with children, but he had looked after his younger brothers and sisters in another life, a lifetime ago. A childhood memory flashed in front of him, but he instantly suppressed it. He didn't allow himself to go back there anymore. He held the child closely to his chest, remembering children did not feel safe unless held firmly. The boy's face nuzzled into his shoulder as he dozed. King looked back at the nurse and pointed to the floor with the pistol. She hesitated, then reluctantly knelt. He rounded her, then struck the same blow he'd done earlier to her lover. The woman fell forwards, her head hitting the floor with a thud. There was no time to check if she was alive. If she was, then he had spared her; and if she wasn't, at least he had tried. That was the limit of his analysis and of his compassion. He didn't kill indiscriminately, but the people working here knew that what was happening was not right. He was not going to lose sleep over any of them.

Grogol led the way without protest, and they walked swiftly down the tiled corridor, King following several steps behind. As he kept his eyes on the Indonesian sergeant, he glanced down momentarily at the sleeping baby, surprised that he had not woken during the disturbance. His eyelids twitched, and he gave a mellow yawn as they walked, which reassured King that he was well.

Grogol paused at the double doors and King motioned the man through into the sparse corridor where Abdul Tembarak was sitting on the polished concrete floor, his back to the wall. Todi was eyeing the corridor in both directions, his large rifle held loosely in both hands.

King kept the silenced Colt aimed at Grogol, then looked down at Tembarak, who was rubbing the side of his neck. "Abdul. I think this little chap will want to see you..."

CHAPTER SEVENTY-SIX

King watched, his heart fluttering as he experienced an inexplicable emotion, for the first time in what now seemed a lifetime. There was no logical reason for his joy, for the matter was of no direct concern to him and offered him no direct benefit. Yet as he watched Abdul Tembarak cradle the infant in his shaking arms, he was swept back to memories of his childhood and the love of his mother. Then came the pang of anger, of disillusionment, as he recalled his childhood. There had been no warm feelings such as this. His mother had been a drug addicted whore, who maintained her drink, heroin and then crack habit by selling her body and neglecting her children. The warm feeling which he was experiencing at this moment was only a projection of his impossible desire to have experienced a father's love. He looked away from the loving father and his child, suddenly feeling uneasy, intrusive.

The Indonesian looked tearfully at the Englishman, then stretched out a hand and touched him on his shoulder. "Thank... you..." he stammered, choking back tears. "Words cannot begin to express my gratitude..."

King nodded awkwardly, suddenly jealous of the man's happiness, and in the same instant, ashamed of his envy. "Don't mention it," he replied. "We are not out of the woods yet though..."

The Indonesian looked at him quizzically, unfamiliar with the metaphor, but realised that King had not noticed his expression. He turned back to his son and continued to stare lovingly into the boy's eyes.

The vehicle rocked gently, then slowed considerably, as Jusi pulled into the side of the road and allowed a much larger armoured vehicle to pass in the opposite direction. He turned around in his seat and looked at King, then glanced at Grogol seated beside him. "He says that this is it," he paused. "This is General Soto's living quarters."

King moved forward ducking his head under the metal struts which spread across the canvas roof. He stepped past Todi, who was covering Grogol with his rifle, then perched himself on the opposite bench seat.

"This is it, Grogol," he paused. "Double-cross me now and you die a second later. You told me that there would be only two bodyguards in Soto's quarters. Do you stick by that?"

"Yes," he nodded emphatically, then winced as a bolt of pain lanced through his wounded thigh. "Two, both in uniform."

"Armed with what?"

"They are *Kopassus*, Special Forces. They use mainly Sig Sauer .40 pistols and Steyr AUG rifles. Sometimes Heckler and Koch MP5 9mm machine pistols as well."

"Body armour?"

Grogol nodded. "Lightweight Kevlar vests, front and back. Femoral armour as well."

King thought for a moment. He needed to get this done, and he was poorly equipped. From the moment Soto's agents picked him up at the airport he'd had to improvise. It was not the ideal approach for taking on such a protected target. Surprise was to their advantage, but to escape the compound, they would have to maintain perfect silence. The lightweight Kevlar vests would stop the pistol rounds but would pose no problem for the powerful 7.62 mm bullets of the SLR, nor the 7.62mm (short) of the AK47. However, start firing the rifles in the dead of night and the entire military base would be alerted within seconds. He was left with little choice, he would have to use the knife and the two pistols, and he would have to enter the building alone. Todi was a good fighter and had not let him down at the railway station, but he had used overkill on his designated target. King could not leave anything to chance, if he was to assassinate General Soto and escape safely, then he would have to go in solo.

He placed both pistols beside him on the bench seat, then quickly tucked his shirttails into his trousers, before picking up the tiny Rohrbaugh 9mm and checking the chamber. He had six bullets at his disposal, but it was a well-made, accurate little weapon. He tucked it into his back pocket. Having shot the guard in the interrogation building he was left with six rounds in the .45. However, it did not give him any more than the element of surprise. The weapon needed cocking each time it was fired. If it came to a shootout, he was at a distinct disadvantage. He quickly tucked the Colt into the shoulder holster and slung the Uzi over his shoulder and tucked the spare magazines into his pocket. If it went noisy, he would bring some of his own. "Right," he said to Todi. "I want you to escort Grogol to the front entrance." He turned to the Indonesian soldier and stared at him coldly. "I want you to get the door to his quarters open. Tell the bodyguard that you have a matter which requires General Soto's immediate atten-tion. If he refuses to open the door, threaten to put him on a charge. If that doesn't work, well you better improvise damned quickly..." He looked back at Todi. "When the bodyguard opens the door, get Grogol back into the vehicle. Tembarak and Jusi will be covering you from the truck," he paused, looking back at the soldier. "So, don't get any ideas about trying to escape."

"What about my wife?" Tembarak stared at him. "I have to try and save her!"

"Forget it," King paused. "This is far too personal. If she is in there, then I will get her back to you. Just stay in the vehicle with your son." He looked down at the boy who was wedged between the front seats with the sheet wrapped around him. He smiled to himself, as he noticed the child's face break into a tiny grin as he looked around the cab of the vehicle. "He needs his father..."

————

King breathed deeply, taking in a huge lungful of the humid air. He needed to ready himself, to calm his nerves and ease his mind. There was so much that should have been done, so much that had gone wrong. The operation should have been carefully planned, carefully orchestrated, but Tembarak's betrayal had put a halt to that. Instead, he had been forced to rush in like a fool and strike while the iron was hot. He should simply have aborted the mission and gone to ground, blend in with the tourists and work out his exfiltration. It was pride that had made him continue. And pride came before a fall. If he was honest with himself, it was the Iraq affair that had spurred him on. To have been sent back to kill the Faisal brothers grated on him. He did not want this operation to be seen as a failure. But now, inside a military base in an unfamiliar country, about to try and kill a figure like General Soto, he could care less about pride and failure. But he was here now and the only way to go was forwards with the plan, such as it was. If General Soto had got wind of his team's failure at

Purwodadi, then the man might have gone to ground indefinitely. King had seen no other option; he had made the best
of the situation as it stood.

Grogol turned around hesitantly and looked at him as
they reached the entrance to the house, which looked like any
other storage hut in the compound, except for the fact that it
was surrounded by a white picket fence and flowering
gardens. Among the other utilitarian buildings, it looked
peculiar to say the least. "This is your last chance," he grated,
looking at the two men. "Give yourselves up, and I will see
that your lives are spared."

"You're just worried that if we fail, General Soto will have
your life for helping us." King stepped aside, allowing the
soldier enough room to stand at the solid looking door. "Well,
just remember this, if an assassin fails to take down a target,
the next course of action is a cruise missile or a laser guided
bomb," he paused. "Hardly as selective as a bullet. Could you
guarantee that you would not be standing near General Soto
in such an event?"

Grogol stared at him curiously, then nodded. "Well, if you
put it like that, you leave me very little choice in the
matter..." He winced as he took the weight off his injured leg,
which seemed to have stopped bleeding.

King watched the man carefully, then felt a little relieved,
as Sergeant Grogol stepped forwards purposefully and
knocked hard upon the heavy wooden door.

CHAPTER SEVENTY-SEVEN

"This is Sergeant Grogol! I need to speak with the general urgently!" He gazed nonchalantly into the lens of the surveillance camera, then waited for the reply.

"General Soto does not wish to be disturbed," the bored voice replied. *"Leave a message, and I will pass it on to him in the morning."* The voice came from the intercom.

"On your head be it, soldier!" Grogol growled. "But if I do not see General Soto immediately, your neck will be in a noose!"

There was a long pause, as the soldier obviously weighed his unhappy options. At last, *"What's it about?"* came the reply.

"What's it about?" Grogol stared into the camera and sneered. "It is about something way above your pay grade, soldier! Now open this door, let me in and get the boss out of his damned bed!"

There was another delay, then came the sound of several bolts being unlocked. King stepped forward and pushed Grogol out of the way, then kept the Colt held firmly between both hands, as he waited for the door to open.

Todi prodded the Indonesian in the ribs with the barrel of

his SLR, then nodded his head towards the vehicle, where Jusi and Tembarak were keeping their rifles at the ready.

King breathed deeply as the last of the bolts was unlocked and the door opened slowly inwards. He took his chance and barged the door with his shoulder, in a bid to catch the bodyguard by surprise. The door gave way as the bodyguard was caught off balance, then suddenly halted, as the brass security chain locked tight.

King's mind raced as he quickly assessed the unforeseen obstruction. He had never encountered something so simple, something so out of place in a military scenario. A ten-pound security chain from Yogyakarta's equivalent of B&Q had thwarted him. Millions spent on his training, but MI6 hadn't trained him for something as simple as that. He barged the door again with his shoulder, then struggled to regain his balance as he was met with the same effect. The chain held firm, allowing a gap of only a few inches. He stepped back from the door, aimed the weapon at the middle of the door and fired a single shot. He cocked the weapon again, moved his aim quickly to the right by a foot or so, then fired one more controlled shot. The bodyguard cried out as he was hit, and King cocked the Colt again and fired a third shot. He heard the bodyguard fall to the floor, but King could still hear the man moving. He put the muzzle of the silencer on the chain, pushed the door as hard as he could to alleviate any slack and fired. The door gave way, and as he charged his way in, he pulled back the slide and manually engaged the next bullet.

The bodyguard had been hit twice, both times in the chest, but the bullets had been slowed considerably by the thick wooden door and had merely embedded themselves in the man's Kevlar vest, leaving their tails sticking out. The guard had fallen onto his back, thoroughly shocked and winded, and was now struggling backwards, reaching for the pistol in his belt holster.

King darted forwards to kick the man's hand away from the pistol, then dropped down onto his knees, straddling his chest. He wrapped both legs over the man's thighs, his insteps pinning the man's legs to the floor. The guard couldn't even attempt to knee him in the back, all four limbs were pinned down tightly. The bodyguard looked up at the intruder, completely helpless. King looked away, keeping the pistol aimed at the hallway, as he searched for a second target. Satisfied that the man had been alone, he returned his stare to the helpless soldier, then drove a left hook into his temple. The man went limp, concussed by the powerful blow, but King hit him again for good measure and then rolled back onto his heels, satisfied that the bodyguard was out of action. He laid the heavy .45 on the ground and picked up the man's Heckler & Koch MP5-SD machine pistol. It was a silenced version with a thick integral silencer. King checked the magazine, saw from the inspection ports that it was full, then checked the breech for a round and flicked the selector to single shot. Now the weapon would fire one 9mm bullet each time the trigger was pulled. Thirty of them. He felt more confident now. This addition would make him feel a little more comfortable as he went in search for his next target.

The next target was not long in coming. As King stepped over the unconscious bodyguard's outstretched legs, the man's partner came charging into the room with a Steyr-AUG carbine held firmly to his shoulder.

King raised his weapon, doubting that the bodyguard had learned that method of room entry from the SAS instructors at Hereford. He sighted quickly, almost instinctively, and fired a double tap into the man's face. The force of the two bullets spun the dead man like a top and sent him spinning into the wall behind him where he suddenly halted, then slumped in a sitting position.

Two bodyguards down, but he could not take Grogol's word for it, there might well be more security to take care of. His eyes darted everywhere, but wherever he looked the MP5 followed as if it were an extension of his vision, viewing everything through the peephole sights.

Grogol had briefed King on the layout of building. The rooms were lavishly furnished for military accommodation, the actual structure was deceptively large. According to Grogol, General Soto's bedroom was the fourth room on the left, between the kitchen, the dining room and the bathroom. There were also more bedrooms, some occupied by a rotation of security personnel.

He walked slowly, breathing deeply and steadily as he advanced. The kitchen was small but functional and looked to be used only for preparing snacks and beverages. It was also empty, which was all the British agent was looking for. He continued, listening out for the slightest sound.

The bullets impacted in the wall near his shoulder. It was a short burst from a machine pistol, but unsilenced in the confined space it sounded like canon fire. King dropped to one knee, using a desk as makeshift cover. The second burst came from the end of the lounge from behind a large leather sofa. King saw the muzzle flashes, aimed at them and sent four rounds into the wall. He lowered his aim to the sofa and fired three rounds into each of the four segment cushions. He heard a shout or cry of pain and aimed a couple more in the same direction. A man charged out from cover but made it into one of the rooms before King could take aim. He was a soldier with body armour and a machine pistol. King got up and ran towards the doorway. He flicked the selector to full-auto as he ran. As the man swung out of the doorway with his weapon aimed King fired a full burst from just a few feet away and the man went down. The man had looked shocked. Clearly, he hadn't expected King to charge at him so fast. The MP5 was empty. King threw it down and tugged the tiny 9mm pistol out of his back pocket. The soldier was lying dazed having taken the brunt of the bullets in his body armour. He was reaching for his pistol on his low-slung leg holster as King dropped on top of him, tucked his pistol under the man's chin and caught hold of his arm in time to stop him drawing his pistol. King fired once, and the top of the man's head painted the wall behind.

He breathed a few deep breaths and quickly took stock. It had gone noisy now, so he unslung the Uzi and tucked his pistol back in his pocket. In his left trouser pocket, he had the two spare magazines for the Uzi. He was thirsty, hot and tired. His heart was thumping through his chest. Still, the deep breaths calmed him a little. He edged his way along the wall, listening intently for any giveaway signs. There was much at stake now. It would be too easy to burst into the target's room and fire the weapon into the man's bed, but Abdul Tembarak's wife was supposed to be here, he had to make sure that she was safe first. It was also a different scenario now that the gunfire had erupted throughout the building. If it had been heard outside, then he was done for. He had to work fast, but Soto would know he was under attack. He could have alerted help or be armed. King eased the handle of the bathroom door, then felt his pulse race as it gave way and slowly opened inwards. He edged himself closer, then peered inside and relaxed a little when he saw it was empty.

It was all to be found in the main bedroom. The house was effectively clear. General Soto, if he was inside, was most probably sleeping with the Indonesian agent's young wife. He could not just burst into the room and shoot, he had to iden-tify then take appropriate action. The woman's husband was waiting outside in the truck, cradling their first-born. It would be all too easy to simply get the job done in his customary manner, but he had seen the Indonesian's happiness at being reunited with his child; not only seen, but somehow felt a part of it. His world was so bitter, so vicious and cruel that he had felt a sudden urge to see more happiness.

He stepped forwards hesitantly, feeling a strange concern, that another person's life was under threat. To date, it had simply been a question of his own life, or the target's. Now there was a third life in the equation, and he was suddenly nervous. Not that his own life was without value, but death was something which he had never seriously considered. He was confident, sure that he would always win against any opposition.

He took another deep breath, then reached for the door handle. If the room was lit, then he would be able to identify the target immediately, if the room was dark, then hopefully the light from the hallway would be sufficient. His mind raced as he attempted to recall what the Indonesian sergeant had said. The bedroom was approximately twenty-eight feet by twenty and doubled as the General's private office for more 'sensitive' matters. These matters usually involved prisoners' wives'. The double bed was situated directly ahead and slightly to the right of the doorway. There was only so much he could take on trust, and if the truth be known, he would rather have gone in blind. At least he would not be relying on information from one of the target's personal aides. He took another deep, calming breath, then gently pulled down on the door handle.

The first gunshot caught him completely by surprise, as they always do. The woman screamed hysterically, and the second gunshot drowned her out for a moment. King had to decide what action was best to take. There was only a split second for that, as the third bullet would surely find its target. King barged the door with his shoulder, then dropped to the floor and rolled into the room out of the light of the lounge which was flooding a patch just inside the dark room. He brought the Uzi up to aim, then frantically searched for his target. The next two shots were fired in quick succession. His ears were ringing. A painful thud each time a gunshot sounded. He knew it was a magnum revolver simply by the noise. He processed the information to be sure – sharp report, no metallic sounds of working parts or ejected cases, obviously a revolver and not a semi-auto. Loud. Incredibly loud. A .357 magnum for sure. Not that the calibre really mattered; bullets were bullets. But a magnum handgun round was a game changer. The only handgun round that could completely penetrate the engine of a truck.

Down on the floor, his ears ringing, King tried to work through what he'd seen and heard. The woman was making a noise, but she was muffled. Maybe Soto had his hand clamped against her mouth. There had been muzzle flashes to his left, four shots fired in total, two shots left in the cylinder. He rolled forwards again, then aimed the Uzi exactly a foot above the last muzzle flash and about six inches to his left. Soto was right handed, he would be behind the woman with his left hand keeping her quiet. King fired a short three round burst. A shot fired back, briefly lighting the bed up in the darkness. There was no time to hesitate, no time to assess his marksmanship. He dived forwards on his belly and took refuge behind the bed as he listened intently for any trace of a sound, anything which could give him information and an edge.

The silence was deafening. King's ears were ringing from the gunshots and the blood which pumped and thudded in his ears from the release of adrenaline made it almost impossible to hear anything in the silence. But then came the whimper, the high-pitched snivel of a woman trying to suppress her tears. The sound was audible and had changed direction. Soto had moved, was moving around the bed. How was that possible? King realised that the bed was centred and not against the wall. He had not imagined that. Instead he had pictured the traditional set-up. But Soto was a beast, a man who raped women. Who raped the wives of his prisoners. Nothing was going to be traditional about this man's sleeping arrangements.

"I have a hostage!" The voice was deep, and highly accented. "Abdul Tembarak's woman!"

King breathed quietly. He tried to be as silent as he could. There was always more to a close quarter battle than simply shooting at your target. Mind games always came into play at some stage – Soto's was to declare the presence of an innocent; King's was to play dead.

"Shoot at me, and you will hit the woman," a pause. "That wouldn't be very British of you, would it?"

King kept still, the next move would have to be Soto's. He would have to confirm his hit at some stage. There was an underlying tone to the man's voice, as if he were under more than extreme duress. And then King heard it. Faint, but easily identifiable in the eerie silence - a sharp intake of breath through the man's teeth. He was injured, fighting to control his emotions as the simultaneous dull ache and burning of the gunshot kicked in and started to burn like acid on raw flesh, becoming more unbearable by the second.

King gripped the Uzi and closed his eyes, heightening his senses to hear more. The man would have to make his move soon. The pain of his wound would affect his judgement, a mistake would soon follow. But King could not stay indefinitely, he was sure the alarm would be raised at any moment.

"I will count to three, and then I will shoot the hostage!" There was a long pause, and then; "I mean it, I *will* kill her!"

King remained silent. Mind games were the worst, the other man could never feel lonelier than he did at that moment.

"One... Two..." This time the pause was long, but decidedly more desperate. "Three..."

King waited but was confident the man would not shoot. He had counted off five shots. He only had one left. The man would be a fool to throw away his only bargaining chip and he most probably knew it as well.

"I *will* shoot her!" There was a grunt as he moved, the pain obviously biting at his resolve. "Throw out your weapon, stand up and put your hands on your head!" There was a faint click, then suddenly, the light flickered briefly and illuminated the room brightly.

King kept still, lying on his stomach, completely masked by the bed. He heard a tentative footstep, then cursed inwardly. The light had changed his hand, he was no longer holding the trump card. From this position, he would not be able to make a move quickly enough in the brightness. If Soto eased himself forwards a pace or two, he would be able to see the lower half of King's body as he neared the bed.

There was nothing else for it. He still had an advantage but would just have to play the game a little differently. He threw the weapon into the middle of the room, then slowly rolled onto his back. "All right, I'm coming out! Don't shoot, I am unarmed!" He slowly eased himself up, then stared into the eyes of the evil, would-be dictator.

General Soto smiled wryly, keeping the barrel of the nickel-plated revolver against the woman's head. "I still have one shot left, stand up slowly," he smiled. "Do you feel like talking? Because I have many questions to put to you, many matters which need answering..." He held the woman close to him by her hair. She was naked and her shoulder and part of her breast blocked half of Soto's chest from view.

King knew that he would have to be quick, a simple shot would not do. He would have to be moving as he fired, he would have to eliminate himself as a target. He moved his feet, testing the rubber soles of his lightweight walking boots against the floor tiles, then made as if to stand. There was no room for mistakes, at this close range, Soto could scarcely miss. King pushed himself upwards, then drew the tiny pistol from his back pocket, as he dived to his left. The big revolver swung out in an arc away from the woman's head and towards King as Soto tried to aim. King fired twice. He landed the dive rolling onto his left shoulder in a judo break fall. He came up onto his feet with the pistol aimed on Soto's chest. He fired three more shots all grouping above the first bullet hole which had hit the man to the right of his sternum. One of his first shots had missed. Soto stared blankly at him, swaying unsteadily on his feet, the revolver still outstretched as he continued to aim. King knew that his own weapon was now empty but was left with the bed between himself and the threat. There was barely time to react, as the dying man continued to hold his gun steady, desperately focusing his last reserves of life on both aim and trigger.

King darted to his left, noted that Soto was slow in bringing the pistol around on him. He was losing a critical amount of blood. King looked to the Uzi on the floor, but it was too far away. He dodged again, keeping the big magnum moving in the Indonesian's hand. He had closed the gap between them. Again, he dodged, this time to the right. The woman elbowed Soto in the face, and he wobbled as she pulled away from his grasp. King was just feet from the man now. And as the man struggled to bring the heavy revolver to aim, he lashed out and knocked it downwards. He was on him now. He struck the man's neck with his ridged left hand and swiped the gun away with his right. King sidestepped and hooked the man's foot off the floor with his right foot, at the same time he clutched his throat and forced him downwards. Soto hit the floor hard. King caught hold of his head with both hands wrenched it up and slammed it back down onto the hard, tiled floor. He did it again and again. Five times in all. Then he stood up and looked down at him. Blood and matter oozed out from under his head and his eyes stared up at him lifelessly.

King stepped away and felt a sudden elation as he saw the woman sitting down on the floor hugging her legs with her head tucked down. She was sobbing and rocking gently. She raised her head and looked back at him. She was naked, her arms covering her breasts. King could see the bandaged toe. Her wrists and ankles were rubbed raw from ropes or cuffs. She was crying.

"It's all right, sweetheart," King paused, whipped the bedsheet off the bed and wrapped it around her shoulders. "He can't hurt you anymore." He bent down and lifted her to her feet, adjusted the sheet around her to cover her below the waist and held her arm. "Abdul is outside, waiting for you," he said quietly. "He is with your son."

The woman forced a tearful smile, then looked at him pleadingly. "Please," she paused, searching for the words. "Don't tell him what you saw, he must never know what that vile pig has done to me..." She stared down at the corpse, then looked back at King. "Please..."

King shook his head. "Of course not."

She wiped a stream of tears away from her face, then stared at him. "It is a great dishonour for a Muslim, to know that another man has been with his wife.

I am a Christian, but we share many values..."

King nodded, aware that the feeling it was not exclusive to Muslims, or indeed any religion for that matter. "I won't tell him," he paused. "And you don't have to either. It isn't as if you had a choice and I think Abdul will always know that it was his doing, that this happened to you. It was his work which brought you *both* here..." He spun around suddenly, as he heard the noise behind him, then sighed with relief as he saw the Vietnamese standing in the doorway. "Todi!" he paused. "You're a bit late..."

"We heard gunshots," he explained, staring at the General's body. He lowered his rifle, then smiled at the Englishman. "Mission accomplished?"

King glanced down at the blood-soaked body, then looked up and returned the man's smile. "Mission accomplished," he replied, then gently guided the woman forwards with his hand and bent down and retrieved the Uzi. "Now, let's get the hell out of here..."

CHAPTER SEVENTY-EIGHT

Emotions were running high in the stifling heat of the vehicle and King could not help finding the celebrations a little premature. Abdul Tembarak was embracing his family and tearfully pledging his undying love for wife and child, while Jusi and Todi's celebrations were merely for the death of General Soto and an end to another potential communist uprising amongst the poverty-stricken people of Indonesia.

"Right, quieten down everybody!" King shouted. "If you heard the gunshots, then I am sure you were not alone." He looked at Jusi and nodded his head towards the driver's seat. "Get back behind the wheel, get us out of here. Don't race, we don't want to draw attention to ourselves." He turned back to the Vietnamese, but the man had stopped smiling and was covering Sergeant Grogol with his rifle once more. King looked at the soldier and nodded. "You're going to get us out of here," he paused. "Don't try anything stupid. General Soto is dead, it just wouldn't be worth it."

"Give yourselves up," Grogol said. "You are all dead men. You just don't know it yet."

"No, I'll take my chances thanks," King reloaded the Uzi

and hung the strap over his neck, keeping the weapon across his chest. He took out the last spare magazine, thumbed out six bullets then started to load the magazine of the tiny R9 Stealth pistol.

Grogol looked at him dubiously as Jusi started the noisy engine and pulled away steadily. He kept the lights dimmed to draw less attention. "You will kill me when I am of no further use to you," he shook his head despondently. "Why would you let me live?"

King put the pistol back in his pocket and looked at him. "How many people have you killed?"

The man shrugged.

"How many people have you tortured? How many did you make beg to die?"

Again, the man shrugged.

"Well stop your bitching. You live by the sword; you die by the sword." King stared at him coldly. "My job is done, I will fly out from Jakarta today or tomorrow and never come back." He leaned back against the canvas covering, having casually laid this false information. He was in fact leaving via Bali, to the East, not Jakarta to the West. But King never knew what was around the next corner and it paid to prac-tice deception in his profession. He shook his head and looked at the man intensely. "I don't care if you live or die, but I said that I wouldn't kill you, and I will not," he paused. "Now, get us through security at the main gates and don't try anything stupid. You will not live to regret it if you do," King lied easily. He would not kill him, but he would have no qualms about leaving his fate to Abdul and Wyan Tembarak...

Security was conspicuously present as they made their way through the compound, but as they watched, it seemed less of an orchestrated investigation into the gunshots and more chaotic by the second. Troops ran around covering the fence with automatic weapons and a group of MPs were darting between the huts hastily rousing sleeping soldiers.

Grogol sat up in his seat, constantly reminded of his plight by the barrel of Todi's rifle prodding painfully into his back. He looked back warily at King, then turned towards the approaching gates and breathed deeply. The guard stepped out from his booth, glanced at the three soldiers who were acting as cover on the other side of the road, then held up his hand to halt the approaching vehicle. King and Todi craned their necks to see the soldiers. Todi looked at King, nodded his head towards the three guards on his side. King nodded, both sensing and agreeing with his concerns and Todi took the weapon away from Grogol and shouldered it, the muzzle pointing in the general direction of the soldiers. King tightened his grip on the Uzi. At the same moment the young boy started to whimper. Tembarak and his wife shushed him quietly, all three lying on the floor in a close embrace. The more the couple tried to silence the child, the more the child became agitated. The moaning was about three whines from becoming a full-blown cry and both parents knew it. They soothed him and cooed gently, but their faces were panicked, and the child picked up on the desperation in their mood.

Grogol leant across Jusi's lap and shouted out of the open window, as the vehicle slowed down to a halt. "Soldier! Come here at once!" Everyone tensed as the soldier walked up to the vehicle. "There have been shots fired on the base!" He looked at the guard, realising that it was the same man he'd chastened earlier. "Corporal Gandok, hurry!" Grogol looked at Jusi next to him, then flung his elbow into the man's face sending the man reeling into his door. "Gandok! The intruders are in here, they have taken me hostage! Help! Help!"

The young soldier hesitated, then flinched as gunfire ripped through the canvas side of the truck and the three soldiers, caught off guard on the other side of the road started to fall. The stunned guard went for his weapon, but King buffeted Grogol forwards onto the dashboard and got the Uzi in front of Jusi and the barrel out of the window. The guard fumbled his weapon up to aim, but he knew he had been too slow. He started to kneel, remembering his training to present a smaller target, but a moment too late. The last thing he saw was the muzzle flash of the machine pistol, then he fell backwards and lay still.

Jusi screamed as his ears caught the full blast from the Uzi. He held both hands up and cupped his ears in agony. King beat Grogol on the side of the head several times with the butt of the machine pistol and turned to Jusi. He shouted over the gunshots as Todi finished the soldiers off with single, well aimed shots. "Get moving! Drive man, drive!"

Jusi could hear only ringing in his ears, but he got the gist. He floored the accelerator and the heavy truck lurched forwards towards the gates. Jusi spun the wheel at the last moment and drove parallel to the fence. They bumped along the grass and he turned hard to the right bringing them back deep into the base.

"What the hell are you doing?" King shouted. He was holding on to a grab handle and bracing himself against the inertia as the vehicle turned a wide circle, its tyres squealing as they mounted tarmac once more.

Jusi battled with the large steering wheel. He couldn't hear King shouting, but he yelled; "Not enough speed! We need to go through the gates! Without speed we'll just bounce off or get stuck in the wire!"

Soldiers outside various huts were watching the scene unfold. Startled by the gunshots at the gate, they seemed to get the idea and a few started firing at the truck as it almost completed its arc. A few bullets pinged off the metal sides, then bullets started to rip through the canvas sidings. King and Todi hit the deck for cover simultaneously alongside the Tembarak family, then Grogol, who was stirring from his beating and attempting to hold on in the cab screamed as bullets ripped through the door and into his legs.

"I'm hit! I'm hit!" he shouted but seeming to realise that he was of no concern to anyone in the vehicle he pushed himself upright and went for his door. His door opened and almost at once impacted against the guard hut and was wrenched from its hinges. Grogol went to jump through the open door but found himself gripped tightly by the collar. He fought against Jusi, who held him tightly with his left hand while struggling to steer the vehicle with his right. Grogol elbowed him repeatedly, but the wiry Indonesian kept a firm grip, ignoring the blows as the vehicle bounced and veered towards the gates. Grogol pulled, and at the same moment Jusi pushed the man through the door opening as the vehicle hit the metal gates and smashed its way out of the compound.

Grogol travelled through the air, free from the vehicle. The gates were flung wide open at a terrific speed but hit the concrete curb on either side and were flung back into the truck with as much force and momentum as the initial impact. Grogol found himself sandwiched between the metal gate and the side of the speeding truck, severing his leg, pelvis and buttock, and his arm at the shoulder.

King watched out of the open rear of the truck and saw the man's limbs fall near his body. He turned back to Jusi and watched as the man struggled to correct his steering, clipping a curb as he swung the heavy vehicle into the road leaving the notorious Yogyakarta Military Installation and Intelligence Centre in a heightening state of chaos.

CHAPTER SEVENTY-NINE

There was a coolness to the light breeze, a welcomed addition to the burning heat which seared down from the azure blue sky and reflected brightly off the shimmering sea.

For the first time in weeks, Alex King felt alive. Few things in life could better the feeling of wading towards a sun kissed beach after a swim in the ocean, and in King's opinion the temperate waters of the Indian Ocean lapping at the rugged southwestern coast of Bali could rank with any spot on earth.

The past few days had come as a welcome relief after the tense happenings on the neighbouring island of Java and King had decided to take refuge amongst the hordes of tourists in the coastal town of Kuta. It had not been his intention to take a short sabbatical, but for the purposes of a successful exfiltration, a less than hasty departure would give the security forces more chance to settle back into their traditionally somnolent approach to their work. Kuta was an ideal place to lie low, it was a town which served as a stopping off point in Asia before going on to Australia or Europe. It was a backpacker's Mecca where drink, music and cheap accommodation was plentiful and where soft drugs could be easily purchased and taken publicly with little consequence, and where shady characters would entice gullible tourists into becoming drugs mules who sometimes paid the ultimate price.

After their escape from the military compound, they had driven back to the village of Purwodadi by a devious route, arriving shortly after daybreak. Their overriding priority was one of self-preservation. It would not take the military long to discover that General Soto's killer, along with his accomplices, had escaped the compound in one of the army's own vehicles. A detailed search would naturally ensue, and the incriminating vehicle would have to be abandoned well away from Purwodadi if the village's inhabitants were to be spared from reprisals. This would be a two-man task, and Jusi and Todi had both volunteered for the duty. Todi knew of an abandoned Bauxite mine where the vehicle could be hidden permanently. The task included taking the bodies of the dead soldiers killed at the railway station from where they had been earlier hidden. In the heat, this would have been a repulsive task. The two men had done this stoically and returned four hours later in the Suzuki four by four.

Abdul Tembarak, his wife and their son had waited with King, making effective use of Jusi's small living quarters to the rear of his vehicle hire premises. After a refreshing shower and a basic meal of steamed rice and curried vegetables along with fresh papaya and bananas, King had walked to the station, where he bought four tickets. Three were one-way rides west to Jakarta, the fourth was a single east to the port town of Banyuwangi.

Abdul Tembarak was heading straight to his intelligence service's headquarters in the Manui district of East Jakarta, where he would give his superiors a full account of his ordeal, but carefully avoid details concerning a certain British agent.

Even after such events, Tembarak could never inform his service that he was also on the British SIS payroll, on however casual a basis.

King on the other hand was to take the hot, uncomfortable and arduous train journey through the mountains to Banyuwangi, where he would board the ferry to Gilmanuk, a mere mile and a half away, on the Island state of Bali.

King had bid his farewells, much the same as before, knowing full well that those he thanked, whose hands he shook, and even promised himself to remember, would soon be a distant memory, never to be seen again. Such was his life, such was his profession.

He had arrived in the tourist town of Kuta by taxi from the port town of Gilmanuk and had known instantly that he could disappear into the hordes of *travellers* - for that seemed to be the name for the few tourists who simply took a longer holiday than most on a tighter budget. Surfers, gap-year students and retirement aged couples searching for their hidden youth now that they were free from the restraints their children had put on them.

With a cheap yet comfortable room secured and having spread the legend of being a recently divorced traveller on his way to Australia, King had simply fitted neatly into the hustle and bustle of the town. He felt at ease as he openly walked through the streets to the numerous restaurants and trendy bars such as *Tubes*. There he found he could eat excellent value meals washed down with ice cold bottles of *Bintang*, watch the latest film releases or football matches on a large screen television, and eye the groups of traveling Europeans.

King waded through the knee-deep water and rubbed salt from his eyes as he searched the beach for his towel. He looked up for the beachfront bar which had been his landmark, then realised that the powerful current had taken him almost one hundred metres down the beach. He walked out of the water and started along the damp sand, which the intense heat was quickly drying to a hard crust that broke with a loud crack under every footstep.

The traders watched his progress intently, brandishing their wares every time he looked up. Governed by a law which forbids them to venture past the high tide mark, the traders tended to swamp visitors to the beach, creating a human barrier of shouts, offers and occasionally insults. King had already politely refused a man's offer of a wooden blow-pipe. But the man had him marked. He couldn't look up without seeing the man grinning at him and holding the blowpipe in the air.

King could see the trader looking at him again. He turned away from the man, then caught sight of his towel, which was now nestled between two large groups of youths, who were playing overly loud music on an iPad with speakers and, judging from the empty bottles, knocking back enormous amounts of beer. He walked casually between the groups, picked up his towel and continued his walk up the beach. There were a few remarks behind his back, a few ultimatums and a challenge to anyone who didn't like their music, but King had heard idle threats many times, shouted by men in large groups. Men who could not stand alone. He ignored the remarks, comfortable in the knowledge that idle threats only rose from idle throats. Besides, he was a trained killer; for him there was no fulfilment in a pointless confrontation which could go nowhere. The challenge had never really been there at all. He stopped walking, turned towards the shim-mering ocean and stared out to the horizon. The light was inspirational, reflecting off the water and bathing the coast-line in brightness. He had always found stimulation when he contemplated something beautiful; it seemed to open the gates to his mind, making him want to paint, or more recently to write. He had found writing cathartic. A way to unburden emotion, deal with what he had done for his country and the death of his wife.

He towelled himself off briskly, then walked towards the barrier of traders. It was time to return, time to convert his thoughts into action. He wanted some normality. He did not want to be alone anymore and was ready to open-up to someone, to be with someone. He was ready to move on. His future was his own, and he suddenly realised there was no place in it for MI6 and the work he did. He had done his penance.

CHAPTER EIGHTY

In his luxurious suite on the top floor of the Ritz Hotel, Charles Bryant turned the pages of *The Times* then froze as he saw the article. His hands shook, the nerves inside making him feel nauseous. He was excited, yet also fearful and full of regret as he read. He had not planned for this mixture of emotions.

A high-ranking Indonesian soldier was killed by arresting officers four days ago in Yogyakarta, Java. It was recently uncovered by Indonesian intelligence that General Madi Soto was planning a military coup and resisted arrest along with nine other soldiers. A small group of military intelligence officers loyal to General Soto were killed by security forces in a separate operation.

General Soto, 58, of the Republic of Indonesia Army was to be arrested for planning a hostile takeover of government as well as his alleged involvement in the disappearance of two Australian journalists two years ago. He was also to be questioned by police about the disappearance of Indonesian citizens near military bases in Java and

*Sumatra and the disappearance of over one hundred political pris-
oners from the on-going conflict in East Timor.*

*His openly communist views and recent anti-government
comments as well as his alleged involvement with resurrecting the
PKI, Indonesia's communist movement are being investigated. Abdul
Tembarak of the Indonesian Intelligence Service commented. "We are
investigating thoroughly and looking into possible accomplices into
General Soto's attempt to destabilize a free and hard-working nation.
The balance of our diverse country, its investors and fellow trading
nations was at significant risk because of one man's own, outdated
ideology."*

Bryant folded the paper, then dropped it lazily on the bed. It
was over, he had nothing more to do in London except pay
the second instalment to his old friend Sandy.

He reached for the tall glass of freshly squeezed orange
juice and took a long sip, before eyeing the food on the silver
breakfast tray. Somehow, after reading of the man's death,
breakfast was no longer foremost in his mind. Other men had
died as a result of going after Soto. He had not been prepared
for that. He felt numb, as if he had just been given the news
of a loved one's death, or that a good friend had been
involved in an accident. He did not know the men but
knowing that he had played a part in their deaths, filled him
with an almost unbearable feeling of regret. At first glance,
the article had filled him with joy. The threat to his future
business in the archipelago had been wiped out, for the time
being at least. His offshore bank account in the Cayman
Islands had never looked better and would soon be credited
with a substantial amount, as would his accounts in Geneva
and Panama as he broke up his fee. So why the regret? Why
the overwhelming feeling of sorrow? Bryant wasn't entirely

sure, but at that moment, it felt as if he had pulled the trigger himself. Men were dead, had been deliberately and wantonly removed from existence, and the fact had made him feel sick to his stomach. He had taken away all the men had, all they would ever have.

His smartphone rang on the bedside table and he reached out, dismissing the guilt from his mind. He had known what he was getting into and it was too late to worry about the details. He pressed the green telephone logo on the screen and answered with his usual tiresome; "Hello?"

"Hello, Charles," Sandy greeted him warmly. "Read the papers yet?"

"I have."

"Like what you saw?"

Bryant paused, the guilt rising within him. "Yes," he lied. "Your man did well."

"So, he did. Now we just have the matter of my final instalment. Is tonight all right with you?"

"Fine," Bryant paused. "My hotel for a drink, and perhaps a bite to eat?"

"Lord no!" there was a long pause. "Jolly sensitive subject, this. Do you remember our first meeting venue?"

Bryant thought of the small unkempt park and the windswept bench where they had first discussed the arrangement. Not like such well-kept parks as St. James's or Hyde, the area was far from desirable for a night time meeting place. "I remember the place, but I'm sure we can come up with a more civilized, if not warmer location."

"Of course, we could, old boy!" Sandy laughed. "But I have official business in Roehampton and have to be at a late-night meeting soon after. The park is just up the road, I cannot disappear for too long."

Bryant relented. "All right Sands, give me a time."

"Nine o'clock should do it," he paused. "Listen, I'm short on time, must dash okay?"

"Sure, see you later." Bryant pressed the off icon and tossed the phone onto the bed. "Great," he said out loud. "Twelve more hours to kill."

CHAPTER EIGHTY-ONE

The walk up the infamous lane Poppies II which cuts through the centre of Kuta to the beach, was much the same as it had always been. King thought it unchanged since his first visit to the town ten years previously. Street traders hassled for the weary tourists to buy their merchandise - some original and well-priced, but mainly poor copies of designer labels at knock-down prices. The heat was stifling, as the relatively shaded walkway picked up the fumes from passing vehicles and the heat which was trapped below the walls to either side of the narrow road.

King had stopped to buy a bottle of lemonade from one of the many traders and drank the refreshing drink as he walked the last few metres to his accommodation.

His chosen room was part of a growing complex catering for travellers of limited means, but King didn't mind. He wanted to fit in and welcomed the hordes of tourists, which were now unwittingly providing the cover which he so desperately needed. The rooms, which mainly on ground level, were arranged inside a walled garden. An open *warong* sheltered from rain by a palm roof offered a suitable dining room where a simple, inexpensive breakfast of green tea and toasted banana sandwiches was served on request every morning.

King walked down the narrow lane leading to his room, then noticed the tiny Balinese man who looked after the complex and was known to the tourists simply as Dan. King seriously doubted if that was his real name, but never questioned it. He sipped another mouthful of lemonade, then caught Dan's eye. "Hi Dan," he smiled.

"Ah, hello," the man paused, picking up a small machete from the toolbox next to him. "Good swim?"

King nodded amiably. "Yes, a bit crowded though."

"Busy, busy, busy!" Dan smiled. "You go to Nusa Dua, much quieter. Many sharks though."

"Then I think I'll pass, thank you." King smiled as he sipped more of his drink. "I need to go to Sanur, to book and confirm my flight. I have an open ticket," he paused. "Do you know where I can hire a cheap vehicle?"

The tiny Indonesian frowned. "You get taxi, or bus, much cheaper."

King shook his head. "No, I want to drive myself, maybe have a swim at Sanur Beach."

"Ah," the Indonesian exclaimed. "You hire bike, motorcycle. Is cheap, I get you bike."

"OK." King glanced at his watch, then looked back at the man. "Will the Qantas office be open tonight?"

"Yes, yes. They close at seven o'clock, I get you bike now." He dropped the machete back into the toolbox, abandoning his pruning efforts and trotted off down the lane towards the town.

King smiled, then turned back and walked through the gardens towards his room and the welcome fan, which had been taking the edge off the stifling heat all day.

The climate in this part of Indonesia seems strange to most visitors. The humidity is among the highest on Earth, yet at times the sun bakes the ground so dry that it could well be concrete. The rainy season is not like the driving monsoon season in India, or the wet season in the Caribbean. Bali's rainy season is merely a pattern of weather, by which you can set your watch. By day, usually throughout the morning the sun shines, the clouds then cover the sun around mid-day and the humidity rises considerably. After that, generally between three and five the heavens open, the rain beats down like gunfire and the ground soaks into a quagmire of warm, murky water, and then mud. Lots of mud. Then the clouds move on, the sun shines once more and within minutes the ground is hard and the whole event easily forgotten.

Having forgotten about the late afternoon downpour and its predictability you could set your watch by, King had got caught in an almighty rainstorm, almost losing control of the Honda 250 cc trail bike. Fortunately, he regained control at the last second and then pulled onto the side of the road, bowed his head and meekly waited for the drenching to cease. As the clouds parted and the sun bore brightly onto his soaked shoulders, he restarted the motorcycle's engine and continued on his way, letting the warm wind dry his shirt and damp skin. The road dried quickly and before long King was riding the agile bike hard, leaning into the corners and banking all the way through the bends, until he corrected his weight and evened the motorcycle out into the opening straight. The air was now slightly cooler, but the sun baked his neck as he turned his back on it and rode into the small town of Sanur.

The town was barely a village but was home to the most expensive hotels and private houses on the entire island, with abundant neatly mown lawns and private gardens. There were several golf courses nearby, all expensive, even by European standards. King slowed, keeping his eyes peeled for the Qantas offices. Personally, he had never heard of anything more ridiculous but then, this was Indonesia. It would be all too simple to locate an international airline's office at the airport, rather than in a hotel, some eight miles away. But then again, perhaps it had something to do with the expensive hotels located here.

He wove the motorcycle between two parked cars, then pulled in to the hotel's entrance among a vast array of expensive cars. Finding a suitable parking spot was not a problem and he was glad he had agreed to hire the bike. A car was far too much hassle in the volatile traffic, and he did not want to rely on Indonesian taxi drivers. For some reason, possibly connected with Abdul Tembarak and Soto's military intelligence officers, King was now very dubious of Indonesian taxis.

One of the most pleasing features of the tropics must be the advent of modern air-conditioning to just about every major shopping centre or office. The icy air hit him like a blast from a freezer as he entered the building, relieving him and relaxing him in one sudden wave of coolness. He paused underneath, making the most of the experience. He could feel his damp shirt cooling quickly under the air. Soon it had chilled him too much and he set out in search for the airline's elusive offices.

———

Across the road, parked on the grass verge and out of the way of any traffic, a man in a black Nissan Patrol four by four replaced the A4 photograph to the centre console, then frowned at the man next to him. "Was that him?"

His companion hesitated for a moment, then shrugged. "I'm not sure, it's hard to tell. We'll need to get confirmation. Give him a few minutes, then go inside."

————

King waited patiently for the German couple to complete their booking to New Zealand then smiled at the pretty Indonesian woman, as she beckoned him forwards to take a seat in front of the large desk.

"Hello, how can I help you?" she asked in perfect English.

King smiled and handed her his passport and return open tickets to Heathrow, via Bangkok. "I need to confirm my flight," he paused. "I understand that you confirm open tickets approximately twenty-four hours before the flight, but would it be possible to be on a flight tonight?"

The woman smiled, then sat down behind her computer terminal and started to type the details onto the screen. "You don't have to confirm from here, but I can book and confirm if you wish. Or you could do it online. If you have a smartphone you can download the app."

"My boss told me I had to confirm flights from here." King said, somewhat irritated.

"That's not necessary, Sir," she said as she typed. "It used to be but changed quite a few years ago. But as you require a flight tonight it's probably best to do it from here," she said pleasantly. King frowned. That wasn't what Stewart had said. The woman looked up as an Asian man entered the office and sat down on one of the comfortable waiting chairs against the wall, he picked up a Qantas magazine and started to read. The woman turned her attention back to her screen and read the relevant information. "Yes," she paused. "The flight is quiet tonight, you can leave on a flight from Denpasar at twenty-three hundred, which gives you an hour and a half at Bangkok, before departing for Heathrow."

"That will be fine," King smiled. The world has many worse airports than Bangkok, and an hour and a half could be easily killed browsing in the many shops.

The woman started to fill out his flight details on the screen, then glanced up and frowned as the Asian man stood up and walked out through the open doorway. She turned back to her booking form, then looked up and smiled warmly at him. "You must check in at least three hours before the boarding time." King nodded, familiar with the formality. He picked up his passport, then stood up as the woman handed him his tickets. "Have a safe journey," she smiled.

King slipped the documents into his back pocket, then returned the woman's smile. "Thank you," he said. "I certainly hope to."

———

Outside the hotel and the Qantas offices King looked at the deep blue cloudless sky and decided that he would get another swim in before returning to Kuta and getting ready to leave. He didn't have much luggage to pack but wanted a long shower and an authentic Indonesian meal at a decent restaurant before heading to the airport at Denpasar. He swung his leg over the Honda's frame, then felt the hot plastic seat burn into his thighs. He flinched momentarily, then grit his teeth against the discomfort, as the heat of the saddle became more bearable.

The ground had dried in the brief time since the downpour and in places where the overhanging trees sheltered the road from the sun's rays, the ground steamed as if it had been drenched with scalding water. King watched, marvelling at the sight. He pressed the motorcycle's start button, then kicked the stand away as the engine fired into life. As he slowly pulled away from a standstill, he noticed the large Nissan Patrol and its three occupants across the street. Each of them wearing dark aviator style sunglasses. Not that there should be anything suspicious about wearing sunglasses in the tropics, but the vehicle's windscreen was slightly tinted, and had been parked in the generous shadow of one of the huge trees lining and shading the road. King studied the vehicle out of the corner of his left eye, using his peripheral vision. He paused at the entrance of the hotel, then rode carefully out into the road and gently accelerated along the quiet tree-lined avenue.

The Nissan Patrol rocked as it dropped hastily off the curb and filled his near-side mirror, then accelerated after him, allowing nothing like a safe distance between them. King changed up through the gears and settled the speedometer at around sixty miles per hour. The four by four followed, dropping to approximately thirty metres. King's heartbeat raced, as he was suddenly aware of the impropriety. The man in the passenger seat looked like the man who had walked casually into the Qantas office, but had only stayed for a moment. He accelerated heavily, putting a further fifty metres between himself and the Nissan, but looked into his mirror in horror, as the big off roader quickly shortened the gap.

There was no question of this being a moment of para-noia. King knew that he was being followed, but what concerned him the most was the blatancy. There was no finesse, no covert attempt to watch him, it was a simple case of high-profile intimidation.

King concentrated on the road ahead. His motorcycle was severely out powered with top end speed. King would be able to accelerate twice as quickly, but the vehicle would soon catch up. However, King was wearing cargo shorts, trainers and a T-shirt. The last thing he wanted to do was fall off on the rough, hot tarmac. For now, he would have to use his acceleration to keep ahead. Fortunately, there were many bends and corners to slow the big Nissan down.

He could only guess at their intentions. They could be security forces, or the police, or even General Soto's own intelligence agents out to seek revenge. Either way, he had to get off the road if he was to avoid capture. He watched the road layout ahead then noticed a narrow sandy lane which broke off to the left.

It would be tight, the lane veered off at a right angle. He slowed the bike by shifting down a gear then swung out erratically to the right. Judging it to the last possible second King leaned hard to the left and veered straight in front of the gaining vehicle. The Nissan's brakes momentarily locked and there was a shriek as the tyres skidded on the dry tarmac, ploughing past the turning before it came to a halt.

The sand was deep and the sudden reduction in speed as he slewed over the soft surface almost threw him out of the saddle. He changed down through the gears, steadied the motorcycle and then accelerated along the narrow lane towards the glimmer of sea which darted between the trees ahead. The Nissan reversed, crunched its gears noisily, then drove into the sandy lane and thundered towards him, gaining distance by the second. King glanced in his mirror and caught a glimpse of the huge metal grille, which was rapidly approaching. He turned his attention ahead of him once more, then noticed the sudden widening as the lane opened out into a turning spot and the picturesque beach which lay beyond. He kept accelerating towards the sea and then at the last moment, leaned to his right and hit the rear brake with his foot. The motorcycle skidded into a wide arc, then spun around almost one hundred and eighty degrees. He changed down a gear, then started to accelerate towards the Nissan as the driver fought for control on the soft sand.

There was little time and certainly no room for mistakes as King reached behind his back and pulled the tiny 9mm pistol he'd taken from Sixties Rocker from the waistband of his shorts. He kept the bike in second gear despite the whining protest from the over-revved engine, then brought the pistol up to aim as he gently steered towards the left, out of the oncoming vehicle's path.

The expression on the driver's face was one of pure shock, even bemusement but it did not bother King as he squeezed the trigger, he had seen the look a dozen times before.

The bullet smashed through the windscreen and slammed into the middle of the driver's chest. He slumped against the steering wheel, then leaned to his left, steering the vehicle away from the turning area and into the thick belt of trees.

King struggled to steer the motorcycle with his left hand but succumbed to fate or inevitability as the front wheel entered a thick tyre rut and wobbled uncontrollably in the deep sand. He plummeted forwards as the bike halted and he was thrown gracelessly from the saddle. He landed flat on his stomach and slid through the sand then as he slowed inertia threw his legs in the air and he rolled over and over, coming to an undignified halt against a fallen tree.

Dazed and somewhat confused, he slowly came to his senses, then realised that he was under fire. The sand blew in his face, as someone fired erratic, but rapid shots at him through the shattered rear window of the Nissan. He dived to his left throwing himself flat to the ground, quickly reducing his target profile, then brought the pistol up to aim, but paused, his training kicking in. He quickly ejected the magazine into his hand, pulled back the slide, keeping the barrel facing downwards. Already sand was coming out of the barrel. Another shot hit the ground near him, followed by two more ever closer. King blew into the breech, cleared the debris as well as he could under duress and inserted the magazine again. He knew that the sand could have caused the bullet to block the barrel resulting in a blowback which could even have blown the gun apart, taking his hand with it. He aimed carefully and fired. The bullet hit the middle of the door and King heard the open window smash within the door. The seated gunman slumped, and King followed it up with another shot for good measure.

King pushed himself to his feet, this time feeling a twinge in his ribs. He had injured himself in the crash, but only now was the pain starting to kick in. He ran forwards, keeping his pistol trained on the figure in the passenger seat. The man struggled to open his door, but the vehicle had halted beside a tree and it was never going to open. He was bleeding from his forehead, and when he looked up into King's eyes, his expression lost all hope.

"Get your hands up!" King shouted, ramming the pistol into the man's face, as he leaned across the dead man in the driver's seat. "Keep still!" He scoured the vehicle for the man's weapon, then noticed a small Smith and Wesson .38 snub nosed revolver in the foot well. He couldn't reach it, but he knew where it was. "All right, are you?"

The man started to shake. "Pulaki," he paused. "Trunyan Pulaki."

King stared at him, then tightened his finger on the weapon's sensitive trigger. "Why were you following me?" He sighted the pistol at the man's forehead. "Don't bullshit me, tell me why!"

"Bullshit?" the man frowned. "I..."

"I mean *lie* to me!" King growled. "Why were you following me?"

The man bowed his head. "We were going to rob you..."

"Crap! Three men, armed with guns and driving a flash

car, do not rob tourists on motorbikes!" King stared at him coldly. "I'm a westerner on my own, dressed for the beach, and obviously carrying little in the way of money or valuables. Now, tell me, why were you really following me?"

The man looked at him pleadingly. "Please, don't kill me!" He shook his head and sobbed. "I wasn't going to kill you," he glanced at the dead man, slumped across the rear seats. "*He* was. I was just riding as back-up."

"So, who hired you?" King asked through clenched teeth. "Who wanted me dead?"

"I don't know, we never know who wants the person..." he trailed off, started to sob. "We usually beat people up, scare them. I've never killed anybody before. These two have," he nodded to the two corpses. "We were just given your details and told to do it."

It all sounded vaguely familiar...

"And what details were those?" King asked.

The man nodded towards the photograph, which had slipped down beside the driver's feet. "We were told that you would be leaving from Denpasar airport and that you had to confirm your tickets at the Qantas office in Sanur. We have been watching for four days..." He shook his head. "Please, spare me, I have a wife and four children to support!"

King reached down and picked up the photograph, then slowly turned it over in his hand. The sight shocked him to the core, sending his heart into a rapid flutter. He stared at the man in shock. "Where the hell did you get this?"

"It was emailed to him..." he motioned towards the body behind the wheel. "... I don't know who, or why, or anything!"

King glanced back at the photograph. He was sweating profusely, but strangely it had nothing to do with the heat. He looked down and noticed his hand had started to shake visibly. Enough to waft the photograph as if it were held in a breeze. The man named Pulaki noticed this too and foolishly went for the revolver in the foot well. King fired, too close to bother aiming. The bullet sliced cleanly through the side of the man's neck, and he fell back against his seat starting to convulse violently. He couldn't breathe and both hands clamped the wound as he attempted to stop the rapid flow of blood, which made breathing even more impossible. He looked hatefully at King as he died, but King was staring only at the photograph.

King felt a wave of nausea wash over him. His legs felt as if they would give way, and he quickly caught hold of the vehicle's wing mirror to steady himself. He could never remember having felt this way before. He forced himself to stand upright, then started to breathe deeply to control his emotions. It couldn't be true, but where else would this hit-team have gotten the picture of him? He forced himself to look at his official SIS/MI6 service photograph once more, but it was no good. Another wave of nausea washed over him, threatening to drown him at any moment.

CHAPTER EIGHTY-TWO

The night air offered little in the way of relief from the heat, as the humidity rose dramatically, soaking the shirt to his back. He sipped another mouthful of cold beer, then watched a large trickle of condensation run down the frosted glass into a pool on the heavily stained wooden table. His mind was racing, but he felt safer in the bar than in the solitude of his own single room. There is truth in the adage about safety in numbers. Outside, the streets swarmed with tourists, all intent upon a good night out. The music from various bars amalgamated into a constant, monotonous drone and the sound of car, motorcycle and scooter engines emitted a vibrant hum through the wooden floorboards of the building. Here, he was merely another face, another single traveller relaxing after a day at the beach.

King knew what he had to do, although it seemed that if he did, and he did not like the outcome, then he was truly out in the cold, abandoned. He picked up the bottle and downed the remnants in one huge gulp. The telephone centre was directly opposite the bar and now that the group of German tourists had left the building, there were two empty booths clearly in view. The telephone centre was of its time, King wondered how long it would last. Most people had mobile phones but in Indonesia data roaming was still expensive and the signal could vary greatly. Many Indonesians used the exchange, but its low rates kept the long-term tourists with a cheaper option. He slammed the empty bottle decisively on the table, picked up his sports bag and walked across the busy street.

The attractive Indonesian woman looked up expectantly at King as he entered, then smiled, baring a set of oversized white teeth, shattering the initial illusion of beauty. King returned the smile, unfazed. He had considerations of a higher priority than the woman's dentition. He glanced up at the multilingual tariff, then looked back at her. "I want to call England."

She nodded silently, then slid a piece of laminated card across the counter. The card offered ten of Britain's major area codes, but King ignored the information. "No, it's okay I have the codes that I need."

The woman smiled, then silently pointed to the booth ahead of him. King guessed that the woman could speak little or no English and returned her smile as he crossed to the telephone. He opened the glass door and dropped his sports bag inside then stepped in, closing the door carefully behind him. The booth was a tight fit for his frame and King felt a wave of heat engulf him, almost drenching his clothes in an instant. He wiped his forehead with the back of his hand, then picked up the receiver and dialled the number from memory, remembering to leave off the 'O' on the area code after dialling the international code.

The dial tone rang for a moment and was then answered by the polite, but somewhat irritating voice of a bored secretary. "Good morning, Callington and Co. Solicitors, Marcia speaking. How can I help you?"

"Err, hello," King paused, suddenly not knowing where to start. "Could I speak to Mister Callington please?"

"I'll see if he is free," there was a short pause, and then, "Who may I say is calling?"

King hesitated. He knew that the solicitor had been dubious about taking on the security blanket and had always made it clear that although he would act accordingly, should the necessity arise, he never wanted to know the details personally. He tensed as he spoke. "Alex King," he paused. "I'm calling from abroad and would appreciate a quick word, if he has the time."

"Oh, Mister King!" the secretary exclaimed. "I'll put you straight through, Mister Callington said to give your call priority."

King tensed, his heart starting to flutter. His pulse raced, and he felt another wave of nausea wash over him, taking his mind back to the damning photograph and the failed assassination attempt. Once more he wiped his brow, now streaming with perspiration.

"Mister King, are you all right?" the man's deep voice was genuinely concerned.

"Yes, fine." King paused. "Is there a problem?"

Callington hesitated for a moment too long. "There most certainly is," he paused. "Your, err ... documents have been stolen. I'm terribly sorry, but we were broken into last week. The burglars by passed our security system, but only took *your* files." King felt sick. He *was* alone. "Mister King, are you still there?" Callington asked.

"Yes."

"I'm dreadfully sorry. I know that you are involved in *sensitive* work, so I haven't contacted the police yet. Do you want me to report the crime? Nothing else was taken, and there has been no real damage to our premises, so I waited to see if I would hear from you."

"Thank you," King replied distantly. He wiped his brow again, then tried as best he could to pull himself together. "No. No, I don't want the police involved, thank you. I'm sorry that you were burgled..." he paused but could think of nothing more to say.

He felt cut off by the tide. Doomed to drowning in a hostile sea. There was nobody who could help him, nobody to throw him a lifeline. His security blanket had been lifted and he knew who was behind it. Donald McCullum was in line for the position of Director and he could not afford dirt on his hands. He was no fan of Alex King. He would have given the order months ago and the lifting would have been simultaneous. It would be no use lifting a few files, then searching for another location. King had scattered the files and documents for that very reason. MI6 would have records of all his contracts, and once they had located all the components of his security blanket and matched them accordingly, only then would the files be lifted.

The photograph. That was what really twisted the knife. His official SIS photograph. Circulated to diplomats in every British embassy throughout the world, it was his passport to sanctuary within a hostile country. And now, that very photograph had been used to mark him out for slaughter. To give a hit-team a positive ID of their intended target. From the hunter to the hunted with one email.

Alex King was not going to remain the hunted for long. *He* was the hunter, *he* was the killer, not the victim. The SIS had taught him well. The instructors had taught him everything they knew, but not everything that *he* knew. He had been trained to enter and exit countries without a trace. To raise sufficient funds in a crisis. To kill without mercy. To live by his wits. To stay alive. None of this had changed and none of it would. He wiped the sweat from his brow, took in a deep, calming breath, then reached for the telephone receiver once more.

CHAPTER EIGHTY-THREE

The night air was suddenly biting cold, a sure signal that the mildness of autumn was giving way to winter chill. The willows swayed in the wind and somewhere in the distance a gate swung wildly on its rusted hinges, whining out into the night-time silence.

Charles Bryant watched the lights of the traffic moving in the distance. Progress seemed to be slow, as it always is in the city, and every now and then a horn would sound as a driver grew impatient.

He thought of the dense traffic in Jakarta, then smiled at the comparison. Road rage was now less of a phenomenon in Britain and becoming the norm. The result of people's irrationality and inability to cope with pressure. Someone would sound a horn, another would retaliate, and a confrontation would follow. In Jakarta there were so many horns sounding at once that nobody could retaliate even if they tried. Bryant had worked in Indonesia's capital for many years and had travelled through the myriad streets every day but had not once witnessed a bout of road rage. If people came to accept that traffic within the city is slow by nature and if the same people used their horns to let off steam more frequently, would road rage become a thing of the past?

A sudden gust of icy wind cut through his body and he shivered involuntarily, now acutely aware that his suit wasn't up to the task. It had become a habit over the years simply to leave his house or office without thinking of what he was to wear. All too often, he found that he was indeed over-dressed, and started to perspire as soon as he stepped into the outside air. Even the lightweight linen suits which he had tailored for him in Jakarta were outrageously hot for wear in the streets and he had adopted, as many expatriates do, a pattern of life which ensured he spent much of his time under air conditioning ducts. Bars and restaurants were useful for meetings because the best places were air conditioned and golf courses where he could be attired in polo shirts and tailored shorts, allowed him respite from a suit.

A beam of light suddenly strafed a pathway across the dark common, illuminating him against the dark backdrop of trees and he found himself squinting as the car pulled to a halt on the narrow roadway some fifty metres or so distant. Bryant strained to see against the powerful lights but gave up, as they remained on full beam. The engine died, and the lights disappeared, leaving Bryant with two yellow after images burned onto his retinas. He cursed out loud, rubbed his eyes for a second or two and then looked back towards the vehicle, as he heard a solid-sounding door close.

The car was a silver Audi A6 saloon. There was a figure moving in the dark and as Bryant squinted in the infuriating blackness, he suddenly felt extremely uneasy with the situation. He watched the figure move silently towards him then suddenly recalled hearing somewhere that the park was a renowned meeting place for homosexuals on the lookout for casual sex.

"Sands?" Bryant called out meekly, finding himself a little intimidated at the approaching figure. "Is that you Sandy?"

"Don't worry yourself Charles," Sandy paused. "Friend, not foe..." He walked decisively towards him and sat down beside him on the wooden bench. "Sorry I'm a tad late, business matters and all that."

Bryant nodded knowingly. "I'm not bothered about you being late Sandy, I never trust someone who is always on time anyway. What I *am* pissed off about, is this godforsaken meeting place. For Christ's sake, haven't you heard of hotel bars, or pubs?"

"I have," he stated flatly. "But, as I mentioned earlier, I had business in the area and have very limited time. I must be back at the office within the hour." He swept his hand towards the distant glow of lights. "And I think that little lot out there is self-explanatory. Bloody traffic..."

Bryant shrugged. "Fair enough, I suppose," he paused. "I'm on a flight from Heathrow tomorrow afternoon, any chance of a drink at the airport?"

Sandy swept a hand through his receding hairline of wispy blond hair. "I'll have to see what is happening," he paused. "What time do you have to check in?"

"Three o'clock."

"All right, I'll try to meet you at two. Which terminal?"

"Four."

"Fine, but just so as you know, it's your round."

Bryant laughed raucously. "It always is, old friend!"

Sandy smiled. "Listen, I don't want to seem rude, but I *do* have a meeting to get to." He glanced at his watch, then looked back to his old friend. "Sorry to rush you..."

Bryant nodded as he reached down and picked up the plastic carrier bag, then dropped it between them. "Sorry about the bag, but you got to keep the briefcase last time."

Sandy picked up the supermarket carrier, then peered

inside. Hampered by the darkness, he reached into his jacket pocket and took out a slimline pen torch, which he shone into the bag. "Splendid," he announced with a warm smiled. "I'll take your advice on investing it. After all, you *are* the businessman."

Bryant smiled, but remained seated and watched his old friend as he rose to his feet. "And *you* are the spy!" he laughed.

MI6 Joint Deputy Director Martin Andrews pulled the silenced Walther PPK out of his inside jacket pocket, aimed quickly and shot the man twice through his forehead. He stared down at the body, which had slumped lifelessly across the park bench. "Very astute of you Charles," he smiled wryly. "As usual..."

CHAPTER EIGHTY-FOUR

He bowed his head, resting his chin in his hands. There was nothing which could have prepared him for this moment. He had hoped, prayed, even deceived to prevent it from happening, but still he had not been prepared. He felt hot, the perplexity of the moment threatening to sicken him to the stomach. He felt dread, anxiety, and a feeling of woe, not experienced since his days at boarding school. Alone. Abandoned and scared witless of what was to follow. It seemed as if there was no light at the end of this tunnel, no horizon for which he could set a course.

He turned back to the stack of newspapers, picked one from the top and then tossed it aside to read the headline of another, which simply read: MI6 Dirty Tricks.

He looked at the pile, feeling a deep anger suddenly rise within him. He pushed the entire stack to the floor, then looked at Marcus Arnott, who had tactfully remained silent.

"How on earth could this have happened?" he asked, perplexed. "I don't see how they could have got hold of this stuff!"

Arnott bent forwards in his seat and picked up the scattered copy of *The Daily Mail*. "It says here that their source remains confidential, but is a well-respected retired barrister, now living in the Channel Islands. Apparently, he has been holding, and updating, Alex King's security blanket for the past eight years."

McCullum shook his head in bewilderment. "But why should King give the order to release the files? And where the hell is King at this moment?"

Arnott shrugged. "I made some formal inquiries just over an hour ago and he seems to have disappeared. His flight was confirmed under his legend, but he never checked in. He must still be on Bali, or at least somewhere in Indonesia."

"But *his* security blanket would have been set up to be released upon news of his untimely death, that's the whole point of a bloody security blanket!" McCullum banged his fist down onto the table. "Why the hell would Alex King give the bloody order! He has cut himself off from the rest of the world! His possessions, his home, *his* life! Why?" He shook his head in bewilderment. "He completed his mission, ex-filtrated to Bali and should have been home by now. Why did he do this to us, and where the hell has he gone? All right, I was shafting him, leaving him out to dry. I hoped a bullet in Iraq or Indonesia might even have his name on it, of course I did. But he's bloody well spun this round on me, hasn't he?"

Marcus Arnott looked at the Deputy Director General and raised an eyebrow. "You ordered his security blanket be recovered. Perhaps he contacted one of his solicitors? It was always going to be a possibility. He's a survivor, he wouldn't have taken the news lying down. As far as he is concerned, someone was out for his blood."

"But how was this 'retired barrister' overlooked?" McCullum pulled out a drawer, then reached towards the back and retrieved a half bottle of Bells whisky and a glass.

He raised an eyebrow expectantly to Arnott, who shook his head.

"It was always going to be a long shot, Donald. Stewart's team located all the components of his security blanket, but realistically there was always going to be the chance of more files stashed away somewhere," Arnott paused. "King just happened to hedge his bets, that's all. Maybe he chose the three offices near places he was either stationed for training, or near where he lived because it was obvious..."

"Obvious? Obvious! Do me a favour, old boy... Write that little observation down and drop it in the internal mail on your way out, will you? Make sure you send it to two weeks ago when it would have bloody well meant something!" McCullum slammed his fist on the desk. "I'm bloody well finished! I have just received a telephone call from the Prime Minister's personal assistant ordering me to meet him at Number Ten at midday. *Ordering* me! I always speak to the Prime Minister personally, now, the bastard's sending messages through his damned secretary!" McCullum picked up the whisky, then swiped the empty glass away with the back of his hand, unscrewed the cap and took a huge gulp from the bottle. "I'm out of the game for the Director's chair. If I'm lucky I'll be sorting files and writing action plans in an embassy, in some fly-bitten, sun-scorched country, in a town in the middle of nowhere that's the next fucking target for Islamic State! That, of course, is if Alex King isn't alive. If he is and he finds out that it was me who pulled the plug on him and took away his security blanket, I'm a dead man. How in God's name will I sleep at night knowing that?"

"Come on Donald, you don't know that." Arnott shifted awkwardly in his chair as he watched the Deputy Director take another drink, almost finishing the bottle. "The Prime Minister has to cover his back, he wants to speak to you before he has to face the opposition in the House of

Commons. He knows your job is tough, he will understand. As for King, if he is alive, then he'll lie low, he certainly won't chance coming after you. Besides, explain the situation to the Prime Minister, and he'll probably grant you diplomatic protection. This time tomorrow, you will have a team of the best bodyguards in the country."

"The Prime Minister, understand? Many of the things described in the papers dates from when the opposition was in power. The Government will have a bloody field day with some of those details! No, my head is on the chopping block. I'm finished, plain and simple..." He shook his head as he stared distantly towards the pile of newspapers on the floor. "It isn't just a question of newspaper headlines. It was on the morning news, on *all* channels. And they reported that the files are already circulating on the Internet. Well, you know as well as I, if it goes on the Internet, it stays. If we can get it off, it will simply crop up on another site. You can't just remove it overnight. It's been downloaded by now, saved and stored and ready to be channelled through God knows how many anorak spy and conspiracy theory websites."

"What does the boss say about it?" Arnott asked. "Surely he can back you up?"

McCullum scoffed, then took another mouthful of whisky. "I can't get hold of him," he paused. "Nor for that matter, can I locate Martin Andrews. His voicemail informs me that he is in meetings all day and will call me back later. But it's me who has been signing off on these ops for the past decade. I'm operations, and the director gave me a free rein years ago when it looked like we were getting nowhere with Al Qaeda. We've had many triumphs over the years, but they'll all count for shit now..."

Marcus Arnott shifted awkwardly again. He recognised the signs, McCullum was the hot potato, and everyone was trying to avoid getting their fingers burnt. He glanced at his watch, suddenly overtaken with an urgent desire to look to his own survival. If McCullum was going down, he was not going to be around when it happened. He rose casually to his feet, then frowned. "I'm sorry, Donald. I truly am. But it must be business as usual, I'm afraid. We'll talk later, I have a meeting in Procurement, vitally important..."

McCullum looked up at him dubiously, then sneered. "I understand, don't worry about it." He picked up the bottle, then swivelled the chair, turning his back to Arnott and facing him towards the murky waters of the Thames. "Close the door on your way out, there's a good chap..." He smiled to himself cynically, then raised the bottle to his lips and started to drink, not pausing until he had drained it.

CHAPTER EIGHTY-FIVE

The last glimmer of sun had just edged its way selfishly over the horizon, bringing the day to a reluctant close. Unwelcome night fell abruptly. He watched the shades of blue gradually turn to black, then closed the curtain, bidding farewell to what had been a beautiful late summer day.

Peter Stewart looked back to his wife, who was busy knitting their neighbour's daughter a yellow blanket to match her growing collection of baby clothes. Her hands worked quickly, bringing the wool around the point of the needle, then pushing it through with the other. *Clickety click, clickety click,* all night long...

That had been the only noise above the television. No conversation, not tonight, nor for the past few nights. Or weeks. The more he thought of it, the longer it now seemed.

His ejection from work had been sudden. Little warning, no talking, merely a dismissal which had come as a complete shock. No blame, nor explanation, simply a memo in his internal mail, which curtly explained the circumstances. Of course, there had been a golden handshake in the form of full pension; the service rarely let anyone go without seeing that their immediate financial future was moderately secure. However, one was never truly ready for redundancy.

His wife had taken the news worse than he had. The sudden and dramatic change in routine had come as a shock. They would both need to find separate hobbies and interests, or the future looked bleak. Perhaps they would adjust, but Stewart doubted it more and more each day. Some couples seemed to get on better with periods apart. His time in the service had given them just that.

Stewart sat back down in his seat and switched channels with the remote control.

"I was watching that!" Margaret protested without looking at him. "Why don't you ever ask?"

Stewart flicked back onto the channel and attempted to find interest in the mating habits of Emperor Penguins. He glanced across at the woman and frowned. *How the hell can you watch anything whilst concentrating on knitting that bloody blanket?* He thought, but wisely resisted saying anything. He rested his feet on the coffee table, then glanced up and encountered her horrified stare.

"Do you mind? You're not in some grubby barracks now!" she blurted. "I don't know what's happened to you since you retired from the army." She dropped the knitting into her bag, then stood up suddenly. "I'm going to bed. Let Mindy out for a run, she's been corking it up all night. Why don't you stay down here and watch a film?"

Peter Stewart watched her as she turned and walked up the stairs. He had served in both the Parachute Regiment and the SAS. He had never told his previous wives of the switch to military intelligence, and then to MI6. The legend he had created held up well with unsociable hours, periods of training and stationing abroad. He had kept the legend going with Margaret. There seemed little benefit in ever telling her now.

He looked at the Golden Retriever who was whining quietly and wagging her tail as she looked expectantly towards the door. Here, at least he had a friend. He smiled at the neurotic dog, then stood up and walked to the door.

"Come on girl, come on, walkies!" He placed a hand on the door handle and was almost knocked off his feet as the dog bounded across the floor and started to scratch at the glass panel in the lower half of the door.

He opened the door, then stepped outside and waited for the animal to do all those things which animals do. Scratch, sniff, dig, eat something discarded on the lawn, then start to look for a private place in which to conclude its principal business uninterrupted.

He watched the dog, distantly wishing that his life was nearly as simple. How world weary, how pitiful, yet how true? He stepped onto the gravel pathway, crunching the loose stones under his hard-soled shoes. He called the dog and walked out of the gate. Their house was the last at the end of the cul-de-sac and he walked through an open gateway which led down a narrow grass and mud pathway to the canal. The canal had been drained, cleaned and refilled and was soon to be an expensive mooring place for both narrow boats and river cruisers. Stewart walked out on to the canal bank and looked at the calm, dark water. He fancied a boat. Perhaps that could be his new hobby. Gently cruising the rivers and waterways, a Scotch in one hand, the rudder in the other.

The metal was cold, as it pressed hard against the nape of his neck. He almost jumped with surprise, but his years of training had taught him better. He tensed, knowing the scenario, and what would likely ensue if he reacted to the threat.

The voice was calm, commanding, and eerily familiar. So familiar, for it had featured in his waking dreams over the past ten months.

"Turn around." The cold metal was gone, and instantly replaced by a crunch of footsteps as the man stepped back three professional paces. "Slowly, Peter, don't rush!"

Stewart turned around slowly, then stared into the man's familiar face. "Hello, Alex," he paused, eyes on the silenced Beretta .380. "What brings you to this neck of the woods?"

King stared at him coldly, then forced a cynical smile. "Fate, I guess."

"Yours or mine?"

"Both." King levelled the weapon to the man's forehead. "Decided by you, when you led a team to take away my security. My bargaining chip." The retriever came over to King, wagging its tail. King reached down and patted its head without taking his eyes off Stewart. The dog sniffed and wagged its tail between the two men, then mooched off to sniff something in the hedgerow. He smirked, then commented, "She's no fucking Lassie, is she?"

Stewart looked at the dog and shrugged. "Maybe she's hatching a plan..." He looked back at King and the thick end of the silencer. "What did you need the bargaining power for? It's not how it's done," Stewart sighed. "I've been to the same places and done the same things as you Alex. I don't have details of assignments spread all over the place. I wasn't going to write a book."

"McCullum was going for the top job. He's the one who signed the orders. It was obvious he would start cleaning house," King stated flatly. "And the writing was therapy. It helped me deal with some of the things I've seen, put it into context. The world has changed over the years since I joined the service. Those extremist bastards aren't human. The atrocities... Their actions burn deep in your brain. You can't just take the edge off with drinking like in your day..."

"It's always been tough, Son."

King shook his head. "I needed that security. I needed a safety net."

"Just following orders, Alex. *You* know how it's done."

King smiled. "Friends know when to toe the line, and when to step back from it," he paused. "You were my friend."

"Don't be a prick, Son. There *are* no friends in the espionage game, you should know that..." Stewart stared at him, returning the assassin's stare for icy stare.

"No, only enemies it would seem," King paused. "And you taught me never to leave an enemy alive..." He stepped back another pace, keeping the pistol aimed steadily at the man's forehead. "Cover your tracks and snip the loose ends. Isn't that what you used to say?" King shrugged. "So how was I going to get it in Iraq?"

Stewart took a step forward, stopped when King moved the pistol and took a step backwards. There was nothing the man could do. "The CIA was going to shut it all down. Insisted on it. They're pissed they lost their agent. What happened to Juliet Kalver?"

"I gave her an out. She didn't take it," King looked at him closely. The light was almost gone, he couldn't see Stewart's features anymore. "Did you know?"

Stewart shook his head. "Not at the time. It came up later. I think McCullum thought it a convenient end to things."

"What about Indonesia?"

"The thinking was the job was so improbable, had so little chance of you getting out if you actually managed to kill General Soto in the first place, that the mission would do it for them."

"For you."

"Not for me. For MI6."

"Well it didn't."

Stewart kept his eyes on the pistol. "I can see that..."

"What about the hit team? Who signed off on that?"

"What hit team?"

"The one in Bali," King paused. "They had my service file photo."

"First I've heard."

"Bollocks!"

Stewart shook his head. "We heard about Soto. We got a detailed report from Abdul Tembarak, just before it was breaking news on the television networks. The next thing your security blanket is in the papers, sent by that retired barrister in the Channel Islands. There was no attempt to rub you out from MI6... Not directly, anyway."

King looked thoughtful. "Andrews," he said. "His old school and university friend was killed in a park here in London while I was in Indonesia."

"So?"

"The man was called Charles Bryant. His Indonesian business associate was killed in those same few days while I was in Indonesia also. I did some checking, and both had money moved about during that time. Andrews must have had a deal going with Bryant. They'd done business before, intelligence reports in return for cash. I traced it. I've had plenty of time on my hands..."

"McCullum is dead. Died just before Christmas. But you'll already know about that," Stewart said. "He slipped in the bathroom and hit his head."

"Shame."

"Isn't it? Trouble with bathrooms is everything around you is so hard."

"And wet floors. Death-traps."

"Corner of the tiled shower step," said Stewart. "What are the chances of that?"

"He drank a lot..."

"Make yourself a hammer out of mosaic tiles and a rubber

mallet, did you?" Stewart shrugged. "Get behind him and smashed his head in? I didn't think it was worth mentioning at the time, but I'd seen the MO before..."

King kept the pistol aimed at him. "It's important to have a hobby..."

Stewart shrugged. "And Andrews in August? The glorious twelfth! First day of the Scottish grouse season. He went every year, apparently. But you'd know that too. I must say, that was a new one on me. Double pressure misfire on his Holland and Holland. Blew his right hand and most of his face off. Poorly loaded shotgun cartridges, apparently. All powder and shot, no wad. Nearly seven times the powder of a heavy game load in fact. *Like little bombs in the breech,* the coroner said. Gave those poor grouse a sporting chance, I suppose..."

"Dangerous sport. Accidents happen..."

"So just me and that little prick Marcus Arnott left then?"

"That's not what they'll read in tomorrow's papers."

"How did he get it?"

King lowered the pistol a little, but it was still aimed firmly on Stewart's chest. "He had a deviant sexual nature."

Stewart laughed. "Come on Alex, tell me! If there's one thing I'd like to know, it's how that little prick went down!"

"At the flat he kept in Mayfair. Naked and hanging from the back of his bedroom door," King paused. "His iPad in one hand and his pecker in the other."

"Some porn and a bad case of auto-erotic asphyxiation," Steward said, laughing. "*The Sun* will love that story!" Stewart stopped laughing, his mood changing in an instant. He stared at King blankly. "So, I don't get a horrible accident? Why the gun?"

"Professional curtesy."

"Doesn't seem so courteous from this side."

"It never does."

Stewart shrugged. "It all catches up with you in the end Son," he paused. "You'll get yours too, Alex. Some twenty-something ex-SAS shining star all bollocks, cock and muscles will catch up with you one day. He'll be fresh and tough and sharp. He'll be wanting to make a name for himself. He'll make you tremble and beg..."

"Sometime, I'm sure."

"I did what I had to do! I didn't want to betray you!" Stewart looked down at the ground, his shoulders sagging. "Please..."

"Don't beg, Peter. We're better than that..."

Stewart shook his head, then stuck out his chin belligerently. "You're not going to do it, Alex! Even *you* won't bring yourself to do it! We were friends!"

"There *are* no friends in the espionage game," he paused. "Your words, Peter, not mine."

Stewart shook his head in disbelief. He looked at King, but he couldn't see the expression in the man's eyes. The light had gone completely now, and he couldn't see the pistol anymore. He struggled to see the man's features, squinting in the darkness. "What's the point of it all? What purpose would it serve, beyond a moment's satisfaction?"

"Because of the way the firm uses people. Good people like the Faisal brothers. Use them, then silence them. Again, and again. We treat people like commodities. I gave those brave men the chance to die in battle. But I was sent out there to kill them in cold blood and what good would that have done anyone? Because they were loose ends. It's as simple as that. You can never afford to leave loose ends, it's what trips you up later." King tightened his finger on the trigger. He brushed the single trickling tear away from his damp cheek and aimed the weapon at his old friend's heart. "Sorry Peter, it's not for satisfaction. It's the loose ends, you see. It's how I've been trained. I'm an assassin. It's what I do."

AUTHOR'S NOTE

Thanks for reading and I hope you enjoyed the story as much as I enjoyed writing it.

We writers rely on reviews so much these days, so it would be great if you could leave one for me, that way my work will become more visible.

If you enjoyed King's adventure and want to find out what happens to him next, then you can find out more here: www.apbateman.com where you will find buying links, the books to review and much more.

Thanks again,

A P Bateman

Printed in Great Britain
by Amazon